# SNOWFLAKES AND SURPRISES IN TUPPENNY BRIDGE

SHARON BOOTH

Storm

This is a work of fiction. Names, characters, business, events and incidents are the products of the author's imagination. Any resemblance to actual persons, living or dead, or actual events is purely coincidental.

Copyright © Sharon Booth, 2023

The moral right of the author has been asserted.

All rights reserved. No part of this book may be reproduced or used in any manner without the prior written permission of the copyright owner.

To request permissions, contact the publisher at rights@stormpublishing.co

Ebook ISBN: 978-1-80508-198-2
Paperback ISBN: 978-1-80508-200-2

Cover design: Debbie Clement
Cover images: Shutterstock

Published by Storm Publishing.
For further information, visit:
www.stormpublishing.co

## ALSO BY SHARON BOOTH

### Tuppenny Bridge Series

*Summer in Tuppenny Bridge*
*Second Chances in Tuppenny Bridge*
*Snowflakes and Surprises in Tuppenny Bridge*

### The Kearton Bay Series

*There Must Be an Angel*
*A Kiss from a Rose*
*Once Upon a Long Ago*
*The Whole of the Moon*

### The Skimmerdale Series

*Summer Secrets at Wildflower Farm*
*Summer Wedding at Wildflower Farm*

### The Home for Christmas Series

*Baxter's Christmas Wish*
*The Other Side of Christmas*
*Christmas with Cary*

### The Bramblewick Series

*New Doctor at Chestnut House*
*Christmas at the Country Practice*
*Fresh Starts at Folly Farm*

*A Merry Bramblewick Christmas*

*Summer at the Country Practice*

*Christmas at Cuckoo Nest Cottage*

## The Moorland Heroes Series

*Resisting Mr Rochester*

*Saving Mr Scrooge*

## The Witches of Castle Clair Series

*Belle, Book and Candle*

*My Favourite Witch*

*To Catch a Witch*

*Will of the Witch*

*His Lawful Wedded Witch*

*Destiny of the Witch*

## The Other Half Series

*How the Other Half Lives*

*How the Other Half Lies*

*How the Other Half Loses*

*How the Other Half Loves*

*For my writing family, The Write Romantics
Alys, Deirdre, Helen P, Helen R, Jackie, Jessica, Jo, Lynne, and Rachael
We believed we could, so we did!*

# ONE

'You know, I think this is probably my favourite carol,' Clemmie said, sighing contentedly as the band struck up 'O Come, All Ye Faithful'.

Her aunt Dolly laughed and squeezed her arm affectionately.

'You say that about every single carol! Honestly, it would be easier to tell me which one isn't your favourite.'

'Hmm.' Clemmie tilted her head slightly, considering. 'Nope, don't think I can do that.'

'Thought not.' Dolly sniffed the air appreciatively. 'Ooh, those hot dogs smell good. The fried onions are making my mouth water! Do you fancy one?'

'Not really. I'd love a jacket potato, though. With cheese or chilli. I'm not really bothered which. Surprise me.'

'All right. I shan't be a jiffy.'

Dolly hurried off towards The White Hart Inn. The pub was serving a selection of takeaway foods for the Christmas Eve event on the village green, a large area of grassland between Green Lane and River Road. Clemmie's stomach gave an involuntary rumble as someone passed her, tucking into a bowl of chilli con carne and rice. She hadn't realised how hungry she was until that moment.

She glanced up at the sky, wrinkling her nose in disappointment. No sign of snowflakes. Apparently, it wasn't going to be a white Christmas this year. What a shame. She turned her attention back to the brass band, smiling as music blasted out across the green, filling her soul with Christmas spirit. Her mind wandered vaguely to the Regency romance she was secretly writing whenever Dolly wasn't around. What, she mused, would Christmas look like in Bannerman Hall?

*I wonder if I should write a Christmas scene for Rollo and Emmeline?*

'You're not here on your own, are you?'

An arm went around Clemmie's shoulders, and she leaned against her best friend, Summer Fletcher, closing her eyes for a moment as the band sounded its final note of the carol.

Only when the sound had faded away did she open them again and respond to Summer.

'Nope. Dolly's gone to get us some food. Oh, hiya, Ben. That looks good.'

Summer's boyfriend, Ben, was busily shovelling a cheeseburger into his mouth. He gave her a thumbs up and nodded enthusiastically, before his comical facial contortions revealed that the burger was too hot, and he should perhaps have been more cautious when eating it.

'Serves you right,' Summer said, giggling. 'Anyone would think you hadn't eaten for a month the way you stuffed that in your mouth.'

Ben gave her an indignant look but couldn't quite manage to reply, so Summer turned back to Clemmie.

'Isn't this amazing?' she said, tucking a stray strand of her chestnut hair under her woolly hat. 'I remember last year when Mum and—' She broke off when Clemmie squealed as the band began to play 'Ding Dong, Merrily on High'. Rolling her eyes she continued, '—When Mum and Rafferty got engaged right here at this event.'

'Have you heard from them? Are they enjoying Australia?'

Sally and Rafferty, who owned The White Hart Inn, had jetted off to Melbourne to spend Christmas week at the home of Summer's elder sister, Billie, and her husband Arlo. Then they were spending the first two weeks of the new year in Sydney.

It was, by most people's standards, a dream holiday, but Clemmie didn't envy them. She couldn't imagine spending Christmas away from home. It just wouldn't feel right.

Summer nodded. 'Mum rang yesterday. They're loving it. Gran got quite jealous and said she wished she'd gone now, but it's too late for that.'

Clemmie grinned. 'How are you coping with your gran being here again?' she asked, knowing that Mona—Summer's grandmother—could be a bit much to cope with sometimes.

'She's behaving herself,' Summer said. 'She's been really good helping in the bar, too. She's got Chris wrapped round her little finger,' she added, referring to the pub's chef. 'She even sent Dad a Christmas card. Can you believe it? When you think how much she hated him when he was married to Mum! Ah well, I suppose a lot's happened since then.'

'Not least you moving to Tuppenny Bridge,' Clemmie said. 'Which I, for one, am very glad about.'

'You're not the only one,' Ben managed, having finally swallowed the cheeseburger. He took Summer's hand. 'Where would I be without you, eh?'

'Aw, the feeling's mutual,' Summer assured him, leaning over to plant a kiss on her boyfriend's cheek.

'Ugh, give over. I'm about to eat.' Dolly nudged her way between Summer and Clemmie and handed her niece a jacket potato topped with chilli. 'Thought that would keep you warmer than the cheese,' she said.

'I like being cold,' Clemmie told her. 'It should be cold, shouldn't it? For Christmas Eve, I mean. I wish it was colder still, though. No chance of snow.'

'No chance at all, thank God,' Dolly said with feeling. 'That's the last thing we need.'

'How can you hate snow?' Clemmie demanded. 'It looks so lovely. It makes everything look pretty and clean and—'

'It doesn't matter what it looks like,' Dolly said. 'It's a bloody nuisance. Don't you remember the other year when we were snowed in? What a palaver that was.'

'Oh, it was such fun.' Clemmie beamed at the memory of cosy evenings around the fire and the thrilling feeling of being cut off from the outside world. She'd got through a lot of books that week. In fact, that had been the week she'd tentatively picked up a pen and jotted down the first words of her secret novel, *The Marquess Wants a Wife*. Hard to believe that three years on she was still working on it.

'Fun! Honestly, it was anything but. You want your head read if you think being stuck indoors for days on end with no way of getting back to civilisation is fun.'

'Have the houses in Tuppenny Bridge ever been snowed in?' Summer asked with interest.

Dolly and Clemmie lived in a cottage some miles away from the town, outside a small village called West Colby. Their home, Wintergreen, was some distance from the village centre, and being in a valley meant they'd been cut off by snow several times in the past.

'Not to my knowledge,' Dolly said cheerfully. 'Not in recent years anyway. The farmers are straight out with the snow ploughs these days, and the roads through the town are passable. Mind, the town itself has been cut off a few times, but never for long. Tuppenny Bridge is a different prospect from West Colby.'

'Oh, that's a shame,' Summer said.

The expression in Ben's blue eyes showed he thought differently. 'It's hard enough, believe me. Try getting to some of these outlying farms to deal with a sick animal when the roads are feet deep in snow. And there's the worry of sheep getting buried in the stuff and freezing to death. I'm glad it's not a white Christmas, and I hope it's a snow-free winter. Though the chances are we'll see some at least.'

'These two have no romance in their souls,' Clemmie told Summer, although she could see Ben's point in a way. He was, after all, a vet. It was different for him. She began to tuck into her jacket potato, relieved to discover that the chilli wasn't too spicy.

'Shall we have a wander around? See who else is here?' Ben suggested.

Summer nodded. 'Why not? Are you two coming?'

Dolly lifted a long string of fried onion from her hot dog and dipped it enthusiastically into a pool of ketchup. 'No, you're all right, thanks. I'm happy here while I stuff my face. You go with them, Clemmie, if you like?'

'I'm okay enjoying the music for now,' Clemmie said. 'You two go. I'll have a walk round later.'

'Fair enough.'

Ben put his arm around Summer's waist and they walked away, just as the band began to play 'Once in Royal David's City'.

'Ooh, I love this one,' Clemmie said, and Dolly laughed.

'Of course you do. Hey, you could have gone with them, you know. I wouldn't have been offended.'

Clemmie prodded her jacket potato and shrugged. 'No, I'm fine. Two's company and all that. The last thing I want to be is a gooseberry.'

'Bless you,' Dolly said, dabbing ketchup from her chin with a paper napkin. 'Time you found yourself a bloke if you ask me. Now, I never met a fella yet who could persuade me that shacking up with him would make me happier. I've got a business to run, and a writing career to maintain, and plenty of friends, and *you*. You on the other hand—well, you're a born romantic, and all them romances you read are no substitute for the real thing.'

Clemmie laughed. 'I've told you before, no real-life man can ever match up to a book boyfriend. I'm perfectly happy with Captain Wentworth, Mr Rochester, Mr Darcy, John Thornton, Gabriel Oak, oh!'

She stepped back, alarmed, as the chilli she'd been balancing on her fork landed on her coat, thanks to some clumsy clot knocking her arm.

'I'm so sorry!'

Clemmie looked up and her heart sank as she saw Ross Lavender gazing down at her. For a moment his dark eyes were full of sympathy and apology, but even as she watched, the warmth in them vanished and his expression became cold.

'Sorry,' he said stiffly. 'I got pushed by someone in the crowd and... Well, anyway, I apologise.'

She had no words, and merely nodded awkwardly at him, grateful when he headed away from her.

Dolly handed her a tissue and Clemmie busied herself wiping away the spilled chilli, glad of the distraction.

'Now there's someone I thought you'd be happy with,' Dolly said thoughtfully, nodding after Ross who had now reached his brother, Noah, and Noah's wife Isobel, who were listening to the carols. 'You *were* happy with him for a time. Your real-life romantic hero you called him. Maybe you could be happy with him again.'

As Clemmie gave her a look of horror she asked, 'Well, why not?'

Clemmie's eyes filled with tears, and she hastily blinked them away as she half-heartedly used her fork to toy with her jacket potato, which was becoming less appealing by the second.

'You know why,' she said quietly.

'You've got to get past all that, love. After all this time! Besides, the right man wouldn't care about all that. He'd just love you for who you are if you gave him a chance—'

'Dolly, stop it,' Clemmie said, annoyed to find that her voice sounded shaky. 'It was years ago. We've both moved on.'

Well, he certainly had, and it hadn't taken him long to do it, either. Grimly, she spooned potato into her mouth, remembering those dark days, six years ago, when she and Ross had separated. She'd made such a fool of herself. Never again.

As her treacherous eyes filled with tears once more, she was relieved when Zach and Ava Barrington arrived at her side with their children, seventeen-year-old Dion, and thirteen-year-old Beatrix. At least they would provide a distraction.

Zach, who was the vicar of All Hallows, was a handsome man, tall and broad-shouldered with tawny coloured hair and bright blue eyes. Ava, meanwhile, was dark-haired and hazel-eyed, with delicate features and a slender figure. Really, Clemmie thought, they were the perfect romantic couple. If they weren't so old of course. They must be in their mid-forties and probably past all that sort of thing.

'Isn't this lovely?' Ava said, smiling at Clemmie and Dolly. 'I honestly think I prefer Christmas Eve to Christmas Day. I get to see more of Zach, anyway, and I do love the band.'

'I've got a raffle ticket,' Bee told them, waving it in the air. 'I want to win the chocolate hamper.'

'I think you'll be eating more than enough rubbish over the Christmas holidays,' Zach told her, his eyes twinkling. 'We really appreciate your donation of the signed copies of your books, Dolly. It was very generous of you.'

'Well, it's for a good cause,' Dolly said. 'They won't be to everyone's taste of course. Can't imagine someone like Clive or

Joseph being grateful for a wartime romantic saga series, can you?

Given that Clive was a vet in his mid-fifties who, by his own admission, read nothing but veterinary textbooks and crime thrillers, and that Joseph—owner of the Whispering Willows Horse Sanctuary—had told Dolly on many occasions that he had no time to read books and therefore no reason to visit her bookshop, she had a point.

'But if the winner would prefer something else I'll let them choose a couple of books from the shop instead. Can't say fairer than that, can I?'

'I'm sure whoever wins your books will be delighted,' Ava said firmly. 'I'm sort of hoping I win the main prize, but I doubt I shall. And even if I did I suppose I'd have to be a noble vicar's wife and let it be re-raffled. That's the trouble with being married to a saint. One is always expected to be just as generous and selfless as he is. How can I possibly compete?'

'Don't be daft, love.' Zach grinned at her, and Clemmie thought, as she often had, how odd it was that someone as working class and broad Yorkshire as him could be married to someone as posh and well-to-do as Ava.

'What is the main prize anyway?' Dolly asked, and Clemmie realised she had no idea either. Quite honestly, she hadn't paid attention to what any of the prizes were.

When the Lavender Ladies—Ross's great aunt, Eugenie Lavender, and her friends, Rita and Birdie Pennyfeather—had barged into The Corner Cottage Bookshop one morning in early December, waving the raffle tickets in their faces, and begging them to be generous because all proceeds would go to the Tuppenny Bridge Fund, she and Dolly had simply handed over their money to get rid of them. They'd shoved the tickets behind the till without even looking at them.

In fact, she realised, they might still be there. She hadn't seen them since. Maybe they'd been thrown away when Dolly dusted the counter.

'Didn't you know? It's a painting. Well, more than that.' Ava beamed at them. 'One lucky resident is going to have their portrait painted for them by Ross Lavender!'

# TWO

'Are you sure you don't want anything to eat?' Noah's voice was gentle and coaxing, but his wife, Isobel, wasn't having it.

'I'm not hungry.' She glanced at the cheeseburgers he and Ross were eating and pulled a face. 'Frankly, even if I was starving I wouldn't touch those. God knows what's in them.'

'Best quality meat, I should think,' Ross said, trying not to sound annoyed. 'Sally and Rafferty are very particular about the food at The White Hart Inn.'

'Maybe, but they're not here, are they? And when the cat's away...'

'Chris has an excellent reputation, and he's not likely to jeopardise that for a quick buck, is he?' Ross snapped.

'Huh.' Isobel folded her arms and stared stonily at the band as they played 'Hark! The Herald Angels Sing'.

Ross felt his brother slump beside him, and annoyance turned to anger. Somehow, Isobel always managed to spoil everything for Noah. Why was she never happy?

Ross eyed his brother worriedly. Noah was a bit shorter than him, slender, with sandy coloured hair and blue eyes. He knew Noah had always envied Ross his height and broader build, and the black hair and dark eyes he'd inherited from his Italian mother, but Ross thought Noah did himself down. He was a good-looking man and had his own charms. Now though, he couldn't help noticing how tired and drawn his brother looked. Ross knew he worked hard. Noah was headmaster of the local primary school, All Hallows' Church of England School on Chestnut Lane, and that carried a great deal of responsibility. Even so, he couldn't help feeling that it wasn't work that was robbing Noah of his sparkle. He wished his brother would confide in him, but he was nothing if not loyal.

If Ross hadn't seen for himself what a bitch Isobel could be, he could be forgiven for thinking they had a wonderful relationship, given the way Noah talked about his wife. Honestly, she was enough to put Ross off marriage for life.

Not that there was any prospect of that anyway. Without meaning it to happen, his gaze slid over to where Clemmie Grant was standing with her aunt. She was still tucking into her food and looked as if she didn't have a care in the world.

He couldn't believe he'd had the misfortune to bump into her, of all people. The way she'd looked when she gazed up at him... He swallowed, recalling the shocked expression in her blue eyes and the way she'd not even acknowledged his apology. An onlooker would never believe they'd once meant something to each other. That they'd once meant *everything* to each other.

'Are you listening, Ross? What on earth are you daydreaming about?'

'Aunt Eugenie!' He hadn't even noticed her approaching, and found his face burning with embarrassment, as if she knew all too well what he'd been thinking. 'Sorry, I was miles away.'

'So I saw,' she said, eyeing him curiously. 'And what a peculiar expression you had on your face, too.'

He gaped at her, unable to think of anything that would satisfy her curiosity. To his relief, she waved a hand dismissively

SHARON BOOTH

at him and said, 'Never mind. Are you ready to make the announcement?'

'Announcement?' He blinked, not entirely sure what she was talking about.

Her hooded blue eyes narrowed as she shook her head slightly. 'Yes, Ross. The announcement. You're going to draw the ticket for our grand prize, remember?'

'Oh, that.'

'Don't say it like that! You're far too modest. People would love—'

She broke off as her friends, the Pennyfeather sisters, hurried up, looking as outlandish and odd as ever in matching purple anoraks, with stripy woolly hats over their dyed red hair. Aunt Eugenie, a couple of years older than them at eighty-two, looked immaculate and stylish as ever in her smart winter coat, court shoes, and an elegant grey wool cloche hat over her silver hair. She was so different from her friends that Ross often wondered how they'd ever chummed up in the first place.

'Yes, what is it?'

'They've started playing 'O, Holy Night',' Birdie said.

'Well spotted. What of it?'

Rita and Birdie exchanged glances.

'That's the last one on their list,' Rita pointed out. 'It means the raffle tickets are getting drawn as soon as it finishes. Are you ready?'

'Of course I'm ready,' Aunt Eugenie snapped. 'I've been ready for hours. I'm just reminding Ross here that he's announcing the winner of the grand prize.'

'I hope it's me,' Rita said with a chuckle. 'If it is, will you paint me and Birdie together, Ross?'

He smiled. 'Of course, if that's what you want.'

'Two for the price of one, eh?' Rita said, nudging Birdie, who rolled her eyes.

'Well, if I win, I want a portrait just of me,' she announced. 'My prize. My painting.'

'Of all the selfish...!' Rita looked incensed, and Aunt Eugenie immediately took control.

'With any luck neither of you will win it. Ross's talents would be wasted on capturing the likeness of you two old fools.'

She smoothed her skirt then eyed him with obvious concern. 'Now, I know we've had this conversation before, dear, but are you quite sure about moving into Monk's Folly in the new year? I know work's started on the place, but there's a long way to go, and it's not exactly a welcoming place to be. Wouldn't you prefer to stay at Lavender House until it's ready?'

'We've been through all this, Auntie,' he said patiently. 'Better to have me on site so I can make sure it's all done to our taste. Besides, I'm nearly thirty. Time I lived on my own, don't you think?'

'I suppose...' She sighed. 'I shall miss you, though. Still, the important thing is that the house is done to our taste and satisfaction, and I know how these workmen can cut corners if they're not watched like hawks. You're quite right.'

'Eugenie,' Birdie said, 'this carol's nearly finished.'

'You need to get a shifty on,' Rita informed her.

'I know, I know!' Aunt Eugenie glared at them for daring to suggest she wouldn't be ready when duty called. 'Instead of standing here like spare parts you could have rounded up the vicar, but I suppose that's down to me, too.' She glanced at Ross. 'Ten minutes at the most. Be ready.'

He nodded and the three Lavender Ladies, hurried away.

'That's you told,' Noah said, nudging him, a grin on his face. 'Glad you stuck to your guns, though. About moving out, I mean. You need a place of your own. Mind you, I don't envy you living in that old pile.'

'It's not an old pile,' Ross protested. 'At least, it won't be when we've finished with it. It's going to be returned to its Regency glory.'

Isobel frowned. 'I thought it was Georgian?'

'Work started on it in 1812, the year after Prince George became Regent. I'd like to see the house looking how it would have looked when it was first built. Aunt Eugenie's got some of Arabella's sketches and paintings that show her children in various rooms of the house, so we're using them as a template.'

Arabella Lavender had been the granddaughter of Josiah Lavender, a renowned Georgian artist who was Tuppenny Bridge's most famous son. Arabella had married one Henry Panton, who'd built Monk's Folly on land bought from Arabella's former sweetheart, Edward Monk. Panton had refused to allow Arabella to paint, despite her obvious talent, so any work she managed had been smuggled to Lavender House, where her parents had lived, and which Aunt Eugenie now ran as a museum and art gallery, dedicated to Josiah's memory.

Monk's Folly had been purchased recently from the Callaghan family, and was going to be turned into the Arabella Lavender Art Academy, with Ross in charge. It was quite a big responsibility, and even though it was a challenge he relished, he had to admit to mixed feelings about it. Aunt Eugenie had invested a lot of money in the project. He just hoped he didn't let her down.

'Must be nice to have a house bought for you and a bottomless pot of money to fund the renovations,' Isobel remarked.

'Isobel,' Noah said quietly. 'The house hasn't been bought for Ross. It's a business, and Aunt Eugenie owns it.'

'*Now* she does,' Isobel said. 'But when she pops off, it's going to be his, isn't it?'

'And Lavender House will be Noah's,' Ross reminded her coldly.

Isobel tutted. 'Lavender House! It's a museum, for goodness' sake! People traipsing through the place every day, even walking round the gardens. And Eugenie stuck in that poxy little flat at the back of the house. Are we expected to live in that? Well, I shan't.'

'Monk's Folly will have people staying there, too,' Noah pointed out hastily, clearly seeing the look of anger on Ross's face. 'It's going to be an art school, so hardly his own private property.'

'But he could sell up if he wanted. It's his choice to run an art school. And no doubt his living quarters will be a lot bigger than the flat at Lavender House. We won't be able to sell that place, will we? It's a condition of inheriting. We all know Eugenie's going to make damn sure that nothing gets altered in her precious museum. We'll be nothing but caretakers when all's said and done.'

Considering Isobel already owned her own flower shop, Petalicious, and that she and Noah had a beautiful house not two minutes away, Ross couldn't see that she had anything to complain about. It was as he'd long suspected. Isobel would find something to moan about, no matter how many good things came her way.

'The raffle's started,' Noah said, nudging him. There was a pleading expression in his bright blue eyes, and Ross's shoulders dropped, aware that the last thing he'd want to do was upset his big brother, no matter how much his wife annoyed him. 'Get ready to go up there.'

Aunt Eugenie and Zach Barrington were on a temporary platform that had been constructed on the green earlier that day. Ross watched as Zach thanked the band for the wonderful music, and everyone else for attending the event.

Ross and Noah exchanged amused grins as he carefully thanked Miss Lavender for organising the raffle and for all her sterling work for the Tuppenny Bridge Fund.

Zach then handed the draw over to Aunt Eugenie, who

began to take tickets from a small barrel between herself and Zach.

Various prizes had been donated by local residents. Sally and Rafferty at The White Hart Inn had given a meal for two, while the landlord of The Black Swan had offered free drinks for two people for an hour every Thursday night for a month.

Isobel had graciously donated a bouquet of flowers. The staff at the Bridge Bakery had offered a takeaway tea for two, including fresh jam and cream scones and a variety of tasty sandwiches and nibbles. Millican's were giving away a fish and chip supper for up to four people. McQueen's Quality Cards and Gifts had donated a chocolate hamper.

Local farrier and blacksmith, Jonah Brewster, had donated one of his handmade iron wall signs. Bluebell at the Cutting it Fine Salon had offered a free cut and blow-dry. Dolly Bennett had pledged signed copies of some of her books. Ross glanced at her as the clearly delighted winner of Dolly's books was announced, feeling a pang as he saw Dolly's smiling face. A small, plump woman with shiny black hair and a silver fringe, Dolly had always been good to him when he'd been seeing Clemmie. He'd really liked her.

His expression hardened as he recalled that she'd barely spoken to him since his break-up with Clemmie. So much for genuine friendship.

As prize after prize was announced, Ross experienced a sudden fluttering of nerves. He'd better make his way towards the platform. His own prize couldn't be far away now.

'And now we come to the main prize,' Aunt Eugenie said. She scanned the crowd, her eyes narrowed until she caught sight of Ross pushing his way to the front. She gave a beaming smile and announced, 'And to make the draw, we have the man himself, talented local artist—and direct descendant of Josiah Lavender, no less—Ross Lavender.'

As the crowd clapped, Ross jumped onto the platform and

smiled, determinedly not looking in the direction of Clemmie and Dolly.

'A very generous prize,' Zach said, holding the microphone once more. 'Ross has pledged to paint the portrait of the lucky winner, which I'm sure you'll all agree is definitely a prize worth having. Good luck, everyone.'

Aunt Eugenie theatrically swept her hand over the barrel and Ross dipped his hand inside it. He felt around, realising there were still plenty of tickets left, even though so many prizes had been given out. They must have sold loads. The Tuppenny Bridge Fund should do well out of this.

'And the winner is...'

His fingers curled around a ticket and he pulled it out.

'Number three hundred and seventy-four.'

His eyes scanned the crowd as everyone checked their tickets. There was a long pause, and Ross wondered if the winning ticket holder had gone home already.

Then a cry went up, and he stared in dismay as Dolly Bennett's hand waved from the crowd.

'It's our Clemmie! Clemmie's won the prize!'

Ross swallowed, his heart racing. Of all the people in this town, it had to be her!

# THREE

Clemmie's legs had turned to water. She clutched Dolly's arm and gave her a beseeching look.

'It can't be me! I don't even know where my tickets are.'

'Doesn't matter,' Dolly said cheerfully. 'I had them with me the whole time. Go on. Go and collect your prize.'

'You collect it,' Clemmie pleaded. 'How do you know it's not your ticket that won?'

'I memorised my numbers,' Dolly said, not quite meeting her gaze. 'It's definitely yours. Go on, get up on that platform. Stop being a wimp.'

Clemmie's eyes widened. Why was Dolly being so horrible? 'But I don't want the sodding prize. You have it.'

'Are you coming up, Clemmie?'

Miss Lavender's voice boomed through the microphone. She sounded thoroughly disapproving, and Clemmie was aware of several dozen heads turning to stare at her, clearly all wondering why she wasn't moving.

'Are you really still so hung up on him that you daren't share a platform with him for ten seconds?' Dolly asked.

Clemmie glared at her. 'I'm not hung up on him at all!'

'So prove it.' Dolly held out the ticket and waited.

Unable to think of an alternative course of action that wouldn't confirm Dolly's suspicions, an angry Clemmie snatched the ticket from her and pushed her way through the crowd towards the front.

Ross, she observed, as she stepped onto the platform, had no welcoming smile for her. Miss Lavender, however, was beaming in obvious delight.

'Congratulations, Clemmie dear. Ross, will you give Clemmie her prize?'

If Ross's expression had been murderous, if she'd seen fury in his eyes, she thought it would have been easier to deal with. As it was, his expression was hard to read. The deep brown eyes—so dark they were almost black—that had once flashed and glittered with passion, humour, and love, stared at her with something she couldn't fathom. His mouth refused to curve into a smile, and his voice was cold as he handed her a piece of card with beautifully written calligraphy, taking great care not to touch her in any way.

'Congratulations,' he muttered.

Miss Lavender stuck the microphone under his chin and Clemmie sensed him gritting his teeth in frustration.

'Congratulations to Clemmie Grant,' he said, facing the audience rather than her. 'This voucher says she is entitled to have her portrait painted by me entirely free of charge.'

'Isn't that wonderful?' Miss Lavender asked the crowd, before turning her gaze back on poor Clemmie, who wanted to fade from existence never to be seen again. 'You must make arrangements for your first sitting, dear. I'm sure you'll be delighted with the finished result.'

Clemmie was shaking so hard she thought the hastily constructed platform would collapse. She gave Ross a sideways glance to see if he'd noticed and swallowed hard. He was staring at her with such obvious contempt that she could only long for his previous expression of cold indifference.

Once, they'd loved, laughed, and talked together for hours at a time, needing no one else. Once, he'd looked at her as if no one else in the world existed. Those days were long gone.

They were strangers. Worse than strangers. At least if they'd been strangers meeting for the first time they might have had a chance to become friends. There was no chance of that now.

Well, who needed him anyway? Clemmie tilted her chin and turned to Miss Lavender.

'Thank you very much,' she said. 'I'll get round to it when I have some spare time.'

As Miss Lavender gave a rather indignant gasp, she left the platform with her head held high.

Let the mighty Ross Lavender pick the bones out of that.


Ross pushed his way through the crowd towards Noah, who was eyeing him warily. Isobel, he noted, had a smirk on her face.

'Well,' she said, the second he reached them, 'that was a surprise, wasn't it? Bet you're over the moon.'

Ross had always thought how odd it was that, on paper, Isobel and Clemmie would sound similar—both around five foot four, with fair hair and blue eyes. In reality, though, they looked completely different, and that wasn't just down to the ten years or so between them. Whatever his personal feelings towards Clemmie, he couldn't deny that her face always had a kind, innocent expression, whereas Isobel seemed to wear a permanent sneer. There was no warmth radiating from her at all.

It hurt him to admit it, for Noah's sake, but he didn't like his sister-in-law. Not one bit. He wasn't going to give her the satisfaction of seeing how rattled he felt. Instead, he shrugged.

'Makes no difference to me who wins it,' he said. 'It's a job, that's all.'

'Course it is,' she said, before turning to Noah. 'I'm going back inside now. I'm bored. Are you coming?'

'I'll be home in a few minutes,' he promised.

Isobel hesitated, then flounced off to Peony Cottage, their charming, detached house, which faced the green.

Noah watched her unlock their front door and go inside, then turned to Ross.

'This could be the best outcome if you ask me,' he said gently.

Ross stared at him. 'For whom? Not me, that's for sure. Can you imagine? I'm going to have to stand there and paint her while she—'

He broke off and shook his head. 'I should never have offered to do a portrait,' he said gloomily. 'I should have trusted my instincts. Aunt Eugenie insisted—you know how she goes on and on. She said it would be publicity for the academy, but I don't see it's going to be very good publicity when I unveil a portrait of *her*.'

'Maybe it will give you a chance to resolve things,' Noah pointed out. 'It seems such a shame that you and Clemmie haven't spoken in years when you used to be so close. Hopefully, if you spend time together, you'll at least become friends again.'

'Friends? I don't want to be friends with Clemmie Grant,' Ross said furiously. 'Frankly, just the idea of spending time in the same room as her brings me out in hives. Of all the people to paint! She's so dreamy and vague. I might almost say insipid. Always has that expression on her face. You know—head in the clouds. It would have been nice to paint someone with spirit.'

'Ross,' Noah said urgently.

'Someone with a bit of fire in their eyes, someone interesting. Instead, I'll have to paint someone with nothing fascinating about them at all.' He gave a bitter laugh. 'Maybe I should just paint a romance novel on legs, because that's basically what Clemmie Grant is. There's nothing more to her than a head full of dreams about stupid romantic heroes that she wouldn't have a clue what to do with if one was standing in front of her. Give Clemmie a real-life flesh and blood man and she'd run a mile. No wonder she spends all her time in that bookshop or tucked away at home with her head in another Jane Austen novel.'

'Ross, don't!'

'Don't defend her. You don't know her like I do. I just wish someone a bit more spirited had won. I'd have loved to paint a woman with some earthiness and substance.'

Noah groaned, and Ross frowned.

'What's up with you?'

'That's what's up with me,' Noah said, nodding over Ross's shoulder. 'I did try to warn you.'

Ross spun round and saw Clemmie pushing her way through the crowd in the opposite direction as fast as she could manage.

'She heard me?' he asked faintly.

'I believe she did,' Noah confirmed. 'And if you don't mind me saying so, Ross, you weren't very kind. I don't know what's got into you.'

No, he hadn't been. He knew it. He'd known it even as the words poured forth from his mouth. Anger and humiliation had loosened his tongue and he bitterly regretted it. He would never have said those things if he'd known she could hear him. He shouldn't have said them at all.

Noah put his hand on Ross's shoulder. 'Maybe you can go after her. Apologise. Tell her you didn't mean it.'

Ross shook his hand away. 'No way! I'm sorry she heard me, and I'm sorry if I upset her, but I can't take it back. I meant every word.'

As Noah frowned, Ross shifted uncomfortably. Okay,

maybe he hadn't meant *all* of it. But some of it was true. And anyway, if he tried to explain, it would only make things worse. It was better to let sleeping dogs lie. Wasn't it?

He couldn't let himself worry about why it was that Clemmie still had the power to make him lose control of his emotions, even after all these years.

It must have been the carols, the crowds, and the raffle that did it.

Blame it on Christmas.

# FOUR

Dolly kindly didn't speak on the long journey back to Wintergreen. Clemmie sat quietly in the passenger seat, her arms folded, the rage bubbling within her fighting for ground with grief and humiliation.

Ross had made her sound pathetic. *Insipid!* What a horrible word to use about her. Like some no-hoper who had no idea about the real world. About real love. About real men.

Huh! She knew about real men all right. If you could call Ross Lavender a real man. They'd dated for eighteen months, and he'd taught her everything she needed to know, thank you very much.

How dare he? How dare he humiliate her like that in front of Noah? She'd seen the pity and embarrassment in Noah's eyes, and it had made her turn around and walk away.

The hordes of people still milling around on the green had made her escape slower than she'd wanted, but at last she'd found her way back to Dolly, who'd eyed her curiously and said, 'Well, did you do it?'

Summer and Ben were standing next to her aunt. Summer must have fought her way back to them, no doubt anxious to know if Clemmie was okay after being thrust into such close proximity to Ross. Now she gave Clemmie a suspicious look.

'Did you do what?'

Clemmie swallowed as Dolly said, 'She was going to tell Ross that she didn't want her portrait painting and he was welcome to draw another winning ticket. Or words to that effect.'

'I can imagine,' Summer said. 'So did you?'

'Didn't get the chance. He was too busy chatting to Noah, so I left it.' Clemmie shrugged, trying to sound nonchalant. 'Maybe I can give the prize to someone else. What about you, Summer? Do you fancy having your portrait painted?'

'By that git? No chance,' Summer said with feeling.

'Ross is all right,' Ben said tentatively.

Summer swung round to stare at him. 'All right? After what he did to Clemmie? He dumped her! Cheated on her! And he's paraded loads of other women in front of her ever since.'

Ben looked uncomfortable, but not as uncomfortable as Clemmie felt when Dolly raised an eyebrow and held her gaze for what felt like an eternity.

'It doesn't matter,' she said. 'Anyway, I'm sure I'll find someone else to sit for him. There'll always be some willing fool who'll simper over him and massage his fragile ego, while telling him how wonderful he is.'

Dolly had said nothing, and Clemmie was grateful for her silence, even though she was pretty sure that, before too long, her aunt would voice her opinions on the subject. She wouldn't be able to help herself.

Clemmie was relieved to pull up into the drive of Wintergreen, a three-bedroomed stone cottage with a long drive and a front garden that, in the summer, was a riot of colour. Now, the only colour came from the Christmas lights around the window, which Dolly refused to switch off when they went out, despite Clemmie's dire warnings of fire and disaster.

'Right,' Dolly said, as she unlocked the front door, 'let's get that kettle on.'

'I'm just going upstairs to have a quick shower and get into my Christmas PJs,' Clemmie called from the hallway, as Dolly hurried into the kitchen. 'Shan't be long.'

As Clemmie entered her bedroom, she took a long, deep breath, then leaned against the door and closed her eyes.

How had she got through that? The Christmas carol event on the green, which she looked forward to every year, had turned into a nightmare. Now, she'd always remember it as a time of stress and embarrassment, and it would be forever spoiled.

She sank onto her bed and stared at the ceiling, thinking it was just her luck that it would be her raffle ticket that won the prize. What was Dolly doing with her ticket anyway? Thinking about it, she still wasn't convinced that the winning ticket hadn't been her aunt's. She wouldn't put anything past her. Surely, she could have stepped up and said it was hers, to save Clemmie the embarrassment?

Before she could stop herself, she dropped onto her knees and reached under the bed, feeling around for the box, and hoping there weren't any spiders lurking on the carpet.

Her hands found their target, and she pulled the box out, staring at it as if it were alive and would bite her at any moment. It was just a simple box, the size of a shoebox, but decorated in pink roses and tied with a pink satin ribbon. So why was it making her heart race just to look at it?

What was the point? Why had she even removed it from its place of safety under the bed? It would only cause her pain and bring back too many memories. Yet, even as the thought occurred to her she found herself untying the ribbon, prising off the lid, and staring at the contents within.

Six years. Six long years since she and Ross had parted. Looking at the fresh faces of the two people in the photographs she now held in her hand it might as well have been decades ago. She felt so much older now. Weary, really.

Her thumb stroked the face she'd once loved so much, and known so intimately. Those dark eyes sparkled back at her. The mouth she'd loved to kiss was open with laughter. Arms that had held her close were wrapped tightly around the girl in the photograph who was laughing back up at him.

The girl who used to be Clementine Grant.

His darling Clementine.

He used to sing the song softly to her — the only person who ever called her by her full name. She'd always hated it, but he said it was pretty, and after that she'd stopped hating it. At least when he used it.

But that nineteen-year-old girl in the photograph, laughing up at him, her eyes so full of love and happiness, had no idea what lay ahead of her. His darling Clementine really was lost and gone forever.

She replaced the photos and eyed the other items through a mist of tears.

A button from the blue shirt he'd worn that night they'd gone to a dance at the town hall. She'd got tipsy and had almost fallen, grabbing him to stop herself. The button had come off in her hand and she'd slipped it in her bag for safekeeping but had never got round to giving it back to him.

Dolly, she recalled, had been less than impressed that she'd had a few too many glasses of punch. She'd given Ross quite the lecture, which wasn't really fair, as he was only just twenty-three himself at the time and why should he babysit his own girlfriend? He'd stuck by her side and got her home safely. Surely that was enough?

She picked up the small teddy bear wearing an *I heart Mr Darcy* T-shirt, bought on their trip to Bath. He'd booked them a hotel room as a surprise for her twentieth birthday, knowing how much she loved Jane Austen, and that she'd always wanted to visit the city so synonymous with her.

He'd even endured a tour of the Jane Austen Centre, gently teasing her as she'd listened, enraptured, to the actor in Regency clothing telling them about the author's life, and only moaning a little bit about the endless flights of stairs in the Georgian townhouse in which the centre was housed.

Kissing the teddy bear gently on the nose, she replaced him. He'd been in the box for years now. It seemed cruel to keep him in there. Maybe she should take him out and put him back on her bookshelf...

Sharply, she reminded herself that the teddy bear didn't care one way or the other. This was the kind of fanciful thinking that Ross had mocked her for to Noah. A dreamer. A romantic. Well, maybe she was, but he hadn't always minded that.

She gazed down at the tissue paper next to the teddy bear and forced herself to unwrap it. Just to prove to herself that it had no special powers. That it couldn't hurt her.

A lock of Ross's raven black hair lay within its folds.

A smile tugged at her lips as she recalled the moment she'd cut it.

'What the heck did you do that for?'

'I needed it. A memento. Just in case.'

'Just in case what?'

'In case something awful happens to you. You could die a tragic death. This lock of hair would be all I had left of you.'

He'd burst out laughing. 'You read way too many romance novels, you know that? Okay, you can have the hair. I guess I've got enough of it to spare.'

With a strangled sob, Clemmie rammed the lid back on the box and shoved it under the bed, just as Dolly tapped on the door and opened it.

She peered round and sighed, then walked in, carrying a

cup of tea in her hand. As she sank onto the bed she said softly, 'Thought you were getting a shower?'

'I am. I will. I just...' Clemmie shrugged. Dolly placed the cup on her bedside cabinet then put her arms around Clemmie.

'You need a shower before you put your Christmas PJs on. Father Christmas won't visit if you're all mucky. What have you been doing up here then? Please tell me you haven't been wallowing in misery all by yourself.'

'I'm allowed to wallow in misery if I want to,' Clemmie said, managing a smile.

'Of course you are, love, but not by yourself. You should have come downstairs, and we could have wallowed in misery together.'

'What have you got to be miserable about?' Clemmie asked, looking round at her aunt for the first time.

Dolly's eyes gleamed with tears.

'I'm miserable that my beautiful, clever, kind, amazing niece is so unhappy, and so lonely, when she deserves so much more.'

Clemmie wiped her eyes. 'I'm okay. It was just the shock of it, you know? I never expected to come face to face with him, and then...' She got to her feet. 'Anyway, I'm okay now.' She eyed her aunt suspiciously. 'Are you absolutely sure it was my ticket that won and not yours?'

'Cross my heart,' Dolly said solemnly. 'So what are you going to do about it? Are you going to book a sitting after Christmas?'

'Of course not. I'll ask around. I'm sure someone will want a free portrait.'

'So you're still in love with him then? Thought so.'

Clemmie gasped. 'I'm not in love with him! I have no feelings about that man whatsoever.'

'Yet you're too afraid to be in the same room as him? Come off it, Clemmie, that doesn't ring true. And what was all that rubbish Summer was spouting earlier?'

'What do you mean?' Clemmie felt the blood rush to her cheeks as her aunt pursed her lips.

'You know full well. Why does Summer think Ross cheated on you?' She frowned suddenly. 'He didn't, did he?'

'Not exactly.' Clemmie squirmed.

'What's that supposed to mean? He either did or he didn't. Which is it? Because I'm confused here, Clemmie. My memory of your break-up is clearly different to yours.'

'If he hadn't, it would only have been a matter of time until he did,' Clemmie said unhappily.

'That's your reasoning?'

'I didn't tell Summer he cheated on me,' she said miserably. 'She just assumed and I...'

'Didn't bother to put her straight. That's a pretty poor excuse for letting Summer and Ben think Ross did that to you.'

Clemmie said nothing, her face burning.

Dolly let out a long sigh. 'It's not fair, love, can't you see that? I know he hurt you, going out with all those other women so soon after you split up, but that's no reason to let people think even worse of him than they do already.'

She let Clemmie go and gave her a stern look. 'You need to put Summer right. Because you and I both know that Ross didn't break up with you at all. You broke up with him. And if anyone's heart was broken back then, it was his.'

# FIVE

The string of Yorkshire flags that hung below the upper windows of The Corner Cottage Bookshop flapped wildly in the bitter January wind that blew around the market square.

The shop stood on the corner of Little Market Street facing the market place—a solid stone building, with a single, large bay window to the left of a glass front door, and two smaller windows on the first floor. In the summer, pink rambling roses climbed the stone walls, but now only the pink and white striped canopy above the shop window, and the rather weathered looking flags, added much-needed colour to its wintry, grey exterior.

Clemmie kept her head down, wishing she'd taken her aunt's advice and worn a scarf. At least her coat had a hood, and she was wearing gloves.

Really, she thought, they ought to bring a packed lunch with them to work. It would save one of them trekking off to Bridge Bakery every day for a sandwich and a cake each. It would be cheaper too. She'd put it to Dolly, see if she agreed.

Pushing open the door of the bookshop, she gave a sigh of

relief as the warm air encircled her. She loved this shop with all her heart, and its welcoming interior never ceased to delight her.

Painted in cream throughout, and with warm oak shelving, it felt homely and spacious, despite the narrowness of the main room. Much longer than it appeared from the outside, there was a second room through an archway, and a sign above the entrance revealed the smaller room where customers would find the children's books.

In the main room, on the right, a glamorous spiral staircase snaked its way to the first floor, which housed even more books, plus a selection of stationery. Whenever Clemmie opened the shop door she felt as if she were stepping into another world, full of magic and possibilities. She was sure that, no matter how long she worked there, she would never grow tired of that delicious 'new book' smell.

The jingling of the bell must have alerted Dolly to her return, as she looked up from whatever she was writing in a notebook on the counter, directly opposite the door.

'By heck, love, you look nithered. Come on in and I'll make us a brew.'

There were no customers. January was always depressingly quiet in the shop. People had spent their hard-earned money on pointless Christmas presents, unnecessary food, and parties that left them hungover and probably full of regrets. There was nothing left for anything as useful, wonderful, and vital as books.

She mentally shook her head. When did she get so small-minded? It was Christmas, and people were entitled to spend their money on whatever they pleased. So what if they'd spent it having fun? Wasn't that up to them? Why should everyone be as miserable as she'd been?

'You okay, love?'

Dolly eyed her worriedly and Clemmie forced a smile.

'Course I am. Just thinking how drab everything looks now

the Christmas tree and lights have been taken down in the market square. You stay there and I'll make the drinks and sort out our dinners.'

She headed into the little kitchen at the side of the shop and put the carrier bag on the counter. As she flicked on the kettle, she unpacked the bag, thinking about Christmas, and how dull it had been.

It wasn't anyone's fault, of course, least of all Dolly's. She'd gone all out to make it as happy as possible. She'd treated Clemmie to some lovely presents, and they'd cooked the Christmas dinner together and agreed it had turned out perfectly. They'd each eaten their own body weight in chocolate Brazil nuts, Dolly had drunk too many glasses of Bailey's, and they'd both enjoyed some great programmes on the television.

But it wasn't...

Wasn't what? Clemmie couldn't place what had been missing. She only knew there was a gnawing feeling in her stomach that told her Christmas had lost its magic, and there was no way she was ever going to get it back.

She spooned sugar into Dolly's mug, scowling. It was all Ross Lavender's fault. Nothing had felt right since she'd overheard him making fun of her to Noah. She would never have believed it of him if she hadn't heard him with her own ears.

But why not? Hadn't he proved that she'd never really mattered to him at all? Yes, she'd been the one to end their relationship, but he'd done nothing to change her mind, had he? No attempt to fight for their relationship or persuade her she was wrong.

No. Just...

She dropped teabags in the mugs and swallowed down her own tears as she relived that day in her mind. His face, she recalled, had gone very pale, and he'd stared at her with eyes that had seemed not just dark brown but black as jet.

And that voice, quiet but steady.

'Is that what you really want, Clementine?'

'It's what I really want.' She remembered turning away from him, not able to look him in the eyes. There'd been a long silence. An endless silence.

Then, 'If that's what you want, I'll go.'

And he had. She'd heard the door close behind him. He hadn't even done her the courtesy of slamming it. He'd just shut it as if he was popping out to the shops.

It took her just a day to learn that she'd made a mistake, and that she'd made a complete fool of herself.

Then, a few days later—she wasn't sure how long exactly—he'd been seen out and about with a pretty redhead. She'd turned out to be the first of many. Ross had made it very plain to Clemmie, and to anyone else who was interested, that he was far from heartbroken about their split, and had moved on quite easily, thank you very much.

She'd sadly realised that, although she'd misjudged him in one way, she'd still been right to end it with him. There could be no future for her with someone like him and she just had to accept that.

Oh! What did it matter now? It was over six years ago, and they were both older, if not wiser. She'd had a lucky escape. Clearly, Ross wasn't one for settling down. He would never have stayed with her anyway. She'd probably got out just in time.

She poured hot water and milk into the mugs and squeezed the teabags with the back of the spoon. Dolly would be annoyed if she knew. She was forever telling Clemmie to pour the water in then leave them to brew before removing the bags and adding milk. Clemmie didn't have the patience. Far quicker and easier to do it this way.

She dropped the teabags in the bin, gave the tea a quick stir, then put the mugs on a tray, along with two plates of sandwiches and Yorkshire curd tarts.

Carrying them through to the shop she said, with forced though convincing cheer, 'Grub's up!'

As she placed them on the counter she noticed Dolly pushing some letters behind the till. If Clemmie didn't know better she'd say her aunt looked shaken, but that wasn't like her. Dolly was always in control of everything. Nothing flummoxed her.

Sure enough, a smile was immediately forthcoming.

'Curd tarts!' Dolly picked one up and nodded in approval. 'Not had one of these in a while.' She put it back on the plate. 'Did you tell them I wanted salad cream on my ham salad sandwich, not mayo?'

'Naturally, although I think they know that by now,' Clemmie said wryly. 'How many years have we been getting our sarnies from that shop now?'

'I suppose you're right.' Dolly nodded and glanced around the shop. 'Bloody hell, it's like Piccadilly Circus in here today. I'll be shattered when I get home. Rushed off my feet.'

'No need for sarcasm,' Clemmie said. 'You know what it's like after Christmas. It will pick up again soon enough.'

'I know, I know.'

They ate their sandwiches in companionable silence. Clemmie watched her aunt warily, sure that something was nagging at her.

'You okay, Dolly?'

Dolly looked startled. 'Me? Of course I am. Why wouldn't I be?'

'I don't know.' Clemmie shrugged. 'You just looked a bit rattled when you were reading the post, and you've been very quiet since. Not like you. You've always got something to say when we're having our dinner.'

'Don't be daft. I'm right as rain. Tell you what, I'm glad we work in this shop all day. Imagine having a job like Ben's, or Jonah's, in this weather. They'll be crippled with rheumatism before they're fifty.'

'Cheerful soul, aren't you?' Clemmie decided not to remind her aunt that it was her fiftieth birthday later this year. They had a few months to build up to that. Let her ease her way into the year.

'Birdie Pennyfeather popped in while you were out,' Dolly said suddenly, picking a few currants from her Yorkshire curd tart.

'Did she buy a book?' Clemmie asked, surprised. As far as she could remember, neither of the Pennyfeathers had ever bought a book—at least not from The Corner Cottage Bookshop.

'As if!' Dolly popped the currants into her mouth and ate them, then said casually, 'She was just in the wool shop, having a look at the work that's going on in there. Says it's coming on nicely, despite the Christmas break. The two rooms have been knocked through into one now, and the decorators are coming in later this week. Won't be long 'til Pennyfeather's is open again.'

Pennyfeather's—once owned by Rita and Birdie—had been run as a wool shop for over eighty years, having been started by their mother just before the second world war. Recently, the flat above the shop had been sold to a young woman called Daisy Jackson, and the shop itself had been signed over to the Pennyfeathers' great-niece, Kat.

Kat and Daisy planned to turn the whole thing into a craft shop, with a craft café upstairs. Clemmie thought it sounded like just the sort of thing Tuppenny Bridge needed, and although she didn't know Daisy, who was a newcomer to the town, she was very fond of Kat, and hoped the business would thrive.

'I'm glad to hear it,' she said.

'I think,' Dolly said carefully, 'that what Birdie really

wanted to know is if you've contacted Ross yet, about that portrait.'

Clemmie broke a little piece of pastry crust off the curd tart but made no attempt to do anything with it. She kept her eyes firmly fixed on the plate.

'Well?' Dolly asked. 'I don't know why I'm asking really, cos I'm pretty sure I know the answer. But just on the off chance that you're going to astound me, have you?'

Clemmie dropped the crust back on the plate and sighed. 'No. I—I've been busy. And it's been Christmas. And anyway, what's the rush?'

'It's Miss Lavender,' Dolly said. 'She's got a bee in her bonnet about you not taking up the prize, so Birdie says. Apparently you didn't look grateful enough when you got that voucher from Ross. She was quite disappointed apparently. Expected you to be thrilled to bits.'

'That's *her* problem,' Clemmie said abruptly. 'Everyone knows she thinks the sun shines out of Ross's backside. Always has done. Gives him everything he wants, doesn't she? He's spoilt rotten. No wonder he's so—'

'So what?' Dolly asked curiously.

'Well, you know. Everything's easy come, easy go with him, isn't it? I mean, nothing has any real value because it can always be replaced.'

'Like you, you mean?' Dolly asked, sounding sympathetic.

'I wasn't talking about me,' Clemmie replied, even though she had been. 'I mean money, possessions. Look how he's had Monk's Folly handed to him on a plate.'

'Which Isobel, according to Birdie, is not very happy about,' Dolly said with some relish. 'Seems the promise of Lavender House isn't enough for her. Now, *she's* the spoilt one if you ask me. Ross and Noah might have had an affluent childhood, but neither of them has ever struck me as being particularly spoilt. Be fair.'

Clemmie took a ferocious bite out of her curd tart and chewed in silence. Dolly, she noticed, gave a sideways glance to the till and shifted a little. Clemmie frowned.

'What's up with you, really? Have you had bad news?'

Dolly's eyes widened. 'Bad news! Such as what?'

'Well, I wouldn't know, would I? You haven't told me what's in the post that's got you so rattled.'

'I'm not rattled.' Dolly hesitated then said, 'I've just had a reminder that I'm invited to a publishing event in London in early February. I totally forgot about it, and I realised I hadn't mentioned it to you. That's all.'

Clemmie wasn't convinced. 'That's it? Really? Why would that bother you?'

'Well...' Dolly shrugged, 'It would mean leaving you on your own for a few days. I'd be staying in a hotel.'

Clemmie laughed. 'So what? I'm nearly twenty-seven! I can look after myself for a few days, Dolly. Besides, you've done it before and it's never worried you. Is there something else I should know?'

'Like what? You want to watch it. You sound paranoid. If you're sure you don't mind me going then that's fine. Nothing to worry about is there?'

No, there wasn't. If that was really the problem. Trouble was, Clemmie wasn't entirely convinced there wasn't more to it than that. It didn't add up. Dolly had never fretted about going to publishing events without her before.

She couldn't help feeling grateful that her aunt had something else to occupy her mind. It had, at least, stopped her from questioning her further about that bloody portrait sitting.

Of course she hadn't booked in with Ross. She couldn't imagine anything worse. She was sort of hoping everyone would forget about it, Ross included. It had occurred to her that she should offer to give her voucher to anyone who wanted it, but Dolly had cut that escape route off by insisting that, if Clemmie had no feelings for the man left, it wouldn't bother her to be painted by him.

If she gave the voucher away it would convince Dolly that Clemmie still cared about him, and that was the last thing she needed. Especially if Dolly had a few too many sherries and aired her opinions to someone like Bluebell from the Cutting it Fine hair salon, or—God forbid—one of the Lavender Ladies.

No, the only hope was that the townspeople would forget all about it. Ross wouldn't, but maybe he'd be glad if the subject was quietly dropped too. She couldn't imagine he'd be any happier about painting her than she'd be sitting for him.

So let Dolly worry and fuss about her being left on her own while she went off to London. Any distraction was a good one, after all.

Her aunt briskly slid the letters out from behind the till and shoved them in her handbag.

'Well,' she said, giving Clemmie a bright smile, 'that's that little problem sorted then.'

If only, Clemmie thought ruefully, all their problems could be solved so easily.

# SIX

'I can't believe you persuaded Jennifer to interview the applicants for the household staff.' Noah shook his head in wonder as they peered in through the window of the study and watched the art academy's new chief cook, Jennifer Callaghan, sitting behind a desk talking animatedly to a young woman of about twenty.

Ross grinned as they walked on towards the front door of Monk's Folly, both well wrapped up against the biting wind that was blowing off the river in their direction. Frankly, he was glad to hear his brother speak at last. He'd been so quiet since he'd arrived with Isobel that Ross had wondered if he was ill.

'She was a bit nervous at first,' he admitted, keen to keep the conversation going, 'but when I pointed out it was she who'd be working with them, not me, she saw the sense in choosing her own staff. She seems to be relishing it now, doesn't she? I think she's going to be amazing, I really do.'

Jennifer had lived at Monk's Folly for decades, since marrying her late husband, Julian Callaghan. After his death from illness, and the death of their eldest son, Leon, in a car accident some fourteen years ago, Jennifer had become reclusive, relying on her second son Ben for everything.

Last summer, Ben had finally taken steps to ease the burden he was carrying and had sold Monk's Folly to Eugenie Lavender so she could turn it into the Arabella Lavender Art Academy, and Ross had hired Jennifer—an excellent cook—to work for him, preparing meals for the staff and students when the academy opened. The Callaghans had moved into a lovely little cottage closer to the market place, and Jennifer was finally coming out of her shell.

They pushed open the front door and headed, with some relief, into the warmth of Monk's Folly.

'So glad we got the heating fixed in time for winter,' Ross said, shrugging off his coat. 'It would have been intolerable without it. I don't know how the Callaghans stood it for so long. The boiler was so inefficient, and the radiators were completely inadequate for a house of this size.'

The house now boasted underfloor heating, while the upper floors also had a mixture of cast iron and steel column radiators, painted and positioned to be as discreet as possible. It had been a big job, and expensive, too, but Aunt Eugenie was determined Monk's Folly would be a thing of beauty by the time it was finished, while Ross's priority was to ensure his students would be warm and comfortable.

After hanging their coats in the cupboard off the hallway, the two of them headed into the living room, where they found Isobel waiting for them, along with a tray of sandwiches and mugs of tea.

'You made these for us?'

Noah sounded genuinely surprised, and Isobel beamed at him.

'Of course. I thought you'd be in need of refreshments after walking around the grounds in this awful weather. Is it all taking shape, Ross?'

Ross wondered what she was up to. It wasn't like Isobel to be so pleasant. Still, it made a nice change, and at least Noah seemed to have brightened a little, so he reached for a sandwich and nodded.

'It's getting there, slowly but surely. I've just shown Noah the studio.'

'It's looking grand,' Noah confirmed. 'When you think of that awful old double garage that used to stand there, and now there's this smart, deluxe building that's going to make an amazing art studio.'

'Won't you need a garage?' Isobel queried. 'And what about car parking? There's hardly going to be enough room for the students' cars here, especially since you're insisting on buying that minibus. What for, I can't imagine.'

'The students can park their cars in town and then they'll be driven here in the minibus. We've negotiated a long-term parking discount with the landlord of The Black Swan. He's going to let them park behind his pub. Anyway, we'll also need the minibus for student excursions.'

'Thank heavens for the improvements to the lane then,' Isobel said. 'It's vastly improved, I must say. It used to be awful bumping along here to Monk's Folly, didn't it, Noah? Do you remember when you got your first car, and we jolted along the lane to see Leon? We were terribly worried about the suspension.' She gave a tinkling laugh which sounded, to Ross, entirely fake. 'I don't suppose he'd recognise the road now.'

'No,' Noah said quietly, 'I don't suppose he would.'

Ross's stomach churned. He hated to think about Leon, because it inevitably led to memories of his and Ben's friendship, and why it had ended. He reached desperately for a change of subject.

'Jennifer's interviewing the kitchen staff and cleaners, Aunt Eugenie's going to be interviewing for a gardener stroke handyman, and I've got to find some admin help. I don't suppose you'd like to help with that, Noah? You'd be better at it than me.'

To his relief, Noah laughed. 'Are you joking? Don't you think I'm buried in enough admin at work?'

'But that's my point,' Ross said, more to keep the light-hearted conversation going than having any real hope of his brother agreeing. 'You do so much of it at that school of yours that you'd be the perfect person to find me some decent staff.'

'It sounds to me,' Noah said, 'as if you're having the easiest time of it. While you've got all these other people around interviewing potential staff members for you, what exactly are you going to be doing?'

'I have to look for another art teacher,' Ross said, slightly offended. 'Not only that, but I'm scouring local artists to see if they'd like to exhibit their work here, and also persuade them to do some demonstrations of their medium.' He grinned at Noah. 'Believe it or not, I've finally persuaded Jonah to let us bring students to the forge to watch him at work.'

'Shoeing horses?' Isobel asked, clearly perplexed.

'Not his work as a farrier,' Ross said patiently. 'He's also an artist blacksmith. I think it will be fascinating to see him in action. Also,' he added, turning back to Noah, 'I'm still project managing the restoration and redecoration of this house, of course, which is easier said than done. Aunt Eugenie's being so particular. She really wants it to look like a proper Regency house, just as if Arabella could walk into the place and recognise it. My view is that, although some Regency features would be nice, the priority is comfort, warmth, and suitability as an art school. We're having some fairly heated debates.'

Isobel shuddered. 'I hope you win! Aren't you worried about living here, seriously? Rumour has it that Monk's Folly is haunted by the ghosts of Arabella and her awful husband, Henry Panton. Fancy bumping into those two when you're creeping along the landing at night! It would finish me off.'

'Why would I be creeping along the landing at night?' Ross asked.

'The bathroom, naturally,' Noah said.

Isobel laughed. 'This is Ross we're talking about. All those female students he'll have staying here! Bound to be at least one in every intake that he ends up hooking up with.'

'There most certainly will not!' Ross almost choked on the last bit of his sandwich. 'Business and pleasure definitely don't mix, and this is going to be a professional establishment. The last thing I need are any sordid complications.'

'Hmm.' Isobel sipped her tea. 'Talking of sordid complications—has Clemmie Grant booked her portrait sitting yet?'

'Maybe we shouldn't talk about that,' Noah said quietly, earning a look of reproach from his wife.

'Why on earth not? It's not a big deal, is it?' Her china blue eyes narrowed as she smirked. 'Or is it?'

Ross picked up his mug and took a gulp of tea.

'Don't tell me you're still carrying a torch for the girl after all these years?' Isobel said scathingly. 'You can't be!'

'Of course I'm not,' Ross said, trying to inject as much scorn into his voice as he could muster. Hell, what a ridiculous idea that was! He had no interest in Clemmie whatsoever and wished with all his heart the prize had been won by anyone but her. 'It's just awkward, that's all. And let's face it, she's not exactly interesting to paint.'

'Well, no, I suppose not,' Isobel acknowledged. 'I mean, she's pretty enough in her own way, but she doesn't stand out, does she? There's nothing special about her. You're going to have to dig deep to make any portrait of her worth looking at. Good job you're such a talented artist.'

Ross glanced at Noah, who was nibbling half-heartedly at a sandwich, looking as if it tasted mouldy. He wondered again why his brother was being so quiet, and why Isobel was being so friendly. Friendly by her standards anyway.

'So whereabouts are you going to be living?' Isobel asked. 'Have you decided?'

'For now I've just nabbed one of the first-floor bedrooms and put a kettle and microwave in there since the kitchen's been ripped out. When I talk to the interior designer tomorrow we're going to be making firmer plans about my quarters. I'm not sure which floor I'll be living on, but I daresay Aunt Eugenie has already got it all worked out. She's attending the meeting with me.'

'Rather you than me,' Isobel said. She glanced around the living room, which had been stripped of its dismal wallpaper and was awaiting the transforming talents of the designer and decorating team Aunt Eugenie had hired. 'It seems such a shame,' she said thoughtfully. 'I mean, this house always seemed cold and ugly to me, but it could have been beautiful, and I'm sure if your aunt throws enough money at it she could make it as elegant as it was when it was first built. But then it's going to be ruined again by turning it into an art school! How much better it would be if it could remain a home.'

'Well,' Ross said bluntly, 'it can't. It wasn't bought for pleasure, Isobel.'

'Oh come off it! We all know Aunt Eugenie's been itching to get her mitts on this house all her life. She's always said the Lavenders should never have sold it to the Callaghans in the first place.'

'Maybe so, but it still needs to earn its keep. Aunt Eugenie's investing a lot of money in this place, and it has to start paying her back. It might be a labour of love for her, and for me really, but it's a school first and foremost. That must be the priority.'

'I think it will look amazing when it's done,' Noah said, giving him a genuine smile. 'I'm sure you'll make a great success of it, Ross.'

Isobel's own smile was undoubtedly forced as she inclined her head towards him. 'Oh, I'm sure you will, too. It goes without saying. After all, you've had so much help, how can it possibly fail?'

She took another sip of tea. 'And I'm sure the portrait you paint of Clemmie Grant will be a useful advertising promotion. After all, that's why you offered the prize, wasn't it? As advertising for the school, I mean. Not so you can paint Clemmie. Well, good luck with it, Ross. I'm sure I don't have to tell you that it's not going to be easy.'

Ross gave her a brief nod in return. He wasn't entirely sure whether she was referring to running the art academy, or painting Clemmie. Both tasks were going to be a challenge. Truthfully, he knew he had his work cut out for him either way.

## SEVEN

Ross would never admit it out loud but there was a huge part of him that was delighted and excited that Monk's Folly was being restored to its Regency glory. He remembered it from when he was a child, and Ben Callaghan had been his best friend. He used to visit regularly back then and had thought it a gloomy old pile even in those days.

If he'd ever imagined a Regency house before—and he couldn't say he had really—he supposed he'd have had in mind a Bath townhouse. Elegant and narrow, with at least four storeys. Monk's Folly didn't fit the bill at all, being more squat and solid.

Then again, it wasn't a townhouse. It had been built to withstand the Yorkshire Dales' climate, and that could be harsh. The weather had beaten the house until it resembled a large, country farmhouse more than a Regency home, and the Callaghans' hideous old furniture, threadbare carpets, and drab wallpaper hadn't helped.

Ross had considered it exceptionally ugly, and with more than a hint of the gothic about it.

Time—and age—had made him look at Monk's Folly through different eyes. He supposed the limitless enthusiasm of

Aunt Eugenie had helped him to see what it could be, and browsing through the paintings and sketches that Arabella Lavender had created (far from the watchful eyes of her disapproving husband, naturally) he'd felt a growing enthusiasm as he gazed at the background of her subjects, which had almost invariably been painted inside the house while Henry Panton was away on business.

She'd inadvertently left a record of what some of the house had looked like in her day, and it was enchanting. He could picture it in his mind's eye and was keen to see it returned to the charming place it had once been. The trouble was, he had no idea where to start, so he was gratified to hear his interior designer so enthusiastic and brimming with ideas.

Meg McKenna was tall, voluptuous, dark-haired, and green-eyed, with a sharp eye and a stack of credentials to her name. Highly recommended by someone Aunt Eugenie knew and respected, she'd sailed into Monk's Folly like a magnificent galleon sailing into harbour, and Ross had known immediately that if she didn't share his vision he was in big trouble, because he couldn't imagine for a moment that Meg would be easy to talk round.

Luckily for him, an in-depth discussion as they walked around the house revealed that the two of them were very much of one mind. Meg had experience in working in period homes, restoring them to their former glory, and she was looking forward to getting started on Monk's Folly.

'Although,' she admitted, as they headed back down the stairs, 'it's such a shame that so many of the original features have been removed. At least the cornicing and ceiling roses are still in place. What's the story with the windows? They're not original, are they?'

Ross ushered her into the living room so they could talk some more. 'Sadly,' he told her, 'the original windows were removed just after the Great War by the Callaghans, who'd bought the house in 1905. We've had a lot of discussions with the council, but they're happy for us to take out these windows and put high-quality Regency reproduction sash windows in place. We've had a manufacturing survey and we're just waiting for a delivery and installation date. They'll be timber framed naturally, and we'll have internal shutters fixed too. That should let in more light. When the Callaghans lived here they had heavy, dark curtains up at the windows and I remember it was always gloomy in here.'

He inwardly shuddered at the memory. 'Tea? Coffee? Can I offer you something to eat?' He'd bought a few packets of biscuits—more in case he got peckish and couldn't be bothered to cook than for his guest's sake—and there was a kettle in the study, along with some cups. He wasn't sure someone as sophisticated as Meg McKenna would settle for instant coffee or teabags though. He should have bought a coffee machine.

'No thank you. Not right now.' She sat down without waiting to be asked, which he thought refreshing, and continued to talk. 'I'm surprised it's not listed, I must say. Most houses built before 1820 are.'

'I know. Lavender House—that's my great aunt's house which is now also a museum—is listed, but somehow Monk's Folly escaped, which is lucky for me. Although obviously, we're still running everything by the planning department, to be on the safe side.' He gave her an almost apologetic smile. 'Luckily Aunt Eugenie's very well-connected, and they've been most accommodating.'

*Well-connected and highly demanding as well as being bloody scary when she puts her mind to it, but probably best not to mention that.*

'I see you've already made a start on some things, like stripping the wallpaper. I couldn't help noticing the radiators upstairs, as discreet as they are. You're okay with having them despite the wish for a Regency look in the house?'

Ross nodded. 'We want to do a sympathetic refurbishment but at the same time we must be practical. We have our students to think of, apart from the fact that I'm going to be living here soon myself. I mean, let's face it, if we were being total purists we wouldn't have electricity, or the internet, would we?'

She smiled. 'Fair enough. I just wanted to be sure how far you want to go. For example, that fireplace. You do know it's Victorian, not Regency?'

'I didn't actually, though looking at it now I should have guessed,' Ross admitted. 'It was already here. We didn't buy it.'

'And do you want to replace it? There are a few either missing or from the wrong period. Are you planning to replace them all?'

He considered. 'I don't think there's a need for a fireplace in every room, and it would be more work and expense to open them up again. Maybe we could just replace the ones in the two front living rooms and the dining room but leave the rooms currently without alone. I'm not sure how much that would cost.'

'I know somewhere very reputable. They do reproduction and restoration, so it would be up to you which you'd prefer.'

Ross frowned. 'Which would be cheaper?'

'Honestly? It depends. You might be surprised to find that some restored antiques are around the same price or even less than well-made reproductions. I can show you the website later, see what you think. We could go there, have a look around. Make a day of it. And since I know the man in charge, I might be able to get us some sort of deal on the Victorian fireplaces. Make some money back. What do you think?'

'That sounds amazing,' Ross said enthusiastically.

'Then there's wallpaper,' she continued. 'Surprisingly little is known about Georgian and Regency wallpaper, in comparison to other eras. I wonder if you're intending to paper the walls or if you want to simply paint them? In which case we should look at some appropriate paint colours.'

'To be honest,' Ross said, 'I'm happy to paint them. My thinking is this is going to be a place of business, and there will be a lot of people staying here. There's not much point spending a lot of money on wallpaper. If it was going to be a family home then I'd think differently, but as it stands...'

'So we're looking at softer, more muted colours. Lots of cream, pale lilac, powder blue, that sort of thing. Which reminds me, have you given any more thought to where you'd like your living quarters to be?' she asked. 'Maybe you could make more of a splash in your own private space. I understand the public areas should have less money spent on them, but surely your own home is a different matter?'

Ross sighed. 'I still haven't made my mind up about that,' he said. 'There's a lot more to think about than I'd realised. And of course, Aunt Eugenie will be here soon and will definitely have her own opinions.'

She nodded. 'Maybe while you're thinking about it we should have that coffee after all?' Her smile was quite dazzling. 'You know, Ross, I think you and I are going to make the perfect team.'

He smiled back, noticing the light dusting of freckles on her nose, and the flecks of gold in her green eyes. 'I'm sure we will,' he agreed.

'Perhaps we could meet up one evening for dinner? We could discuss more over a decent meal. Truth is, I'm staying at a tiny hotel in some town called Lingham-on-Skimmer about ten miles away, and I don't like being stuck in my room every evening. It's hardly five-star, but it does have an okay restaurant. My treat naturally. I do think it's more civilised to discuss these things over food, and it would be a break from those four walls upstairs. Unless you know somewhere better?'

'There's The White Hart Inn or The Black Swan,' Ross

suggested, as he flicked through the paint brochures she'd pushed towards him. 'They both do good food. They're only across the river. In fact, The Black Swan's just across the road from the riverbank. You can see this place from the window.'

'That sounds perfect. You'll have to check your diary and let me know when you're free.' She glanced up as the door opened and his aunt stomped into the room.

'Aunt Eugenie, allow me to introduce Meg McKenna,' Ross said. 'Meg, this is my great aunt. She's the one holding the purse strings.'

Aunt Eugenie nodded firmly and held out her hand to shake Meg's. 'Very pleased to meet you, er, Miss McKenna? Mrs McKenna? Or perhaps you go by that dreadful term, Ms?'

'Why don't you just call me Meg?'

'Perfect. So how are we getting on? Ross, be an angel and put the kettle on, would you? I'm longing for a cup of tea.'

Ross nodded as Meg added, 'Coffee for me please. Black, no sugar.'

As he walked out of the room he thought vaguely that he still didn't know if she was Miss, Mrs or Ms. And it also occurred to him suddenly that he'd agreed to have dinner with her one night at The Black Swan. He could imagine what the Lavender Ladies would make of that if they got wind of it, which they no doubt would, because Meg was bound to mention it in front of his Aunt Eugenie.

Oh well, he was used to gossip about his supposed love life. Let them speculate. It had never mattered to him before, and he wasn't going to let it bother him now.

# EIGHT

Dolly, thought Clemmie, had been behaving oddly all day. In fact, scrap that, she'd been behaving oddly all week. Back home at Wintergreen, settled in the living room each evening, Clemmie would sometimes look up from her book and catch her aunt staring at her, a most peculiar expression on her face.

At work she was distracted, blaming her writing schedule when Clemmie challenged her. Clemmie didn't buy it for a second, though she had felt a bit guilty when Dolly asked her if she minded looking after the shop alone for a couple of days, as her aunt was so behind with the first draft of her latest novel.

'I didn't realise,' she'd said, rather ashamed of herself. Since she'd started working on *The Marquess Wants a Wife*, what felt like an eternity ago, she'd developed a much greater appreciation for Dolly's craft. 'You should have mentioned it if you were struggling. Anyway, we're hardly swamped with customers, are we? Go ahead and take as many days as you need.'

'Two should be enough,' Dolly had assured her. 'I just need to do some catching up, that's all. Thanks, love.'

Today, Dolly was coming back to The Corner Cottage Bookshop, but her eyes still held that worried look, and as they drove towards Tuppenny Bridge that morning, Clemmie couldn't help feeling concerned.

'Are you sure you're all caught up with the writing, Dolly?' she asked, noting the tightness in her aunt's jaw as she gripped the steering wheel.

'What? Oh, 'course I am. I said so, didn't I? Mind you, I need to put in a few extra hours of an evening, what with me going to London next month. Don't want to fall behind again. No more *Corrie* and *Emmerdale* for me for the next few months, I'm afraid.'

Clemmie grinned. 'How will you manage? Look, you can take some more days away from the shop if you—'

'No, no. It's fine, honest, love.' Dolly glanced at Clemmie and gave her a warm smile. 'You okay? I haven't really spent much time with you lately, have I?'

'But you're busy. We both know the score, and besides, I've been reading when I get home from work. I haven't even missed you.'

'Bloody charming that is.' Dolly laughed good-naturedly. 'What is it this time? Are you mooning about over Darcy, or fantasising about Heathcliff?'

'Heathcliff?' Clemmie shuddered. 'You know me better than that, I should hope.'

'Of course. What was I thinking? What any bugger sees in that sadistic sod I have no idea. So who's the hero of the week right now?'

Clemmie blushed a little, all too aware of what her aunt would say when she admitted the truth.

'Er, Captain Wentworth,' she said hesitantly.

Dolly burst out laughing. 'By heck, you've had your money's worth out of that book! How many times have you read *Persuasion* now? I've given up counting.'

'I love it,' Clemmie said dreamily. 'It's such a romantic story. Just when you think Anne's going to be alone forever, Captain

Wentworth finally finds it in his heart to trust her again, and they get the new beginning they deserve.'

'Have you ever thought of reading something a bit more contemporary?' Dolly suggested. 'I mean, I wouldn't want to frighten you or anything, but I do write sagas set during the Second World War and you said you enjoyed them. Why not read a few more by another author?' Her eyes narrowed. 'Unless you were just being kind to your poor old auntie, of course.'

'Dolly, I love your books,' Clemmie assured her. 'It's just that the Regency and Georgian eras are so romantic.'

'Hmm, but not exclusively. You read *North and South*,' Dolly pointed out. 'That's Victorian, and you fell madly in love with John Thornton as I recall. And I swear I once caught you having a sneaky look at *The Importance of Being Earnest*. You want to be careful. At this rate you're going to find yourself in the twenty-first century before you know it.'

'I'm not that bad!' Clemmie protested indignantly. 'I've read some modern books. You know I have. I just like to alternate contemporary with historical romance. Nothing wrong with that is there?'

'No, love.' Dolly sighed. 'Nothing wrong with that. You and your romances...'

Clemmie shuffled uncomfortably in her seat. There was no way she was going to tell Dolly the real reason she was devouring so many Regency novels lately. If her aunt discovered she'd almost finished writing her own she'd never hear the last of it. It was definitely something Clemmie was keeping to herself.

They drove over the stone structure that gave Tuppenny Bridge its name, and Clemmie couldn't help but give a sideways glance at the riverbank, where she could just about make out Monk's Folly before Dolly turned down Green Lane and the riverbank vanished from her view.

She wondered if Ross was there, and if he'd moved into the house yet, and was about to ask Dolly when she realised it would only stir up a hornet's nest. Her aunt was bound to ask if she'd arranged a date for her portrait sitting yet, which was the last thing she wanted. Best keep off the subject of Ross Lavender altogether.

The morning passed without incident. There was a slow trickle of customers to the bookshop, and Clemmie thought the post-Christmas dearth might finally be ending. Trade usually picked up by the end of January so, fingers crossed, the shop would be busier before too long.

She passed the time between serving by dusting the shelves, pausing now and then to withdraw a book she liked the look of, and giving it a quick once-over to see if she wanted to buy it.

When Dolly went upstairs to clean the first floor of the shop, she whipped her notebook out of her bag and added a couple of hundred words to her work in progress. It was, she thought, nearly done. Her hero, Rollo Bannerman, Marquess of Wolchester, had already won her heart and might even replace Captain Wentworth in her affections one day. She chewed her pen thoughtfully. She wasn't so sure about the heroine, Emmeline Balfour, though. Something was missing there. She just couldn't figure out what.

By the time her aunt came back downstairs it was lunch time, and she and Dolly settled themselves to eat the ham and tomato sandwiches Clemmie had packed for them, washed down, naturally, with a good strong mug of tea each.

'Well,' Dolly said, looking around, 'the shop's nice and tidy at any rate, even if we have made about fourteen pence profit today so far.'

'I think we've made a bit more than that,' Clemmie said wryly. 'That red-haired woman bought the entire *Chronicles of Narnia* for her goddaughter, and the young bloke in the duffel coat bought three books of air fryer recipes, so cheer up.'

'You're right! What was I thinking? Let's book a holiday to Mauritius.' Dolly laughed and took another swig of tea, just as the bell above the door jangled and a man walked in.

'Here we go. Maybe he's after the full backlist of Terry Pratchett,' Clemmie said hopefully, giving Dolly a nudge.

Her aunt gulped down the tea and coughed, and Clemmie eyed her with concern.

'You okay, Dolly?'

Dolly's eyes were fixed on the man, and to Clemmie's surprise she rushed towards him, her arms outstretched.

'Reuben! I don't believe it. What are you doing in this neck of the woods?'

Reuben? Who the heck was Reuben? Clemmie watched as the man stood awkwardly while Dolly gave him air kisses. Air kisses! Dolly never did that. Whoever this bloke was he'd got her aunt rattled.

Clemmie eyed him dubiously. On the surface he seemed okay. He was probably about thirty, she thought. Fair-haired and casually dressed, she had never seen him before, and couldn't imagine where Dolly knew him from.

Her aunt spun round, dragging the man with her. 'Clemmie, love, this is Reuben Walker. He's the son of an old friend of mine. Reuben, this is my niece. Clemmie Grant.'

Reuben made no move towards her, but simply stared at her. She noticed he had blue eyes and a round face, and was probably about five foot nine, although he looked a lot taller standing next to Dolly, who was basically five foot and a peanut.

'Pleased to meet you,' she said, since he obviously wasn't going to say anything.

Dolly gave Reuben a slight nudge, and he blinked and stepped towards Clemmie, holding out his hand.

'Clemmie. It's so good to meet you,' he said, and she thought he sounded genuine at least. Maybe he was just shy. She could relate to that.

'Pleased to meet you, too,' she said, aware that her voice was a little croaky. She cleared it and turned her questioning gaze on Dolly. 'What old friend?'

Dolly looked blank for a moment, then said, 'Oh! Oh, no one you know, love. He was my accountant many moons ago. Sadly, he passed away some years ago now. Haven't seen Reuben for ages, have I? How are you doing? What brings you here?'

Reuben's expression softened. 'I—I recently lost my mum, and I thought I could do with getting away from the world for a bit. I remembered Dad telling me about this place and I thought it sounded just the job, so here I am.'

Clemmie's heart went out to him. She could empathise with his loss all too well. 'I'm so sorry about your mum,' she said. 'How awful for you.'

'Thank you. It was. But the way I look at it is, at least she's not in pain any longer. It was a rough couple of years for her. For all of us. She's at peace now.'

Clemmie's eyes filled with tears and Dolly said briskly, 'I'm sorry to hear that, Reuben. Here, let me put the kettle on. Nice cup of tea's what you need.'

As she hurried into the kitchen, Clemmie smiled at Reuben and said, 'That's her answer to everything. No matter what's going on, nothing's so bad it can't be made better with a cup of tea.'

'If only that were true,' Reuben said, but at least he smiled back at her.

Clemmie wasn't sure what else to say to him. Small talk was never her strong point, and she wasn't good with strangers. She'd often wondered who she got this shyness from, because Dolly was one of the most outgoing and sociable people she knew. She supposed it must have come from either her mum or dad, but it was hard to remember.

She hadn't known them as an adult, as they'd died of carbon

monoxide poisoning when she was only thirteen. They'd been staying in a caravan in Scotland and there'd been a fault with a heater. Her parents had been found side by side in bed, holding hands. Dolly had been responsible for her ever since.

To her, both her parents had seemed remarkably self-assured, but then she'd only seen them from a child's perspective. They were just Mum and Dad, and she'd had every confidence they could handle any situation they found themselves in.

Anyway, they'd had each other. Her parents were devoted to one another and had a blissfully happy marriage. The only comfort Clemmie had ever taken from their deaths was that at least they'd died together. She was sure they'd have wanted it that way because she couldn't imagine how one of them could have carried on without the other.

Reuben shuffled uncomfortably and Clemmie's attention was dragged back to him immediately.

'Would you like to sit down behind the till?' she asked politely. 'There's a chair there if you—'

'I'm fine, thanks.' Reuben gazed around him. 'Nice shop. Love the Yorkshire flags flying outside.'

Clemmie laughed. 'Dolly decided to keep them up all year round. We used to put them up for Yorkshire Day, but then a customer made the mistake of telling her they didn't approve, so now she keeps them up permanently. They're looking a bit bedraggled after the weather we've had recently. Lots of rain and it's been quite windy. Are you from Yorkshire then?'

'London,' he said briefly.

'London? Quite a trip. Are you staying long?'

Reuben was saved from answering as Dolly returned with a tray of drinks. Clearly she'd decided this was a special occasion which merited a second mug of tea for herself and Clemmie.

'There you go, lovey. Milk and sugar if you need it. Now, are you two getting to know each other?'

Clemmie blushed. 'Reuben was just telling me that he's from London.'

'Oh yes,' Dolly said, nodding. 'He's in foreign parts here.'

'Whereabouts in London?' Clemmie asked, just as Reuben took a sip of tea.

She turned to Dolly, but Dolly gulped down some tea, too, so she had to wait for a moment until one of them was ready to speak.

'Hampstead,' Reuben said eventually.

'Oh, okay.' Clemmie had heard of it, of course, but she had no real idea what it was like. 'Is it nice there?'

'It is,' he said. 'You're not familiar with it?'

'Never been to London,' Clemmie admitted.

His eyes widened. 'Seriously? Never?'

Clemmie shrugged. 'Why would I want to? I'm quite happy here.'

Reuben stared at her, and Dolly said, 'So where are you staying, Reuben? You're very welcome to stay at ours if you want. It's a few miles out of town, but there's plenty of room.'

Clemmie wasn't so sure about that. They hardly knew this man, after all. The thought of sharing her private space with him was unappealing, to say the least. What was Dolly thinking?

Fortunately, Reuben declined the offer. 'It's very kind of you but I've already booked a holiday cottage in Tuppenny Bridge. In fact, I've just been there and unpacked, and it's a nice place. I'll be very comfortable there.'

'Oh, really?' Dolly sounded surprised for some reason. 'Well, if you're sure. Whereabouts is it? We probably know it,' she added.

'Dale View on Lavender Lane?'

'Oh yes, it's not far from Lavender House, is it? Nice.'

'How long are you staying?' Clemmie asked.

'Well, I've nothing to rush back for now Mum's gone,' he

said briefly. 'I can work anywhere, and to be honest, I need the break. I've booked it until the first of March. Luckily, it was available, what with it being winter. That should be long enough.'

'Long enough for what?' Clemmie asked, curious.

He hesitated. 'For me to sort my head out, I suppose. It's been a stressful time.'

She supposed it had, and the sympathy for him returned. 'What is it you do for a living?' she asked, remembering he'd said he could work anywhere.

'I'm a web developer,' he said. 'I create, design, and maintain websites for my clients.'

Dolly looked impressed. 'Really?'

Clemmie frowned. 'Didn't you know?'

'We've, er, never spoken about it,' Dolly said. 'I've only met Reuben once before, when I was in London a while back. I didn't know his mum, you see. It was his dad I knew, and, like I say, he died some years ago. I don't think you were a web developer then, were you, love? Probably still at college or uni.'

'Yeah, I think so.' Reuben nodded. 'Anyway, I just wanted to pop by and let you know I was in town, so maybe we could meet up again—the three of us, I mean. It would be nice to get to know you both better. Any friend of Dad's and all that...'

'Smashing idea,' Dolly said enthusiastically. 'We'd like that, wouldn't we, Clemmie? I'm sure you two will have a lot in common and get on famously.'

Her eyes flashed at her niece, and Clemmie gave a silent groan. Surely, surely Dolly wasn't trying to play Cupid? Reuben had just lost his mother, for goodness' sake, and even if he hadn't, why would he be interested in someone like her?

And, as nice looking and friendly as he seemed, she wasn't interested in him. Not in the slightest. She didn't think she'd ever be interested in any 'real-life flesh and blood man' ever again.

'Great,' he said. 'How about tomorrow night at my place? I'd like to cook for you. I'm quite good at cooking if I say so myself.'

'Are you sure?' Clemmie asked doubtfully. 'We wouldn't want to put you to any trouble.'

'You're welcome to come to ours,' Dolly said, sounding cautious. 'Of course, if you prefer...'

'Maybe next time?' Reuben suggested. 'Honestly, I find cooking helps relax me, but who wants to cook for one? You'd be doing me a favour.'

Dolly and Clemmie exchanged glances.

'Fair enough, love,' Dolly said with a shrug. 'Shall we say six thirty at yours then?'

'Great. I'll look forward to it. Nice to meet you, er, Clemmie.'

'You too.'

As Reuben bid them both farewell and headed towards the door, Dolly flashed her a wary smile. If she wasn't mistaken there was an apology in those eyes.

Clemmie sighed. So she was right. Dolly *had* been trying to play Cupid, and now she was feeling embarrassed about it. Serves her right!

The bell jingled and she turned to call goodbye to Reuben, but the sound died in her throat as Ross entered the shop. There was an awkward moment when he and Reuben tried to get past each other, then both apologised and stepped back at the same time. Reuben laughed and waved Ross into the shop and Ross thanked him, then turned to Clemmie as Reuben closed the shop door behind him.

# NINE

Clemmie's heart achieved the extraordinary feat of leaping up into her mouth before plunging with alarming speed and settling in her boots. Only Ross Lavender, she thought bleakly, could have that effect on her.

She couldn't believe he'd walked into The Corner Cottage Bookshop as if he had every right to be there. Well, technically he did, of course. But morally? After the way he'd spoken about her on Christmas Eve she didn't know how he had the nerve.

Now she came to think about it, she hadn't seen him in here since the break-up. She had an awful feeling she knew exactly why he'd come, and she didn't think for a moment that it had anything to do with books.

She was all too aware of Dolly turning to look at her, her teeth gently nipping her lower lip as she waited to see how this would play out. It was like a scene from a Wild West movie, Clemmie thought suddenly, as she and Ross faced each other in silence. Who would draw first?

When neither of them made a move towards the other, Dolly clearly decided it was time for her to stage an intervention.

She hurried towards Ross, a wide smile on her face. 'Yes, love, what can I do for you?'

Ross looked taken aback by the warmth of her greeting.

'I—er—I need to speak to...' His voice trailed off and he nodded uncertainly towards Clemmie, who could feel the tell-tale burning sensation in her face, and knew she was blushing furiously.

'What about?' she asked, sounding ruder than she'd meant to. The truth was, she was perfectly well aware that he was here to ask about the portrait. What else would he be here for after all?

Ross frowned, and she saw her snappy tone had annoyed him. Well, good. Maybe he wouldn't hang around then.

'I need to fix a date for this sitting,' he said, sounding irritated, as if it was all an annoying waste of time for him which, she guessed, was how he probably saw it.

'I've told you. I'll get round to it.' She doodled a meaningless scribble in the order book on the counter, realising too late that Dolly would be less than impressed with her act of wanton vandalism. 'Soon.'

'Well you'd better hurry up about it. We've got the art academy scheduled to open in a few months and it's all hands on deck there. I've got enough to do without hanging around waiting for you to make an appointment. I thought you'd have done it straight after Christmas. I could have got the preliminaries done by now if you'd got your act together.'

Clemmie glanced at her aunt, hoping for some backup, but Dolly was simply watching them, saying nothing.

'Look, why don't you give the prize to someone else?' Clemmie said coldly, turning back to Ross whose eyebrows shot up in surprise at her question.

'Someone else?'

'Yeah. I'm sure there are loads of people who'd love to get

their portrait painted by you, so why not re-raffle it? I don't mind.'

He gave her a scornful look. 'I'm sure you don't, but if you think I've got time to mess about doing yet another raffle...'

'Well offer it to someone you know then,' she said desperately. 'What about Isobel? Or your great-aunt? I'll bet either of them would enjoy that.'

Ross drew himself up and glared at her, then glanced at Dolly who shrugged. For a moment he seemed lost for words, then he shook his head.

'Can't do that. What you fail to understand is that this is a publicity promotion for the art academy. Your name was announced on social media and in the local press. Everyone's waiting to see this painting—this painting of you. If I produce a painting of someone else, people are going to want to know why.'

'So tell them I was too busy,' she muttered.

'Too busy? What kind of excuse is that? People will talk. They'll start casting aspersions on me and my work. What if they think it's because I tried to paint you and it was a disaster? Or they'll think the whole raffle prize was a scam. You know what people are like. No smoke without fire and all that. My reputation as an artist could be trashed.'

'I think you're being a bit dramatic,' Clemmie said sulkily.

'*I'm* being dramatic? What about *you*? You're the one making a song and dance about this. Why can't you just do the sitting so we can get this ordeal over and done with?'

'Ordeal? Wow, you make it sound so irresistible who could possibly refuse?'

Ross took a steadying breath. 'We both know this isn't an ideal situation. I probably wouldn't have offered the prize if I'd known you were going to win, and I'm sure you wouldn't have entered at all if you'd thought you'd hold the winning ticket.'

'No,' she said bluntly. 'I wouldn't.'

He paused, and for a moment she thought she saw a flash of something in his eyes. Was he—hurt? But no, he couldn't be. Why should he care whether she wanted to be painted by him or not? He'd already admitted it wasn't an ideal situation. No doubt if there'd been no publicity he'd have been begging her to let him find another subject.

'I promised that the winner would get their portrait painted by me,' he said icily. 'A promise is a promise, remember? At least, for most people.'

The heat in her cheeks increased as she stared back at him, seeing the challenge in his eyes. She knew all too well what he meant. Hadn't they once promised they'd always be together, and that nothing would come between them? She'd broken that promise. She couldn't deny it.

Even so, she'd hardly broken his heart, had she? Whatever Dolly believed, Ross had got over Clemmie so quickly it had taken her breath away. If anyone had been hurt it had been her, and she'd never stopped hurting since.

Every time he paraded another gorgeous woman around town it was like a splinter of glass in her heart. She wouldn't admit it to anyone, not for the world, but Ross had had his revenge, whatever he believed.

Dolly stepped forward, clearing her throat. 'Tell you what, love,' she said to Ross, 'why not let Clemmie and I have a little chat about when's best to fit her in, and then she can text you and let you know, and you can go from there.'

'When?' he asked, clearly not taking her word for it that something was actually going to happen.

'She'll text you after tea tonight,' Dolly said firmly, ignoring Clemmie's frantic facial gestures. Clemmie only just managed to straighten her face as Ross turned back to her.

'Do you still have my number?'

'Of course not,' she said dismissively. 'You'd better write it down for me.'

To her dismay, he took his phone from his coat pocket and made a few taps on the screen. Instantly, Clemmie's own phone began to vibrate loudly from its shelf under the counter, where it nestled on top of *Persuasion*.

'There you go,' Ross said. 'That's my number. Make sure you let me know as soon as possible.'

With that, he spun round and pulled open the door, leaving The Corner Cottage Bookshop as suddenly as he'd arrived.

Clemmie exhaled and slumped against the counter, all too relieved that he'd gone. Dolly put her elbows on the counter and leaned over, eyeing the phone with evident curiosity.

'You could have helped me,' Clemmie said accusingly.

'Helped you? How?'

'What do you mean, how? You could have told him to stop hassling me for a start.'

'He's hardly hassling you, love. He's got a business to run, and this is promotion work for that. If you didn't want your portrait painting you shouldn't have bought a ticket.'

Clemmie gasped. 'Neither of us knew what the prizes were going to be when the Pennyfeathers came round begging us to buy tickets from them!'

'Then let that be a lesson to both of us in future,' Dolly said cheerfully. 'Always check what you're buying a ticket for. Could have been worse. You might have had to go skydiving, or swimming with sharks.'

'Swimming with sharks? Isn't that just about the same thing?' Clemmie muttered.

'Don't be so mean. Poor lad's got a job to do. This can't be any easier for him than it is for you. In fact, it's probably worse, given that he was the one who got dumped.'

'Will you stop saying that?' Clemmie said crossly. 'You know what happened. You know why I had to do it. And you know he didn't take long to get over me, too.'

'I know you've never been the same since,' Dolly said firmly.

'I know you've never trusted any other man, and you've never loved anyone the way you loved that fella.' She sighed. 'Why not give him a chance, love? Have you ever thought that, just maybe, he's still missing you?'

Clemmie snorted with laughter. 'Missing me? How's he got time to miss anyone? He's never without some gorgeous model type by his side. I'm sure they keep him all too preoccupied.'

'You sound very bitter,' Dolly observed. 'All I'm saying is, he's never settled down, has he? Yes, he's had lots of girlfriends, but how long have any of them lasted? Everyone knows Ross Lavender never goes on more than two dates with anyone. Yet he was with you for eighteen months. That's got to mean something, surely?'

She took Clemmie's hand in hers. 'Whatever you say, I know you still have feelings for him. You wouldn't be making all this fuss about spending time alone with him if he didn't matter to you. Isn't it worth finding out if there's a way back for you both? You never know.'

Clemmie shook her head. 'Even if I was still interested in him—which I'm not—it would never work. What Ross and I had was special at the time, but it's all spoilt now. It can't ever be the same again. You can't go back when something's no longer perfect. What's the point?'

'No relationship's perfect, love,' Dolly said. 'You're asking for the impossible.'

'Mum and Dad's relationship was,' Clemmie said firmly. 'You know as well as I do that they were soulmates. They had the happiest marriage, and they'd been together since they were teenagers. Anyway, Ross and I are finished. He's over me and I'm over him. End of story.'

'Hmm.' Dolly straightened and rubbed her chin thoughtfully. 'Just seems a bit odd, doesn't it?'

'What does?'

'Well, you said you didn't have Ross's number, so he rang you.'

'Yes?'

'*He rang you*. He still had your number in his phone book after all this time.'

It hadn't occurred to Clemmie, and her heart raced at the realisation. So he had! But why?

As Dolly gave her a slow smile and headed back to the shelves she'd been stocking, Clemmie could only be grateful that her aunt hadn't spotted that Ross's name had flashed up on the screen of her own phone. Because of course she still had his number in her phone, along with all the messages he'd ever sent her. She'd backed them up, so she hadn't lost them when she got a new phone a couple of years ago. Every single one.

Wild horses wouldn't make her confess that to Dolly, or anyone else. She wouldn't want them to get the wrong idea after all.

# TEN

The Black Swan wasn't too busy, and Ross and Meg easily found a table, which was fortunate, as Ross had totally forgotten to book one.

While Meg browsed the menu, he brought out an envelope full of photographs which he'd printed off.

'So these are the paintings by Arabella,' he explained, placing them on the table in front of her. 'As you can see, she's included some very helpful details for us to make use of. The colours—'

Meg put down the menu and gave him a patient smile. 'That's wonderful, Ross, but shall we eat first? I didn't have any lunch and I'm ravenous.'

'Oh. Sorry.' He scooped the photos up and put them in the envelope, shoving them back inside his jacket pocket. He wasn't sure whether he'd had lunch or not himself, but he wasn't feeling particularly hungry.

'Cheer up,' she said lightly. 'This is supposed to be a pleasant evening. A distraction from work. I don't live round here, remember? If I'm not at Monk's Folly I'm stuck in that hotel, watching rubbish television on my bed. Give me a break.'

He immediately felt ashamed. She was right, of course, and he should be more thoughtful.

'Sorry,' he said again. 'Right, let's have a look at this menu.'

They perused the selection of dishes on offer. Ross decided to have fried halloumi followed by sea bass fillet. Meg went for tempura vegetables and a ribeye steak.

Their orders taken and their wine glasses topped up, Meg glanced around the room and smiled.

'Isn't this place adorable? A proper country inn, isn't it? So rustic and charming. I hope the food's as good as the décor.'

'It's got a great reputation,' Ross assured her. 'We're very lucky in Tuppenny Bridge. The White Hart Inn does excellent food, too. Then there's The Farmer's Arms over in West Colby, and a few other restaurants dotted around various villages in the vicinity. What's the food like in your hotel?'

'Not too shabby,' she said. 'You'll have to come over one evening and we can have dinner there. I'll pay though, since you're insisting on paying for tonight, even though it was my suggestion.'

He smiled. 'Sounds good to me. Since I moved out of Lavender House I've eaten far too many sandwiches and Pot Noodles for my own good. It feels a bit like I'm camping out at the moment.'

'What made you move out of Lavender House so early?' she enquired. 'I'd have thought you'd have preferred the comfort of your old home until Monk's Folly was ready.'

'I've been itching to move out of there for a long time,' he admitted. 'I'm nearly thirty. Aunt Eugenie's lovely, and she's been brilliant to me, but sharing a flat with her has its disadvantages, believe me. Sharing a flat with her two Yorkshire terriers being one of them.'

Meg laughed. 'I met Boycott and Trueman. Lovely little things, although they did cock their leg against my car, which wasn't too endearing.'

'They have a habit of doing that,' he told her. 'They leave their mark wherever they go. Still, at least they're housetrained, which is a blessing.'

'I'm sure it is.' Meg took a sip of wine and eyed him thoughtfully. 'So will you be getting a dog?'

'At Monk's Folly? I highly doubt it.' Ross rolled his eyes. 'I really must stop calling it that, you know. It's the Arabella Lavender Art Academy now. Well, it will be soon.'

'Bit of a mouthful, though,' she said, her eyes twinkling. 'Maybe you could give it a nickname.'

'Like what?'

'Arabella's?' she suggested.

'If I told people I was going home to Arabella's they'd definitely jump to the wrong conclusion.'

She grinned. 'Oops! Yeah, you're right. Especially with your reputation.'

He raised an eyebrow. 'Sorry? My reputation?'

She shook her head slightly. 'Oops again. I shouldn't really have said that, should I? But you must know, surely, that in this town you're seen as quite the lothario.'

Ross sighed inwardly. Not this again!

'Who have you been talking to?'

'Nobody in particular. Just, wherever I go round here people seem to want to know who I am and what I'm doing here. Pop into the newsagent's for some chewing gum, it's like an interrogation. Head to the supermarket for a meal deal for lunch, someone practically shines a light in my eyes. I called at the bakery yesterday to buy a sausage roll and a pasty, and I was practically pinned to the counter while they demanded to know if I was that designer woman who was working up at Monk's Folly.'

'I should have warned you,' he said. 'This town is full of gossip. Everyone knows what everyone else is doing.'

She laughed. 'Don't worry. It was all done very politely and kindly. Main thing I learned was, "That Ross Lavender has had more women than hot dinners". I'm quoting a woman who I bumped into as she was coming out of the library, just as I passed by. I think her name was Mrs Millican? Anyway, she made sure I knew all about you and your many conquests.'

'Oh, God.' He groaned and shook his head. 'Take no notice. Especially not of Mrs Millican. She's almost as bad as my aunt and her friends, and Bluebell at the hairdressing salon.'

'So it's not true then?' she teased. 'I'm safe after all?'

'Of course you're safe! Good grief, what do you think I am?'

'I'm not sure yet, Ross,' she said, leaning forward slightly. 'I'm looking forward to finding out.'

There was a light in her eyes that he understood all too well. He felt a stirring of interest. He knew this game and was used to it. It was something he usually enjoyed—the first signs of attraction, the light flirting, the back and forth between him and whichever woman he was with at the time. It was fun. More than that, it was a distraction. It took his mind off his loneliness and frustration. It took his mind off Clemmie.

There she was, back in his head again. He thought about their meeting in the shop, and how dismissive and rude she'd been about sitting for the painting. She hadn't texted him after tea yesterday to arrange a sitting, even though Dolly had assured him she would.

She clearly didn't want to be in the same room as him, not even for a few hours. He wondered how they'd got to this state after all they'd once meant to each other.

Meg's eyes were still shining, her pupils dilated, her lips slightly open. He knew the signs and normally he'd have flirted right back with her. Why not? He was single. He didn't owe anyone anything.

But tonight...

He just wasn't in the mood for all this. Clemmie had done it again. Sabotaged him. He knew from bitter experience that once she'd lodged in his brain there was no point in even attempting to respond to another woman.

He breathed a sigh of relief when the waitress brought them their starters.

They could eat, they could drink wine, he had the photos to show her of Arabella's paintings. He would steer her away from anything too personal. Then he'd go home to Monk's Folly alone, because the last thing he needed was another complication.

Meg was beautiful, but she wasn't Clemmie. And right now, while his meeting with his ex was still so fresh in his mind, he had no room for anyone else. Not even for one night.

# ELEVEN

Dale View was a sweet little cottage on Lavender Lane, not far from Lavender House. It had belonged to the Wilson family for generations, but when Mr and Mrs Wilson passed away, their children—who had long moved away from the Dales—decided it was time to sell up.

Unfortunately, they'd sold it to someone who hadn't wanted to live in it but planned to turn it into a holiday let. Yet another home lost to the locals.

It had caused some resentment at the time, but there seemed to be nothing anyone could do about the growing trend. And although the residents of Tuppenny Bridge weren't happy that Dale View had been lost to them, they bore no ill will to the multitude of holidaymakers who'd since rented it. After all, it wasn't their fault.

Besides, they invariably spent plenty of money in the town, which eased the sting a little. For some residents at least, if not all.

Clemmie was quite looking forward to seeing what it looked like inside, as she had endless curiosity about other people's houses, but it didn't stop her feeling a bit nervous about the dinner with Reuben. She'd deliberately dressed down, sending a clear signal to both him and her aunt not to get any ideas. As she pulled on a thick, pink woollen jumper and a pair of jeans, she hoped Dolly would get the message. She wasn't interested in Reuben, or anyone else.

Dolly, to her relief, didn't even seem to notice what she was wearing. She had a pensive look on her face and rattled the car keys impatiently as Clemmie ran downstairs.

'Come on, we're going to be late at this rate. And look, it's bloody raining. Typical.'

Clemmie frowned. 'Well, I'm sure he won't mind waiting a few minutes if we're a bit late. Not that I think we will be. Are you okay? You sound really stressed out.'

Dolly took a deep breath and closed her eyes for a moment. When she opened them again she gave Clemmie a bright smile and said, 'Sorry. I'm all right really. Just got a nagging plot point that I'm trying to fix in my head and it's playing silly buggers. You know how it is.'

*More than you realise.* 'Are you sure you want to go tonight? I'm sure Reuben would understand if you didn't.'

'I'm sure he wouldn't! How would that look, eh? He's cooking for us and it's too late to back out now. Come on, let's get going.'

They drove through the darkness towards Tuppenny Bridge, the windscreen wipers swiping away the rain which was coming down steadily.

'I hate January,' Dolly said fervently. 'Miserable month. Roll on spring.'

Clemmie glanced at her aunt, puzzled. No matter how many assurances Dolly gave her, she couldn't shake the feeling that there was something big worrying her. All these excuses about writing and deadlines and her approaching trip to London didn't ring true. She couldn't help fretting that maybe Dolly was ill and was doing her best to cover it up.

The more she considered it, the more certain she was, and by the time they drove over the bridge and towards River Road she couldn't hold in her anxieties any longer.

Shifting in her seat she said, 'Dolly, please don't lie to me. Tell me what's going on.'

Dolly glanced at her, her eyes wide with surprise. 'Going on? Meaning what?'

Clemmie swallowed. 'You're keeping something from me. I can tell. If you're ill I need to know. Please, please don't let me find out through someone else.'

Dolly's expression softened and she patted Clemmie's knee. 'Aw, bless you, love. I swear to you, I'm not ill. There's nothing wrong with me at all.'

Clemmie couldn't suppress the sigh of relief at her words. Even so...

'You're sure? You promise?'

'I swear on my—oops, I'd better not say that, had I? Okay, I swear on my next publishing contract that I'm not ill. At least, not as far as I know. And no, before you jump to conclusions, I've not got any symptoms. I'm right as rain.'

'It's just, you're not really yourself,' Clemmie said hesitantly. 'You've been funny for ages, and I can't help feeling you're holding something back.'

Dolly laughed. 'You're imagining it.'

When Clemmie didn't reply she tightened her hold on the steering wheel and stared grimly at the road ahead of her.

'Okay,' she said at last. 'If you must know, I've won an award.'

'An award?' Clemmie squealed in delight. 'What sort of award?'

'Best saga book of the year. I've got to give a bloody speech. Can you imagine?'

'Dolly, that's wonderful news. You'll be great!' Clemmie beamed at her. 'I'm so proud of you.'

'Aye well, it's not bad, is it?' Dolly allowed herself a smile.

'It's fabulous! My aunt, the award-winning novelist.' Clemmie grinned. 'I can't believe you didn't tell me. Fancy fretting about that all this time. I could have told you straight away that there was nothing to worry about.'

'You think?' Dolly raised an eyebrow.

'I know! You're smart and funny and outgoing. You'll smash it, honestly you will. Hey, we can practice together if you like. I'll be your audience and you can make the speech to me. I'll give you feedback and suggestions if you want.'

'Hmm, well I've got to write the thing first,' Dolly pointed out.

'Haven't you even started?'

'Not yet. There's plenty of time. Well, a bit of time. Well, not much time at all really. I'd better get cracking.' She gave a hearty laugh and Clemmie smiled.

'See? You're already sounding more confident now you've told me. A problem shared is a problem halved, remember?'

Dolly's eyes crinkled with humour. 'I'll remember that in future, lovey. Thank you.'

Clemmie leaned back in her seat feeling happier. Fancy Dolly worrying about that, of all things! It was brilliant news, and she was surprised her aunt hadn't told her before.

'Here we are then,' Dolly announced at that moment. 'Dale View. I hope he's as good a cook as he says he is, don't you? What will we do if his food tastes like pig swill?'

Clemmie giggled. 'I've got a tote bag folded up in my coat pocket. I'll put it under the table and we can scrape it into there if we have to. I'll ask him for another drink and when he goes into the kitchen we'll tip our plates in.'

'Leaving him wondering how come we didn't have a bag when we walked in, but we've got one now when we're walking out, and it's got a distinct whiff of stilton soufflé and sprout supreme about it.'

Clemmie gave a horrified gasp. 'That's not what he's cooking is it?'

'Don't be daft!' Dolly rolled her eyes. 'Mind you, I say that. Who knows? Only one way to find out. Ready?'

Clemmie nodded and they climbed out of the car, slamming the doors shut behind them. Clemmie pulled up the hood on her coat while Dolly opened her umbrella. Together, they headed up the path towards the front door.

After knocking, they waited a few minutes before the door opened and Reuben stood there, looking rather too smart for Clemmie's liking in a cream shirt and dark trousers, a rather awkward look on his face.

'Come in. Great to see you both again,' he said, stepping back so they could come inside.

Dolly folded her umbrella and shook it slightly before stepping into the hall, which was little more than a tiny square, barely big enough for the three of them to stand in. Luckily, the living room door was open, and she backed into that, giving Clemmie the opportunity to move further away from Reuben, who was standing too close to her for comfort.

'Shall I take your coats?'

'Never mind our coats, love, do you want us to take our shoes off, with us being wet?' Dolly asked.

'No, that's fine. As you can see it's wooden floors. It will easily wipe down.' Reuben collected their coats and hung them on a rack above the radiator in the entrance. 'Go through, please. Dinner's nearly ready so it's perfect timing.'

Something definitely smelled good. Clemmie's nose twitched even as she noted that the living room was another small space, barely able to hold two two-seater sofas. There was a lovely fireplace, though, and it was smart but homely, with pictures on the walls and a selection of books on shelves in one of the recesses.

'Come through,' Reuben said, leading them through another door.

Clemmie and Dolly exchanged glances as they followed and found themselves in a huge kitchen diner.

'I wasn't expecting this!' Dolly admitted. 'That front room's a bit of a con really. You expect another tiny room and walk into this.'

'Nice and modern too,' Reuben said. 'I'll admit when I first arrived and saw the size of the hall and living room I panicked a bit, but this space more than made up for it. Drink? Which of you is driving?'

'I drove here, but Clemmie can drive us home,' Dolly said comfortably. 'She doesn't like the taste of alcohol, so she'll be happy with a soft drink, whereas if you're offering a glass of wine I'll not say no.'

'Wine it is,' Reuben said. He gave Clemmie an appraising look. 'So you don't like the taste of alcohol? Interesting.'

'Is it?' Clemmie couldn't see why, unless he was just being polite.

'Yes it is.' Reuben paused, the bottle of wine tipped enticingly over Dolly's empty glass. 'Oh hell, I should have asked. You're not vegetarians or vegans, are you?'

'Do I look like a vegan?' Dolly said, raising an eyebrow as she gestured to her shapely figure. 'Aren't they all emaciated and leaning on counters cos they're too weak to stand up?'

Reuben laughed. 'I think you're having me on,' he said wisely.

'Yeah, I am, love. But no, I'm not a vegan or a veggie, and neither is Clemmie. What have you got in store for us then? Smells good, whatever it is.'

'Mushrooms stuffed with cheese, bacon, and breadcrumbs and a salad for starters,' Reuben said. 'Followed by chicken chasseur and mashed potato, and finally a lemon baked cheesecake for dessert. That sound okay?'

Dolly looked as if she was practically drooling, and Clemmie couldn't blame her.

'Wow! You really can cook.'

He laughed again. 'Well, you haven't tasted it yet, so you can't know for sure, can you?' He finally poured Dolly's wine, much to her obvious relief. 'How about you, Clemmie?'

She shook her head. 'A soft drink's fine, honestly.'

'No, I mean, do you cook?'

'Not really. I can do basic stuff, but nothing like stuffed mushrooms or a baked cheesecake. Wouldn't even occur to me,' she admitted.

'She does a mean fishfinger, chips and peas though,' Dolly said, taking a large gulp of her wine and raising her glass in Clemmie's direction.

'I expect you could cook if you put your mind to it,' Reuben assured her, his eyes warm as he smiled at Clemmie, making her feel suddenly awkward and rather uncomfortable.

What if Dolly had said something to him? What if he thought she was on the lookout for a new boyfriend? Why else would he be so interested in her?

Then again, he'd just lost his mum. Surely he wasn't in any mood to flirt with any woman, let alone start a relationship with one? She must be imagining things.

'So, I have apple juice or blackcurrant squash, or tea or coffee of course,' he offered.

'Just apple juice would be fine,' she assured him.

'Great.' He indicated the table and chairs that were in the other half of the large room. 'Take a seat, both of you. I'll just get Clemmie's drink and then dinner will be served. I'm really looking forward to hearing all about you both.'

Dolly gave Clemmie a reassuring smile and nudged her towards the table. It almost felt, thought Clemmie, as if they were in on this together. She mentally shook her head. She was being paranoid. It was seeing Ross yesterday morning that had done it. He always did mess up her mind until she couldn't think straight.

And that was another problem. She hadn't texted Ross last night even though Dolly had told him she would. She knew that, at some point soon, she was going to have to make time for this rotten portrait sitting. He wasn't going to let her get away with it. Maybe, she reflected, he knew how uncomfortable the thought was to her, and was determined to make her go ahead just to watch her squirm. Well, she wouldn't give him the satisfaction. She would make the appointment and hold her head up —unless he wanted her to look down while he was painting her of course.

Wistfully, she remembered sitting on the riverbank some years ago, when he'd drawn her as she'd gazed out over the water, watching the ducks and swans paddling by. She hadn't even realised he'd done it, but he'd captured her so perfectly in such a short space of time. She'd been delighted and touched by it, and he'd kissed her so passionately after she'd thanked him that they'd got catcalls from a group of teenagers sitting near them.

'Apple juice,' Reuben said, placing the glass on the table. 'Just say when you need a top-up of wine, Dolly.'

He was a very pleasant and kind-hearted man, Clemmie thought, determined to put Ross from her mind. They were going to have a nice evening together and she wasn't going to give her ex another thought.

Not if she could help it anyway.

# TWELVE

Reuben, it turned out, was good company. He was thirty years old—three years older than Clemmie—and had lived in Hampstead all his life. His mum and dad had divorced when he was fourteen, but he'd stayed close to his father until his death when Reuben was twenty-one.

His mum had been artistic and fun and had worked as a potter.

'They were chalk and cheese really,' he admitted. 'Mum was all vague and dreamy, and loved anything arty and creative. Dad was all about facts and figures and business. Somehow, they got together, and it worked well for ages. I think Dad sorted Mum's life out for her and kept her grounded, and she brought out the fun side of him. For a while at least.'

'But it didn't last,' Clemmie said sadly. 'What a shame.'

'I think Dad just got tired of always having to be the sensible one. Mum had unrealistic ideas and no clue about paying bills or sorting finances, or any of the grown-up stuff. Dad tried to teach her, but she wasn't interested. They started arguing a lot and eventually he moved out. They stayed good friends, though.' He laughed. 'He was actually her accountant right up until the day he died, which was a good job because we'd have been homeless if he hadn't been.'

'I'm so sorry they divorced,' Clemmie said. 'It must have been horrible for you.'

'Not really. The arguments were much worse, and I could see how tense Dad was about everything, whereas Mum was getting edgy, and it was affecting her work. When they separated, it was much easier on us all. Anyway, like I said, they stayed good friends. They got on much better actually, and Dad was always there for me. I was very lucky,' he said firmly. 'He really was the best dad I could have wished for.'

'I'm glad to hear it,' Dolly said, raising her glass to him. 'He sounds wonderful.'

'I thought he was your friend?' Clemmie asked, puzzled.

Dolly stared at her then flapped her hand, as if dismissing the question. 'He is. Was! What I meant was that he sounds wonderful as a father. I knew him as an accountant and a good friend, remember. Very different thing.'

Reuben smiled. 'I expect it is. How's the chicken chasseur?'

Clemmie and Dolly both assured him it was delicious. Clemmie couldn't fault his cooking. The stuffed mushrooms hadn't particularly sounded like something she wanted to eat, but despite her trepidation she'd thoroughly enjoyed them, and the main course was, if anything, even better.

'If the pudding's half as good as this I'll be very happy,' she told him.

'Fingers crossed then. So,' Reuben took a sip of wine and eyed her thoughtfully, 'tell me about *your* parents. Were they happily married?'

The fact that he spoke about them in past tense told Clemmie that Dolly had already tipped him off that they were dead, so at least she'd be spared that. There was nothing worse than seeing people's sympathetic expressions when she had to explain to them that her parents were no longer alive, inevitably followed by questions about their deaths. As if she'd want to talk about all that! She was glad Reuben had given her a different question, and one she could answer with honest enthusiasm.

'Oh yes! They absolutely adored each other. They met at school, you know. They started going out together when they were just teenagers. They were engaged at eighteen and married at twenty. It was true love.' She sighed. 'I really don't think they could have borne to be apart, so in a way I'm glad they died together, even if it did leave me an orphan.'

Reuben was quiet for a moment. 'It must have been terrible for you,' he said at last. 'I'm glad you had Dolly to take care of you.'

'Oh, so am I.' Clemmie gave her aunt an affectionate smile. 'I don't know where I'd have been without her. She's one in a million.'

'That's me,' Dolly said cheerfully, raising her glass before taking a large gulp of wine. 'Mind if I have another, love?' she asked Reuben, nodding at the bottle on the table.

'Help yourself,' he said. 'Clemmie, would you like another apple juice?'

'I'm fine thanks.' Clemmie said. 'Anyway, what about you? Do you take after your mum or dad? I mean, are you artistic or more businesslike?'

Reuben considered the matter. 'I suppose I'm a mixture of both. I love designing websites, and that allows my creative side to flourish, but then there's a lot of technical stuff involved in that too, and I'm self-employed so I have quite a business head on me. I had to learn pretty fast, because after Dad died I was the one responsible for sorting Mum's finances out.'

He rolled his eyes. 'It was a steep learning curve, I'll tell you. Mum always thought things would work out somehow, no matter what. She bought me a pony for my twelfth birthday, with no clue where we were going to put it. Dad was fuming. He had to sort out livery and pay for my riding lessons. They had a heck of a row that day as I recall.' He laughed. 'I must admit, though, I was glad she'd done it. I loved that pony. But you see what I mean? Like I said, chalk and cheese.'

'My parents were both quite practical,' Clemmie admitted. 'Dad was a mechanic and Mum worked in a carpet shop. Although Dad was interested in poetry, and Mum had loads of books.' She thought about it, remembering. 'I don't really know who I take after to be honest.'

'You get your love of reading from me and your mum, and your romantic nature from your dad,' Dolly told her.

'Your dad was a bit of a romantic, was he?' Reuben asked.

'Well, he was very romantic with Mum,' Clemmie said. 'He used to bring her flowers all the time, and he was always telling her how much he loved her. They used to walk down the street holding hands, and I was always telling them off about it.' She sighed. 'I shouldn't have. I didn't mind really.'

'I'm sure they knew that,' Dolly said gently. She turned to Reuben. 'Greg was a mechanic by trade, but he had the soul of a poet. He loved all that hearts and flowers stuff. My sister Lucy was always rolling her eyes at him while he quoted poetry to her or cried at the soppy bits in films.'

'Needless to say,' Clemmie added, 'he was the one responsible for my name. And what a commotion that caused!'

'Oh?' Reuben's eyes crinkled with amusement. 'In what way?'

'While Mum was pregnant she'd been determined to call me Jeannie after my gran, but she ended up having a caesarean and was quite poorly after she had me, so Dad went to register the birth and he registered me as Clementine Jay instead. Mum was livid and didn't speak to him for days!'

Dolly burst out laughing. 'He said the Jay was short for Jeannie, so he'd done his bit. Lucy couldn't believe he'd saddled their little girl with a name like Clementine and if she'd not been feeling so crap I reckon she'd have thrown him out there and then.' She sighed, suddenly sad. 'They laughed about it later. He got round her. He always did. Besides,' she added, 'Clementine is popular again now, so maybe he had a point.'

'It's a lovely name,' Reuben said softly. 'It suits you.'

Clemmie felt herself blushing and hurriedly spooned up some chicken chasseur.

'It does suit her,' Dolly agreed. 'Though for all his protestations, she was always Clemmie to Greg, right from the minute he gave her the name. His little Clemmie. She could wrap him round her little finger.'

Clemmie's eyes stung with tears. Most of the time she could live with the loss of her parents. It never went away of course—the sense of grief and loss—but she'd learned to put those feelings into a box and get on with her life. Just now and then, though, they burst out of that box, and she would give way to a paroxysm of grief and pain. She didn't want now to be one of those times, so she blinked away the tears and forced herself to think about something more cheerful.

'Maybe you could design a website for Dolly, Reuben. She's always saying what a mess hers is, and she needs something more professional. What do you think?'

She was aware that her voice sounded croaky, but she hoped neither of them had noticed. If they did they very kindly didn't mention it.

'Are you looking for a website designer?' Reuben asked.

Dolly chewed some chicken while she thought about it. 'My site does look a bit like it was designed by two schoolkids who had an hour to spare before their next lesson,' she admitted. 'Mind you, I'm not sure I could afford professional prices. How much do you charge?'

Reuben's eyes twinkled. 'I'm sure we could come to some arrangement,' he said.

Dolly shook her head. 'No, no favours,' she told him. 'We all have to earn a living, love, and it's hard enough when you're a small business. I should bloody know. I'll give you my email address and you can send me your details tomorrow. That sound fair enough?'

'Sounds great to me,' he agreed. 'Now, more wine?'

'I'm going to be tiddly at this rate,' she said, nevertheless holding out her glass for a refill.

Reuben obliged then turned to Clemmie.

'And apple juice for you?'

She smiled. 'Yes please. If it's no trouble.'

'No trouble at all,' he assured her. 'Like I said, you've both done me a favour. I didn't fancy wallowing in misery all evening, and it's been great to do some cooking. If you weren't here I'd have been forcing down a microwave meal for one. Fate worse than death.'

Clemmie thought about the contents of hers and Dolly's fridge-freezer at home and wondered what Reuben would say if he saw how many microwave meals there were in it. She noticed Dolly didn't contradict him, even though she was a fiend for a frozen chicken curry.

As he pushed back his chair and headed over to the fridge for apple juice, Clemmie sat back and sighed, thinking this was turning out to be a much pleasanter evening than she'd anticipated.

Without warning, Reuben's friendly blue eyes were replaced by dark brown ones, cold and challenging. Reuben's round, smiling face and dimpled chin morphed into a face that bore an angry glare, short, clipped beard, and sharp cheekbones. Fair hair became raven black as her host's image was fully replaced by the image of Ross, standing on that platform on the village green, clearly angry that she'd won the prize he'd so generously offered.

He hadn't wanted her to sit for that portrait, so couldn't he find another way to appease his aunt? Surely, as an intelligent man, he could think of some other means of getting publicity for the academy?

Why couldn't he just leave her alone? Because no matter how hard she tried, somehow Ross Lavender always nudged his way into her thoughts. Even now, when she was having such a nice time with Reuben. Maybe especially at moments like these, when it became all too clear to her that no matter how much she tried, she still wasn't over him.

And just maybe she never would be.

# THIRTEEN

The evening had been a successful one, and Dolly had clearly been quite taken with Reuben, going on and on about him the entire way home from Dale View.

'You'll have to arrange another get-together,' she'd told Clemmie as they headed along dark, winding roads towards West Colby. 'Maybe we should invite him over to ours? I'm sure you two have lots to talk about.'

'Like what?' Clemmie had asked worriedly. 'Look, Dolly, he's very nice but—'

'I'm glad you think so. I do too.' Dolly sat back in her seat, folded her arms, and gave a satisfied smile. 'I knew you'd like him.'

Clemmie had wanted to warn her that if she was harbouring any ideas about her and Reuben getting together she was barking up the wrong tree. However, she was too tired and eager to get home to bother. Besides, she'd had a feeling Dolly wouldn't listen.

As they'd sat together at breakfast that Friday morning, Dolly had urged Clemmie to invite Reuben to the forthcoming opening of Pennyfeather's Craft Shop and its upstairs eatery, the Crafty Cook Café.

Kat and Daisy had worked hard to turn the old wool shop into something spectacular, and many of their friends and neighbours were planning to attend and show their support for their new venture.

Clemmie was pretty sure that this was another attempt by Dolly to throw her into Reuben's path.

'Why would he want to go to that?' she'd demanded, convinced that he wouldn't be in the slightest bit interested.

'He's got nothing else to do, has he?' Dolly pointed out. 'He doesn't know anyone here, and he's in danger of becoming a hermit if we don't lure him out of that cottage. Come on, Clem, don't be mean. Poor lad's just had a bereavement. I owe it to his dad to help him through it. Just ask him if he'd like to go. Tell him there's free fizz on offer, and that should do the trick. Give him a call. I've got his phone number.'

So Clemmie had, reluctantly, called Reuben to ask him if he wanted to attend tomorrow's event, and to her amazement he'd seemed ridiculously enthusiastic about it.

'That would be great,' he told her, smiling warmly. 'I'll meet you outside, shall I? Looking forward to it.'

She wished she could say the same, but she couldn't deny that her aunt's obvious keenness for her to get together with Reuben had quite put her off him. She just hoped he didn't have any funny ideas of his own.

The morning at the bookshop had flown too fast for her liking. As the time on her phone showed it was less than five minutes to Pennyfeather's opening time, Clemmie cast a desperate look at Dolly.

'Are you sure you don't want to go instead?' she asked. 'I don't mind staying here if you'd rather—'

'What have you got against Kat?' Dolly said, her eyes narrowing.

'Nothing! Why would I have anything against Kat?'

Clemmie gave her an exasperated sigh. 'Stop messing with my head. You know why I don't want to go.'

'I'm sure I have no idea.' Dolly settled herself on the chair behind the counter and gave Clemmie an innocent smile.

'Okay, I'll tell you. Two things. Ross Lavender and Reuben Walker.'

Dolly rolled her eyes. 'For goodness' sake! Firstly, Reuben's done nothing to you, and he's had a bad time lately, losing his mum like that. All he wants is a friend or two, and if we can't be there for him we should be ashamed of ourselves.'

Clemmie looked down at the floor, feeling guilty. Her aunt did have a point, after all. Poor Reuben had been through an awful experience, and he needed compassion. Maybe she'd misunderstood her aunt's intentions, and after all, Reuben had been nothing but a gentleman. He was just a kind man, that's all. She was being very selfish.

'And as for Ross...' Dolly hesitated, then said, 'You needn't worry there. He's not going.'

'Oh.' Clemmie angrily dismissed the pang of disappointment she experienced at the news. She was glad he wasn't going. Of course she was. Especially since she still hadn't phoned or texted him to make any arrangements for the portrait sitting, which would make any meeting with him even more awkward than usual. 'How do you know? I mean, are you sure?'

'Absolutely sure. He's too busy at Monk's Folly. Miss Lavender told me so herself. Well, she didn't actually tell me, but I heard her talking to Rita and Birdie about it in the market place as I was on my way to the post office the other day. Rita wanted to know final numbers, you see, so they could order enough fizz from Sal and Rafferty. I thought I'd better ask them if it was okay to invite Reuben and they were delighted. I told them I wouldn't be going, but I said you'd be there with him.'

'Oh, did you? Before you'd even asked me to invite him? That was a bit presumptuous of you.'

Clemmie chewed her lip for a moment, wondering whether or not she ought to say something. In the end, though, she couldn't help herself.

'Look, Dolly, you do know I'm not interested in Reuben, don't you? I mean, he's a very nice man and everything, but I really don't want to go out with him, so if you're harbouring any hopes...'

'Go out with him?' Dolly sounded genuinely aghast at the idea. 'Who said anything about that? He needs a friend, not a girlfriend, and besides, we all know you've only got eyes for Captain Wentworth.'

She grinned, and Clemmie relaxed a little.

'Okay, fair enough. Sorry. I suppose I'd better get off then. Reuben will be waiting.'

'Have a good time and give my love to Kat. Tell her I'm sure it's going to be a huge success.'

'Will do.'

'Oh, and if Sally's there, tell her I want to see her photos from Australia ASAP. I could do with a bit of sunshine, even if it's only from looking at other people's holiday snaps.'

Feeling a little easier, Clemmie headed out of the bookshop, where she found a small crowd had already gathered outside Pennyfeather's, which had a pink ribbon tied across its front door, and cheerful bunting strung above its shuttered window.

She waved as she spotted Reuben standing outside the shop, looking around him in interest. His face lit up when he saw her, and she felt mean for having such ungenerous thoughts about him earlier.

'Are you sure you don't mind attending this event?' she asked him doubtfully. 'I wouldn't have thought the opening of a craft shop would be your cup of tea.'

'Better than sitting in that holiday cottage moping, and I like to support small businesses,' he said, then grinned at her. 'Besides, you never know. They might decide they need a new website.' He patted his coat pocket. 'I've brought my business cards to hand out anyway.'

'All right, Clemmie?' Bluebell, who owned the Cutting it Fine hairdressing salon on the other side of the market square, gave her a big smile before turning her gaze on Reuben. 'No Dolly then?'

'She's minding the shop,' Clemmie explained. Seeing the curiosity in Bluebell's eyes she added, 'This is Reuben Walker. He's the son of an old friend of Dolly's. He's here from London.'

'London!'

As Bluebell said the word, several heads turned to stare at Reuben, as if he were an alien from outer space.

'Fancy that!' Bluebell's nineteen-year-old daughter, Clover, sounded thoroughly impressed. 'I'd love to go to London.'

'What for?' Frank, who ran the post office but had clearly left it in his assistant's capable hands to attend this event, gave her a scornful look. 'Nothing there worth leaving the Dales for. Waste of time and money if you ask me.'

'When did you last go to London, Frank?' Ava gave him a knowing look.

Frank shuffled. 'Don't have to go to London to know it's not my cup of tea. I've seen enough of it on telly. It's all gangsters and skyscrapers and pubs charging a small fortune for a pint of southern beer that's weak as water.' He gave Reuben a friendly nudge. 'No offence, like. But if you want a decent pint, you ought to try our Lusty Tup.'

Reuben blinked. 'I'm sorry?'

'Lusty Tup. It's the local brewery and by heck, it puts any London beer to shame.'

'Not that he's biased of course,' Ava said, smiling. She held out her hand. 'Ava Barrington. I used to be a frequent visitor to London, and I love it. Take no notice of Frank. He thinks you need a passport if you go as far as Ripon.'

Reuben laughed. 'I'll bear that in mind.'

At that moment the Lavender Ladies arrived and quickly drew attention to themselves with their outfits.

'Blimey,' Reuben murmured, 'who got them dressed?'

Clemmie giggled. Eugenie Lavender was dressed as if for a film premier, with a long dress in an appropriate shade of lavender, and a silver fox-fur coat, which Clemmie could only pray was fake. Knowing Miss Lavender, she suspected it was.

With a pillbox hat perched on top of her silver hair, she was the picture of elegance, if rather overdressed for the occasion. Clemmie wouldn't have been at all surprised if she'd worn long white gloves and carried a cigarette holder.

Rita and Birdie on the other hand looked as if they'd dressed for a rummage sale. With brown nylon trousers and purple anoraks, and striped woolly hats pulled down over their dyed red hair, they'd obviously decided that today was Kat's day, and they weren't going to steal the limelight by looking too smart.

At least, that's what Clemmie told Reuben. The truth was that they usually looked far worse, but she didn't think he would believe her if she told him. If he stuck around in Tuppenny Bridge for long enough, he'd realise for himself.

The Lavender Ladies were soon holding court, assuring everyone that Kat and Daisy were on their way and the opening would take place within a few minutes. There were several pointed remarks about the cold weather and mutterings about brass monkeys in response.

'It's quite busy,' Reuben said, glancing round. 'Looks like it's going to be a popular shop.'

'I hope so,' Clemmie said. 'I don't really know Daisy—she's the one who's going to run the café upstairs—but Kat's lovely, and she's got a young baby, so she needs for this to work. Pennyfeather's wool shop has been in the market place for over eighty years. Her great-great-granny started it, so she's keen to make a success of this and keep the name going.'

'Quite a lot of pressure then,' Reuben remarked. 'I hope it

works out for her. There's nothing more important than family, is there?'

'No, I guess not. I don't know where I'd be without Dolly,' Clemmie admitted.

It still made her shiver when she thought about how differently her life might have turned out if her aunt hadn't willingly taken her in after her parents died. After all, Dolly had never wanted marriage or children, valuing her freedom and independence, so it had been a lot to ask of her.

Clemmie didn't think she'd realised at the time just how much of a sacrifice Dolly had made for her. Her aunt never made her feel as if she'd been a burden or an inconvenience and had shown her nothing but love and kindness. She'd been very lucky.

'What about you?' she asked suddenly, realising that, for all she knew, Reuben had no one in the world now his mother had died.

He frowned. 'What about me?'

'Well, have you any family left? Or is there just you...' She trailed off, realising he might not want to dwell on all that, and she was supposed to be cheering him up, not bringing him down.

'Oh, I see. Well, I've got family, but I don't really know them. My grandparents died when I was very young, and I don't even remember them. Mum was an only child, so there's no one on her side, and dad's family... Well, let's just say we barely know each other and leave it at that.'

'Oh.' Clemmie couldn't help feeling sympathy for him. 'I'm sorry. It must be really hard for you.'

'Other people have it worse,' he said. 'I've got great friends, a good job. I can't complain.'

Clemmie nodded, but she couldn't help wondering, if he had such great friends, why was he here in Tuppenny Bridge, grieving for his mother alone? Where were they? And why hadn't he turned to them for help with his grief instead of running away to a town he'd never visited before?

As he smiled at her, she pushed the thought away, feeling disloyal. People grieved in different ways. Maybe the sympathy from people he knew was too much for him to cope with. Maybe he needed time and solitude to heal alone. She shouldn't be so judgemental.

There was a general shuffling and a buzz of conversation as Kat arrived, along with Jonah, her partner, and Daisy Jackson. Kat was holding the hand of Jonah's seven-year-old son, Tommy, and Jonah carried eleven-month-old Hattie, Kat's daughter, in his arms.

'Oh, gosh! I wasn't expecting so many people.' Kat sounded flummoxed, and Daisy—a newcomer to Tuppenny Bridge— went quite pink as she gazed at the crowd in obvious surprise.

'Don't worry. There's more than enough champagne to go round,' Birdie assured her. 'Now, who's going to cut the ribbon? You, Kat, or Daisy?'

There was an awkward silence as everyone realised that Miss Lavender had produced a pair of scissors from her bag. It seemed she'd been expecting to do the honours herself, and it was clear that the thought hadn't occurred to anyone but her.

That was so typical of Miss Lavender, thought Clemmie. She just naturally assumed that everything in Tuppenny Bridge revolved around her. Just because of her famous ancestor! Every year she got to stand on the town hall balcony and switch on the Christmas lights, and no one could object because she'd paid for them, and for the tree that graced the market square every December.

Kat glanced at Daisy, who shrugged.

'Miss Lavender,' Kat said graciously, 'would you do the honours?'

Miss Lavender beamed at her. 'But of course, my dear. It would be my pleasure.'

As Birdie and Rita rolled their eyes and nudged each other, Miss Lavender's hand hovered over the pink ribbon strung across the door and she cleared her throat.

'Oh heck,' Clover muttered. 'She's going to make a bloody production of it, isn't she?'

'Ladies and gentlemen,' Miss Lavender said, her already cut-glass tones sharpened to new levels of grandiosity, as befitted the occasion, 'I take great delight in welcoming you to the opening of our beautiful town's newest venture. Pennyfeather's Wool Shop opened its doors back in nineteen thirty-seven, and it proudly served the people of Tuppenny Bridge throughout even the darkest of times. Now it's time for a new generation of this family to take the business into a new era. I'm sure you'll all join me in wishing Katherine Pennyfeather and our new resident, Daisy Jackson, every success in this wonderful venture. I now declare Pennyfeather's Craft Shop and the Crafty Cook Café open.'

With that, she cut the ribbon and everyone cheered, while Hattie whooped with joy and tugged Jonah's hair in excitement.

Kat hurried forward and unlocked the door, and everyone poured into the shop, eager to see the difference between the old business and the new. Jonah handed Hattie to Birdie then pulled up the shutters, and as light flooded the premises, people gasped and gazed around them in surprise.

'You lot certainly know how to do things properly,' Reuben remarked, staring round him and taking in, as was Clemmie, the bottles of fizz and orange juice, and the dozens of champagne flutes on the counter.

'This is amazing,' Ava said, patting Kat's arm. 'What a difference, darling!'

'Do you like it?' Kat was clearly thrilled as everyone began to issue compliments and expressions of amazement at how much the place had changed.

Clemmie had known there was a lot of work going on while

the shop had been closed, but she hadn't realised how much it had been altered. It looked more than twice the size of the old shop. The back room had been knocked through to the front, so the actual square footage had increased, but it no longer looked as if it was being smothered in wool and bits and pieces that Rita and Birdie had spread haphazardly around.

When they'd run the shop while Kat was on maternity leave, they'd crammed every available space with stock, and there seemed to be no order or reason to their display at all. Now the shop was neat and spacious, light and welcoming. Clemmie could already see that it stocked everything the eager crafter could desire. She had a very good feeling about it.

'If you'd like to go upstairs when you're ready,' Daisy said, rather shyly, 'you'll find the Crafty Cook Café open, and I've a wide selection of sandwiches and cakes and other treats for you to sample, free of charge.'

'Lead us to it!' Bluebell nudged Ava. 'Champagne my eye. This is Prosecco. Maister's own brand, if I'm not mistaken,' she added, with all the confidence of one who'd spent a lot of time in the local supermarket's wine aisle. 'What a swizz.'

She nevertheless drained her glass, filled it with more of the sparkling wine and nudged Ava towards the stairs. 'Come on, let's see what's on offer up there.'

Kat and Jonah laughed, and Clemmie couldn't help but feel a pang of envy as Jonah put his arm around her shoulders and kissed her tenderly, while Hattie chuckled and waved at Tommy from Birdie's arms. They looked like the perfect family. Kat was so lucky to have someone who obviously loved her so much.

Not that Clemmie begrudged her that. Kat had been in love before, with Ben's older brother, Leon Callaghan, but he'd been killed in a car accident years ago. It had taken Kat a long time to get over him. Jonah had been Leon's best friend, so he'd been hurt too. It was kind of nice that they'd found true love with each other after all this time. After all, everyone deserved a second chance, didn't they?

Her mood dipped and she dejectedly turned away from Kat and Jonah. *Not everyone.*

'Are you coming up for some cake?' Reuben asked. She noticed he'd taken some of his business cards out of his pocket and smiled knowingly.

'Sure. Why not?'

Clemmie turned round to put down the empty glass of orange juice, and as she did so she glanced at the window, noticing Summer outside with her mum, Sally. She smiled in anticipation of her friend's arrival, but her smile dropped as she realised Summer looked upset. Sally was obviously trying to comfort her, but Summer shook her head, seeming inconsolable.

'You go on up,' she told Reuben. 'I've got to do something first.'

He looked surprised but shrugged. 'Fair enough. I'll see you up there.'

Clemmie hurried out into the market square.

'Summer? What's up?'

Sally looked relieved to see her. 'Aw, she's a bit upset, love. She's had some bad news. I thought coming to the shop opening might cheer her up a bit, but I was daft. She's not in the mood for this. I'll take her home.'

'What's wrong, what's happened?'

Summer's face was streaked with tears, and she shook her head. Clemmie's heart sank. Surely Ben hadn't dumped her? They seemed so happy together. He wouldn't. Would he?

'Why don't you go to the opening, Sally?' she suggested. 'I'll take Summer back to the shop and make her a cup of tea. Would you like that, Summer?'

Summer wiped her face. 'That would be good. Thanks, Clem.'

'Are you sure?' Sally looked worried. 'I can take you home if you'd prefer, love?'

'No, it's okay. You go to the shop opening. Tell Kat I hope it all goes well. I'll go with Clemmie.'

Sally nodded. 'Fair enough, love. If you need me you know where I am.' She kissed her daughter's cheek and stroked her hair. 'I'm so sorry, sweetheart.'

Summer wiped her nose with a tissue and managed a faint smile. 'Thanks, Mum.'

Clemmie put her arm around her friend's shoulders and together they walked back to The Corner Cottage Bookshop. She'd forgotten all about Reuben. All she cared about right now was Summer. What on earth could have upset her so much?

# FOURTEEN

Dolly looked up in obvious surprise as the bell jangled and Clemmie walked in, with Summer trailing miserably behind her.

'By heck, that was quick! What are you doing back so soon? Don't tell me they scrimped on the cake...' Her voice trailed off and she frowned. 'Are you okay, Summer?'

Clemmie thought Summer looked ready to burst into tears again. She glanced quickly around the shop, noting that there were no customers browsing the shelves. She heard footsteps above her head, though, and realised there were some upstairs.

'I'm just going to take Summer through to the kitchen and make some tea,' she said.

Dolly nodded, giving them a worried look, and Clemmie led Summer into the small kitchen, where she immediately burst into tears.

'Oh, Summer!' Clemmie put her arms around her and gave her a comforting hug. 'What is it? What's he done?'

'What's who done?' Summer's voice was muffled against Clemmie's shoulder.

'Ben of course.' Clemmie leaned away a little. 'I take it he's said or done something to hurt you?'

Summer sniffed and shook her head. 'Of course not! It's nothing to do with Ben.' She wiped her eyes and stepped back. 'It's Joseph. Oh, Clemmie, it's just awful.'

Clemmie's heart thudded. Joseph was Summer's boss at the Whispering Willows Horse Sanctuary, and she knew her friend thought the world of him. 'What's happened to him?'

'Can I have that cup of tea?' Summer asked plaintively, and Clemmie hurriedly filled the kettle and flicked it on, dropping teabags in three mugs.

Summer waited until she'd poured the boiling water then said slowly, 'He's dying, Clem.'

Clemmie banged the kettle on the worktop and turned to face her friend, feeling sick.

'Dying? What—I mean, how...?'

'Clive told me,' Summer said, straightening. 'Apparently he's known for months. Back in the summer when Joseph was going to hospital—when he told me he was absolutely fine and it was just a bit of anaemia—well, they told him then. Cancer.'

As the word left her mouth the door opened and Dolly walked in. Her face paled.

'Who's got cancer?' she murmured, an expression of dread in her eyes.

Summer hung her head and Clemmie handed Dolly a mug of tea.

'It's Joseph. He's dying.'

'Joseph!' Dolly slumped, looking dazed. 'Oh bloody hell, Summer. I'm so sorry. When did this happen?'

'He's known for months!' Summer burst out. 'He never said a word to me. And Clive knew. Clive went with him to the hospital, but he never said anything either. He reckons Joseph made him promise. Why would he do that? I thought we were friends!'

She began to sob again, and Dolly put down her mug and enfolded her in her arms.

'Bless you, love. You've had a proper shock. Clive was bound to know, being Joseph's best mate, wasn't he? I'm sure they were both just trying to protect you. But look, maybe they can do something? There's all sorts of new treatments these days. You never know—'

Summer shook her head. 'I asked Clive all that. Apparently it's too far advanced to cure him, but they offered him treatment to give him more time.'

'Well,' Dolly said, sounding subdued, 'that's something.'

'He refused it.' Summer gave a bitter laugh. 'Can you believe that? He actually refused treatment that would have given him a few more months. I'm so angry I don't know what to do with myself. I can't believe he kept all this from me, and that Clive went along with it. What am I supposed to do now? What about all the horses? What's going to happen to them? How could he be so bloody selfish?'

As Dolly soothed her, Clemmie stood watching them both, feeling helpless. She realised that Summer's anger was born of grief and shock. She felt pretty shocked herself. Joseph was a nice man. He kept himself to himself, but he had a heart of gold. He'd devoted his life to animal welfare. He was only in his mid-sixties, and it didn't seem fair that he should be taken from them so young.

And Summer was right. What would happen to the horses, ponies, and donkeys that Joseph had rescued? Who would take care of them when he was gone? What would happen to Whispering Willows?

It was a small sanctuary, funded by what was left of Joseph's inheritance, donations from kind-hearted individuals, and money from local charities, such as the Tuppenny Bridge Fund. With Joseph gone how could the place continue? The house and land might have to be sold, and Summer couldn't possibly keep the place going on her own anyway. How awful.

She realised that Joseph's illness had huge implications for the welfare of his animals, and stared anxiously at her friend, wondering how she was ever going to cope with this.

She heard the bell jingle and was about to head back into the shop when a voice called, 'Hello? Anyone there?'

Dolly patted Summer on the back and said, 'Think that's your mum, love. In here, Sal!' she called over her shoulder. The kitchen door opened, and Sally headed in.

'Aw, love, look at the state of you,' she said, and Summer went from Dolly's arms to her mother's.

'Terrible news, Sal,' Dolly said, and Sally nodded.

'I couldn't believe it. Fancy him keeping it quiet all that time, bless him.'

'Bless him?' Summer spluttered. 'It was mean and selfish! I never thought he'd be so cruel. I'm supposed to be his friend, not just his employee!'

Sally put her hands on her daughter's shoulders and gazed steadily into her eyes.

'You know as well as I do that Joseph *is* your friend. He thinks the world of you. He probably didn't know how to tell you, love. It's not an easy thing to say, is it? And maybe he didn't want to talk about it. Maybe he was still coming to terms with it all himself.'

'But why would he refuse treatment, Mum? It doesn't make sense.'

Dolly took a sip of tea and sighed. 'I don't know about that, love. If they can't save his life, well... Thing is, treatment's not exactly pleasant or easy is it? And if it's a case of just adding a few months, when those few months are going to be full of hospital appointments and drugs and tests... It's not Joseph's style, is it? Be honest. Does it really surprise you that he'd say no to all that?'

Summer was trembling, and Clemmie handed her the mug of tea. 'Drink this. I've put extra sugar in. I've no idea why but they reckon it helps with shock.'

Summer took a sip and pulled a face. 'Yuck! It's like syrup.'

'Get it down you,' Dolly said brightly. 'It'll put hairs on your chest. That'll give Ben something to think about.'

Despite her grief, Summer managed a smile. She took another sip then put the mug down. 'I suppose I'd better call Dad.'

'Your dad? What for?' Sally asked, wrinkling her nose in surprise.

'I'm supposed to be flying off to Australia with him in April,' Summer pointed out. 'That's not going to happen now is it?'

Clemmie saw the look Sally and Dolly exchanged.

'Don't go making any decisions just now, love,' Sally warned. 'We don't know what's going to happen yet, do we?'

'Well, I think we do actually,' Summer said bitterly. 'And from what Clive said I haven't got time to be jetting off to the other side of the world.'

'But your dad's really looking forward to taking you,' Sally said. 'And Billie and Arlo can't wait to see you.'

'I can't wait to see them,' Summer said, 'but Mum, surely you can see that Whispering Willows has to be my priority now? Joseph's too ill to work there any longer—that's probably why Clive told me when he did. He's run out of excuses. There's only me to take care of twelve animals. And there's Viva to think of too,' she added, referring to Joseph's Bichon Frise dog. 'She'll still need walking every day. This is only going to get worse. I can't leave Joseph now, and Dad needs warning.'

'All right, love, all right,' Sally said, patting her arm as she eyed Dolly worriedly. 'I'll give your dad a ring, tell him what's what. You just concentrate on the stables for now.'

'Might be worth having a chat with Clive,' Dolly murmured

as Summer—despite her assertions that the tea was like syrup—took another long gulp from her mug.

Sally nodded. 'I'll pop round to see him this afternoon. I wish he'd warned me he was going to tell her today. I'd have been there with her.'

'I just don't know how I'm going to cope,' Summer admitted. 'I'll have to drop the rest of my shifts at the pub, Mum. I'm sorry, but—'

Sally held up her hand. 'No need to worry about that, love. We'll manage. You just concentrate on Whispering Willows.'

Clemmie nibbled her thumb. Even with Summer working full-time at the sanctuary, it was a lot to deal with on her own. If only she knew something about horses, she'd offer to help, but she didn't. Not only that, but she had to admit she was a little bit afraid of them. She'd be worse than useless at the stables. Even so...

'I can give you a hand,' she said, wondering even as the words left her mouth what the hell was wrong with her.

Three pairs of eyes fixed on her.

'You?' Dolly gave her a doubtful look. 'You don't know anything about horses, love.'

'But surely a lot of it is common sense?' Clemmie asked. 'I mean, shovelling horse muck into a wheelbarrow, putting down fresh straw, making sure they have water and food—it can't be that hard, can it?'

'Are you sure, Clem?' Summer asked. 'I know you're a bit wary of horses.'

'Well there must be something I can do that doesn't involve being in close proximity to them? They won't have to be in the stables when I clean it up for them will they?'

Summer smiled. 'It's really good of you, but—'

'I mean it,' Clemmie said desperately. 'You're my friend and I want to help you. You can spare me for a few afternoons a week, can't you, Dolly?'

'Well,' Dolly said, sounding far from certain, 'if you're sure.'

'I am.'

Sally gave her a bright smile. 'Well, that's lovely of you, isn't it, Summer?'

'Of course it is,' Summer agreed.

Clemmie could practically hear her thinking, *It would be even lovelier if only she knew something about horses.*

Then a thought crossed her mind and her heart lifted. Reuben! Hadn't he said he used to own a pony? Surely he'd know how to feed them and groom them and whatever else they needed? Maybe, if she asked him very nicely, he'd give them a hand? Between the two of them, they could surely ease the burden on Summer.

It was a lot to ask, considering she hardly knew him, but her friend was in dire straits.

What the heck. It was worth a shot.

## FIFTEEN

Luckily for Clemmie, Reuben hadn't given up on her and gone home. He was still in the Crafty Cook Café and seemed to be enjoying himself. He was sitting at a table chatting to Ava, and the two of them looked as if they were thoroughly absorbed in conversation, while a bored-looking Bluebell sat opposite Ava, sipping Prosecco, and twirling a strand of her hair around her finger.

They all looked up and smiled as she joined them at the table.

'Clemmie! I was just telling Reuben here how dreadfully dated the church website is. He's come up with lots of suggestions to improve it. Now I just have to sweet-talk Zach into spending some funds on it.' Ava giggled. 'I might have to cook him his favourite meal for dinner tonight.'

'I appreciate that funds are always low for church spending,' Reuben said. 'I'm sure we could come to some sort of arrangement.'

'Really? Aren't you kind? I'll talk to Zach tonight,' she promised.

'Reuben, I'm sorry to interrupt,' Clemmie said, 'but do you mind if we go outside? I need to talk to you.'

Bluebell sat up straight, her interest clearly piqued at this development.

'Don't mind us,' she said, her eyes shining. 'You've finished talking about church business now. *Haven't you, Ava?*'

There was the hint of a threat in her tone, as if she was daring her friend to say anything else on the subject.

Ava gave her an apologetic smile. 'Would you like some more cake, Bluebell?'

'Love some.'

Reuben got to his feet. 'Excuse me, ladies.'

He followed Clemmie down the stairs, through the craft shop, and out into Market Place.

'Something wrong?' he asked, his brow furrowing as she turned to face him.

'Very wrong. We've got a bit of an emergency, Reuben, and I think you might be the only one who can help us.'

'Sounds intriguing.'

She led him back to The Corner Cottage Bookshop, where Summer and Sally were waiting.

'This is Reuben,' she explained. 'Reuben, this is my friend, Summer, and her mum, Sally. Summer's had some bad news today, and that's why I had to leave you alone at the opening. I'm sorry about that.'

Reuben nodded politely at Summer and Sally. 'I'm sorry to hear that.' He turned to Clemmie. 'You said I could help you?'

'Yes. You see, Summer works at the local horse sanctuary, Whispering Willows, and—'

'Oh, I know the place,' Reuben confirmed. 'It's just down the road from Dale View. I've passed it a few times and noticed the sign.'

'Yes, well, the man who owns the sanctuary, Joseph, he...' Her voice trailed off and she gave Summer a sympathetic look.

'He's dying, I'm afraid. And the thing is, Reuben, he's too ill to do any work at the stables, and there's only Summer. I've volunteered to put some hours in, but I don't know anything about horses, and I thought maybe—'

'You want me to work at the horse sanctuary?' he asked in surprise.

'I know it's a bit of a cheek,' Summer said desperately, 'but you'd be doing us a huge favour. Even if you could only spare a few hours a week it would be something.'

'Oh.' Reuben smiled at her. 'I reckon I could spare you a bit more than that.' He tilted his head, thinking. 'I've got a bit of work on now, and the promise of more to come, but I think I could give you a full day and maybe two afternoons a week for starters. I'll see how it goes after that. Might be able to increase it once I finish a website I'm working on at the moment for a doctor's surgery. That's heavy going, but it shouldn't take me much longer.'

'That would be amazing,' Clemmie said in delight.

'But we can't pay you,' Summer added cautiously. 'You do realise that? It would be voluntary.'

'I miss my old pony,' Reuben told her. 'And to be honest, I miss getting my hands dirty. I'm getting too soft. Some manual labour would do me the world of good. When would you like me to start?'

'Reuben,' Summer cried, her relief palpable, 'you're a star! Isn't he a star, Clem?'

As Reuben beamed at her Clemmie had to admit he'd played a blinder. Thank goodness he'd arrived in Tuppenny Bridge when he had.

# SIXTEEN

Ross could hardly take it in, but even as he murmured, 'Are you sure?' to his great aunt, he could tell by the pinched look on her face that there was no mistake.

He sank down on the chintzy sofa next to her and took hold of her hand.

'I can't believe it. Joseph? He's not even that old is he?'

'Sixty-six, sixty-seven or thereabouts,' she said briefly. 'It's hard to accept, I know.'

'I'd heard he wasn't well,' Ross admitted, 'but I thought someone said he was anaemic or something. I had no idea it was so serious.'

'Apparently only he and Clive knew,' she said. 'Joseph didn't want a fuss.'

'How long...?'

She shrugged. 'Weeks, according to Ben. He popped round this morning to check up on Boycott,' she said, nodding at one of her two Yorkshire terriers, who were lying on the thick, pink carpet of her living room. 'He's not been eating well, and I was worried.'

'Is he okay?' Ross asked automatically, though he was sure

he would be. Aunt Eugenie was always worrying about her two precious boys, Trueman and Boycott, and had poor Ben running ragged after them. He must have the patience of a saint, Ross thought, and sighed inwardly.

'Ben thinks it's a problem with his teeth. He's booked the poor darling in for a proper dental examination and a possible extraction,' she said briefly.

Knowing how many cakes and treats Aunt Eugenie gave the dogs, Ross wasn't at all surprised.

'How was he?' he asked, almost reluctantly. 'Ben, I mean. He probably sees a lot of Joseph through work, and with Summer working for him...'

'Very upset,' she confirmed. 'Everyone is, of course. Clive is being stoic, but he's Joseph's best friend. It's going to hit him hardest of all. And Summer, too. She's devastated according to Kat. Sally's quite worried about her. And Jonah and Ben are going to miss him deeply.' She paused. 'Maybe you should give Ben a call. I'm sure he'd appreciate a friend at a time like this.'

Ross steadied himself. 'I'm hardly a friend, Auntie.'

'You were once,' she reminded him.

'A long time ago. We were just kids. We're not the same people we used to be.'

'All the same...'

'What about you and Joseph?' he said quickly.

She gave him a sharp look. 'What about us?'

'Well, given the situation, are you going to pay him a visit? I know you don't like him, and I've honestly never understood why. Everyone loves Joseph, and you can't deny he's done a lot of good things for those horses of his.'

'He has,' she acknowledged. 'I'm not denying it.'

'So what is it?' he persisted. 'Why did you fall out with him?'

'I didn't exactly fall out with him,' she said, waving the question away with a brief hand gesture.

'Well, you don't speak to him. You usually change the subject when he's mentioned. To my knowledge you've never even been to Whispering Willows.'

'Oh, I've been there,' she said. She was quiet for a moment, and Trueman and Boycott watched her, their heads tilted as if they sensed she wasn't quite her usual self. 'I wonder if anyone's told Bethany...'

'Who's Bethany?' Ross asked, surprised.

His aunt blinked. 'Why, Joseph's sister, of course.'

'He has a sister?'

She tutted impatiently. 'I'm perfectly certain you already know this, Ross. It's hardly a secret. Yes, he has a sister. She's much younger than him—probably ten years or so. I haven't seen her for a long time.'

'Where does she live then?'

'I have no idea. She left Tuppenny Bridge decades ago and never returned.'

'But surely she and Joseph are still in touch?' he asked, finding it difficult to believe that siblings could be apart for that long without any communication. He couldn't imagine life without Noah. There was quite an age gap between the two of them, but even so he would be lost if his big brother left town and didn't keep in touch with him.

'I highly doubt it,' she said. 'Anyway, the point is I think you should be there for Ben. Maybe this is the chance you've been waiting for.'

He reared away from her. 'What chance?'

'To make it up with him,' she said quietly. 'To put the past behind you and start again. Ben's come on in leaps and bounds recently. You were just teenagers, Ross. Time to forgive and forget, surely?'

Ross frowned. 'Some things can never be forgiven, Aunt Eugenie.'

'Oh but, Ross...'

He shook his head. 'What about Summer? How's she going to manage without Joseph? She can't deal with all those horses on her own, surely?'

'Naturally, there are going to be big changes,' his aunt acknowledged, thankfully seeming to accept that the subject of Ben was closed. 'When Joseph's—gone—who knows what will happen? I should imagine Whispering Willows will be sold and the horses will have to be rehomed, or... Well, let's not think about that just yet.'

'Oh no! Poor Joseph. He must be worried sick about their future,' Ross said, closing his eyes as he imagined the terrible strain the poor man must be under.

'Well for now at least there's help at hand,' his aunt said, smiling faintly as Trueman trotted over to her and gazed up at her appealingly. 'Summer has a couple of new stable hands.'

'Oh?'

'Clemmie—'

'Clemmie!' Ross's eyebrows shot up in surprise. 'But she's scared stiff of horses! What's she going to do at Whispering Willows? Read the horses a bedtime story?'

'Sarcasm really isn't an attractive quality, Ross,' his aunt reproved. 'At least she's making an effort. A good heart should always be appreciated.'

Ross shifted, feeling ashamed. She was right of course, but Clemmie? Really? He couldn't imagine it. She'd be terrified. His heart melted at the thought of her trying to help, her pulse racing in fear at being so close to the various equines at the stables.

'Also, Reuben's stepped in. You know, Reuben Walker?'

Ross dragged his thoughts away from Clemmie and gave her a puzzled look. 'Who?'

She shook her head impatiently. 'Do you know nothing about life in this town?'

'I've been rather busy lately,' he reminded her with a grin.

'Besides, I always know that if there's anything juicy happening you'll tell me all about it. You're the resident oracle of Tuppenny Bridge after all.'

She rolled her eyes and gave his leg a playful slap.

'I don't know what you mean by that,' she told him, a gleam in her eye. 'But anyway, Reuben Walker is a friend of Clemmie's. He's staying in Dale View for a couple of months, and by all accounts he's a very personable young man.'

Ross's stomach did an involuntary flip. 'What friend of Clemmie's? I've never heard of him.'

'Well, why should you have done?' She eyed him knowingly. 'It's not as if you've had much to do with Clemmie lately, is it? And by the way, you still haven't started that portrait. People will talk, and I'm not having accusations that our raffle was a fake and our prizes non-existent, so you need to sort that out.'

'Yes, I'm on it,' he said quickly, 'but who is this Reuben?'

'I'm quite sure I don't know,' she said innocently. 'As I said, he's a friend of Clemmie's and he's staying in the town for a while. I know they've had dinner at Dale View, and he's been to Wintergreen a couple of times.'

'How on earth do you know that?' he asked, then sighed. 'Forget it. Of course you know.' *They've had dinner together? Clemmie and this man? In his holiday home?* 'So,' he asked, trying to sound offhand, 'why is this total stranger working at Whispering Willows?'

'It was Clemmie's suggestion.' She stroked Trueman's silky ears then placed him lovingly on her lap. 'Apparently Reuben used to have his own horse and he helped at a livery stable when he was younger. He was happy to volunteer at the sanctuary as a favour to Clemmie.'

'How noble of him.' Ross knew he sounded ungracious, but he couldn't help feeling suspicious. His mind raced as he wondered exactly how this Reuben character had become friends with Clemmie, and why he was so keen to ingratiate himself with her. 'Doesn't he have a job to go to?'

'He's a web designer according to Dolly.' She leaned back in the sofa and gave a big sigh. 'I would love a brandy, Ross, if you're offering. For shock, naturally.'

'A web designer?' Maybe that was how they knew him? Maybe he was creating a website for Dolly? But why would he be staying in Tuppenny Bridge for a few months if that was the case? Surely he could create a site from anywhere? Why was he trying to integrate with the community all of a sudden?

'Some people just do things out of the kindness of their hearts,' his aunt told him, eyeing him shrewdly as if she knew exactly what he was thinking. 'I must say, he's rather an attractive young man. Probably around the same age as you or thereabouts. Clemmie took him to the opening of the craft shop; did I mention that?' She gave him a sweet smile. 'It's nice to see Clemmie moving on at last.'

'Moving on?' he said faintly.

'After you and she—I mean, it's been a long time, and while you seem to have got over it quite quickly, poor Clemmie hasn't been out with anyone else to my knowledge. Until now.' She held up her hands. 'Now, I'm not saying they're courting, naturally. You know me; I'm not one to speculate on other people's lives.'

*Wow, she actually said that without a trace of irony.*

'But people *are* talking, and of course they're bound to be curious.' When he didn't respond she said, 'Well anyway, I'm just glad he's able to help Summer out. We must think about poor Joseph first and foremost. We may not have been friends exactly, but I wouldn't wish this on my worst enemy. If Reuben can ease his burden in any way at all then I for one am extremely grateful to him.'

She put Trueman back on the floor. 'And I can see I'm going

to have to get that brandy myself,' she grumbled as she got to her feet.

She strode into the kitchen, leaving Ross sitting on the sofa, wondering exactly who this Reuben was, and—more importantly—why the hell it bothered him so much.

# SEVENTEEN

Summer handed Clemmie a bottle of water and leaned against the loosebox wall with a relieved sigh.

'I definitely need a break.'

Clemmie, who was sitting on an upturned bucket, gave her a sympathetic look. 'You're knackered. How long are you going to be able to keep this up?'

'As long as I need to,' Summer said quietly, and Clemmie blushed, realising that was probably a tactless question.

'Sorry.'

'It's okay.' Summer shrugged. 'How are you doing anyway?' She glanced around, noting the wheelbarrow piled high with dirty straw and manure. 'I'd take some of that off before you take it to the muck heap,' she said. 'Best not to overload it. It can be heavier than you'd expect.'

'I was just trying to save time, but I expect you're right,' Clemmie acknowledged. 'I never thought using a pitchfork could be so painful. My blisters have blisters. How do you do this every day?'

'You get used to it.' Summer lifted her head as a car pulled into the stable yard. 'Oh, who's this? We should charge for parking.'

She strolled over to the open door and Clemmie followed her gaze, noting the dark blue SUV that had pulled up next to the red Mini belonging to Joseph's nurse, who was at that moment inside the house with her patient.

'It's Clive,' Summer said. 'Looks like he's brought someone with him.'

Clemmie got to her feet and joined her. 'Teenagers,' she said suspiciously. 'What do they want?'

Summer frowned. 'No idea. Come on, let's find out.'

She strode out of the loosebox and Clemmie followed her, bottle of water in hand. At least it was a chance to get out of the stables and breathe fresh air for a few minutes. She didn't think she'd ever get the smell of manure and soiled straw out of her nostrils.

Clive beamed at them.

'Summer, Clemmie, good to see you.'

'Hiya, Clive. What brings you here?' Summer asked, eyeing his companions with interest. Her animosity towards Ben's boss had vanished once she'd got over the shock, and she'd accepted his apology and his reasons for keeping Joseph's illness from her for so long. She'd had to admit that she would have done the same if her employer had asked her, so how could she stay angry?

'This is Lennox and Maya. They're here to volunteer,' Clive explained, indicating the two teens who were standing, hands in pockets, their eyes darting around the stable yard with interest.

The girl, thought Clemmie, looked confident and eager. The boy a little less so. She had a feeling he'd been nagged into joining her and wondered how long his altruism would last.

'Hiya,' Maya said cheerfully. 'We can't come here during the week cos of school and homework and stuff, but we can be here at weekends. We're happy to do whatever you need us to do. We love horses, don't we, Len?'

Lennox nodded. 'Yeah. Love 'em.'

'We can't pay you,' Summer explained. 'You do realise that?'

Lennox frowned and glanced at Clive, who gave him a reassuring smile. 'The deal still stands,' he said.

'What deal?' Summer asked.

'Mr Browning's gonna pay us. Twenty-five quid each per day. Right, Mr Browning?'

'I'd do it for nothing,' Maya assured them. 'I just want to be around horses. This is a dream come true for me.' She blushed fiercely. 'I mean, not a dream exactly. God, that sounded awful.' She hung her head. 'I'm sorry about your friend,' she said quietly.

'Yeah, me too. It's proper crap,' Lennox agreed.

'Thank you. You're right. It is.' Summer eyed Clive warily. 'Are you sure about this?'

'One hundred per cent. It's the least I can do. Kids, why don't you have a quick look around? See what's what, then meet me back here in say, half an hour?'

Lennox rolled his eyes as Maya hooked her arm through his and said, 'Ooh yeah, great! Thanks, Mr Browning.'

Clemmie watched them head straight to the paddock behind the stables where some of the donkeys were grazing.

'Is this a good idea?' she asked. 'Do they know what they're doing? Then again,' she added, as the thought struck her, 'they probably know a lot more than I do.'

'Ach, don't worry about those two,' Clive said in his soft Scottish accent. 'They're horse mad. Well,' he added with a grin, 'Maya is. Lennox is Maya mad.' He winked. 'But they're good kids. I've been looking after their families' pets since those two were in nappies, and I know they're both kind and caring.'

'Maya reminds me of myself at her age,' Summer said

thoughtfully. 'I volunteered at a local animal sanctuary when I was a teenager. Anything to be around animals, especially horses.'

'So you understand then. They won't let you down. Anyway, how's it going?' Clive asked. 'Settling in, Clemmie?'

Clemmie wrinkled her nose. 'I'm not sure if I'm more of a help or a hindrance to be honest,' she admitted. 'But I'm doing my best.'

'You've been brilliant,' Summer assured her. 'And Ben's been lovely, not minding when I haven't got a moment to spend with him and giving up his free time to help out too. And we've got Reuben of course.' She took a sip of her water. 'He's been a godsend. He's given up two afternoons and one full day a week to help, and when you think he's got his own business to run too...'

'Yeah, it was good of him,' Clemmie admitted. 'I didn't expect him to volunteer for so many hours. I just thought a few here and there would help you, so it was as much of a surprise to me as it was to you.'

'He's really good around the horses. Very gentle. Obviously loves them to bits, and he knows what he's doing which is useful. Between us all we'll manage. For now anyway.'

'How's Joseph?' Clive asked. He nodded at the Mini. 'I see the nurse is here.'

Summer hesitated. 'You know Joseph,' she said at last. 'Doesn't give much away, does he? Ava and Bluebell have been popping by to check up on him, and he's not best pleased about it. Well, he says he isn't, but I think he's quite grateful really. They've been brilliant making sure he eats something and that he's taking his painkillers and stuff. I don't think I'd be very good at all that. Horses I can deal with. Sick people...' She sighed. 'This is horrible, Clive.'

'I know,' he said gently. 'I know. I think I'll go in and see how he's getting on. Have a wee chat with the nurse and find out where we're at. If the terrible twosome return, tell them to wait by the car. I won't be too long.'

He headed towards the house and Summer and Clemmie returned to the loosebox. Clemmie offered her friend the upturned bucket, but Summer shook her head.

'If I sit down I might never get up again,' she said, half laughing.

'Poor Clive,' Clemmie said, sitting down and opening her bottle of water. 'He looks shattered. I can't imagine how awful it must be, losing your best friend.' She gave Summer a look of compassion. 'I know it's awful for you, too. How did it go, by the way? When you and Joseph finally had the talk, I mean? I've been meaning to ask you, but you never mentioned it and I didn't like to bring it up.'

Summer leaned against the wall and closed her eyes for a moment. 'It wasn't easy. There were a lot of tears—mine mostly. I understand now why he didn't want to tell me, and why he kept it from me for the longest time he could, but even so I wish he hadn't.' She stared out into the yard, clearly reliving the moment she'd found out. 'It must have been an awful burden for Clive, too, and I wasn't very nice to him. I'm relieved we made it up. At least we're all on the same side now.'

'I'm sure he understood. You were in shock. We all were. What's the nurse like?'

'Lovely. Really kind and practical. You'd have to be a pretty special person to do her job, wouldn't you? Palliative care they call it.' She shivered. 'Horrible word, palliative. All those connotations. I can't believe it, Clem, I really can't.'

Clemmie didn't know what to say. As far as she was aware, this would be Summer's first real taste of bereavement. Clemmie was all too aware how painful it was going to be for her friend, and wished she could make the whole thing go away. She took a sip of water, feeling desperately sad for Summer.

'When's Reuben here next?' she asked, hoping to change the subject.

'Tomorrow afternoon, thank God! I'd give him a medal if I could.' She frowned suddenly. 'How well do you know him, really?'

Startled, Clemmie wasn't quite sure what to say at first.

'Well,' she admitted at last, 'I don't really. But I'm sure you can trust him around the horses, and—'

'Oh no, it's not that,' Summer assured her. 'But you've not known him long, right?'

'No. Just a few weeks,' Clemmie admitted. 'Why?'

Summer watched her from under her chestnut fringe, and Clemmie was surprised, and not a little relieved, to see a familiar twinkle in her friend's eyes.

'What?' she said, half laughing.

'Well,' Summer said, a sudden spark of excitement in her voice, 'it's just that he's been asking an awful lot of questions about you for someone who's barely an acquaintance.'

'Questions? What sort of questions?'

'All sorts,' Summer said. 'Like what sort of music you listen to, and what you do in your spare time, and did you always want to work in your auntie's bookshop or did you have other plans, dreams, ambitions. That sort of thing.'

Clemmie thought about *The Marquess Wants a Wife* stashed away in her bedroom drawer. She'd finished it just the night before and had no idea what to do with it now. Did she have plans for it? Dreams of becoming a published writer? An ambition to perhaps one day be as prolific and successful as Dolly? She couldn't imagine it, and right now she'd rather die than reveal all that to Reuben, or anyone else for that matter.

'Why would he ask that?'

Summer grinned. 'Well, isn't it obvious?' She winked at Clemmie. 'I think you've got an admirer there.'

'Don't be daft!' Dread washed over Clemmie, making her

palms sweat and causing her to put her bottle on the floor before it slipped from her hands. 'As if!'

'What do you mean, as if? I don't get you. You're always so self-deprecating, but you're an attractive woman. Why shouldn't Reuben fancy you? Why shouldn't any man? Except Ben of course,' she added, as if Clemmie needed that pointing out to her.

Clemmie's face burned with embarrassment. 'He came here to see Dolly, not me. I'm just some random woman who got caught up in it all, so he had to be polite to me. He doesn't like me in that way.'

'Says who? You're completely blind to male attention, aren't you? I've seen loads of blokes giving you admiring looks, but you never pick up on it. Or if you do you deliberately ignore them.' She frowned suddenly. 'Is this because of Ross?'

Clemmie gulped, horrified. 'What would it have to do with Ross?'

'The way he treated you. The way he cheated on you and dumped you. Has it put you off men for good? You see, I think he's damaged your self-esteem, and now you're convinced no man will find you attractive. Ooh, honestly, I could throttle him! What he's done to you is unforgivable.'

Clemmie stared at her in horror, as Dolly's words came back to her. Her aunt was right. This had gone far enough, and Summer should know the truth. Ross deserved that much at least.

'About that,' she mumbled. 'I might not have given you the full picture there.'

Summer's eyes widened. 'About what?'

'About me and Ross. About the break-up.' Clemmie nibbled her thumbnail, not entirely sure how to tell Summer what had really happened.

'Well go on then,' Summer urged. 'Tell me.'

Clemmie didn't think it was possible for her face to burn

any more fiercely yet somehow it seemed to be managing it. She must look almost purple by now.

'Thing is,' she said carefully, 'Ross didn't exactly cheat on me.'

'Exactly?' Summer frowned. 'What's that supposed to mean?'

'It means—it means he didn't cheat on me at all. Well, not really. That is, he didn't go out with someone else until after we broke up.' She could barely look at her friend. 'But he would have done sooner or later! It was only a matter of time,' she burst out.

Summer looked baffled. 'How do you know that? So if he wasn't cheating on you, what did he dump you for exactly?'

Oh blimey! This was getting worse and worse. If Clemmie hadn't emptied the cold water out of that bucket she'd have plunged her scorching face straight into it.

'All right,' she said, her eyes pleading with Summer to understand, 'he didn't dump me. I dumped—I mean, I broke up with him.'

There was a silence as Summer processed that new and unexpected information. Clemmie picked up her water and gulped half of it down in one go. For the first time ever she wished she drank alcohol.

'O-kay,' Summer said slowly. 'So Ross didn't dump you, and he didn't cheat on you. You broke up with him.' She shook her head. 'Help me out here, Clem. Why do you hate him so much?'

'I don't hate him exactly,' Clemmie protested. Oh heck, if Summer could have read her thoughts sometimes she'd know all too well that Clemmie didn't hate him at all.

Maybe, just maybe, it was herself she hated for the way she'd hurt him. She'd had no choice, but it didn't make it any easier knowing she'd treated him so badly. And even worse, she hated the fact that she was angry with him for pulling himself together so quickly and going out with other women, rather than pining for her. She was a horrible person.

'That's not the impression you've always given me,' Summer said pointedly.

'No, well...' Clemmie took a deep breath. 'After we broke up, I thought—I thought he might fight for me. At least put up a bit of a protest. But he didn't. He just accepted it. Well, that is, he asked me why, but when I told him he just... left. And then,' she added hurriedly, 'he started dating other women. Within a week! And it's been one after the other ever since. Well, you know what he's like. You can see what sort of man he is, and that he's never going to settle down. I had a lucky escape really.'

Summer looked stunned. 'You're seriously telling me that you've been treating Ross like public enemy number one on the off chance that he might have cheated on you with some mythical woman at some point in this alternative future?'

Clemmie didn't reply. She wished she could tell Summer everything, but it was impossible. Things were bad enough as it was.

'And you let me be horrible about him!' Summer cried. 'I've said some awful things about him. I've even argued about him with Ben. Why did you tell me he cheated on you?'

'To be fair,' Clemmie said hastily, 'I didn't. Not exactly. You just assumed.'

'And you didn't put me right, did you?' Summer sounded angry, and Clemmie supposed she couldn't blame her. 'I can't believe you did that, Clem.'

'I know, I know,' Clemmie said miserably. 'I just find it really hard to talk about him. And you must surely see how hurt I was when he didn't fight for me, and went out with all those other girls?'

'Did you *expect* him to fight for you?' Summer demanded. 'Is that what you wanted?' Her eyes narrowed. 'Is that why you broke up with him? As some sort of ridiculous test to see if he'd behave like a romantic hero out of one of your stupid Jane Austen books?'

Clemmie flinched. 'Of course not!'

'Then why did you break up with him?'

There was nothing she could say to that. Instead, she hung her head, wishing she'd never come here in the first place.

There was an uncomfortable silence that hung between them for what felt like forever. Just as Clemmie was about to make her excuses and leave, Summer cleared her throat.

'Well,' she said, 'at least you managed to take my mind off Joseph for a few minutes. Thanks for that anyway.'

Clemmie risked a peek at her friend, and relief flooded through her as she saw Summer smiling.

'You are a banana.' Summer crouched down beside the bucket and put her arm around Clemmie's shoulders. 'You should have just told me the truth.'

'I know,' Clemmie agreed. 'I really am sorry.'

Summer nodded. 'I can see that by your beetroot red face. You're practically fluorescent. Seriously, though, Clem, *did* you break up with him so he'd fight for you? Was it a test to see how much he loved you or something?'

'No, honestly it wasn't! I didn't really expect him to fight for us...' Her voice trailed off, because she knew that wasn't strictly true.

Those few months six years ago had been the most difficult time in her life, apart from when her parents died. She'd been so stressed, and Ross had been away visiting his mother, and by the time he got back... There wasn't a day went by when she didn't wish things could have been different. Even so, she knew she'd made the right decision. For both of them.

'Then why did you break up with him?' Summer asked curiously. 'I don't get it. Even after all this time I can see he still bothers you, and looking at it through the lens of this new information, it makes me wonder if you've still got feelings for him.'

'I haven't!' Clemmie said quickly. Perhaps too quickly. She could see Summer wasn't convinced. 'We weren't compatible,' she said eventually. 'It would never have worked long-term.'

'It worked for eighteen months,' Summer said reasonably. 'And it's not as if either of you has found true love with anyone else since, is it?'

'He's had a bloody good go at it though,' Clemmie said bitterly.

'There you go! It's stuff like that which makes me think you're not really over him. What do you mean, you weren't compatible?'

'He wasn't romantic enough,' Clemmie said. 'I mean, he didn't say romantic things.'

'Seriously?' Summer burst out laughing. 'You should hear some of the things Ben comes out with. We can be kissing quite passionately one minute, then the next minute he's telling me all about a pig castration he's performed earlier. He'd definitely fail your test, which,' she added, 'I'm quite glad about. Poor Ross. He didn't stand a chance.'

'I think he thought I was a bit of a drip,' Clemmie said defensively. 'Said I was a dreamer.'

'Well, you are. That doesn't mean he thought it was a bad thing. I've said it too. Do you believe I think you're a drip?'

'Possibly,' Clemmie admitted. 'Particularly after today.'

'Hmm, you've got a point.' Summer laughed and got to her feet. 'It seems to me a bit of a stupid reason to dump the man of your dreams. No offence.'

'Maybe he wasn't the man of my dreams.'

'No, I guess not.' Summer stretched her back. 'I mean, let's be honest, even you wouldn't be daft enough to let the love of your life slip through your fingers for no good reason. I'm sorry, Clem. It's your life and your decision. I'm just glad I know the truth now. I'll have to be a lot nicer about Ross, you know. I feel pretty awful about the things I've said. But look, whatever happens, you're my best friend, and I'll always be on your side, okay?'

Clemmie nodded, feeling grateful but also completely wretched. If Summer knew the truth—that she had indeed let the love of her life slip through her fingers—what would she say then? Would she understand?

Not if Clemmie didn't explain the real reason why she'd had to let him go. And somehow, she doubted that would ever happen.

# EIGHTEEN

Ross wished, with all his heart, that he hadn't agreed to meet Meg at her hotel for dinner. He'd almost cancelled on her at the last minute but knew that wouldn't be fair to her. It wasn't her fault, after all. Besides, it was only dinner. He could get through it, even if he wasn't the slightest bit hungry.

'Aren't you going to look at the menu?' Meg asked lightly. She looked, he realised, quite beautiful. Her glossy dark hair hung in waves over her shoulders, she'd gone for a smoky look with her make-up, which really enhanced her green eyes, and she was wearing a tight-fitting dress that showed off her voluptuous figure to its full advantage. She'd clearly gone to a lot of trouble for his benefit. What was wrong with him that he couldn't bring himself to care?

'Sorry,' he said guiltily, picking up the menu where he'd dumped it on the table after the waiter handed it to him. He gave it a quick look but soon realised his appetite hadn't miraculously returned. Maybe he should just look at the light bites section.

'I think I'll have the sirloin steak,' Meg said. 'You know me and red meat.' She laughed and Ross looked at her blankly. He had no idea what she was talking about.

'Just a tuna and cheese melt for me,' he said, putting the menu back in its wooden holder. 'I'm not very hungry.'

'Oh, no! Now I feel greedy,' she said, tilting her head and pouting. 'Can't you try to eat something from the main menu? For me?'

'There wouldn't be any point...' His voice trailed off as she raised her eyebrows, an appeal in her eyes. 'Okay. I'll have whatever you're having.'

'Excellent. And shall we share a bottle of Pinot Noir?'

He nodded, not really minding one way or the other. Right now, he could down a pint of Randy Ram, but he thought she wouldn't appreciate that.

'You're not yourself tonight, Ross,' Meg observed some time later, as she sliced through her steak. 'Is something wrong?'

Ross thought that was a good question. There wasn't anything wrong, as such. It was just him being an idiot. Even so, he couldn't get the conversation he'd had with Bluebell earlier that day out of his mind, which was stupid because it had nothing to do with him. None of it should matter. Not any more.

'No, just work,' he said lightly. 'A million and one things to do and very little time left to do them in. You know how it is.'

'I do indeed,' she agreed. 'But that's even more of a reason to relax tonight and forget all about it. Work can wait. You know what they say about Jack. You wouldn't want to be thought a dull boy, would you?'

Ross was hardly listening. In his mind he was replaying, for what felt like the hundredth time, the conversation he'd had with Bluebell earlier that day.

He'd only popped into Cutting it Fine for a quick trim to appease his Aunt Eugenie, who had informed him that he'd let himself go to seed and was in danger of looking like one of those hippies from the sixties.

'If you're having dinner with Meg this evening the least you can do is have a decent haircut,' she told him sternly. 'Anyway, I've taken the liberty of booking you an appointment at the salon for this afternoon. Be there at two sharp.'

It worried Ross how eager she was for him to look his best just to go out for dinner with Meg. He knew his aunt was keen for him to settle down, but he really hoped she hadn't pinned her hopes on him choosing his interior designer.

Even so, he'd decided to keep the appointment, and had settled back in the chair and let Bluebell get on with it, while he'd mused over the colour schemes for the students' bedrooms.

At some point he'd realised she was talking about Joseph and had pushed thoughts of Monk's Folly away to concentrate on what she was saying.

'And that nurse deserves a medal. Honestly, what a hard job that must be, don't you think? I'm in awe. Ava and me, we just bob in to check up on him, take him some treats to coax him to eat, that kind of thing. Ava's better at it than me to be honest, but then, that's her job really, isn't it? Being a vicar's wife, I mean. Ministering to the sick of the parish, that sort of thing.'

'How's he doing?' Ross had asked tentatively.

'Joseph?' Bluebell queried, as if he could be talking about anyone else. 'Well, he's a lot happier in himself now he's not so worried about them blooming horses. He was fretting like mad when he thought Summer couldn't cope, but now she's got all them people helping her he's feeling a lot easier. Good job, cos as Clive told him, he needs to concentrate on himself and leave the horses to other people now.'

Ross had hesitated. 'I—I heard Clemmie was working there,' he ventured.

Bluebell nodded. 'She is. Only part time, like, cos of the bookshop. And they've got two teenagers to work weekends now, so that'll be a big help, and then there's Reuben.' She smirked and nudged him, and he saw in her reflection in the mirror a gleam of excitement in her eyes. 'Have you met him?'

Ross was about to shake his head, but seeing how close the scissors were to his neck he changed his mind. 'No, I haven't.'

'Ooh, well, he's lovely. Very nice looking. Fair hair, gorgeous blue eyes. And from London! Clemmie took him to the opening of Pennyfeather's, and he was ever so nice. Mind you, he never missed a trick. He was handing out business cards, left, right, and centre. Touting for business at someone else's opening! But then again, he did it in a nice way, and he's volunteered to work for nothing at Whispering Willows so he must have a good heart.' She winked. 'Well, Clemmie obviously thinks so.'

Ross tried hard to keep his face expressionless. 'Really? Are she and this Reuben together then?'

'Well, Dolly says he's just a friend of theirs, but I don't know so much. He and Clemmie seemed very close at the opening, and then she asked if she could see him in private outside, like. And ask yourself, why would someone who's got a successful business of his own volunteer to work for nothing for some fella he's never even met, if not to impress Clemmie? Now, think on that.'

He had thought on it and it had depressed him immeasurably. In fact, it had gnawed away at him ever since, and the fact that he was giving it so much headspace was annoying him.

Meg pushed her plate away and he realised he hadn't even answered her.

'Sorry,' he said sheepishly.

'If you want to leave you're free to go,' she said, clearly wounded by his lack of manners.

'No, honestly.' God, what was he thinking? He couldn't let Clemmie rule his thoughts like this. It was none of his business who she saw. What did he care anyway?

'This steak is delicious,' he told Meg, enthusiastically carving a slice as if he couldn't wait to taste it again.

She eyed him doubtfully. 'Are you sure? Because if you want to leave—'

'I'm sure,' he said firmly. 'Besides, we've got a lot to talk about.' He needed to get her opinion on those student rooms for starters.

She smiled widely. 'Great. You finish that and I'll order us another bottle of wine. Same again?'

As he chewed his steak, barely tasting it, he thought he really was going to have to sort himself out. He couldn't go on moping like this, dwelling on the past. He needed to get this portrait of Clemmie done and then it would all be over, and he could focus on the art academy. He need never give her another thought.

If only he could believe that...

Despite Meg urging him to have a dessert, Ross refused, stating he was far too full to even contemplate it.

A smile tugged at her lips. 'Well, I suppose we don't want you to be too full,' she said, and he heard the seductive note in her voice and realised she had plans for tonight. Plans that definitely included him.

'Shall we have coffee?' she asked him. 'We could take it up to my room, if you like?'

He considered her for a moment. She was stunning, there was no doubt about it. He also found her good company. At Monk's Folly she was witty and intelligent, and he loved how professional she was and how good at her job. She understood his vision and seemed to respect his opinions. He respected her, in turn. He thought, at any other time, he'd probably have taken her up on that offer.

But there was Clemmie.

There was always Clemmie, and it made him angry. He'd been able to, if not forget her, at least keep her at bay for a long time—while in the company of other women anyway. They'd helped to take his mind off her, giving him a much-needed break from brooding about her, missing her. He'd managed to go on without her all these years, determined to enjoy his life and not waste time wanting someone he could never have.

But since she'd won that raffle ticket and they'd been thrown back in touch again, everything had changed. She was in his orbit once more, and somehow she'd managed to fix herself back in his mind and heart. He was struggling to think about anything else, even Monk's Folly. The gossip he'd got from Bluebell today had thrown him. His mind was in turmoil.

'Meg,' he said quietly, 'I don't think that would be a good idea.'

She looked surprised. 'I don't see why not. We're both adults, both single. Are you saying you're not attracted to me?'

He couldn't lie about that. 'I am,' he admitted. 'You're a very beautiful woman.'

'Well then. You're a handsome man,' she said, smiling. 'I like you. A lot. Hey, don't look so worried, I'm not asking you to marry me. I just think we could have some fun, and what's the harm in that?'

What *was* the harm in that? She was right, wasn't she? It was just fun. No strings attached. Maybe he needed the release.

But going up to Meg's room would be a disaster. The more logical side of him knew that. Besides, even if he'd wanted to go through with it, it was hardly fair to Meg. She'd be a substitute, nothing more. He couldn't do that to her.

'I just—'

'Maybe,' she purred, 'I want to know if you live up to your reputation. Are you really the sex god the people in this town seem to think you are?'

He gave a mirthless laugh. 'The people in this town know very little about me,' he assured her. 'They make most of it up. Believe me, I'm not what they think I am.'

'Well, let me find out for myself,' she said, her eyes glittering with obvious lust.

Ross sighed, wishing things could be different.

'I just think it would be a mistake. You work for me,' he explained. 'It's never a good idea to mix business with pleasure. I honestly would prefer it if we kept things professional.'

She leaned back, clearly disappointed. 'Oh, I see.'

'It's really not that I don't find you attractive,' he said quickly, anxious that her feelings weren't hurt. 'You're a stunning woman. Any man would be lucky to have you.'

'But yet you still resist my charms,' she said mockingly.

'It's a rule I have,' he said ruefully. 'Sorry.'

She blew out her cheeks, looking fed up, then threw her napkin on the table. 'Okay, I get it. Well, if that's the way you want it.' She hesitated, then leaned towards him, smiling. 'And after all, I won't be your employee for much longer, will I? Who knows what will happen then?'

He managed a smile in return. 'Indeed.'

Maybe by the time she'd finished working at Monk's Folly she'd have fallen for someone else. Or maybe he'd have got Clemmie out of his system and would be more than ready to take Meg up on her offer. Who knew?

But as she called the waiter over to ask for the bill, Ross thought sadly that *he* knew. He would never get Clemmie out of his system.

And where did that leave him?

# NINETEEN

Clemmie couldn't deny she felt relieved when Summer assured her that she wouldn't be needing her at Whispering Willows any longer.

'Are you sure?' she asked, more because she felt she ought to check, rather than because she was hoping her friend would change her mind.

'Quite sure,' Summer said firmly. 'You've been brilliant, Clem, and I can't tell you how grateful I am, but we've got Reuben, Maya, and Lennox now, and they all like horses, whereas you—well—don't. Not,' she added quickly, 'that that's a bad thing. Each to their own and all that. But it's really not fair on you. I can see you're a bit scared of them.'

Clemmie grinned. 'That's one way of putting it. Thanks for being so polite about it.'

Summer put her arms around her. 'And thank you for being such an amazing friend. I know it wasn't easy for you, and I'll never forget that you stepped up for me when I needed you.'

'You're welcome,' Clemmie said. 'Any time.'

Dolly was glad to have her back at the bookshop, too.

'I'll be away next week,' she reminded her, as they sat at the table in Wintergreen's cosy kitchen the following morning, eating a full English breakfast, their usual Sunday treat. 'I've got a lot of writing to fit in between now and then, not to mention preparing that bloody speech, and finding something to wear for the event. I think a trip to York or Harrogate might be on the cards today. I'm going to treat myself to a fancy frock.'

'Good for you,' Clemmie said. She glanced out of the window at the grey sky and wrinkled her nose. 'Maybe a woolly jumper and a new winter coat might be a better idea.'

'Oh, it won't be this cold in London,' Dolly said confidently. 'Them southerners don't know what a cold winter is. No doubt they'll all be shivering in their thermals, and I can knock 'em all dead in my sexy dress.' She laughed and helped herself to more cornflakes. 'I was wondering,' she added, suddenly sounding hesitant, 'if you'd think about staying with Reuben at Dale View while I'm away. I don't like to think of you stuck out in the back of beyond all alone.'

'Dolly, I'm a grown woman!' Clemmie burst out laughing. 'Honestly, you have to stop seeing me as a little kid. I can look after myself.'

'Yes, of course you can. Even so, I'd feel easier if you were with someone you know.'

'I barely know Reuben,' Clemmie pointed out. 'He could be a serial killer for all we know.'

'Hardly, love.' Dolly sighed. 'Are you sure you won't think about it? He's already said he wouldn't mind you taking the spare room.'

'You've spoken to him about it?' Clemmie asked, horrified. 'Why would you do that?'

'Calm down. I was just sounding him out, that's all. I was going to ask him if he'd like to stay at Wintergreen, with it being bigger, but then I thought about you getting in to work and him being at Whispering Willows, and it made more sense.' She glanced out of the window, eyeing the sky worriedly. 'They reckon there's going to be snow soon, and I can't say I'll be surprised. It's been getting colder and colder here. If the worst happens and you get cut off out here...'

'Oh, Dolly! Even if that did happen I'd be fine. And I'd rather be here on my own than stuck at Dale View with a man I barely know, especially in such a small space. Can you imagine? What if he...'

Her voice trailed off and she bit her lip.

'Trust me, love, Reuben wouldn't touch you.'

'How could you possibly know that for sure?' Clemmie demanded.

'He just wouldn't. I know.' Dolly shook her head. 'I—I have a feeling about him, that's all.'

'Forgive me if I don't trust your feelings,' Clemmie said. 'Besides,' she added, picking up a triangle of toast from the rack and taking the lid off the butter dish, 'that's not what I meant.'

'Then what did you mean?' Dolly frowned, then her face cleared as she realised what her niece was talking about. 'Like I said, you'd have your own room. Your own space.'

'In that tiny cottage?'

'There's no reason he'd find out,' Dolly assured her. 'But even if he did, would it be the end of the world?'

Clemmie paused, her knife hovering over the dish of butter as she stared at her aunt, hardly able to believe she'd asked the question.

'Yes,' she said incredulously. 'It bloody would.'

Dolly sighed. 'Okay, okay, point taken. If you're sure. I'll let him know that you're okay on your own. Mind you, I might ask him to pop over, just to check on you.'

'Don't you dare,' Clemmie said.

She couldn't help but remember what Summer had said. Was it really possible Reuben had a bit of a crush on her? The thought made her feel nauseated. Reuben was a nice man, and she wasn't denying he was attractive, but she had no romantic interest in him whatsoever. She had no intention of encouraging him, or of allowing Dolly to, however unintentionally.

Dolly said nothing and after a moment Clemmie bit into her toast. For a while there was nothing but the sound of clattering coffee cups, contented chewing, and the odd slurp from Dolly.

'What are your plans for today then?' her aunt asked eventually, after draining her third cup of coffee.

Thank goodness, Clemmie thought, that she mainly stuck to decaf.

'Do you fancy coming into town with me? You can help me pick out a dress. We can take the train, make a day of it.'

Clemmie hesitated.

Dolly seemed to sense her indecision. 'Go on. I'll treat you to tea and cake at Betty's. How does that sound?'

'Wow, you fight dirty,' Clemmie said, laughing. 'All right, why not?'

'Great! We'd best get ourselves ready then.' Dolly gave her a sly smile. 'And since I've promised to treat you to cake, can I ask you a favour in return?'

'I've already said I'll listen to you reading your speech,' Clemmie reminded her.

'It's not that, love. Will you promise me you'll ring Ross and fix a date for the portrait sitting?'

Clemmie gazed at her in dismay.

'Why would you bring that up? Just as we were planning a nice day too.'

'It needs sorting, love. I was talking to Allison Fisher—you know, her with the hooked nose whose husband breeds Labradors? Him with the breath that could stun a grouse at fifty paces? She cleans for Miss Lavender, and she reckons the old girl's getting a bit het up about this portrait, because people are beginning to suggest the whole thing was a scam, and she's worried Ross's reputation will be ruined.'

'I don't believe that for a minute!' Clemmie laughed scornfully. 'Anyway, what people? I've not heard anyone suggest any such thing, and surely if they suspected fraud they'd be asking *me* about it? I'm the one who won the prize after all.'

'Oh,' Dolly waved a hand dismissively, 'you know what folks are like. Easiest way to shut them up and make Miss Lavender happy would be to get it over and done with. Besides, I'd really like to have a portrait of you in the house. Brighten the place up no end. What do you say?'

Clemmie didn't know what to say. She stared at her aunt in dumb misery.

'It can't be that bad, love, surely? A few hours or so in Ross Lavender's company. It won't hurt you.' Dolly's eyes narrowed. 'Or will it?'

'No,' Clemmie said, through gritted teeth. 'Of course it won't.'

'There you go then.'

'I'll text him later,' Clemmie promised.

Dolly pushed away her empty plate and leaned back in her chair. 'Or,' she said, folding her arms, 'you could do it now, before we get ready to go out.'

There was no escape and Clemmie knew it. Besides, maybe her aunt had a point. Maybe it was time to prove to everyone—particularly Ross Lavender—that he had no power over her whatsoever, and that spending some time sitting for a portrait with him wouldn't be a problem.

'Fine.'

She grabbed her mobile phone and tapped out a message.

> Hi Ross. Think we should fix a date for this sitting. Let me know when's best for you. Clementine.

She stared at the screen. Had she really put Clementine? She quickly deleted it and replaced it with Clemmie, then frowned. *Date?* That sounded all wrong. She didn't want to put those ideas in his head.

> Ross, let me know what day you want me to do this sitting and we'll get it over and done with. Clemmie.

There, that sounded better. He couldn't possibly read anything into that, could he?

She pressed send and put the phone down. 'Done.'

'Good lass,' Dolly said approvingly. 'Right, let's get a shifty on. We've got a train to catch.'

## TWENTY

Aunt Eugenie was clearly delighted by the progress that had been made at Monk's Folly. Even the noise and mess from the window specialists, who were currently in the process of replacing the old 1920s windows with reproduction Regency sash windows, didn't seem to annoy her.

As Ross showed her round, accompanied by an enthusiastic Meg, she nodded brightly, her blue eyes showing enthusiasm as they pointed out the genuine early 19th century fireplaces in the two front rooms at either side of the hallway, the incredibly authentic-looking reproduction fireplace in the dining room, and the gleaming units and two six-burner, dual-fuel, stainless-steel range cookers that had been newly installed in the huge kitchen.

'I know this looks a bit modern,' he explained, 'but the main thing in this room is space, efficiency, and hygiene. Jennifer's going to be doing a lot of cooking in here.' He gave her a wry smile. 'We didn't think a Regency kitchen would cut it.'

'It's marvellous,' his aunt exclaimed. 'Absolutely marvellous. The two of you have done a splendid job. I'm thrilled.'

'I'm delighted to hear it,' Meg said. 'Of course, we haven't started decorating yet as there was no point while all this work was going on, but we've sourced the materials we want, and the decorators will be starting here next week.'

'It looks better just for having that awful wallpaper stripped off,' Aunt Eugenie assured her. 'How the Callaghans lived with that I can't imagine. I'm sure it's going to look stunning when it's all painted.' She turned to Ross. 'Have you decided which rooms you're taking for yourself?'

'Jennifer's old bedroom with the en suite at the front left, and the room directly opposite it on the right.'

'Really?' For the first time she sounded disapproving. 'Don't you think the front rooms would be better left to the guests? After all, that view is a huge selling point.'

'We talked about that,' Meg said quickly. 'But after all, this house is set on a hillside, and they'll still get the views from the living room.'

Ross rubbed his short beard, feeling awkward. Maybe, he thought, he should have gone with his gut and taken the back rooms himself, but Meg had been very persuasive. She was busy persuading his aunt now, just as she'd worked on him. She could be a very persuasive person, as he knew all too well. In other circumstances he might well have ended up staying the night with her at that hotel.

'This is going to be Ross's home,' she was pointing out to his aunt. 'He won't have students here all year round, and why should he be relegated to staring at a hill all the time? They're here to paint, and they'll be mostly outside to do it, or in the studio. Their bedrooms will be for sleeping. They won't care about the view from up there, whereas it might be important to Ross. It's his private sanctuary, away from the communal areas after all.'

Ross had let himself be talked round, but he could see his aunt wasn't convinced, and now he was doubting the decision himself. Maybe the students should be his priority…

'Bear in mind,' Meg continued, 'that each of these students will only be staying here for six days, maximum. Ross, on the other hand, will be here all the time. It's only right that we make his living quarters as aesthetically pleasing as possible.'

'I suppose...' He'd never heard his aunt sound so uncertain before. It was quite something to behold.

'The left front room will be his own bedroom, and we're replacing the old bathroom suite with a new one as the one in there now is pretty ancient. The right front room will be a living room with a kitchenette. There's plenty of space for some units and a basic cooker, as well as a sofa, television, that sort of thing. Maybe even a table and chairs in front of the window. Imagine eating your breakfast every morning gazing out over the river and that adorable little town beyond.'

She sighed, and Ross had a sudden uncomfortable feeling that she *was* imagining it. He hoped she wasn't getting any ideas about waking up to those views herself, because it wasn't going to happen. Maybe he hadn't been clear enough with her.

He couldn't imagine why she'd be interested in him anyway. He'd hardly been the most attentive dinner companion when they'd eaten out, but she hadn't let that put her off, and was angling for them to go out again soon, to 'get away from the hotel'. Ross couldn't help thinking that if her hotel was that bad she really ought to check out and find herself somewhere else to stay. At any rate, it had seemed perfectly fine to him.

'You're right of course.' His aunt's voice, brisk and no-nonsense, brought him back to the present, and he was relieved to see she was smiling at him. 'This will be a fine art school, but after all, it's also your home, dear. Most of the students will be day students anyway. It's silly to fuss about views from the bedrooms when all that matters is that they're warm, well-fed, and get the first class teaching they're paying for. Which, naturally, they will.'

She nodded, pleased with herself for making the decision.

'Yes, excellent idea, Miss McKenna. Excellent. You've done a wonderful job so far. I look forward to seeing it completed. Which, by the way, will be when exactly?'

'Once the windows have been replaced we'll be good to go with the decorating,' Meg said confidently. 'You'd done the main job before I even got here—sorting out the heating. While the decorators are at work we're going to make a few trips to purchase the furniture. Oh, and we've got a company booked to install the new internal window shutters. No more heavy, dark curtains. We can't wait to go shopping, can we, Ross?'

Ross shuffled awkwardly as she slipped her arm through his and beamed at him, for all the world as if she were talking about choosing furnishings for their new marital home.

'Er...'

Thankfully, at that moment, his mobile pinged.

'Excuse me.'

He deftly removed her arm and moved away, leaving his aunt to occupy Meg while he tapped his screen and stared at the name in amazement.

Clemmie! It had been so long since he'd last seen her name pop up like that it stunned him for a moment. His heart raced as he opened the message but sank again when he read what she'd sent him.

Talk about cold and to the point! Well, what did he expect? For a true romantic she *was* cold. Cold and brutal. So she was going to honour him with her presence, was she? How kind of her. Maybe her new boyfriend was having a positive effect on her.

He gazed around the living room, picturing the duck egg blue walls and warm white paintwork that would soon brighten this space, and match the stunning period fireplace. Clemmie, he knew, would adore it. When they added in some Regency-style furniture it would look exactly as if Mr Darcy himself could walk into the room at any moment.

Although, as he recalled, Darcy wasn't Clemmie's favourite Austen hero. That was... He frowned, trying to recall. Mr Knightley? No! Captain Wentworth. That was it. Well, Captain Wentworth would look right at home here. A part of him couldn't wait to see Clemmie's face when she saw it.

Then his heart hardened. Why should he show it to her? He owed her nothing. When she found out that Monk's Folly had been transformed into something that looked like the setting of one of her much-loved Jane Austen novels, she'd be dying to see it, and it would give him the greatest of pleasure to make sure she never set foot inside the place.

He'd been nagging her for weeks to let him get on with this portrait, and now suddenly she was being gracious enough to allow him to do so, as if she was doing him a favour. Didn't she realise he had better things to do with his time?

What was it—Reuben Walker given her a day off had he?

With a jealousy he refused to acknowledge burning inside him he quickly jabbed a message back to her.

> I'm truly honoured that you're finally able to fit the sitting in. Are you sure Reuben can spare you? Or were you planning to invite him along to watch? Well, neither of you are welcome at Monk's Folly, so if you want it doing I'll have to come to Wintergreen. The sooner this is over with the better so let's say next week. Will text you further details when I know when I'm free. Ross Lavender.

He was about to press send, but as he checked it over one last time to make sure he hadn't made any spelling mistakes, his eyes narrowed, and he felt a wave of nausea. Honestly, it sounded petty, spiteful, and pathetic. Cursing himself, he deleted it. The last thing he wanted was for her and her new boyfriend to think he was jealous.

> Okay. Monk's Folly in middle of refurbishment, so will have to do preliminaries at Wintergreen. Next week will be fine by me. Will text you exact day when I'm free. Ross.

*Ross? Or Ross Lavender?*

In the end he deleted three letters and signed the message R. That would do.

'Everything all right?' Aunt Eugenie asked as he shoved the phone in his pocket and wandered back to them.

'Absolutely. Looks like I'll be starting that portrait of Clemmie next week.'

'Oh, thank goodness,' she said. 'That will shut people up. I'm looking forward to seeing it.'

'You're painting someone's portrait?' Meg gazed at him admiringly. 'How wonderful. Lucky girl.'

Tell Clemmie that, he thought wryly. He'd bet anything that she wasn't looking forward to this any more than he was. In fact, he wondered which of them was dreading it the most.

# TWENTY-ONE

As Ross manoeuvred the car into the drive at Wintergreen he wondered what sort of reception he'd get. He was only glad that he wouldn't have to face Dolly.

Maybe, he reflected, as he unclipped his seat belt, he was being a coward, but really Clemmie had asked for this.

Despite her promises, she still hadn't fixed up a date to sit for him. Ross had sent her several texts with possible times he could fit her in, and she'd come up with an excuse for every one of them. In the end, if it had been up to him, he'd have stopped bothering, but Aunt Eugenie wasn't having it.

She'd insisted he sort this out once and for all, and when Ross had heard on the grapevine—the grapevine, naturally, being the Lavender Ladies—that Dolly had gone off to London for a couple of days to attend some writing event, leaving Clemmie alone at Wintergreen, he'd decided it was now or never.

With Dolly not due back until Monday afternoon, he'd seized the chance to visit Clemmie early on Sunday afternoon, knowing The Corner Cottage Bookshop would be closed, and she'd be alone at home.

As he climbed out of the car and stared up at the pretty stone cottage, it crossed his mind for the first time that, just maybe, she wouldn't be alone after all. What if Reuben Walker had spent the night there?

The thought made him feel sick, and he forced himself to walk to the front door, determined that, even if Clemmie had company, he wouldn't let on that it bothered him.

Not that it did bother him. Not in the way Clemmie might assume anyway. It wasn't that he was jealous, or that he wished it was him who'd spent the night with her. No, nothing like that. He was just bewildered, he supposed. Bewildered that she had room in her life and her heart for another man, when she'd treated him so badly, so unfairly.

What had he done to make her hurt him like that? He'd racked his brains many times, going over and over their relationship, trying to work out why she'd decided to end it so cruelly and without warning.

He honestly couldn't understand it. All right, he wasn't the most romantic of men. He held his hands up to that. He wasn't a big reader. He didn't quote poetry or say soppy things to her, that was true. But that didn't mean he didn't feel those things. He *had* felt those things. And the things he'd said to her about his feelings towards her might not have sounded poetic, but they'd come from the heart. Why hadn't that been good enough for her?

Maybe, he thought sullenly, as he knocked loudly on the front door, Reuben Walker could quote vast reams of Wordsworth, Shelley, and Keats to her. Maybe he even wrote his own poetry. Well, good luck to him. Good luck to them both. They deserved each other.

No one answered.

Ross knocked again, then put his head to the door, listening. He was pretty sure he heard something, though he wasn't sure what.

He peered through the letter box and could just about make out footsteps on the landing.

'Clemmie?'

The footsteps stopped and there was sudden silence, then a door shut upstairs.

Ross's heart raced. Were they...

He straightened and took a deep breath. Maybe this wasn't such a good idea after all. Maybe he should leave them to it.

He heard footsteps on the stairs and swallowed, feeling a sudden panic. He wasn't ready for this after all. If Reuben Walker opened the door now he didn't know how he'd react. He should never have come here.

He turned to hurry back to the car, but the door flew open, and when he glanced over his shoulder he saw Clemmie standing there, her face red, an angry expression in her eyes.

'What are *you* doing here?'

He peered over her shoulder for a sight of her *friend*, trying to hide his anxiety behind a façade of irritation.

'What the hell do you think I'm doing here? I'm supposed to be painting your portrait, remember?'

'Not today! We hadn't made any firm arrangement,' she pointed out.

'No, we hadn't, thanks to you. I've tried all week to pin you down to an exact day and you've messed me about non-stop. You won this prize in December, and here we are in early February already. You've had plenty of time to book a sitting. I decided to take matters into my own hands.'

'Oh, did you? And what if I'm busy?'

'*Are* you busy?'

The defiance in her eyes dampened a little and she sighed. 'Well, no, not really. I suppose you'd better come in.'

He stepped, almost reluctantly, into the hall, bracing himself for an appearance by Reuben Walker. There was a part of him that would quite like to meet him. To see for himself what made him so special. Another part of him—the biggest part by far—wanted never to set eyes on the man, particularly in Clemmie's presence.

Clemmie peered past him, and her eyes widened in surprise. 'It's snowing!'

There was a childlike wonder in her voice that almost made him smile despite his annoyance. She'd always loved snow.

'It started just as I left Tuppenny Bridge,' he said, keeping his voice deliberately casual, as if he couldn't care less. 'Are you alone?'

She frowned. 'Why do you ask?'

'I noticed Dolly's car wasn't here,' he said, feeling a pang of shame at his deception. 'I assumed she'd be here on a Sunday. Unless it's in the garage?' He knew it probably was. Dolly had no doubt taken the train to London, because Clemmie would need the car for work.

'She's out,' Clemmie said briefly. 'So how long do you think this will take?'

Wow, she really couldn't wait to get rid of him, could she?

'That depends.'

'On what?'

'On how soon we make a start, how good the light is, if you do your job well—'

'My job?'

'Sitting still while I draw you takes patience. Have you got any patience?'

She stared at him for a moment. 'I guess if it will get this out of the way once and for all it's best to just get on with it, isn't it?'

'I suppose it is.'

'Like bracing yourself for a trip to the dentist.'

'You're seriously comparing having your portrait painted by me to a trip to the dentist? Thanks for that.'

Clemmie shrugged and headed into the living room. Ross closed the door behind him and followed her.

'You've redecorated,' he said, looking round in surprise. 'Didn't this room used to be green?'

'Of course we've redecorated,' she said coldly. 'It's been years. We've probably repainted this room three times since you were last here.'

'It's a bold choice, red. I like it.'

He did, too. He noted the Victorian features and the big, bay window, and thought that Wintergreen was very different to Monk's Folly. He wondered which Clemmie would prefer.

'So,' she said, 'where do you want me?'

The words had no sooner left her mouth then her face began to turn pink. He watched the flush spread from her cheekbones down to her breastbone. A dozen replies suggested themselves to him, but he knew she was embarrassed enough.

'I'm just hoping to do a few preliminary sketches today. Could we have a cup of coffee first and discuss what sort of portrait you want?' he said, deliberately sounding brisk and businesslike so as not to humiliate her further.

She nodded and hurried into the kitchen. Ross wasn't sure whether to follow her or not but decided it might only fluster her more so remained in the living room. He sank into a comfy looking armchair which sat next to one of those old-fashioned standing lamps with a vintage, tasselled lampshade. He'd spotted something similar at Monk's Folly when he'd had a quick viewing with Aunt Eugenie. He remembered looking at it with distaste then, but somehow it seemed to suit the décor at Wintergreen. Maybe Dolly had bought it from Jennifer.

He closed his eyes for a moment, remembering how much time he'd once spent in this house. It seemed like a century ago.

He could see it now—cosy winter afternoons by the fire, curled up on the sofa together while Dolly tapped away on the computer in her study next door. Watching Clemmie's favourite romcoms on the television, or—just as likely—kissing to a soundtrack of their favourite songs, playing just loudly enough so as not to disturb Dolly, but to make sure she couldn't hear them either.

Now that the memories were flooding back he found himself relaxing. Suddenly it seemed no time at all since he was last here, as if everything that had happened since had been a dream.

He blinked as Clemmie nudged the door further open with her hip and walked in carrying two mugs of coffee.

'Thank you,' he said, taking one from her.

'Milk, two sugars. Right?'

He was surprised she'd remembered. 'Er, that's right.'

She perched nervously in another armchair, nursing her mug, and not meeting his gaze.

'So,' he said carefully, 'have you given any thought to what sort of portrait you want this to be?'

'In what way?' she queried.

'Well, head and shoulders, full body, any particular pose, any accessories you'd like included, that sort of thing.'

'Oh.' She shrugged. 'I hadn't thought about it at all. Bad enough getting your photo taken, never mind having a portrait painted.'

He remembered she'd always pulled a face when he wanted to take her photo, but she'd never seemed to mind when he'd taken a selfie of them both. It was as if being next to him had given her confidence.

'Well, maybe you can give some thought to it now? And while you're thinking, I'll start sketching.'

He reached into his bag and pulled out a sketchbook and pencils. Clemmie watched him dubiously.

'You're going to start drawing me now? While I'm sitting here with a mug of coffee?'

He shrugged. 'It's good to get a few different sketches. Different angles, moods, that sort of thing. Just ignore me and carry on with what you're doing.'

'I'm not doing anything,' she pointed out. 'I was doing something before you rudely knocked on the door, but now I'm just sitting here feeling stupid.'

He frowned. 'What were you doing when I arrived?' Without meaning to he cast a wary eye at the door to the hallway, half expecting Reuben to walk through it and announce he'd been upstairs the whole time.

She hesitated. 'Cleaning out my room,' she said at last.

'Well, maybe...' Ross realised that probably wasn't a good idea and clammed up. 'Put the television on?' he suggested. 'Or you could read?'

She gave him a scathing look. 'I'm not always reading, you know.'

'I never said you were.'

Hell, she was prickly! He couldn't say anything right.

'I'll put a film on,' she announced, reaching for the remote control. 'I'll watch that while you draw, and I'll just pretend you're not here.'

'Fine by me.'

If it put her at her ease he didn't care. The main thing was to get a few of her expressions down on paper, some quick sketches of her hands in different poses, to capture the slope of her shoulders, the curve of her neck...

He braced himself for some soppy film, but to his astonishment something quite different came on screen.

*The Muppet Christmas Carol?*' He stared at her, amazed. 'You do know it's February?'

'Never got a chance to watch it at Christmas,' she said, giving him what looked suspiciously like a smirk, as if she knew she'd surprised him and had guessed what he was expecting.

Scowling, he flicked the lamp on, put pencil to paper and tried to concentrate. She knew he loved *The Muppet Christmas Carol*. They'd watched it together over their last Christmas as a couple. Well, there was mean and then there was mean, and this was downright mean. How was he supposed to concentrate now?

Out of the corner of his eye he watched Michael Caine stomping through the streets of Victorian London as a variety of Muppets sang about the miserly Ebenezer Scrooge. His gaze flickered over to Clemmie, and he noticed that she was already captivated. That expression on her face...

He forgot all about the film and started drawing, making various sketches over the next hour and a half or so of her eyes, noting the way they widened and narrowed, sparkled with mirth, blurred with tears. Her hands relaxed one moment, twisted in her lap the next. Her fingers tapping along to the music or wiping away the trace of a tear that suddenly threatened. Her shoulders, relaxed as she enjoyed a love song, hunched with tension at the plight of Tim, shaking with laughter at Mrs Cratchit's attempts to stuff her face with food without her daughters realising.

He realised she'd forgotten all about him and a part of him felt sad that she could push all thoughts of him aside so easily, even though it didn't surprise him. Why should it? She'd pushed him out of her life easily enough after all.

He began to sketch her hair, which was loose over her shoulders. He remembered the days when he'd stroked it and twisted it gently between his fingers and inhaled the scent of her favourite coconut shampoo.

He noticed the way her fringe fell below her eyebrows, brushing her eyelashes. He saw the frosted blonde highlights shimmering among the honey blonde base of her hair, the way it fell in long layers and framed her pretty face. It was slightly darker than she used to have it, he thought. And she didn't used to have layers either. Her hair had been one length. He liked the layers though. They added depth and movement.

He focused on her mouth. She had well-shaped lips. They curved into a smile at the heartwarming moments, silently mouthed the lyrics of the songs, fell slightly open at the tenser parts of the film, turned down at the corners as the Cratchits mourned Tiny Tim.

As the film reached its conclusion, she smothered a yawn suddenly and scratched her head. Her eyes widened and she spun round to stare at him, a look of panic on her face for some reason he couldn't fathom.

'Are you okay?' he asked.

'I forgot you were here!'

She was blushing fiercely, and he said gently, 'It's okay. You were supposed to. I wanted to capture you at your most natural, remember?'

'Yes, but...' her voice trailed off and she mumbled, 'I'll put the kettle on.'

She shot out of the room even before the end credits had finished rolling, which wasn't like Clemmie. She always liked to watch the film right until the bitter end. He supposed she must have changed. It had been a long time after all.

He glanced through the sketches he'd made, almost without thinking about it. She was there on the page, already coming to life. He just needed to know what sort of pose she wanted.

'Would you like something to eat?'

She was standing in the doorway, and her expression now was calm, with no trace of the frightened fawn look she'd had a few minutes ago. He couldn't keep up.

'Something to eat?'

She nodded at the clock on the mantel. 'It's teatime. I'm hungry. If you want something I'll cook for you too. If you're wanting to get off it doesn't matter.'

He looked at her in surprise. Was she seriously offering him tea?

'That would be great,' he said, suddenly realising he was hungry too. 'If you're sure you don't mind.'

She shrugged. 'It makes no difference to me. Don't expect a

banquet. I was just going to heat up some soup and shove some part-baked bread rolls into the oven. Okay?'

'Sounds great,' he told her, and she nodded.

'Can you close the curtains?'

'Of course,' he said, startled to realise it was dark outside.

She went back into the kitchen, and he stared down at the sketch of her wiping away a tear. She was making him soup? Could that be called progress?

As he closed the curtains he noticed it was snowing heavily now, and thought he'd better set off home as soon as he'd had something to eat. Really, it would be better if he set off now. The roads between West Colby and Tuppenny Bridge were always bad in wintry weather.

But she was making him soup, and she'd offered it to him without him so much as hinting. Surely another hour wouldn't make any difference?

He straightened the curtains and sat down again. Just an hour. That's all.

# TWENTY-TWO

Clemmie wasn't sure why she'd invited Ross to join her for soup and rolls. What she should have done, of course, was tell him she was about to have her tea, so if he was quite finished she'd rather like him to leave, thank you very much.

Instead, she found herself standing there asking him to join her. *Well done, Clemmie.*

Now, as she faced him over the kitchen table, she could only hope that she didn't slurp, or drip soup down her front. It certainly wouldn't be the first time. She wondered why she'd chosen something that was so messy and precarious to eat.

'Minestrone! My favourite.'

Ross's face lit up as he realised what she'd made him, and while there was a part of her that was delighted by his approval, she forced herself to sound neutral as she replied, 'I made it last week. Didn't take long to defrost,' just so he knew she hadn't prepared it especially for him. She had, though, scattered it with basil and grated parmesan just before serving, because she remembered he enjoyed it like that.

He never had minestrone soup at Lavender House. Miss Lavender didn't approve of 'foreign food', and even if she had she certainly wouldn't approve of anything that reminded Ross of his Italian mother. She was hardly Giulia Lavender's biggest fan.

Then again, neither was Clemmie. She'd heard enough about her from Miss Lavender, Noah, and a few bits from Ross himself to know that Ross had got a raw deal when it came to his mamma.

As he tucked into the soup, Clemmie watched him surreptitiously. She couldn't help but feel a pang of sympathy for him. She'd been so lucky with her own parents. Her mum and dad had not only adored each other, but her too. She'd never had a single moment when she hadn't felt loved by them.

Ross, on the other hand, had been discarded by his mum and dad almost from the moment he'd figured out who they were. His father, Abel, had always been a bit of an irresponsible player. Ross had confided in her that he'd led his first wife, Hester, who was Noah's mum, a heck of a dance while they were married. Miss Lavender had approved of Hester because she was sensible and practical, and had hoped that she would tame Abel.

Unfortunately, that didn't happen. Instead, Abel rather broke Hester, who ended up divorcing her husband and running off to America with a kindly businessman who was dull but utterly dependable. Unfortunately, his kindness didn't extend to another man's child, so Noah had been left behind with his father.

Abel had played the field, leaving Noah in his aunt's care. Then he'd met Giulia and had, for the first time in his life, fallen in love. Giulia had tamed him all right, and he'd done anything she'd asked. They were married within three months of meeting, despite Miss Lavender's pleas for them to wait, and soon a baby was on the way.

However, once Ross was born, it became obvious that Giulia was just as flighty and unreliable as her husband. Their marriage descended into a cycle of arguments, infidelities, bitter break-ups and passionate reconciliations.

Eventually, Miss Lavender had begged them to put the boys first. Noah and Ross had endured enough, she argued, pleading with them to think of the children's welfare. Abel and Giulia had totally agreed with her, and had responded to her plea, though not in the way she'd expected.

They'd left both boys in her care and continued their game of cat and mouse all over Europe. Sometimes, they lived together. Sometimes, they lived alone. Sometimes, they lived with other lovers. Whatever they were up to, and whoever they were with at the time, it seemed Ross and Noah seldom crossed their minds, and the care of the boys had been left entirely to their great-aunt.

Maybe, Clemmie thought, that was why Miss Lavender spoiled them so much. She absolutely doted on both boys, and had sent them to St Egbert's—a posh public school a few miles from Tuppenny Bridge. She'd made it very clear that Lavender House would be left to Noah, rather than his father, upon her demise, and of course she'd bought Monk's Folly for Ross. They were both set for life.

Even so, it didn't make up for the fact that neither of them had loving parents. Clemmie was grateful for the love she'd received from her own mum and dad, even if that love had been cruelly taken from her at a young age.

'This is so good,' Ross told her, raising his eyes for the first time, and looking a bit taken aback to see her watching him. 'Is something wrong?'

'Of course not. I'm glad you're enjoying it.'

'It's delicious.' He paused. 'Did you say you made it?'

'That's right.' She waited for him to make a sarcastic comment. She hadn't, after all, exactly done much cooking when they were together, and to be honest she was more an egg and chips sort of girl, but this was an easy recipe to follow. It came in handy because she could freeze portions and keep it for a day such as this. It was probably the only real cooking she'd done for months, but she wasn't going to let him know that.

'Well,' he shook his head, 'it's seriously good.'

He smiled at her and something inside her thawed a little. Without even thinking about it, she said, 'Have you heard anything from your mother lately?'

A shadow passed across his face and Clemmie could have kicked herself. Why on earth had she brought that woman up?

He broke off a small piece of bread and held it between his fingers. 'Not for ages. Last I heard she was in Switzerland, shacked up with some Belgian machine manufacturer.'

'Random.'

'That's mia madre,' he said with a shrug.

'And your dad?'

'Buying and selling houses in France. Well, he was four years ago or thereabouts. Haven't heard from him since.'

'I'm sorry,' she said. 'It must hurt.'

'Not after all this time. They never bothered so why should I bother with them? Anyway, Noah's got it just as bad as I have. Dad doesn't keep in touch with him either, and as for his mother—he doesn't even know where she lives. He doesn't even know if she's still alive come to that, it's been so long since she contacted him. He was a teenager, I think.'

Clemmie shook her head, hardly able to believe it. 'I don't understand how any parent could behave like that.'

'No, well. It is what it is. I don't waste time thinking about them.'

'I'm sorry I brought them up.'

His expression softened. 'It's all right. For all you knew I could be in regular contact with them. I guess we've got a lot of catching up to do.'

Clemmie wasn't so sure about that. They were just having soup together. She didn't want to get too deep into conversation with him. She supposed it was her own fault for bringing up his mother.

What were they supposed to talk about? Noah? Monk's Folly? Or the never-ending string of women he'd dated over the last few years? That, she thought wryly, would be an interesting conversation. Not.

'So, who's Reuben Walker?'

The question came completely out of the blue and caught her off-guard. She dropped her spoon into the soup and cursed as splashes of minestrone landed on her jumper.

Dabbing at them with a piece of kitchen paper she said, 'Why do you ask?'

He dipped bread into the soup and said casually, 'Just heard you'd been seen out and about with him, that's all.'

'Out and about with him?'

'Having dinner at Dale View,' he said. 'That's where he's staying, isn't it? That holiday cottage on Lavender Lane? Someone said he'd been here a few times too.'

'Oh,' she said coldly. 'Someone did, did they?'

No prizes for guessing who. Those Lavender Ladies—was there anything they didn't know?

'I just wondered who he was,' Ross said briefly. 'If you'd rather not talk about him...'

What did he mean by that? Why shouldn't she talk about him?

'His late father was a friend of Dolly's,' she explained, even though she was now wondering why she should tell him anything after his last remark.

'Ah.' Ross spooned up more soup. 'So what brought him to Tuppenny Bridge?'

Clemmie stared at him. 'Does it matter?'

'No, of course it doesn't matter! Hell, I was just making conversation, that's all. If I'd realised it was such a big secret I'd never have mentioned it.'

Angrily, he jabbed his bread into the soup and Clemmie tilted her head, puzzled. If she hadn't known better she'd have sworn there was a hint of jealousy in that outburst. But why would Ross be jealous of Reuben?

'His mother died recently,' she said. 'He's come here to get away from well-meaning friends who were killing him with their sympathy.'

Ross chewed his bread quietly, and she thought she caught a brief look of shame in his eyes.

'That's—sad,' he said at last. 'I'm sorry to hear that.'

'He's a nice man,' she said. 'He's helping out at Whispering Willows, what with Summer having to cope with all those horses alone.'

He eyed her doubtfully. 'I heard you were helping out too,' he said. 'Is that true?'

Clemmie's cheeks burned with embarrassment. 'Summer needed me,' she said.

'But you always hated being near horses. You were afraid of them,' he reminded her, as if she'd somehow forgotten.

'People change.'

His eyebrows shot up in surprise. 'So you're not afraid of horses any longer?'

The burning increased. 'Well—a bit.'

His mouth curved into a smile and to her surprise she heard herself laughing.

'Okay, so I'm terrified of them. But what could I do? Summer needed help.'

'It was very kind of you to offer,' he assured her. 'It's awful news about Joseph. Summer must be devastated.'

'She is.' Clemmie's smile dropped. 'I don't know what she's going to do when he's gone. What's going to happen to Whispering Willows? It doesn't bear thinking about really.'

'At least Summer's got Reuben to help her,' he said, an edge to his voice. 'What a blessing he turned out to be.'

'Yes, exactly,' she said sharply. What exactly was he getting at? 'Like I said, he's a nice man.'

'And obviously keen to make a good impression on you.'

Clemmie almost laughed at the implication. Then she remembered what Summer had said and wondered if there was something in all this. Were other people seeing something she was missing? Reuben hadn't seemed romantically inclined towards her. In her opinion he'd been friendly, chatty, and helpful, but there'd been no sense that he was interested in her in any other way.

Summer had read it differently, and it seemed clear that Ross was of the same opinion. Though what did he know? He'd never even met Reuben! Well, he had briefly passed him in the shop doorway that day, but he didn't even realise that, obviously.

'I wouldn't say that. He's just got a good heart.'

'You like him then?'

His voice sounded a little strained and Clemmie watched him, feeling puzzled. Why was he so interested in Reuben?

'I do, yes. There's nothing to dislike.'

'Yeah. He seems to have made an impression on Bluebell anyway. She mentioned he was good looking.'

Clemmie rolled her eyes, knowing Bluebell's flirtatious ways. 'I suppose he is.'

'Hmm. There's more to people than looks though.'

Clemmie hardly knew what to say to that. The cheek of him! This was Ross Lavender, who'd escorted a multitude of attractive women over the last few years. He was a fine one to talk about there being more to people than looks.

'Perhaps,' she said, in a tone of voice she barely recognised, 'but it certainly helps, *doesn't it?*'

Honestly! He was such a hypocrite. Looks clearly meant everything to him. When was the last time he'd been seen with an ugly woman? Never, that's when, because he was vain and shallow, and any woman who didn't meet his standards of perfection would never make the grade.

'So,' she said, when he didn't reply, 'who are you seeing these days?'

She said it as sweetly as she could manage, determined he wouldn't get even a tiny hint that it bothered her.

He didn't answer her for a few moments, then he said, 'The only person I've seen for weeks is Meg. She's an interior designer. We're working together on Monk's Folly.'

Clemmie suddenly felt very cold. 'Right,' was all she could manage. Meg must be the woman Buttercup had mentioned seeing Ross heading into The Black Swan with the other week. 'I heard you'd been out for a meal with someone. Tall? Dark-haired?'

*The very opposite of me.*

Ross nodded. 'Yeah, that's right. We had dinner at her hotel once, but it wasn't up to much. We're lucky to have The Black Swan and The White Hart Inn in Tuppenny Bridge, although I keep meaning to try that new Indian restaurant that's opened on Station Road. Have you been there yet?'

Clemmie didn't even register the question. *Her hotel?* What had he been doing at her hotel? As if she couldn't guess!

Wait, though. That meant they'd been out to dinner a couple of times, so surely that would be the end of it then. Everyone knew Ross Lavender didn't date anyone more than twice.

'Clemmie?'

She blinked. 'Sorry, what?'

'The Indian restaurant,' he said patiently. 'Have you been there yet?'

She shook her head. 'No. Not really my thing. So Meg's your, er, interior designer? How's Monk's Folly coming along?'

His eyes lit up and he leaned forward slightly. 'Brilliantly!

You should see it. It's being completely refurbished, and it's going to look amazing. You'd love it, Clementine!'

They both seemed to realise what he'd called her at the same moment. He pulled back and his eyes dulled, even as Clemmie leaned away from him in shock.

'So, this portrait,' he said at last, finally ending an excruciating silence that had dragged on for what felt like forever. 'Have you decided? Head and shoulders? Full-length?'

'I don't mind,' she said. 'Whatever you think's best.'

'It would be useful to have some input,' he remarked. 'You can't expect me to make the decisions for you.'

'I thought that was a proper artist's job,' she snapped, still shaken from his use of her full name. 'Aren't you supposed to tell me how you want me to look, how you want me to pose?'

'Fine,' he said abruptly, 'I'll make the decision and let you know. In fact,' he added, pushing back his chair and getting to his feet, 'I think I've got all I need from you.'

She stared up at him, shocked. 'Already? But you've barely done anything.'

'You'd be surprised.' He gestured to the empty bowl on the table. 'Thanks for the soup. It was delicious. I'd better go before the snow gets too heavy.'

'Well, if you're sure...' He was slipping away from her again. She was glad about that, wasn't she?

She led him through to the front door and handed him his coat. 'Well, thanks for coming,' she said awkwardly. 'Sorry it took us so long to organise, but at least it's done now.'

'It is,' he said, sounding just as uncomfortable as she felt. 'I'll let you know when the portrait's ready and we can arrange a handover.'

'A handover?'

'We'll need some publicity shots. Aunt Eugenie insists. Firstly for the academy, and secondly to prove that the raffle prize was genuine. You know what she's like.'

There was a note of apology in his tone, and she smiled, relieved to see him smile back.

'Thanks again for that soup. I really enjoyed it.'

It was on the tip of her tongue to offer him a portion from the freezer to take home with him, but how would that look for goodness' sake?

'It was no bother. Like I said, I made it last week. Glad you enjoyed it. Well,' she grasped the door handle, 'thanks for coming. Bye, Ross.'

'Bye, Clemmie.'

She opened the door and they turned to face the outside. There was a shocked silence as they surveyed the garden, which was completely white. The snow was coming down fast, in thick, fat flakes. Ross's car tyres were almost fully buried in snow.

'Oh.'

They both knew what that meant. If it was this bad, the roads to Tuppenny Bridge would be a nightmare. His car might not even make it back from West Colby that night. He could be stranded at the roadside.

Clemmie shivered as Ross pulled his coat a little tighter and straightened his shoulders.

'Right,' he said. 'This is going to be fun.'

He stepped onto the snow which was almost level with the doorstep already. She could hear the crunch of his footsteps as he made his way towards the car.

'Ross!'

Oh hell, why had she said that?

He turned to face her, a query in his expression, but said nothing.

'You can't go home in that,' she heard herself saying. 'It's too dangerous.'

'I'll be fine,' he assured her. 'Don't worry.'

But she *did* worry, and she *would* worry, sitting in her

warm, cosy living room knowing he was out there, trying to make his way along twisting, narrow, isolated roads to Tuppenny Bridge. She couldn't do it.

'You'd better come back inside,' she said. 'It's not worth the risk. We've got a spare room.'

He eyed her steadily. 'Are you sure?'

'It will probably be cleared tomorrow,' she said, with more confidence than she felt. 'I don't think you should drive home in this weather, especially in the dark. Wait until morning. I'll make up the spare bed.'

He hesitated, but it was obvious he was relieved.

'Thanks, Clemmie.'

He crunched back to the cottage, and she stepped aside to let him in, taking his coat from him, half tempted to reach up and brush the snowflakes from his hair.

'What about Dolly?' he asked. 'She'll be stranded, wherever she is.'

Clemmie hung up his coat then leaned against it for a moment, breathing in the woody scent of his cologne without meaning to. He was still using the same one then. She remembered buying him a bottle for his birthday. It was expensive stuff.

'She's in London,' she replied quietly. 'She won't be back tonight anyway.'

She could feel his breath on her neck as he murmured, 'Clemmie, I really appreciate this.'

'Go and put the kettle on,' she burst out, rushing towards the stairs. 'I'll put the bedding on. There's hot chocolate in the cupboard. I think maybe it's hot chocolate weather, don't you?'

She didn't catch his answer as she reached the landing and threw open the door of the linen cupboard, collecting fresh bedding before heading to the small box room at the front of the cottage.

She was going to be under the same roof as Ross Lavender. All night!

Of course nothing was going to happen. God forbid. In fact, she fervently wished she had a lock on her bedroom door. Not that she was afraid of him. He may be a bit of a ladies' man, but he was a decent man too. She knew that. It was just...

Taking a deep breath she began to sort out the bedding. She just hoped the Lavender Ladies never got wind of this.

# TWENTY-THREE

The spare bed made up, Clemmie headed back downstairs, where she found Ross in the living room. He'd made them both hot chocolate as she'd asked, and looked strangely awkward sitting on the sofa, a doubtful expression in his eyes.

'I do appreciate this,' he told her, 'but are you absolutely sure?'

She wasn't. Far from it. Even so she couldn't live with herself if she'd made him go home and something happened to him on the way.

'Don't be silly,' she said, trying to sound as if it was no big deal. 'What's the point of risking yourself in this weather when there's a spare bed here? It's all made up for you, by the way. Whenever you want to go up. Oh, and I've put a toothbrush on the bedside cabinet for you.'

He raised an eyebrow. 'A toothbrush?'

'It's new,' she said hastily. 'We get those battery ones, and they're quite expensive, so we always stock up on them when they're on offer at Maister's.'

'Ah, I see.' He nodded appreciatively. 'Well, I'm very glad you do. Thank you.'

They sipped their hot chocolates, not speaking. Clemmie wondered what Ross was thinking. She reached for the remote, unable to bear the silence any longer.

There were a couple of programmes that she usually watched on a Sunday night, but she didn't think they'd be Ross's sort of thing. She couldn't imagine he'd enjoy *Call the Midwife*, for example, even though it was one of her favourite programmes. She'd have to watch it on catch-up later.

'Watch whatever you like,' he said after she'd fruitlessly flicked through the channels for a while. 'I'll do some sketching.'

Clemmie considered. It would be a good opportunity for her to continue working on *The Marquess Wants a Wife*. She'd been in her bedroom writing when he'd arrived and had hurriedly put her laptop away before rushing downstairs to answer the door. She'd managed to type up all the words she'd jotted down in her notebook in her free time at the shop and had added quite a bit more. She thought that, if Ross was going to be sketching, she might as well get on with her novel. He need never know what she was doing, after all.

She put Spotify on and hastily selected one of her music playlists, then she ran upstairs for her laptop.

When she returned, Ariana Grande was singing 'One Last Time'. Ross was head down, his brow furrowed as he concentrated on his drawing.

She opened her laptop but couldn't resist watching him for a few moments. She'd always loved to watch him at work. To her, what he achieved with just a few strokes of a pencil or paintbrush was miraculous.

She remembered how it used to turn her on, seeing the look in his eyes as he worked, watching the deft movements of his hand as he brought his subject to life. He used to laugh when he realised she was staring at him, knowing the effect it had on her. Although sometimes the laughter had turned to something else, and the painting or sketching would be abandoned in favour of an entirely different pursuit...

She couldn't risk him remembering that now! She forced herself to focus on the laptop and brought up her Word document. Time to get on with her own work.

She quickly read back over what she'd written recently and frowned. She'd honestly thought she'd made it better, but something still wasn't right. The truth was, Emmeline was annoying her.

*Why are you behaving this way? Why are you being so horrible to poor Rollo when it's obvious he loves you? What's stopping you from loving him back?*

She knew Emmeline's secret wound, of course, but even so. The trouble was, she seemed to have too many issues. It was all a bit confusing, and her motivation wasn't clear enough.

'What are you doing?'

She glanced up, startled to see Ross staring at her.

'Just—just playing a game,' she lied.

He nodded. 'Must be difficult. You're sighing a lot.'

She hadn't realised she'd sighed at all. Blushing she said, 'Oh well, it's just a bit tricky, that's all.'

'I didn't know you were into gaming,' he said. 'I wouldn't have thought it would be your thing at all. Who introduced you to that then?'

There was a distinct edge to his tone. What had rattled his cage?

'It's not really gaming,' she amended. 'More a quiz.'

'Ah.' The crease in his forehead smoothed out. 'Maybe I can help? I love a quiz.'

'No, it's all right. I like to do them myself. It's a challenge.'

'Fair enough.' He shrugged and went back to his sketching.

Clemmie almost sighed again but caught herself in time. She stared at the Word document and wrinkled her nose. She wasn't in the mood for this right now. She had no idea where to start, no clue what was wrong with it, and working in front of Ross Lavender was putting her off anyway.

She closed her laptop again and put it on the floor next to her chair.

'Given up?' Ross asked, without looking up from his sketching.

'For now.'

She rested the back of her head against the armchair and closed her eyes, thinking. The strains of Ariana Grande died away and Clean Bandit took over. She found she was smiling as she recognised the opening bars of 'Symphony', one of her favourite songs.

Quietly she sang along with it, knowing all the lyrics, her heart lifting with the chorus. About halfway through she opened her eyes and her face burned as she saw Ross watching her.

'You always did love this one,' he said, smiling.

She shrugged, trying not to show how embarrassed she felt that he'd witnessed her not-so-discreet singalong. 'It's a great song.'

'It is.' To her discomfort he packed away his sketchpad and pencils and leaned back on the sofa. 'It's a great playlist.'

She glanced at the screen, realising that it was her 'Hits of 2017' playlist: 2017, when she and Ross had been practically joined at the hip. Almost every song on it held a memory for them. She was about to reach for the remote but realised that, by doing so, she would only confirm that it still bothered her. That *he* still bothered her. She couldn't let him know any of it mattered.

Not knowing what else to do with herself she took out her mobile phone and browsed through Instagram, not really taking in anything she was supposedly looking at. Anything to avoid looking at, or talking to, Ross. Anything to make it seem as if the music was having no effect on her at all.

Her heart sank as 'Symphony' faded away and, in its place...
Oh no! Ed Sheeran singing 'Perfect'.

She couldn't help herself. She glanced over at Ross and saw that he was sitting very still. Suddenly he turned to her, and for a moment she thought she caught a glimpse of utter desolation in his eyes.

They'd danced to this at the Town Hall that night when she'd had too much punch. Ross had held her close and softly sung the words to her as they swayed, arms around each other, on the dance floor. She'd known, at that moment, that life couldn't be any more perfect, and that she would love this man forever.

If she'd only known what lay ahead of her...

'Clemmie.' His voice sounded odd.

She forced herself to look at him, praying her expression wouldn't betray how emotional she was feeling. 'What?'

'Do you remember? This song...'

'Hmm.' She wrinkled her nose. 'I never liked it.' She grabbed the remote. 'Let's find something decent to watch.'

She could see she'd wounded him and hated herself for it. She hadn't meant to be so dismissive of that night, but really, what else could she do? If she allowed herself to walk with him down memory lane it would be the end of her.

And what good would it do? Nothing much had changed. The main reason she'd ended it with Ross still stood. There was no happy ending on the horizon for the two of them.

She found an action film that she knew was one of his favourites as a way of apologising and forced herself to sit through two hours of it without complaining. Not that she'd paid much attention. Her thoughts constantly strayed to the man who was sitting on the sofa, quietly watching the film, his face revealing nothing about whether he was enjoying it.

It was hard to believe they'd once sat together almost every evening on that very sofa, arms around each other, totally at ease in one another's company.

This, she thought grimly, was painful.

As the credits mercifully rolled, Ross got to his feet. 'I'll go to bed now if it's okay with you.'

She blinked, surprised. 'So early?'

'It's been a long day,' he said, and to be fair he did look weary. He sounded it, too. 'Besides, I don't think my being here has been a pleasant experience for you, has it?'

'I—I don't know what you mean.'

'Oh, I think you do. You're uptight, on edge. You know, you didn't have to ask me to stay. I wouldn't have thought any the worse of you.'

Meaning he *couldn't* think any worse of her? She frowned.

'I could hardly let you drive home in this weather. If something had happened to you…'

'Yes?' He waited. 'If something had happened to me, what?'

She shrugged. 'Your aunt would have blamed me. My name would have been mud all round the town. I wasn't risking that.'

'Right. Well, hopefully, the snow will have melted a bit overnight and I'll be able to go home.'

'Hopefully,' she agreed.

'Wow.'

He shook his head and picked up the empty hot chocolate mugs from the coffee table.

Clemmie prickled with indignation. 'What's that supposed to mean?'

'What should it mean? I was just wondering if I ever knew you at all. I don't remember you being so heartless. Although maybe I'm just kidding myself. Now I think about it you always did have a brutal side to you, didn't you?'

'Meaning what?' she asked indignantly.

'Well, people's feelings never really mattered, did they? It was always about what you wanted. The rest of us just fell into line.'

'The rest of us? Meaning who?'

He sighed. 'Do you really want to go into this now?'

'You brought it up.'

'Okay then.' He put the cups down and sat back on the sofa. 'Meaning me. The way you treated me!'

'The way I treated you? I was good to you! We were good together!' She couldn't believe he was being so cruel. She'd always considered his feelings, always thought about what he wanted, always kept him at the forefront of her mind.

'I thought so, too,' he said. 'But if we really were good together, how come I arrived back from the Netherlands to find I was surplus to requirements? No prior warning. No explanation. Just thank you and *tot ziens*.'

'I don't even know what that means,' she said, exasperated.

'It's Dutch for goodbye,' he said, his eyes narrowed. 'I picked up a bit of the language while I was staying with my mother and her boyfriend. Most of it was obscene, but I remember a few other bits that are more useful.'

'Good for you,' she muttered, not wanting to remember his return from the Netherlands. Another painful memory she could do without. Why had she ever let him stay here? 'Leave those cups. I'll wash them up after you go to bed.'

She gave him a pointed look, hoping he'd remember he'd been about to go to bed.

'I thought we were doing this now,' he said flatly. 'I did ask you if you wanted to, remember?'

'I didn't mean—' She shook her head. 'Oh, you're tying me up in knots! Just go to bed, Ross.'

'But I think maybe we should get this out in the open once and for all,' he said. 'You owe me that much at least. You never explained. You never told me what I'd done wrong.'

'What does it matter now?' She held his gaze, desperately

hoping he couldn't read the pain she was feeling. 'It's in the past. It's over. We've both moved on. I don't see what difference it makes any more. It's not going to change anything. I'm not going to change my mind. Now, leave those cups and go upstairs. Please.'

It felt like he sat there forever, staring at her in silence. She wondered what he was thinking and braced herself for his next words.

To her relief he got to his feet. 'You're right. What difference does it make now? Like you said, we're finished. No going back. Goodnight, Clemmie.'

He left the room, quietly closing the door behind him.

Just like he'd done all those years ago. No fuss. No pleading with her to change her mind. Just a soft, gentle exit.

Well, it was what she'd hoped for, wasn't it? So why was every fibre of her being longing to follow him upstairs and tell him how sorry she was, how she wished things could be different.

But she'd been telling the truth. It wouldn't change anything. There was no point in even thinking about it, and following Ross wasn't an option.

Instead, she picked up the cups and headed into the kitchen.

## TWENTY-FOUR

Clemmie wasn't sure how much sleep she'd got last night, but when she finally reached for her phone to check the time she was still so exhausted she couldn't believe it was almost eight o'clock. Eight o'clock!

She yawned and rubbed her eyes, then panic hit her. It was Monday morning, and she should be at The Corner Cottage Bookshop by nine. Worse, Ross Lavender had spent the night at Wintergreen, and she was going to have to wake him up and turf him out. No time for a long, lingering breakfast.

Her heart thudded as she realised he might already be awake, wondering if he ought to wake her up so she wasn't late for work. He might burst into her bedroom at any moment...

It was enough to make her dive out of bed and rush to her en suite. Locking the door behind her she heaved a sigh of relief. She was safe. Now she just needed to make herself presentable.

Showered, dressed, and ready for a day at the shop, she quickly made her bed, turned off her lamp and drew back the curtains.

The dazzling light made her step away from the window for

a moment, then she peered outside, her mouth dropping open in horror.

The world was white. Trees stooped, their branches bent under the heavy burden of snow. The sky had all but merged into the landscape, all traces of blue washed out and faded to the palest grey. The snow was still falling, showing no signs of slowing down. And Ross's car...

She swallowed, seeing his tyres were completely submerged by the snow, and the roof of the car was hidden under a blanket of white, leaving only the body of the vehicle visible. He would never be able to get home today.

Clemmie took a deep breath. It was okay. It was all going to be fine. She'd got through yesterday, hadn't she? And last night had been okay. All right, she'd not slept very well, knowing he was just down the landing in that little box room, and she'd had a bit of a panic this morning in case he walked in on her, but he hadn't, had he?

She'd got through it, and there was no reason why she couldn't get through it again. Just another day. The snow would stop soon, and the snow ploughs would be out. The roads would be cleared and all would be well.

She just had to deal with today.

Slowly, she walked downstairs, not entirely sure whether Ross was even awake yet. He was in the kitchen, sitting at the table, eating a full English breakfast as if he'd made himself quite at home.

He got to his feet as she walked in, smiling. Clearly, he'd decided to draw a line under last night's unpleasantness. She was grateful for that.

'Morning. I hope you don't mind. I got hungry,' he admitted sheepishly. 'I made you some too, and I've kept it warm. I hope you're as hungry as I am.'

She was about to reply that she couldn't eat a thing, but realised he was offering her an olive branch, and that she should take it. Besides, it wasn't true that she wasn't hungry. Maybe she should have done something more substantial for tea yesterday after all. Soup hadn't been enough to keep her full all night, and she could well imagine that Ross felt the same way. No wonder he'd cooked a big breakfast. She supposed she could forgive him just this once.

'Thanks,' she said gratefully. 'I am a bit peckish.'

Her stomach chose that moment to growl ferociously at her, as if to point out that peckish was hardly the word it would have chosen. Ross's mouth twitched with amusement.

'Great. I've made coffee too. Hope that's okay. I'll make you one. Sit down.'

He'd used Dolly's precious coffee machine, and one of her pods. Clemmie wondered what Dolly would think of that but said nothing as he presented her with a flat white. She supposed being snowed in was an emergency. Dolly would surely understand.

Ross carefully carried over a plate and put it down on the table in front of her. Clemmie's nose twitched at the smell of crispy bacon and succulent sausages.

'There weren't any mushrooms,' he said mournfully, as he sat back in his own chair and picked up his knife and fork. 'It doesn't really feel like a full breakfast without mushrooms, but I did my best.'

'Maybe,' Clemmie said jokingly, 'we ought to ration the food. Looks like we might be stuck here for some time.'

His eyes widened. 'Are you short on food? I didn't really check the cupboards, other than to grab a couple of tins.' He sounded genuinely worried.

Clemmie couldn't help but smile. 'Relax. We've got a fridge-freezer full of food.' She carefully cut up a rasher of bacon. 'Unless the electricity goes off of course. If the power dies we're screwed.'

Ross gave her a knowing look. 'You're winding me up now, aren't you?'

'Well...' Clemmie wasn't quite sure how to break it to him. 'We were marooned here for almost a week once. Do you remember the other year, when we had that bad weather in the January, and Dolly and I were stuck here for days? Well, the power went off then. Luckily, we had the fire and lots of candles.'

'But how did you manage for food?' he asked.

He always did have a big appetite, Clemmie remembered. For all the pleasures in life.

'We opened some tins. I seem to recall we ate a lot of cold beans and rice pudding. Oh, and cream crackers.'

'Are you joking?'

'No, I'm really not.' Clemmie gave him a sweet smile. 'It was fun actually.'

'Fun?'

'Sort of—' She broke off as she realised she'd been about to say *romantic*, and the last thing she wanted was to give him any reason to mock her for her romantic nature again. Remembering what he'd said to Noah about her she scowled and popped some bacon into her mouth, saying nothing else.

If he'd guessed what she'd been about to say he didn't mention it.

'Thanks for letting me stay last night,' he said, prodding his fork into a fried egg so the yolk broke and flowed over his plate. 'I dread to think what would have happened if I'd tried to get home.'

So he really was going to pretend their uncomfortable conversation hadn't happened? She couldn't deny she was relieved, so answered him in a light-hearted way.

'You'd probably be a popsicle by now,' she said.

'I probably would,' he agreed. 'I guess neither of us is going to be at work today. I rang Aunt Eugenie last night to tell her I'm okay and not to worry. She's going to let Meg know I won't be at Monk's Folly. Although,' he added, 'I'm not sure Meg would even try to get to Tuppenny Bridge. She's not used to rural roads and complains about them all the time. I doubt she'll risk driving in this.'

He gazed out of the window at the falling snow, and Clemmie tried to overcome her irritation that he was talking about Meg. What did he have to bring her up for? It reminded her that she'd had a phone call herself though.

'Reuben rang me last night, just to check I was okay. He was worried about me, being out here on my own. See? I told you he had a kind heart. Anyway, I told him I was fine.'

Ross sipped his coffee. 'How nice of him. Did you tell him I was here?'

'Of course,' she said. 'Why wouldn't I?'

'And how did he take that?'

'I don't know what you mean.' Clemmie frowned. 'How should he take it?'

'Another man spending the night with you? I know how I'd have taken it.'

He practically speared a piece of sausage and shovelled it into his mouth, chewing rapidly while watching her closely.

'You didn't spend the night *with* me,' she reminded him. 'You slept in the box room.'

'You know what I mean. Besides, he doesn't know that for sure, does he?'

Clemmie couldn't fathom what he was getting at. Why should Reuben care one way or the other? Or was Ross worried he'd tell Dolly if he thought there was something going on? He had a point, she supposed. Dolly would be a nightmare if she thought that.

'Yes, he does actually, because I told him so and he trusts me.'

'More fool him.'

Clemmie glared at him. So much for their truce. 'What's that supposed to mean?'

Ross dropped his fork and ran a hand through his hair. 'Nothing. Forget it.'

'If you've got something to say—'

'I haven't got anything to say. Can we just try to get along? We might be stuck here for some time and it's going to drag if we're arguing all the time.'

She knew he was right, but his words still rankled. She gulped down some coffee and gazed out of the window, hoping against hope that the snow would stop falling. She really didn't think she could cope with being stuck with Ross for another night.

Food and electricity were the least of her worries.

# TWENTY-FIVE

Ross couldn't help but feel awkward around Clemmie, aware that she hadn't bargained on having him stay at Wintergreen like this. He hadn't bargained on it either and couldn't believe his timing. If he'd just waited another hour or so to visit her, he would never have set off in the first place. It was as if fate was having a laugh at their expense.

Dolly rang Clemmie at around ten thirty, clearly in a bit of a panic that she wouldn't be able to make it to West Colby. Ross was sprawled on the sofa, sketchpad on his knee, making rough drawings of how he wanted his living quarters at Monk's Folly to look when they were finished. He could hear Dolly's voice getting higher and higher from where he was, even though Clemmie was in the armchair furthest away from him.

'I'm fine, honestly. Yes, I know, but it's okay. Well, it was just one of those unfortunate things. Bad timing.' Her voice dropped to a whisper and Ross pretended to concentrate hard on his sketching. 'No, he hasn't. I promise, he's been no trouble.'

Ross wasn't sure whether to smile or scowl at her remark. Just what was Dolly accusing him of?

'You are? Oh, well, that's something. I thought the trains

might be delayed. Where are you going to stay? Oh, that's good of him. No, don't worry about the shop. Maybe you can open it tomorrow. It can't last much longer, can it?'

With those words, she stared doubtfully out of the window, where the snow was still falling. Although, Ross noted, it had eased off a little. Maybe the end was in sight.

'Okay, well I'll see you soon. Just stop worrying, right?' She gave a short laugh. 'Sure you will. Bye, Dolly.'

She ended the call and gave Ross a sheepish look. 'That was Dolly.'

'You don't say.' He sat up a little straighter. 'Where is she? Still in London?'

'No, she's halfway home. Well, I mean, she's halfway to Tuppenny Bridge. The trains are running okay, but obviously she's realised she can't get through to Wintergreen. Still, she's safe, which is the main thing.'

'So where's she going to stay until she can get here?'

'Oh, Reuben rang her and he's going to put her up in the spare room at Dale View,' she said lightly. 'She's not bothering to open the bookshop today though. She's still recovering from a heavy night out with some of her writer pals last night. Those authors sure know how to party.'

'Thank goodness for Reuben then,' he said, aware that he sounded grumpy, but unable to help himself.

'Exactly,' she said primly. 'I don't know what we'd have done without him lately, what with helping at Whispering Willows, setting up a new website for Dolly, and now this.'

'The man's a saint,' Ross remarked. 'Maybe I should paint *his* portrait instead and we can hang it in the town hall.'

Clemmie put her hands on her hips. 'Is something bothering you? You don't seem to have a kind word to say about Reuben, and what's he ever done to you?'

'Me?' He feigned surprise. 'I have no idea what you're talking about. I've got nothing against him. Just making conversation, that's all. How exactly did Dolly know I was here, by the way?' As she looked at him blankly he added, 'I gather she needed quite a bit of reassurance that I wasn't about to ravage you, judging by your side of the conversation.'

There it was again—that tinge of pink to her cheeks that he loved to see.

'She didn't think you were about to... She just worries about me, that's all.'

'And she knew I was here, how exactly?'

The pink deepened. 'Reuben might have mentioned it.'

'I'll bet he did. Well, that wasn't very kind of him, was it? Fancy worrying her like that.'

'He was probably trying to reassure her that I wasn't alone.'

'You're right of course,' he agreed. 'As if Reuben would ever do anything to cause trouble.'

'Now you're being sarcastic.'

He put a hand to his heart. 'I'm wounded that you'd think such a thing of me.'

'Seriously,' she said, 'what have you got against him? It's not like you even know him. You've never actually met him, have you?'

'Not in person, but I've heard so much about him I feel as if I've taken him out to dinner. Everyone's talking about Reuben Walker,' he said, with shameful exaggeration. 'He's made quite the impression. Like I said, I have nothing against him. How can one dislike someone so perfect?'

'Actually, you have seen him,' she informed him with some pleasure. 'He was going out of the shop when you were coming in that day to harangue me about having the painting done. He waved you through like the gentleman he is.'

He scowled. 'He did? I don't remember him.'

'Surely you must do? Fair hair, blue eyes, exceptionally good looking. Makes a huge impression on everyone—except you, clearly. Anyway, I'm going to make a coffee. Do you want one?'

'Please. Milk and—'

'Two sugars. I know, I know.'

She headed out of the room and Ross sank back against the cushions and closed his eyes. He couldn't work out his own feelings, so he was hard-pressed to figure out hers. Right now, his emotions were all over the place. It was so good being here with Clemmie, talking, eating together... It had been years since they'd spent any time in each other's company, and he'd forgotten how much he missed her. Almost.

But when she was snappy, or mentioned Reuben, his heart would harden against her. He'd remember the way she'd broken up with him, completely out of the blue, and with devastating coldness. Then he'd feel angry with her and find civility a struggle, let alone friendliness.

He thought about last night's argument. Part of him wished he'd never brought up the subject of their break-up, but there was another part that desperately wanted to find out exactly what it was that he'd got so badly wrong. Because it must have been something, and he really couldn't work it out.

Almost immediately, he dismissed the idea. He couldn't go over it all again. This was ridiculous. They'd broken up what, six years ago? She obviously had no desire to talk about that time, and if he insisted she would think he was still brooding on what had happened. After all this time it would make him look pathetic.

Perhaps he *was* pathetic.

But she'd also think it was down to male pride, and there was so much more to it than that. His confidence had been well and truly shaken, and he felt as if she'd stamped all over his heart. He'd honestly thought they were meant for each other. How had he got it so wrong? And what if he got it wrong again?

He hadn't often dwelt on why he'd been unable to settle

down with any other woman since Clemmie, preferring to keep things casual and concentrate on work. But deep down there'd been that nagging worry. What if he gave his heart away and some woman broke it all over again?

He didn't seem to be a good judge of how a relationship was going, or what his partner's feelings really were. He'd spectacularly messed up with Clemmie, and still hadn't fathomed out how he'd managed it. There was no way he'd want to risk that again.

Besides, if he was being honest with himself, he'd never been tempted. He'd deliberately chosen women who were nothing like her, but it hadn't helped. He felt no closer to settling down now than he had when he'd found himself unceremoniously dumped all those years ago.

God, it was a mess. Noah had told him loads of times that he should speak to Clemmie. Try to put this thing to bed once and for all. Now was the best chance he'd probably ever get. If he could just make himself ask her...

She was back all too soon, carrying two mugs of coffee.

He couldn't do it. He knew that now. The time had gone. Their relationship was in the past. Well, the romance was. Maybe, if he could keep a lid on his feelings, they could emerge from this enforced house share as friends. It would be good to have her back in his life, even if there was some emotional distance this time around.

'I was thinking,' he said as they sat in amiable silence, sipping from their matching mugs, 'about this snow.'

'What about it?'

'Well, we're doing okay here. We've got food, we've got fuel for the fire, we've got company. Is there anyone nearby who might need any of those things? I'm thinking maybe someone who lives alone? Or someone elderly, or infirm or—'

'There's Mr Francis,' Clemmie said thoughtfully. 'He's all alone and he's getting on a bit. There's only his house, Mulberry

Cottage, between us and the village, and I should think the people in the village are okay, but he's as isolated as us really. Gosh, I never thought...'

'Well, we've thought of it now,' he said. 'Maybe we should check on him. What do you think?'

'We should,' she agreed. 'And take him something to eat, just in case?'

'Good idea.'

She jumped up and looked out of the kitchen window. 'It's not going to be easy getting to him,' she said. 'I've got wellies, but you...'

She stared pointedly at his jeans and brown combat boots.

'I'll be fine,' he said with more confidence than he felt. 'The main thing is we check this Mr Francis is okay, right?'

'Right.' She sounded doubtful, and he wondered if the walk might be too much for her in this weather.

'You don't have to come with me, you know,' he told her. 'I can go alone.'

'He doesn't know you,' Clemmie pointed out. 'He might be worried if a total stranger knocks on his door, even one bearing gifts.'

'Fair enough.' Ross couldn't deny it was a possibility. 'Right, I'll get my coat. What can we take him to eat?'

While he was in the hallway collecting their coats and Clemmie's wellies, he heard her opening and closing doors in the kitchen, looking for something suitable to take to Mr Francis.

'I've packed him a tin of chicken soup and some of those part-baked rolls,' Clemmie announced. 'Plus a frozen roast beef dinner and a packet of biscuits. Oh, and some milk, just in case he's out of it.'

'That should do him for today,' Ross agreed, 'and he might already have plenty of food in anyway. We're probably worrying about nothing, but better to be safe than sorry, isn't it?'

'Absolutely.'

Clemmie pulled on her wellies, and he helped her on with her coat, thinking how adorable she looked all wrapped up against the winter weather.

She squared her shoulders as she glanced out of the window where the snow was falling again. Her nose wrinkled in a cute way, and she said, 'Okay, let's get out there.'

It wasn't, Ross reflected, as he found himself trudging up the lane, shin deep in snow, how he'd expected to spend today at all. He was longing for a hot bath or shower. It was exhausting work, and he could see Clemmie was already struggling. He offered her his arm, certain that she'd refuse it. Surprisingly, she took it with a breathless, 'Thank you.'

As they made their weary way towards Mr Francis's home, Ross wondered how he could be so cold and tired, and yet feel this sudden surge of happiness. His jeans were soaking wet, his feet were frozen, and his face was numb with cold. Yet right now, there was nowhere else he'd rather be than wading through the snow, arm in arm with Clemmie.

# TWENTY-SIX

Mr Francis showed no hesitation in opening the front door. He threw it open within moments of them knocking and beamed at Ross, even though he'd never seen him before.

'Have you come with the shopping? I had a phone call to say you wouldn't be able to make it, but I knew you'd get through if you put your mind to it.'

He frowned and looked over Ross's shoulder where a weary Clemmie was standing.

'Oh. Two of you?'

'It's me, Mr Francis,' she explained, stepping forward. 'Clemmie Grant. You know, from Wintergreen?'

He stared at her then nodded. 'Oh yes, so it is. What are you doing here, flower? It's not very good weather, is it? You shouldn't be out in this.' Then he turned to Ross and asked, 'So where's the shopping?'

Ross reluctantly explained that he wasn't the supermarket delivery man. 'I'm a friend of Clemmie's, Mr Francis. We thought we'd come to check on you; make sure you had everything you needed.'

Mr Francis looked shocked. 'You've come out in all this bad

weather to check on *me*? Well, that's right kind of you. Come in, come in. You must be bloody freezing.'

Gratefully, Ross and Clemmie followed him into his house, noting with relief that it was nice and toasty. Evidently, Mr Francis was safe as far as warmth went. Ross prised off his boots and helped Clemmie out of her wellies, and they hung their coats up in the hallway before heading into a snug living room. Thankfully, it had a large radiator that was blasting out heat, and an electric fire that gave the illusion of real flames and made them feel instantly warmer.

'Now then,' he said, motioning to them to sit down, 'how would you like a nice cup of tea to warm you up?'

'I'll make it,' Clemmie offered, but he waved a hand at her.

'You certainly will not. You look dead on your feet.' He fixed Ross with a stern look. 'What do you think you're playing at, dragging a young lady out in this weather, you rotten bugger?'

'I did tell her I'd come alone,' Ross said defensively, 'but she thought you'd be worried since you don't know me.'

'Did she indeed? Stubborn as a mule. Just like my Freda.' He tutted and headed into the kitchen and Ross and Clemmie exchanged amused glances.

'Well, that told us,' he said.

'At least he's not dying of hypothermia,' she said. 'That's something.'

'Although clearly he's waiting for his weekly shopping to arrive, and somehow I doubt it will do. That's not good. Probably a good job we brought him some food. Speaking of which.'

Ross took the carrier bag into the kitchen where Mr Francis was spooning tea into a teapot.

'I was just about to ask you if you take milk and sugar.'

'One sugar for Clemmie, two for me, and we both take milk,' Ross said. He put the carrier bag on the worktop. 'We brought you these in case you were running low on food. It's not much but it will do you for a day. And we brought milk in case you were running low.'

Mr Francis peered into the bag. 'Well, isn't that grand? Funnily enough, I am running a bit low. I had a supermarket delivery booked for today, but it looks like that won't be happening now. My daughter rang me this morning and I said to her, "Don't fret, Pam. I've got loads of stuff in." But of course that was just to stop her worrying. I was getting a bit worried myself, to be honest, because we don't know how long we're going to be stuck here and I really can't make it to the village shops. Very thoughtful of you, lad. Very thoughtful indeed.'

He patted Ross on the arm and Ross was touched to see tears in the old man's eyes.

'I'd best put this in the freezer,' Mr Francis said, taking the frozen beef dinner from the bag. 'That'll be just the job for my tea tonight. Ooh, and I see we have biscuits. Let's open them up while we have this cup of tea, eh?'

Ross helped him carry the cups of tea through into the living room where Clemmie was slumped on the sofa still looking exhausted.

'I don't know, lass,' Mr Francis said, shaking his head. 'You'd have been better off staying put at home, never mind following your boyfriend all the way here. Can't bear to be apart from him, eh? I know, I know. I remember them days.'

He chuckled and offered her a biscuit.

Clemmie's face was pink, and Ross doubted it was from the heat. He felt embarrassed himself, knowing how she'd be reacting to that little misunderstanding.

'He's not my boyfriend,' Clemmie said firmly, refusing a biscuit but taking her mug of tea from Ross.

'Is he not?' Mr Francis stared at them both, his eyes crinkled in the corners with amusement. 'If you say so. Stubborn as a mule. You put me in mind of my wife, Freda. She was just the same.'

'So you said,' Clemmie murmured.

'She kept telling everyone me and her were just friends.' Mr Francis sank into the armchair and helped himself to a custard cream. 'Nigh on four years we played that game, you know. Her mam and dad didn't think I were good enough for her you see. Well, they owned their own shop, and I were just a farm labourer. Snooty buggers filled her head with rubbish.'

He sighed and bit into his biscuit, crunching contentedly for a moment as he remembered.

'But she came round in the end?' Ross asked, realising, when the old man didn't continue his story, that he wanted to know what had happened.

'Oh, aye. Eventually.' Mr Francis chuckled. 'We'd go out for a bit, then she'd chuck me and go out with someone else. Allus came back though.'

'And you let her?' Clemmie asked incredulously.

'Oh, I knew we were made for each other,' he said comfortably. 'It broke my heart at times, but I knew I had to let her figure it out for herself. She had some boyfriends that worried me, cos they had more money than I did and better prospects, but they never held her interest for long.'

'So what made her come back to you for good?' Ross asked curiously.

'Her cat died,' he said flatly.

Clemmie and Ross exchanged puzzled looks, and Mr Francis chuckled to himself.

'That's made you think, hasn't it? See, that cat meant everything to her, and when it died she were heartbroken. Her mam and dad offered to buy her a new cat, just like that, but it were too soon. Any fool could have seen that. I held her and let her cry, and I understood, see? Cos I knew what it were like to lose someone you love, having watched her walk away from me that many times, and I explained that to her. And that's when she looked up at me, all teary and that, and she said, "Arthur, I'll never walk away from you again". And bugger me, she didn't. Just shows you, doesn't it?'

Ross risked a glance at Clemmie who was staring at Mr Francis, her mouth open in shock. It was hardly a conventional love story, and not one he supposed she'd ever come across in her Jane Austen books, but it kind of made sense. In a way.

He sipped his tea, half wondering if things would have been different all those years ago if Clemmie had owned a cat.

'So,' Mr Francis said, having finished his not-so-romantic tale, 'when do you reckon this road'll be cleared, eh? Any chance of me getting that delivery tomorrow?'

'I wouldn't have thought it would be that soon,' Ross admitted. 'Are you okay for food for tomorrow or—'

He broke off as a telephone began to ring. It was a proper old-fashioned landline telephone with a dial and a cord and was sitting on a small table at the side of Mr Francis's armchair. Ross hadn't seen one of those for years. Even the ones in the museum were push button and cordless.

Mr Francis put down his mug of tea and picked up the receiver.

'Hello, Pam. What can I do for you?' He winked at Ross and Clemmie and mouthed, 'It's my daughter, Pam,' to them, as if they hadn't guessed.

Ross and Clemmie sat quietly, sipping tea while they listened to his half of the conversation. Evidently Pam was worried sick about her dad.

'Now, I've told you, stop worrying. And for your information I'm not on my own. I've got company. You know that little Clemmie Grant who lives at Wintergreen? Aye, that's right, Dolly Bennett's niece. She's here with her boyfriend.'

Ross clutched the handle of his mug tighter, not daring to look at Clemmie.

'They've brought me some food. Not,' he added hastily, 'that I needed it. Plenty in so don't you worry about me.' He tutted suddenly. ''Course I've got my radiators on! What do you think I am? Daft in the head? Oh, bugger the gas bills. What are they going to do to me, eh? I'm eighty-seven for God's sake.'

Ross smothered a grin. He had to admit, he rather liked Mr Francis.

'Right, I'm going to get off, flower, because like I say I've got company and we're just having a nice chat and some custard creams. Don't you fret, I'll give you a ring as soon as the road's clear, and in the meantime Clemmie and Ross are cheering me up and they're visiting again tomorrow.'

He nodded at the two of them as if to confirm it and Ross found himself nodding back. He guessed he'd be making another journey to bring supplies tomorrow. Fair enough.

'Well, that's that sorted,' Mr Francis said, replacing the receiver and sitting back in his chair. 'Now where were we? Oh yes, so tell me how you two first got together.'


Clemmie was exhausted by the time they got back to Wintergreen. Ross helped her off with her wellies, noting with some envy that her socks were completely dry.

His, on the other hand, were sodden, as were his jeans.

'Look at the state of you,' she gasped, having not realised how wet and cold he must have been all this time. 'You need warming up.'

He gazed down at her, and she blushed furiously, having realised what that sounded like. Thankfully, he didn't take advantage of her mistake.

'Do you mind if I go up and have a shower?' he asked instead.

She gulped. 'Not at all. You know where everything is. There'll be a clean towel in the linen cupboard on the landing.'

'Er...' He paused, looking embarrassed. 'Would it be okay if I washed my clothes?'

Washed his clothes? So what was he going to wear?

'Er—'

She couldn't refuse him, could she?

But he'd have to wrap a towel around himself, and he'd be sitting in the living room with her, half naked while he waited for his clothes to wash and tumble dry... Wow, the radiator in the hallway must be really blasting out some heat. It was definitely hotter in here now. As she struggled to dismiss the image of him in a towel inspiration struck.

'Yes, and afterwards you could wear Dolly's old dressing gown.'

He gave her a horrified look. 'Seriously?'

'It's floor-length on her and quite big, and it's navy-blue, not girly in any way.' She managed a grin. 'I'm sure it will suit you. I'll put it on your bed for you while you're in the bathroom.'

'Thanks. If you're sure.' He sounded doubtful but she thought it would be better than him wearing a towel all day. Better for her, anyway. 'Right, shower. I won't be long.'

'Take as long as you like,' she mumbled, trying not to imagine him in the shower. Not that she had to imagine it. It may have been some time ago, but she still had her memories. Sometimes, she wished she'd knocked her head and suffered from amnesia. Though even if she had, she couldn't imagine she'd ever forget the sight of Ross standing in the shower in her en suite, lathered up and looking irresistible...

She waited ten minutes until she heard him in the bathroom, then she hurried upstairs and went into Dolly's room. Her aunt's old dressing gown was still hanging on the back of the bedroom door, and Clemmie quickly snatched it from its hook and placed it on Ross's bed. She noted the pile of wet clothing on the carpet and nearly picked it up to put in the washing machine, but then she realised his underwear would be among it somewhere and didn't feel she could. He'd have to put his washing on for himself.

Frankly, she'd had a stressful enough day, what with having to fend off Mr Francis's insistence on knowing their backstory and having to listen to Ross mumbling a half-baked explanation of their relationship which, he'd insisted, had only ever been friendship.

Part of her had longed to point out that it had been far from that, but then she'd have had to explain to Mr Francis why their romance had ended, because, rather like his wife, Freda, Mr Francis was nothing if not stubborn and wouldn't have taken no for an answer. Ross, she supposed gloomily, had done her a favour really. It was her own fault if his version had hurt so much.

## TWENTY-SEVEN

The dressing gown was ankle-length on Dolly, but barely reached below Ross's knees. At least, though, he was fully covered and could tie the belt around his waist, thanks to Dolly's portly proportions.

As he bundled his clothes into his arms and headed downstairs, Ross just hoped Clemmie wouldn't laugh.

'You look, er...' She shook her head but didn't finish the sentence, instead turning away as if the sight of his bare legs repulsed her.

He sighed inwardly, trying not to feel offended. 'Is it okay if I put these in the washing machine?'

She nodded. 'If you can't figure out the programme, just give me a shout. The washing liquid and the fabric conditioner are in the cupboard under the sink, though I should warn you, the cycle takes hours. Oh, and there's a cheese and tomato sandwich in the fridge for your dinner. I've had mine.'

Ross managed to work out the washing machine and set the cycle to wash and dry. He collected his sandwich and wandered back into the living room where he found Clemmie dozing off on the sofa, no doubt worn out after their trek to Mulberry

Cottage. He left her to sleep and collected his sketchpad and pencils, then resumed sketching, taking a bite of his sandwich every now and then.

Clemmie didn't sleep long, if at all. Within twenty minutes she was on her feet and gazing out of the window. She didn't speak so he didn't either, though he was aware of her every movement and wondered what she was thinking. He glanced up at her and his expression softened as he saw the faraway look in her eyes. There was something so beautiful about her in that moment that he reached for his phone and, without her even realising, he took a photo of her. As far as he was concerned, he'd found it—the perfect pose for her portrait.

At that moment she shifted a little, folded her arms and gave a big sigh, which he tried not to dwell on. Was she sighing because she was bored? Or because she was missing Reuben? That didn't bear thinking about, and he concentrated harder on his sketches. His living quarters were coming to life on the pages, and he could hardly wait to get started on making the vision a reality.

Would a king-size bed fit in his bedroom, he wondered? Did people in Regency times have four poster beds? What sort of bedding would look good in the room?

It was probably a mistake to think about his bedroom while Clemmie was sitting just opposite him. He couldn't help wondering what it would be like to share the room with her. He was sure she'd love a Regency bedroom.

Although, he thought, she would probably prefer it if she didn't have to share it with him. Maybe she'd have another person in mind for that.

His mood darkened at the thought, and when she sighed again he couldn't help but snap. 'What's up with you?'

Oh God, he really hadn't meant to sound so impatient. 'Sorry. I shouldn't have... Are you okay? You keep sighing.'

She eyed him suspiciously, as if uncertain how genuine his apology was and whether or not she should forgive him.

'I'm just bored,' she admitted in the end.

He raised an eyebrow. 'Bored? Well, why don't you read?'

Lord knows, she owned enough books as he recalled, and she'd probably added to the stock by now. She'd always had her nose buried in a book when he visited at Wintergreen. Until she'd realised he was there, when she'd carefully put a bookmark in the book she was reading—because Clemmie would never do anything so disrespectful as to turn down the corner of a page—and put the volume aside to be with him. He'd felt honoured. He'd always known that fictional heroes were his main rivals for her affections.

'I don't want to read,' she said sullenly.

He almost laughed. 'You don't want to read?'

'Don't sound so shocked. There's more to me than reading, you know.'

He bit his lip. 'Well,' he said eventually, 'put a film on or something. There's bound to be something worth watching.'

'Hmm.' She picked up the remote and aimed it at the television.

Ross went back to his drawing, wondering whether he should invest in an antique bed or get a reproduction made. Or should he just stick with a modern divan? Were old beds comfortable enough? Did he really want a bed that goodness knows how many people had slept in previously?

As he pondered the question, he became aware of a cacophony of different voices, accents, and snatches of music, as Clemmie flicked through various channels looking for something to watch.

'Can't you find anything?' he asked, somewhat irritably.

'What do you think?' She glared at the television as if it was being deliberately difficult.

'Why don't you watch one of your old romance DVDs?' he suggested. 'That's if you've still got them.'

His blood chilled as she slowly turned her head to stare at him as if he'd said something unspeakable. Oh hell, what had he done wrong now?

'Oh, you'd love that, wouldn't you?'

'I'm sorry?'

'You think there's nothing more to me than soppy films and books, don't you?'

'I never said that.' Bloody hell, he'd only tried to stop her from being bored. He shouldn't have bothered.

'You never said that? Are you sure?'

Clemmie tilted her head, and he felt a sudden prickling of dread as something stirred in his memory.

'Let me see. What was it now? Oh yes. A romance novel on legs. Just a head full of dreams about stupid heroes that she wouldn't know what to do with if one was standing in front of her. If Clemmie had a real-life flesh and blood man she'd run a mile. I think it was something like that, wasn't it? Words to that effect anyway.'

He froze, mortified by her words. His words. God, he'd been so crass. No wonder she was angry with him.

'I didn't mean that,' he mumbled, staring down at the sketchpad on his lap. 'I'm sorry.'

'You mean you're sorry I caught you assassinating my character to Noah,' she said. 'I think you did mean it. You certainly sounded as if you meant it anyway.'

His head shot up as he heard the catch in her voice, and he was appalled to see tears in her eyes.

'Clemmie, I *didn't* mean it, honestly I didn't. I was just...'

'Just what? Being horrible and spiteful for the sake of it?'

'Being an idiot. I was embarrassed. Isobel had been a cow, winding me up about you, and—'

'*Isobel?* Why would she do that? Winding you up how?'

It was his turn to blush. He seldom did, but he could feel the heat in his face.

'She knew it had thrown me, being on stage with you, having to speak to you like that, and in front of an audience too. We haven't—I mean, we *hadn't* spoken for so long. Not since the break-up. It was a big deal, and she knew it. I felt stupid and I lashed out at the wrong person. I'm so sorry.'

He'd mentioned the break-up again. He saw her flinch as he said the words, and wondered if it still affected her. But why should it? If she was so bothered about it why had she finished with him in the first place? That made no sense.

It occurred to him that now the subject was open once more, maybe this was the perfect opportunity to get some answers to his questions at last.

'Clemmie, the break-up... When you finished with me.' He hesitated, seeing the look of discomfort on her face but then pressed on, feeling a growing urgency. A need to know. 'Why did you? What did I do wrong?'

She looked stricken, terrified.

'Do we have to talk about this *again?*'

'Well,' he gave a half laugh. 'You can't say I've rushed you.'

'We went over this last night. Anyway, you didn't seem to care why when it happened,' she said, sounding surprisingly bitter. 'Why are you so bothered now?'

*Didn't seem to care back then?* Was she joking?

'Clemmie—'

'I really don't want to talk about it. There's no point. It's over and done with,' she said.

He wasn't sure whether to pursue the subject, and while he was trying to decide she snatched up the remote again.

'I think I'll watch a comedy,' she said. 'Oh, I know, *Ghosts* is on catch-up. I love that programme. Have you seen it?'

'Well, yes, but—'

'Great, that's sorted then.' She aimed the remote at the television and selected the appropriate app, not seeming to care which series or episode she started with.

Ross sighed inwardly, realising that she'd shut down the conversation and had no intention of reopening it. Maybe, he thought, it was for the best. She was right. A long time had passed. He needed to get over it and put it behind him, the way she had.

He stared down at the sketchpad in his lap, and silently put it to one side. He couldn't concentrate on planning his home now. Might as well enjoy the antics at Button House and try to ignore the fact that he was none the wiser about the demise of his relationship with Clemmie. And that he probably never would be.

# TWENTY-EIGHT

After a marathon session of old episodes of *Ghosts*, broken only by the odd comment about the programme, an occasional awkward laugh, and a short, light-hearted discussion on whether the UK version of the programme was better or worse than the US one, Ross suggested it might be time for something to eat.

'And this time,' he said firmly, 'something a bit more substantial than soup.'

'I thought you enjoyed the soup,' she said, somewhat defensively.

Ross rolled his eyes. 'I did enjoy it. Just that it didn't really fill the gap, and by the middle of the night I was starving. How about if I cook us something?'

'You made breakfast,' she pointed out reluctantly.

'You made lunch.'

'Sandwiches! Hardly a culinary feast.'

He frowned. 'So do you really want to cook then?'

Maybe it hadn't been such a good idea, starting this discussion. The minestrone soup had been the jewel in her culinary crown. She didn't honestly want to offer him fishfingers and chips, and frankly that was probably the best she could manage.

'Fine,' she said, pretending it was a pain in the arse that he was being so pushy. 'You cook then. Whatever.'

There was a light in his eyes that made her suspicious. It was as if he knew she was secretly grateful to surrender on this issue.

'What are we having?' she asked, rather ungraciously.

'I'm not sure yet. I'll have a look in the cupboards and fridge-freezer, see what's what.'

She wasn't sure whether to follow him when he ventured into the kitchen, but she couldn't resist. Knowing the sort of foods Dolly stocked up, she couldn't imagine he'd be exactly thrilled with what he found.

Sure enough, when he pulled out the first drawer in the freezer his face fell.

'Oh.'

'What's that supposed to mean?' she asked, even though she knew perfectly well what it meant.

'It's just a bit—not what I was expecting,' he said hastily.

Clemmie followed his gaze and bit her lip with embarrassment. Okay, but he had to remember that she and Dolly were working women who often got back late from The Corner Cottage Bookshop, tired and hungry, and in need of food that didn't take forever to prepare and wasn't going to test their admittedly limited cooking skills.

Even so, as she stared at the packs of beefburgers, frozen veg, ready meals and potato waffles, she had to admit to feeling something akin to shame.

He opened another drawer and looked at her blankly.

'You have frozen mash potato.'

It was said without any sort of inflection to his tone. It was merely a statement of fact, but Clemmie bristled.

'We don't always have time or energy to faff around peeling

and boiling potatoes,' she explained. 'Anyway, don't knock it until you've tried it.'

He held up a box of chicken nuggets and raised an eyebrow.

'There are some decent ready meals in there,' Clemmie said. 'I think we've got a few chicken kormas, and there might be a chilli con carne somewhere.'

Ross looked appalled, then his eyes lit up. 'You have salmon!'

'Do we?' No one was more surprised about that than Clemmie. Then she remembered a few weeks ago when Dolly had decided to go on a health kick. She'd stocked up on lots of fish, but after eating a mackerel fillet she'd announced that fish was the food of the devil, and she was going to have a cheeseburger to get rid of the disgusting taste. The rest of the fish had remained forgotten in the freezer.

'I'm not that keen on salmon,' she said faintly. Not that she'd eaten much of it. In fact, she couldn't remember the last time she'd tried it. Even so, it had never really appealed.

Ross ignored her and checked out the cupboards and fridge.

'Right,' he said. 'We have salmon. We have mash potato. We have frozen peas and some frozen herbs, and we have a variety of other basics that I can turn into something you're going to love.'

'Are you sure?' she asked doubtfully. How long had those herbs been in the freezer? She couldn't recall them ever being used. The last thing she needed was to be laid up with food poisoning.

'Watch me.'

'Literally watch you? Only I was going to finish *Ghosts*.'

Ross sighed. 'Okay, you go and finish watching the programme and I'll whip us up something you'll really enjoy. By the time you've tasted these you'll be begging me for the recipe. You just wait and see.'

Clemmie couldn't imagine that happening any time soon,

but she nodded and left him to it, glad to sit on the sofa and watch television without feeling his oppressive presence just a few feet away from her.

It wasn't really his fault, she thought, trying to be reasonable about it. But honestly, why did he have to ask her about the break-up? It had really thrown her. He'd sounded as if he desperately needed to know her reasons for walking away from their relationship, and she hadn't expected that. She'd assumed he'd forgotten all about her within days, and that had hurt her so badly she'd convinced herself she hated him.

How could it possibly still bother him? Deep down she knew she'd hurt him at the time. She just tried not to think about it, because whenever she remembered that day—and she did her best not to—she could recall the look in his eyes. Bewilderment. Confusion. Pain.

But he hadn't tried to persuade her not to end it, had he? And he'd walked away, his head held high, as if pride was all that mattered. Within days he'd found someone else, so he couldn't have been that upset really. Could he?

Yet here he was, all these years later, asking her why she'd done it. What did it matter to him now? Surely he hadn't been carrying that question around with him all this time? What was she supposed to tell him?

Not the truth, that much was for sure. She felt a lurch of dread at the thought of it. Never that. She couldn't face it. Better to let him think it was just one of those things. Incompatibility. He wasn't romantic enough for her.

Well, maybe that was true. Or maybe she'd just forgotten about that surprise trip to Bath. Maybe she'd dismissed the loving texts he'd sent her because everyone knew texts didn't compare to real letters, and he didn't exactly use poetic language.

Maybe, she thought suddenly, she'd been too quick to dismiss a lot about Ross. It was more convenient to remember him as someone who couldn't possibly compare to her fictional heroes. Less painful that way for sure, but maybe not entirely honest.

It couldn't have been more than half an hour before Ross called from the kitchen that dinner was served.

Clemmie wrinkled her nose, uncertain what lay ahead of her. She wasn't exactly adventurous with food, and dreaded finding out what he'd prepared, although she had to admit something smelled good.

'My clothes are dry,' he told her, gesturing to a neatly folded pile on the worktop as she walked into the kitchen. 'I was wondering, though, if you'd mind if I stayed as I am for now? I'd quite like to have clean clothes for the morning.'

'You're decent,' she mumbled. 'It's not a problem.' Wanting to change the subject she said brightly, 'So, what have you made for us?'

Expecting to find salmon fillets laid out before her on the plate, reminding her a bit too much of an actual living fish, she was surprised and undeniably relieved to see fishcakes instead.

'Oh.'

'Salmon fishcakes with minted peas,' Ross said proudly. 'There's bread and butter so help yourself. And for dessert—'

'You made dessert?'

'Well, not exactly. I found a tin of custard in the cupboard and an apple crumble in the freezer. Anyway, the main thing is we're not going to wake up hungry tonight.'

He probably hadn't meant it that way, but it was a reminder that he would be staying over again. He'd be in the room just down the landing from hers. He'd be lying in his bed just feet away from where she would be lying.

It felt surreal. How had this even happened? Clemmie tried to smile as she took her place at the table, aware that Ross had gone to a lot of trouble for her, and that she needed to look appreciative of that fact.

But the truth was, his presence was stirring up emotions she'd fought to bury for years. Feelings she'd almost convinced herself had vanished were whirling around inside her, filling her with a panic she didn't know how to handle.

She couldn't let herself be swept into that maelstrom of emotion again. Couldn't let herself remember the way he'd once made her feel. Couldn't acknowledge how she still felt about him, somewhere deep inside her.

Ross wanted to know why she'd broken up with him, but if he ever found out...

She felt sick at the thought of it, imagining the expression on his face. It was hard enough for her to deal with. How could she expect him to? And when he made it obvious that he couldn't cope, he would break her heart all over again.

Somehow, she had to make absolutely sure that he never discovered the truth. Whatever Ross believed, his ignorance was best for both of them.

'So you admit it then? You enjoyed the salmon fishcakes?'

Ross's tone was gently teasing, and Clemmie couldn't help but smile as they sank back in their respective armchairs, full up after eating a two-course meal.

'Oh, they were all right,' she said, a slight smirk on her lips. 'I mean, I wouldn't want to eat them again, but they filled a gap.'

'That's outrageous! You couldn't wolf them down fast enough,' he protested. 'I thought you were going to grab mine from my plate.'

'Stop exaggerating.' Even so, she laughed. They *had* been delicious. She'd even eaten her peas, and she wasn't a big fan of those normally. Funny how just the addition of some frozen mint had made all the difference.

'Are you denying it?'

She threw a cushion at him, and he ducked out of the way

just in time. 'All right, you win. It was a yummy meal. Thank you.'

'You're very welcome.' He gently threw the cushion back to her. 'So what are we going to do now?'

There was an awkward silence. They'd loaded the dishwasher and had coffee.

'I don't think I can face any more *Ghosts*,' she admitted. 'I mean, it's brilliant, but you can have too much of a good thing.'

She shivered, suddenly realising it was getting colder.

'I'd better add more fuel to that stove,' he said, crouching down in front of it and taking some logs from the basket on the hearth.

Clemmie took a throw from the back of her armchair and draped it over her knees, watching him as he coaxed the fire to burn brighter. He looked, she thought suddenly, incredibly sexy as he concentrated on those flames. Her thoughts strayed to the moment when Ross had strolled back into the living room after his shower. She'd noticed how his dark hair was still damp and curling slightly at the ends, and she'd had to look away. She'd always loved his hair.

She almost jumped when he suddenly closed the stove doors, got to his feet, and turned to face her.

'You okay?' he asked curiously.

'Me? Absolutely fine.' She quickly reached for the remote, not wanting him to guess what she'd been thinking.

He nodded at the screen. 'Find something we can both watch. Your choice. I promise not to criticise.'

'Really?' She gave him a challenging look. 'So if I find a Regency romance you'll be happy with that?'

To her amazement, he sat down again, his face eager.

'Actually, Clem, that's not a bad idea. Lots of Regency houses. I'd love to see that.'

She frowned. Since when did Ross Lavender want to watch a Regency romance with her? Yes, he'd watched a few back in the day, but that was only out of kindness. She'd paid him the same courtesy, watching some of his dreary action films, even though they bored her to tears. It was what couples did after all. But they weren't a couple any more, so why...?

'Are you taking the mickey?'

'No honestly, I mean it. You have a look and I'll make us both a hot chocolate.'

'O-*kay*,' she said uncertainly, staring after him for a moment as he headed into the kitchen. She found the 2020 version of *Emma* and decided that would do nicely. The houses were gorgeous in this film, with different colours in every room. He wanted to see a Regency setting? Well, he'd asked for it. She turned on the lamps and drew the curtains. It looked lovely and warm and cosy in here. Romantic even...

She settled back, snuggling under the throw again, lost in her daydreams.

When her phone rang it startled her back into reality. What on earth had she been thinking?

It was Summer.

'Clemmie, I've been working with Reuben today and he told me you were stuck in Wintergreen with Ross Lavender of all people! Are you okay? How's it going?'

Clemmie smiled, imagining how Summer had reacted to that nugget of information.

'Don't worry. It's going okay actually. He made me a yummy breakfast this morning, and we've just had salmon fishcakes and—'

'Never mind the food,' Summer said impatiently. 'Is he behaving himself?'

'Of course he is. He's the perfect gentleman.' Clemmie could hardly believe how warm her voice sounded as she said that, so she could imagine Summer would be astonished to hear her talking about Ross in such glowing terms.

'Really?' There was a telling silence. 'Are you managing okay? Have you got enough to eat?'

'Plenty. I just told you, Ross cooked for us. We've watched *Ghosts*. We're going to watch *Emma* soon.'

'*Emma?*'

Clemmie sighed inwardly. 'It's a Jane Austen story. It doesn't matter.'

'Wait, Ross is going to watch a Jane Austen story? A romance? With you?'

'Yes. It was his suggestion actually.'

She heard Summer's sharp intake of breath. 'Sounds to me like he's trying to get you in the mood, Clem. You ought to watch him. You know yourself what his reputation's like, and why else would he want to watch a romance with you? I mean, first he makes you food, and now this. If that's not dodgy I don't know what is.'

She was so far off the mark it was laughable. Wasn't she? Clemmie shifted, suddenly uncomfortable. What if she was right? What if Ross was planning to, what, seduce her?

She felt a sinking feeling in the pit of her stomach. Well, good luck with that, mate. You've got no chance.

'Where is he now?' Summer's voice had dropped to a whisper, as if she thought Ross was standing right next to Clemmie listening to their conversation.

'He's making us a hot chocolate.'

'Aha! What did I tell you? Clemmie this has seduction written all over it. He's lulled you into a false sense of security.'

'I thought you liked Ross since you found out he didn't dump me,' Clemmie pointed out.

'I never said I liked him,' Summer said defensively. 'I said I would have to be nicer to him because I'd got it all wrong about him breaking up with you and cheating on you. Still don't trust him, though. I mean, all those women he's been out with! What am I supposed to think? I don't know why Ben persists in defending him.'

Clemmie's eyes widened as Ross came back into the room carrying two mugs of hot chocolate and smiling warmly at her.

Time to change the subject.

'Did Reuben tell you he's letting Dolly stay at his until she could get through to us?'

'Yes, but what does that have to do with... Oh! Is he there? Has he walked in?'

'Yes, that's right,' Clemmie said, keeping her tone even as Ross handed her a mug then settled himself on the sofa.

'Just remember what I said. I'm only at the other end of a phone if you need help. If he tries anything let me know. Me and Ben will be at Wintergreen in no time, snow or no snow.'

Clemmie grinned. 'And how are you going to manage that? I know you think Ben's Mr Wonderful, but Superman he isn't.'

She noticed the uncomfortable look on Ross's face and wondered why he always looked so weird whenever Ben was mentioned.

'We'll be there, even if we have to call in the army,' Summer said grimly. 'Don't let him have his wicked way with you, Clemmie. I suppose it's a blessing that you don't drink alcohol. At least he can't get you drunk.'

'There is that,' Clemmie said. 'I'd better go, Summer. We've got a film to watch.'

'Hmm, haven't you just. If I were you I'd put something else on. How about *Kill Bill*?'

'See you soon, Summer.' Clemmie ended the call and gave Ross an apologetic smile as if he'd heard every word.

'Everything okay?'

'Yeah, that was just Summer, checking I was all right and we had enough to eat.'

He grinned. 'And what would she have done about it if we'd been starving to death?'

'She said she and Ben would make it through somehow, even if they had to call in the army.' Well, it was almost the truth.

'Right. They probably would too. They obviously think the world of you.'

She eyed him curiously. 'You and Ben...'

He looked startled. 'What about me and Ben?'

She hesitated, not sure whether to press the subject. But the truth was, it puzzled her. It always had.

'You used to be such good friends. Everyone says so. I never understood why you fell out, and you never explained. Even when we were—' She stopped, appalled at her slip. 'I mean, I could always tell that there was a part of you that wanted to make it up with him, but something stopped you.'

He was staring at the fire. 'We didn't exactly fall out,' he said. 'We just grew apart, that's all.'

'But you don't speak. Even at social events like the Christmas carol concert on the green, or bonfire night, you avoid each other.'

'And how would you know that? Been watching me, have you?'

'Not in recent years, no,' she said coldly. 'But even when we—'

'Were together?' he supplied.

She blushed. 'Even then you avoided him. Yet I get the distinct impression that you'd like to make it up with him. That you miss him. I always thought that. I can't believe that you still haven't repaired your friendship. What happened? What could be so bad that you could hold a grudge all this time?'

Ross nibbled at his thumbnail.

'Ross?'

'What?'

'You and Ben—'

He turned to her, a look of sorrow in his eyes. 'Leave it,

Clem. Some things can never be forgiven, and some relationships can never be repaired. You should know that.'

She curled up in the armchair, feeling attacked and suddenly strangely vulnerable. There was a long and difficult silence.

*Note to self: don't mention Ben. Or Ross's mother. Or his father. Or our break-up.*

Really, she thought, there were so many taboo subjects it was a wonder they'd managed to hold a conversation at all. Now what?

It seemed Ross had decided that he wasn't going to let their earlier good humour go to waste.

'So, have you found a film we can watch?'

'I have, but I'm not sure you'll approve,' she told him.

'Try me.'

'It's *Emma*. You know the Jane Austen film?'

He frowned. 'Jane Austen film? Can't place it. What else has she starred in?'

Clemmie's mouth fell open. 'Jane Austen isn't an actress!'

He laughed. 'I know. I was having you on. I remember watching *Emma* with you years ago. The matchmaker, right? Mr Knightley?'

She was impressed, she couldn't deny it. Fancy him remembering that!

'Well, yes, but you won't have seen this version. It was only made in 2020,' she told him. 'But it has some lovely sets, and you said you wanted to see some Regency settings.'

'I do.'

'Why?' She leaned forward eagerly. 'Is this something to do with Monk's Folly? Rumour has it that it's being done up to look how it did back in the days of Arabella Lavender. Is that true?'

'Rumour has it?' His lips twitched.

'Well, okay. The Lavender Ladies might have said

something.'

'I'm sure they did,' he said, his eyes twinkling. 'It's all down to Aunt Eugenie. She's footing the bill. Monk's Folly has always meant a lot to her, and now that it's back in the family she's determined to lavish love and money on it. That's what Meg's doing now. Helping us transform it into a Regency home again.'

Clemmie hugged herself in delight. Even the mention of Meg hadn't quite extinguished her excitement.

'How fabulous! So you want to watch *Emma* to get some ideas about decorating, furniture, that kind of thing?'

'Yes, but mostly for my quarters. The decorators have already started on the public areas of the house, using Arabella's paintings as templates, but Meg's still waiting for me to decide how I want my private rooms.'

Clemmie's stomach twisted. Meg was working with him on his own private rooms? *Well, of course she is. She's his interior designer, for goodness' sake. Get a grip!* She forced herself to sound unconcerned. 'You should get some inspiration from this film. It makes good use of colour. The house looks so pretty.'

'Great, put it on then.'

She pressed play and soon they were both absorbed in *Emma*. Now and then Clemmie would sneak a peek at Ross, surprised to see him watching the screen intently.

'Interesting,' he said at one point. 'Meg said that lavender colour was popular back then, and of course it's quite appropriate with my name.'

Then, 'I do like that powder blue. It looks really elegant.'

And a bit later, said with a slight frown, 'I'm not sure about all that white, you know. Meg says the brilliant white paints we use these days weren't used back then. It was more of an off-white. Muted. I'd have toned that down if I was them. Although,' he added almost grudgingly, 'it does look good against the coloured walls.'

Wow, he was really taking this seriously! Clemmie couldn't

help but feel impressed. She'd done quite a lot of research herself in the course of writing *The Marquess Wants a Wife* but had never expected Ross to care that much about historical detail. So Monk's Folly really was going to look like something from a Jane Austen novel? Lucky Ross, living somewhere like that. She just hoped he'd appreciate it. She hoped, even more, that his precious Meg wouldn't be sharing it with him.

'Shall I pause this?' she asked, halfway through it. 'We've got some teacakes in the freezer. I could toast a few. Would you like some?'

'That would be good,' he said, his eyes shining. 'Might warm me up. Even with the fire burning it's a bit nippy in here.'

She supposed he was right. She'd been snuggled up under the fleecy throw, so it hadn't really bothered her, but he was only wearing Dolly's dressing gown, which wasn't exactly thick.

She toasted some teacakes and spread them liberally with butter, then carried them back in. She handed Ross a plate and put the other on the coffee table in front of the sofa. He raised an eyebrow.

'Don't get any ideas,' she warned him. 'I just thought we could share this throw. I feel mean sitting here all warm and cosy while you're feeling the chill. Don't read anything into it.'

'As if I would,' he said dryly.

'Hmm.'

She dragged the fleece over to the sofa and settled down next to Ross, putting it over them both. Contentedly eating their hot, buttery teacakes, they continued watching the film, and she was gratified to note that he'd apparently stopped browsing for decorating tips and seemed to be paying attention to the storyline.

'I have to admit,' he said, as the end credits finally rolled, 'I enjoyed that.'

'Really?'

Clemmie couldn't help but feel delighted that he'd admit

something like that. It felt like a huge breakthrough somehow, though she wasn't sure why.

'So what's next?' he asked.

'Your choice,' she said, feeling warm and generous towards him. 'I've watched my film, now it's your turn.'

'I haven't got a clue,' he admitted. Then he smiled at her. 'How about *Bridget Jones's Diary*?'

Clemmie's eyes narrowed as Summer's words came back to her. Was he deliberately leading her on? Since when had Ross ever wanted to watch a rom-com of his own free will?

'You don't have to do that,' she said slowly.

'No, I don't. But I enjoyed *Emma*, and maybe while I'm feeling so cosy and relaxed I might see Bridget through different eyes. She was one of your favourites, wasn't she?'

'Yes...' Clemmie felt uncertain. 'But we can watch something more to your taste. I really don't mind.'

'Honestly, it's fine.' He took the remote from her hand and did a search, finding the film quite easily. 'There we go. Sorted.'

Despite her misgivings, Clemmie couldn't help but get drawn into the antics of Bridget and it didn't take long for her to forget she'd ever had an issue with it.

'Is it wrong,' she asked at one point, 'to admit that I actually fancy Daniel Cleaver more than I fancy Mark Darcy?'

'Really?' Ross turned to her, clearly surprised. 'I would never have believed it.'

Neither would Clemmie, and if anyone had asked her she'd have denied it outright. Somehow, though, it didn't seem to matter at this point.

'Of course, he's not as *nice* as Mark,' she said quickly. 'Not as reliable, or as kind. Not a catch at all really. But he is rather sexy, and funny. Maybe I have a secret hankering for a bad boy,' she added thoughtfully.

'You have hidden depths,' he said, smiling mischievously. 'I quite like that.'

Uh-oh! The way he said that she wouldn't have been at all surprised if he'd called her 'Jones'. Clemmie knew she should be on alert, but somehow she couldn't quite force herself to pull away from him.

She realised she was sitting dangerously close to him. Their arms were actually touching. The throw was warm and comforting, draped over them both, cocooning them in their own private little nest. The flames danced in the wood burner, and she felt suddenly sleepy and contented. Even Summer's warning didn't seem to matter any more.

There was a part of her—a worryingly large part of her—that just wanted Ross to take control of the situation and kiss her, the way Daniel Cleaver was kissing Bridget Jones right now.

When, she wondered suddenly, had Ross's arm moved? She hadn't been aware of it before, but somehow it had ended up draped over her shoulder. He was watching her with dark eyes burning with an intensity that far surpassed the flames in the wood burner. For some reason the wolf in *Little Red Riding Hood* popped into her mind.

'Clem,' he murmured, and she closed her eyes, aware that this was dangerous territory and she had to be careful, but too caught up in the moment to do anything about it.

She nestled her head on his shoulder and heard him sigh softly with pleasure. His hand stroked her arm, and she was gripped by an aching sensation, low down in her abdomen, that urged her to put aside all her worries and whatever had happened in the past, and just kiss him. To hell with the consequences! What did it matter? What did any of it matter?

He held her tighter, and his breath caught in his throat, as he murmured, 'I've missed you.'

*Oh, God, I've missed you, too. You've no idea...*

His lips brushed the top of her head, and she heard him inhale softly.

'You've changed your shampoo,' he murmured.

Clemmie's eyes snapped open. 'What?'

He smiled at her. 'Your hair used to smell of coconuts. I don't know what scent this is. I can't quite place it, but—'

Clemmie practically threw off the throw and leapt to her feet.

'Clem?'

'What do you think you're doing?' she gasped, distraught. 'Oh my God, Summer was right. This was all about seduction, wasn't it?'

'Seduction?' His forehead creased as he stared at her. 'What are you talking about?'

'Cooking me a meal, stoking up the fire, going upstairs to take a shower, dropping hints about being cold so I'd sit next to you and share the throw. Letting me watch *Emma* and *Bridget Jones's Diary*! Wow, you're a piece of work, you know that?'

'Are you for real?' Ross glared at her. 'Are you saying this was all one way? I thought—'

'Well,' she said, furious with herself as her voice cracked and tears sprang from her eyes, 'you thought wrong.'

'I'm sorry,' he said, his voice softer and his eyes gentle as he held up his hands. 'I would never have—this wasn't planned, Clemmie. We both just got caught up in the moment. There's no shame in that, is there? Look, maybe it just shows that we're not done after all. Maybe there's still something there? Something worth fighting for?'

'You've got to be joking. I finished with you years ago, and it was the right decision then. I don't want to be with you, so get that through your head and leave me alone!'

With a strangled sob she ran from the room, not looking back to see how he was reacting to her outburst.

She just wanted to reach the safety of her room and shut that door firmly behind her. There could be no going back for her and Ross. This had been a huge mistake.

# TWENTY-NINE

Ross sat for a few moments in stunned silence. What the hell had just happened? One minute he and Clemmie had been so close he'd honestly believed she'd wanted him to kiss her; the next she was screaming at him as if he was some sort of sexual predator and had rushed from the room like she was scared stiff of him.

What had he done wrong? He replayed the scene over and over in his mind, but no matter how he tried to look at it from her point of view, he couldn't recall any moment where he'd overstepped the mark or done anything that he believed she hadn't wanted him to do.

He stared miserably at the remains of the fire. He'd done it again, hadn't he? Somehow, he'd committed some terrible faux pas that had sent Clemmie running for the hills. What was wrong with him? What was he missing?

And it wasn't just Clemmie's feelings that were bewildering him. His own had left him pretty rattled too. He couldn't deny to himself any longer that he still wanted her, cared about her. He was obviously still attracted to her. His body's reaction to hers had made that pretty clear.

But it was so much more than that. Every part of him, every cell in his body, remembered her and ached for her. Sitting so close to her he'd recalled the way he used to feel every day when they were together, and his heart longed for her now as much as it had then.

Was it possible that he still loved her, even after all this time? If so, he was lost. If a separation of so many years hadn't made him immune to her what would? And the way she clearly felt about him meant there was no way their relationship would ever come to anything. So now what?

Gloomily, he turned off the lamps and the television then headed into the kitchen. He washed up the empty plates then took out the ironing board and iron and pressed his clean clothes, ready for tomorrow. Maybe, he thought, he should have put them on as soon they were dry. Perhaps he'd given Clemmie the wrong signals by staying in this dressing gown?

Cursing himself for being so stupid, he made sure everything but the fridge-freezer was switched off, and that the doors were locked, then carried his clothes upstairs to the box room and closed the door behind him.

Lying on his bed, he stared up at the ceiling wondering what the hell he was going to say to Clemmie tomorrow. The box room was cold, but he seemed immune to that now, his thoughts occupied elsewhere.

What *could* he say to Clemmie? He'd have to apologise, though he wasn't entirely sure what for. She'd got him all wrong. There'd been no bad intentions in his actions tonight. He'd just been having a nice time and wanted to make her happy, that's all. What it had led to had been entirely instinctive, and—so he'd thought—mutual. There was no grand plan to seduce her, as she obviously believed.

Somehow, he didn't think his denials would convince her. She clearly didn't trust him and hadn't appreciated his affectionate behaviour one little bit. Well, he wouldn't make that mistake again.

He sighed and rolled over onto his side, staring at the door, determined to ignore that plaintive little voice in his head that was saying, 'Yes, but *why* did she do that? What made her react that way?'

Clemmie was just... weird. He couldn't give another answer because there wasn't one. She'd broken up with him for no good reason, even though they'd been happy and in love. Or so he'd believed.

Tonight, she'd been responsive to him, affectionate even. Then suddenly she'd leapt up as if he'd done something unspeakable to her, when all he'd done was kiss the top of her head! It was hardly sexual assault. He would never hurt her or do anything she didn't want him to do. Surely she knew him better than that? What on earth was wrong with her?

Suddenly, his blood ran cold. What if...?

He sat up straight on the bed, his fists clenching. No! It couldn't be that, could it? But the thought persisted, and he was gripped by a sudden feeling of nausea and panic.

What if she'd been assaulted? Was that why she'd dropped him like a stone all those years ago? Was that why she'd reacted so badly tonight, just because he'd got close to her?

The more he thought about it, the more plausible it seemed. But surely Clemmie knew he wasn't that sort of man? He would never do anything to hurt her or frighten her intentionally.

*Oh, Clemmie.* His heart ached for her. It was the only thing that made sense. Someone had hurt her back then, and she hadn't felt able to tell him. He couldn't bear it. He had to put this right.

Without stopping to think, he swung his legs over the side of the bed and strode out of the room, stopping only when he reached her door. His heart raced as he listened for any signs of movement. Maybe she was asleep, and he didn't want to wake her.

But no, he could hear her moving about from somewhere within. He knocked lightly on the door then cautiously pushed it open, entering the room almost apologetically.

She wasn't there, and he frowned before realising she must be in the en suite. It occurred to him suddenly that she might not be dressed, and that he was wearing only the thin dressing gown that just moments ago he'd been cursing himself for wearing so long. He'd scare the life out of her if she walked in and saw him standing there, half naked.

*What the hell are you thinking, you idiot! Get out of here!*

He was on the point of turning when something made him stop dead in his tracks. He stared at the dressing table at the far end of the room and his brow furrowed. Was that...?

He tried to make sense of what he was seeing, but his brain couldn't seem to compute. Why was Clemmie's hair settled on a stand on the dressing table?

*That's not Clemmie's hair, you idiot. It's a wig.*

Before he could ask why Clemmie had a wig on her dressing table, the bathroom door opened, and she entered the bedroom.

He wasn't sure which of them was most shocked. As he stared at her, a thousand questions popped into his mind, but his mouth couldn't seem to formulate a single one of them. He simply gaped at her, too stunned to speak.

Clemmie's eyes seemed huge as she stared back. Then suddenly she screamed.

'*Get out! Get out! Go!*'

He didn't need telling twice. With a startled gasp, he ran from the room and didn't stop until he'd entered the box room, where he slammed the door shut behind him and leaned against it, his mind racing as he tried to understand what had just happened.

Clemmie had no hair. None.

He knew what that meant.

Ross sank onto the bed and covered his face with his hands as the tears began to fall.

Clemmie didn't want to get up. The clock on her bedside cabinet told her it was almost nine o'clock and she ought to have been up ages ago, but she couldn't face it. She'd heard Ross go downstairs at around six this morning, so guessed he hadn't slept much either. Now and then she'd heard movement downstairs, and had hoped with all her heart that, by some miracle, he'd realised the snow had cleared and he could leave.

No such luck. He was still down there. She wondered what he was doing in the kitchen. She was sure she'd heard the oven door closing, and there'd definitely been some clattering of pots or pans.

She thought about him standing in her bedroom last night, wearing only that thin dressing gown of Dolly's, with absolutely nothing underneath. If things had been different she might have appreciated that sight, she realised. Especially after how close they'd got during the evening.

All she could think about, though, was his expression when he finally realised the truth about her. Her secret was out. How could she ever face him again?

The look on his face! Tears scalded her cheeks as she remembered the horror in his eyes when he saw her standing before him. He couldn't get out of there fast enough. She imagined he'd be dreading this morning as much as she was, wondering what to say to her, how to be polite.

Would he mention what he'd seen at all? Or would he pretend it had never happened—too embarrassed to comment? Would she see scorn in his eyes? Or worse, would she see pity?

She wiped her face and sat up. There was no getting away from it. She couldn't hide up here forever, and she might as well get it over and done with. Time to end this once and for all. At least she'd finally have closure. They both would.

Feeling sick with dread, she got dressed and took a deep breath as she sat at the dressing table and stared at her reflection in the mirror.

This was the person Ross had seen last night. This was the real Clemmie Grant. She'd bet he wouldn't want to watch romantic films with her now. Determined not to cry again, she reached for her wig and fixed it securely in place.

There, she was the woman everyone thought they knew again. Time to face the music.

Ross had obviously heard her moving around upstairs because as she walked into the kitchen, her head held high despite the awful churning in her stomach, he gave her a weak smile and said, 'I made you scrambled eggs on toast. I hope that's okay.'

She hardly knew what to say to that. Was he really going to pretend that nothing had changed? That he hadn't seen what she knew he had?

'Thank you.' Her voice was croaky, her throat dry. She cleared it and tried again. 'Thanks. I'm not really hungry.'

'Just eat what you can, I won't be offended,' he said gently. 'Would you like tea or coffee?'

She sat at the table and stared at the plate he put before her. Was he really expecting her to eat?

Yet she found herself saying, 'Coffee please.'

Ross obliged, making himself one in the process. He didn't speak and Clemmie picked up her knife and fork and tried to force some scrambled egg down her throat. Anything to take her mind off this awful silence, and the dread of what he might say next.

He eventually put two mugs of coffee on the table and sat down opposite her.

'It's looking a bit brighter outside today,' he offered. 'I don't think we've had any fresh snow overnight, so that's good news.'

*Yeah, great news. You'll be able to escape sooner rather than later. You must be so relieved.*

'Maybe you should try to get home now,' she ventured.

He shook his head. 'I spoke to Noah earlier. The roads aren't cleared yet, but they're hoping to get through later today, or if not, early tomorrow, providing there's no fresh snow of course.'

He'd spoken to Noah? What the hell had he told him? She stared at him with beseeching eyes, making a silent plea to him to reassure her that he'd kept her secret.

If he noticed he didn't acknowledge it. Then again, he was too busy staring into his coffee. Couldn't face her, obviously. Was she really so hideous to him now the façade had been stripped away?

'You could try,' she said bleakly.

He shook his head, still not looking at her. 'I'm not going to risk freezing to death just because you don't want to talk to me, Clemmie.'

'There's nothing to say,' she said bitterly, prodding her scrambled egg with her fork. 'I could see how you felt about it last night. Don't worry, I'm not going to subject you to the sight again. Let's just forget it happened, okay? You'll be going home tonight or tomorrow, and we need never speak about it again. Or anything else for that matter.'

He raised his head to look at her and she was shocked to see tears glistening in his eyes. The shock, however, soon gave way to anger.

'I don't need your pity,' she snapped. 'Don't feel sorry for me.'

'Why didn't you tell me?' he murmured, reaching for her hand. 'How long have you been going through this?'

She frowned. 'I'm not *going through* anything. It is what it is. I've had to accept it and that's all there is to it.'

Except she hadn't really accepted it, had she? There wasn't a single day when she didn't hope for a miracle, even though she knew, deep down, it was probably never going to happen.

'But—but there must be hope? I mean, the treatment...' His voice trailed off and his hand tightened on hers. 'How bad is it, Clemmie? Can they...?'

He swallowed and tears spilled onto his cheeks. Clemmie's mouth dropped open as she realised what he was thinking, and even though she was still embarrassed and angry, a part of her was moved that he was so upset.

'Ross, no! You've got it all wrong.' She pushed away her plate, having no appetite. 'I'm not ill. This isn't because of cancer or anything like that.'

The look of hope that flared in his eyes warmed her heart, but only briefly. Now she had to explain it all, and she hated the thought of that. It was why she hadn't told anyone—not even Summer. Only Dolly knew the truth. How could she bear to reveal everything to Ross, of all people?

'Then—what?'

She closed her eyes for a moment, gathering strength.

'It's called alopecia totalis.'

'Alopecia?' Ross frowned. 'Hair loss? So you're not ill?'

'No,' she said, trying to keep her voice steady. 'I'm not ill.'

'Oh thank God!' He visibly slumped, but she noted he'd let go of her hand, and thought sadly that now he knew the truth he'd probably experience very different emotions.

'So, what—I mean, how did it happen? What caused it?'

'They don't really know. It's probably an autoimmune thing —my body's defences attacking my hair follicles for some reason.' She was surprised at how calm she sounded. Inside, her emotions were a raging whirlpool, but on the surface she was maintaining a dignity that impressed her. Ross would never believe how hard this was for her. 'I suppose, in a way, I was lucky. I've managed to hang on to my eyebrows and eyelashes. Well, for now at any rate, although there are no guarantees it won't progress. Small mercies.'

He was staring at her hair, which she considered extremely rude of him.

'Do you mind?' she said pointedly.

He looked embarrassed. 'Sorry, I didn't mean... It's just, that's an amazing wig. It looks so realistic.'

'I've got a couple of them,' she said. 'Dolly paid for them. They're exceptionally good quality.' She gave him an impassioned look as fear flared up again. 'You won't tell anyone else about this will you? You didn't tell Noah?'

'Of course not,' he said softly. 'It's not my place to tell anyone. So, who else knows?'

'Just Dolly.'

'So even Summer doesn't know?'

'No, and I don't want her to. You have no idea...' She broke off and shook her head, then gulped down half the coffee in her mug.

'I can't believe this,' he said, cradling his own mug and looking thoroughly bewildered. 'So, what happened? Did you just wake up one morning and it had fallen out?'

'Sort of, although I had some warning,' she explained, trying not to give in to the pain of those memories. 'At first I didn't think too much of it; more hair in the comb, a few extra hairs in the shower, that sort of thing. Then I started seeing it on my pillow when I woke up in the morning and noticed a few bald patches. I covered it over as best I could, and Dolly took me to see a specialist. Everyone was very kind. They said there was a good chance it would grow back spontaneously within a few months. Then, one morning I woke up and it was nearly all gone. My crowning glory was mostly on the pillow and sheet. I was spitting hair out of my mouth. It was disgusting. I freaked out then, I can tell you.'

'Bloody hell.' Ross clearly didn't know what else to say.

'I thought it would grow back,' she admitted. 'I was so sure I'd be one of the lucky ones. But once it had all gone the doctors said it was much less likely to return.'

'And there's no treatment?'

'For alopecia totalis the only treatment likely to be effective is contact immunotherapy, but it's not widely available, and to be honest, the information I've read about it didn't convince me to pursue it. Besides, it has a low success rate, particularly when the disease has progressed as much as mine. After all this time, regrowth is probably never going to happen. That's something I'm still trying to accept.'

'When did it happen?' he asked.

She hesitated. 'A few years ago.'

*About six years ago actually. I was looking forward to my twenty-first birthday, and my life was just beginning. You were just twenty-four and so handsome it hurt to look at you. Until then I thought I was the luckiest woman alive.*

'I don't understand why it has to be a secret,' Ross said, his brow furrowed. 'You're acting as if it's something to be ashamed of.'

'You have no idea how it feels,' she said, determined not to give way to the emotions his words had evoked. 'I don't want people to look at me the way you looked at me last night.'

'How I looked...?' He reached for her hand again. 'Clemmie, I'm sorry if I reacted badly. I was shocked. It was so unexpected, and you were yelling at me to get out. I panicked. But honestly, you look beautiful with or without hair. It's no big deal.'

Clemmie shook her head, hardly able to believe what he'd

just said. 'No big deal? Who do you think you are to tell me what's a big deal to me? You don't know how I feel, what I've been through. How dare you tell me how I should feel?'

She was openly crying now, unable to hold back the storm of emotions that had suddenly overwhelmed her. All those years of shame and pain, and he was just dismissing her feelings like that? As if all the anguish she'd felt for so long meant nothing, had no meaning?

'I'm sorry,' he said desperately. 'Clemmie, I'm so sorry. I didn't mean it to come out like that. I just—the truth is, I don't know what to say. I wouldn't hurt you for the world, and I'm just floundering here. I'm an idiot.'

'Yes,' she said, 'you are.' She wiped her face with the back of her hand. 'I'm going to take a walk up the lane, see how far I can get before the roads are impassable. It might give us some idea of when they'll be able to get through.'

'Do you want me to come with you?' he asked, sounding subdued.

She shook her head vehemently. 'No! Please, Ross, just leave me alone. I need to be by myself for a little while, okay?'

'Whatever you want, Clemmie.'

*Whatever I want? Oh, if only!*

As she pulled on her coat and boots and left Wintergreen, Clemmie's eyes blurred with tears at the realisation that what she wanted was something she could never have. Oh, Ross was being nice to her, but he clearly didn't understand how much this had affected her, or he'd never have told her that losing her hair was 'no big deal'. Besides, she'd seen the horror in his eyes when he'd first seen her without her wig. Of course it had been a shock to him, but even so...

He would never look at her the way he'd looked at her all those years ago, because she wasn't the same person. Someone like him—handsome, rich, charming, with a seemingly endless supply of beautiful women to choose from—would never want someone like her. He might wish to be kinder to her now. Maybe he'd even want them to be friends. But he wouldn't see her as girlfriend material any longer, and she couldn't blame him for that.

But, God, it hurt like hell.

# THIRTY

As Clemmie walked away from West Colby, Ross headed towards the centre of it, carrying a bag with a flask of her minestrone soup, some bread rolls, and a large portion of the shepherd's pie he'd made early that morning during the seemingly endless wait for Clemmie to get up. That should keep Mr Francis going for the rest of the day.

As he trudged through the snow, he considered the way the conversation had gone earlier, realising he'd made a huge error of judgement, presuming to know how she should feel. Alopecia totalis? He wasn't sure what that was, so he googled it as he walked. He'd always assumed that if someone lost their hair they would also lose their eyebrows and eyelashes, but apparently that happened with alopecia universalis, where all body hair was also lost.

Ross clicked on several items about the condition, frowning as he struggled towards Mulberry Cottage, trying to absorb as much information as he could.

It was likely that Clemmie would never get her hair back. How must that feel?

He paused for a moment and gazed up at the sky, mentally

putting himself in her shoes. He tried to imagine what it would feel like to lose all his hair.

He had to admit, he'd always worried about experiencing hair loss as he got older. He'd hung on to the hope that, because most of the men in the Lavender family had apparently had a good head of hair—well, judging by their portraits at any rate—it wouldn't happen to him. But then, he didn't know anyone on his mother's side, and male pattern baldness could come from there. Only time would tell. But he'd always hoped he'd retain his hair for the whole of his life.

How much worse must it be for a woman? Without wishing to be sexist, he knew that many women felt their hair was a vital part of their identity. To lose it must be traumatic for them. Would it change how they saw themselves? Surely it must do? And he'd been crass enough to tell her it was no big deal! No wonder she'd flipped. But he really hadn't meant it the way it sounded. He'd been trying to tell her that it was no big deal to *him*, not to her. Of course it must be a *huge* deal to her.

Clemmie's hair, he remembered, had been thick and fair, and always... He closed his eyes for a moment. *Always smelled of coconuts.* That's why she'd freaked out last night! He'd kissed the top of her head and remarked that she'd changed her shampoo. She must have been terrified that he'd guess she was wearing a wig.

*Oh, Clemmie!*

He continued through the snow, his mind whirling. He had no idea how to fix this for her. He liked to fix things, and when he couldn't it made him feel uneasy. Then again, hadn't trying to fix things been his downfall once before?

He pulled his coat tighter, remembering as he walked a day many years ago, when he'd been determined to fix another sort of problem, and it had led to unimaginable catastrophe. Surely he'd learned his lesson by now?

Grief and sadness overwhelmed him, and he was glad to

reach Mulberry Cottage and push open the gate—with some difficulty. The bank of snow behind it meant it couldn't be fully opened, and he thought he'd better return later with a shovel and clear the path for Mr Francis.

The old man answered the door almost immediately, and was clearly pleased to see him, thanking him profusely for the food.

Ross checked he was warm enough, and that he had everything he needed.

'Shouldn't be long until the roads are clear again,' he reassured him. 'It's looking as if it will be later today or tomorrow morning, so your daughter will be here to see you before you know it.'

'I'm fine, lad, don't you worry,' Mr Francis assured him. 'How's that young lass of yours doing?' He winked. 'Bit of luck, getting stranded in a cottage with her for a few days, eh? Mind, I hope you're behaving yourself. Being a proper gentleman. Nice, decent girl is Clemmie. Still,' he nodded towards the food that Ross had placed on the table, 'I can see you're a good 'un. She's safe with you no doubt.'

'She's safe with me,' Ross assured him. 'I just want her to be happy.'

His eyes filled with tears suddenly and he blinked them away. This definitely wasn't the time or the place, but he couldn't deny Clemmie's pain was hurting him. He wished there was something he could do to take it from her.

'Now, what's happened to make you so upset?' Mr Francis asked. 'You and her had a falling out, have you?'

Ross shook his head, too miserable to reply, and the old man put his hand on his shoulder.

'Whatever it is, it'll all come out in the wash, lad. Trust me. I've lived eighty-odd years on this planet, and I'm old enough to know that most of what we fret about either never happens or doesn't matter a jot in the scheme of things. By heck, when I think of some of the worries I've carried on about over the years. Seems daft now. Waste of time. All that matters is the people you love, and if they're okay you've cracked it. Trust me on that.'

'But you had your Freda,' Ross blurted before he could stop himself.

Mr Francis eyed him thoughtfully. 'Ah, like that is it? Well, lad, if it's meant to be it'll happen, no matter how bleak things seem right now. Clemmie's a good lass and if she's yours she'll find her way to you, like my Freda did to me. You've got to trust in God. Or fate. Or whatever the heck you like as long as you trust in summat. Things have a habit of panning out. If she's for you, the two of you'll make it, and if she's not, no sense in worrying.'

Ross nodded and wiped his eyes. If only he could believe that.

'Mr Francis,' he said, suddenly anxious to have something to do, 'you don't happen to own a shovel, do you?'

It took him half an hour to clear the path, make sure the gate could be opened easily, and ensure there was no snow around the doorstep.

He stayed for a further half an hour inside the cottage, drinking tea with Mr Francis and making small talk. He knew the old man would be alone for the rest of the day, and a bit of human company was essential.

'Now, don't forget to watch that programme I told you about,' he said as he prepared to leave. 'It's on at three and I'm sure you'll find it really interesting.'

'I won't forget,' Mr Francis assured him. 'Anything to do with gardening and I'm all over it. You get back to young Clemmie and don't fret about me, lad.' He patted Ross's arm. 'Don't give up. I can see you two together you know. She's a stubborn bugger like my Freda but remember this. The right one's always worth fighting for. It might be a long, hard fight, but the rewards when you get there are worth it. I had nigh on fifty years with the love of my life. Who can ask for more than that, eh? It's worth the wait, lad.'

Ross smiled and headed back towards Wintergreen, his nerves kicking in the closer he got to the cottage, wondering if Clemmie had returned, and if she had, what sort of mood she'd be in.

Just how was he going to deal with this? He didn't want her to think he was ignoring the issue, but if he mentioned it would he just succeed in making things worse? He supposed the only thing he could do was to take his lead from her. She'd let him know, one way or the other, if she wanted to discuss it further.


As it turned out, when he arrived back at Wintergreen he found Clemmie sitting at the kitchen table, chatting on the phone. She seemed to have composed herself anyway and acknowledged him with a nod as she continued her conversation.

Ross nodded back and gestured to the kettle. She clearly thought a drink was a good idea, so he flicked it on and took mugs from the cupboard.

'Well,' Clemmie said to whoever was on the other end of the phone, 'that's great news. I'm so relieved. Yes, I'll bet she is. How's it been going at Whispering Willows?'

Ah, so it was probably Summer then.

He dropped teabags into the mugs and reached for the sugar canister.

Clemmie giggled and Ross raised an eyebrow as he took a spoon from the drawer. Whatever Summer had said it had obviously amused her.

'I think you're a superstar. What would they have done without you? Especially with all this snow.'

Ross frowned and risked a sneaky peek at her. She caught him looking and gave him a sweet smile.

'Okay, then, Reuben, I'll let you get off. Yes, as soon as it's clear. Oh, we'd love to! Providing there's no more snow of course. You wouldn't want to end up having me *and* Dolly as your house guests for the next few days!'

She giggled again and Ross scowled and poured boiling water over the teabags. So she was talking to Reuben. What the hell did he want? And why was she being all girly and giggly with him? That wasn't like Clemmie at all.

Clemmie ended the call and thanked him as he handed her a mug. 'That was Reuben,' she said, quite unnecessarily.

'So I gathered,' he said dryly, returning the milk to the fridge before sitting down at the table. 'Everything okay in Tuppenny Bridge?'

'Oh yes. Dolly's opened the bookshop, and Reuben's been at Whispering Willows again, helping Summer. He just rang to tell me that the word is the road should be cleared any time now, so you should be able to go home soon. Isn't that good news?'

'Mm.' He sipped his tea, not entirely sure how he felt about that. 'What was that about you and Dolly being his house guests?'

'Oh, he's invited us round for tea tomorrow evening,' she said carelessly. 'I was just warning him that, though we'd love to, it's on condition there's no more snow forecast. After all, imagine if we all got snowed in at Dale View.'

'Imagine.' A knot of jealousy tightened in his stomach, as he wondered exactly how close Clemmie and Reuben really were. 'So,' he said, 'does *he* know? About the alopecia I mean?'

As soon as the words left his mouth he could have kicked himself. Why had he brought that up, when she was clearly making every effort to ignore the issue and act as if he'd never found out about it in the first place?

Clemmie glared at him. 'Thanks for that.'

'It was just a question,' he said defensively. 'You don't have to answer.'

'I told you,' she said coldly. 'No one knows except for Dolly, and I'd quite like it to stay that way if it's all the same to you.'

'It's bound to come out sooner or later,' he said, thinking aloud. 'You can't keep it a secret forever, surely? And why should you have to?'

Clemmie's eyes flashed a warning. 'It's my decision who I tell, if I tell anyone at all. I would never have told you, except you barged your way into my private space and took that choice away from me. Besides, I've managed to hide it for six years so I don't see why I can't do so for another six years, and another six after that.'

'Okay, okay, I take your point.' He held up his hands. 'Sorry. I didn't mean...' He broke off and frowned at her. 'Did you say six years?'

Clemmie's face reddened and she stared at him dumbly.

'Clemmie?'

'Or thereabouts,' she muttered eventually.

'Or thereabouts?'

She swallowed hard then sighed. 'Six years and four months. But who's counting?'

Ross shook his head slowly as pieces of the jigsaw began to fit themselves together.

'I was in the Netherlands, visiting Mamma,' he said slowly. 'It was the last time I saw her. She was living with that Dutch man, Hendrik. They were having relationship problems, and he was quite angry, so I ended up staying on much longer than I'd intended to make sure she was okay. When I got back you were different. Cagey. I thought you were angry because I'd been away for so long. I remember, I kept apologising and you didn't want to know. The next day we...'

'Broke up,' she finished for him, nibbling her thumbnail.

'Because we were too different. Incompatible.' He ran a hand over his face, as if trying to clear his thoughts. He felt sick. Had she been going through all that while he was away?

Suffering all that trauma while he'd been dealing with the temper tantrums and pathetic arguments between his tempestuous mother and her then lover?

'Why didn't you tell me?'

She shrugged, but he could see by the glaze of tears in her eyes that her show of defiance was an act.

'You should have told me!'

'Why should I?' she demanded, suddenly angry. 'So you could come up with some excuse to drop me? I saved you a job. It was easier that way.'

He sat back in his chair, stunned. 'You broke up with *me* because you thought *I'd* break up with you?'

She didn't reply but pushed away her tea and headed into the living room. Ross sat quite still for a few moments, trying to make sense of what she'd said. Then he jumped up, scraped back his chair, and followed her.

She was curled up in an armchair, her feet tucked underneath her, her arms folded. It was as if she was defending herself, and as he saw the look of anxiety in her eyes the fight left him.

'I wouldn't have broken up with you,' he said, dropping onto the sofa. 'How could you ever have thought I would? I loved you. You losing your hair wouldn't have changed that.'

She gave a half laugh. 'Are you for real? Of course it would. You're forgetting, Ross, I was with you for eighteen months. I knew you!'

'What the hell does that mean?' he asked, genuinely puzzled.

'You think I didn't see you?' she asked, unfolding her arms as she leaned towards him. 'I saw the way you looked at other women! Always an eye for a pretty girl. How could I compete with any of them? It was only a matter of time even if I hadn't lost my hair, but once that happened, I knew... I knew...' She broke off as a sob smothered whatever else she'd been about to say.

Ross could barely believe what he was hearing. 'If I looked at other women it was only ever from an artistic point of view! I looked at men, too. Do you think I fancied them? Old men, young men, old women. Interesting faces. An expression in the eyes. A quirk of the lips. A misshapen nose or crooked teeth or, or *anything*! It had nothing to do with being attracted to them. How could you think it was? Why did you never ask me?'

She bit her lip. 'I was going to tell you,' she admitted eventually. 'About the alopecia, I mean. I thought, maybe you'd understand. Maybe it was worth a try. But then...'

'But then what? What changed your mind?'

'I drove all the way to the airport to surprise you. But when I got there, and I saw you in arrivals...' She swallowed. 'You weren't alone. There was a woman with you. A beautiful woman with loads of glossy brown hair. You were arm in arm with her. I saw you smiling at her and I just... I couldn't stand it. I ran out and drove home again.'

'A woman...?' Ross shook his head despairingly. 'Clemmie, that was Hendrik's daughter! She'd had an awful time being stuck in the middle of their arguments and she needed to get out of there. She was going to stay with her friend in York and we shared a flight back together. She stayed at Lavender House for one night and then caught the train the next morning. We were arm-in-arm because we'd both been through weeks of hell with our respective parents, and we were just so glad to be out of there. That's all there was to it. I swear to you—'

'I know, I know,' she said wearily. 'I found that out the day after I broke up with you. The Pennyfeather sisters told me all about her, but it was too late by then.' She wiped her eyes and gave him a sad look. 'I really am sorry about that. I thought— well, you know what I thought. I was wrong and I apologise for misjudging you. When I saw you with her... Oh, Ross, she was so beautiful, and she had all that glorious hair, and I...' She shook her head. 'I just felt so inadequate and stupid. How could I compete with someone who looked like her?'

'Clemmie, when I was with you no one else came close,' he said, meaning it. 'How could you not know that? Why did you send me away? All this time we could have been together, and instead we've been apart because you didn't trust me! You punished me for something I hadn't done and had no intention of doing. Do you know how that makes me feel?'

'I understand that,' she said quietly. 'But you didn't exactly put up a fight for us, did you? Eighteen months we were together, and when I told you it was over what did you do? Go on, what did you do, Ross?'

He blinked, not sure what she meant. 'I—I did what you asked.'

'Yeah, you certainly did.'

'I don't understand what you're getting at.'

'You walked away. You didn't say a word to try to fight for me, for us. You grabbed the chance to be free and made the most of it.'

'That's not fair,' he said, incensed that she was turning this all back on him. 'What did you want me to do? Refuse to listen to you? Ignore what you were telling me? Force you to stay with me?'

'You could have argued! You could have asked why!'

'I *did* ask why! I begged you not to do this, I asked you to think it over. You wouldn't even give me a sensible reason for finishing with me. I could see your mind was made up. I asked you if it was what you really wanted and you said it was. What was I supposed to do after that?'

'Try to talk me out of it? Surely if you'd really cared you would have said something to stop it happening?'

'Are you for real? You must have known, must have seen how hurt I was? How could you *not* see it? I was devastated,

Clemmie. You broke my heart. I walked out of the door because I knew I wasn't going to be able to hold it together much longer, and I didn't want to put that on you. I didn't want you to think I was trying emotional blackmail. You'd made your decision and I respected that. I wasn't going to manipulate you, even unintentionally. I've seen my parents play those sort of games and there was no way I was going to be like them.'

Clemmie shifted in her chair and gazed at the fire. 'It didn't take you long to get over it. As I recall you had a date with another woman within a few days. Don't try to tell me I broke your heart, Ross. I remember exactly what happened. You've not been short of female company since we split up, have you? And your so-called broken heart healed very quickly. We should all be so lucky.'

Ross put his head in his hands, trying to make sense of the way her mind was working. Had she really believed he'd got over her so quickly? How little she'd known him. Maybe what he thought they'd had hadn't been real after all. If it had been, she couldn't possibly have believed he could move on so fast.

'Clemmie,' he said finally, 'I never wanted anyone but you. You've got me all wrong, you really have. Mia madre—I've told you what she was like. Her and my father playing their stupid mind games. They've spent years trying to manipulate each other. They've had affairs just to make each other jealous, anything to provoke a reaction. It's pathetic. And so many people have been hurt by being dragged into their relationship battles.'

He shook his head sadly. 'I vowed never to be like them. When you said it was over I was devastated. I asked you why and you said it was because we were too different. Incompatible. I pushed for an explanation. You got upset. You said I wasn't romantic enough for you, and I had to accept that was true. I asked you—as calmly as I could manage—if you were absolutely sure it was what you wanted. You said it was.'

'So you gave up and walked away.'

'I walked away because I wasn't going to mess with your head the way my parents had messed with each other's heads! I had more respect for you than that. More respect for myself, for us.'

'And the women you moved on with, oh-so quickly? Weren't they about making me jealous? About hurting me?'

'No! I honestly didn't think you'd care one way or the other,' he admitted. 'They were about making *me* feel better. I was still in love with you, but I wasn't going to let myself wallow. My parents' break-ups were always long, drawn-out, furious events. I was determined to draw a line under ours. I wasn't going to engage in arguments and manipulation. I made up my mind to move on and let you do the same.'

Clemmie slumped. 'Oh.' She gazed down at her lap for a few moments. 'I guess I can understand that,' she said at last. 'But there have been a lot of women, Ross. You must have been in love with some of them?'

'I can honestly, hand on heart, tell you I haven't been in love with any of them,' he assured her. 'And before you accuse me of treating them callously, I've always made it very clear to every woman I've dated that I'm not looking for a relationship. I've made it a point of honour never to go out with them for more than two dates, and I've always told them that, too.'

'Did you...' Clemmie's voice trailed off as she stared at him in dumb misery. 'It doesn't matter.'

'What doesn't matter? What were you going to ask me?'

She hesitated. 'I was going to ask you if—did you sleep with them all?'

He smiled and shook his head. 'No, Clemmie. I didn't. I'm not going to lie and say I've been celibate since we broke up, but you'd be surprised how few women there have been these past six years.'

'Oh.'

He wasn't sure whether she believed him, but his conscience was clear on that score.

'Clemmie, now that we know the truth about each other, can't we give it another go? Hear me out,' he pleaded as her eyes widened. 'There was only ever you, and we broke up over something that should have brought us closer together if anything. You didn't trust me and I'm sorry for that. I obviously wasn't good at making you feel secure, and I'm sorry I failed in that respect. I promise I'll do better next time if you'll give me a chance.'

'Don't you understand?' she asked, clearly distressed. She waved a hand over her head. 'My hair will never grow back. Oh, I know they say there's always a possibility, but realistically this is me for the rest of my life.'

'But I don't care about that,' he said. 'It honestly makes no difference to me. Can't we just start again?'

Clemmie closed her eyes for a moment, and he waited, hoping against hope that she would agree. When she opened them again tears spilled from them onto her cheeks, and she rubbed them away.

'It's too late, Ross,' she said. 'It's all spoiled now.'

'What? How is it spoiled?'

'We had our chance, but it didn't work out,' she explained. 'Me breaking up with you over this, keeping my secret from you, not trusting you. You walking away so easily, taking up with all those women...'

'But I explained all that!'

'You did, and I understand now, I really do. But it's been ruined, can't you see that? We had a clean book to write our story on, and we started off so well. But now it's full of scribbles and ink blots, corrections, and crossings out. We can't erase all of that.'

He frowned, trying to understand what she meant. 'Are you

saying that, because we've made some mistakes, we can't ever go back?'

'It's spoiled forever. Don't you understand?'

He gave an incredulous laugh. 'No, I don't, because it's not true.' He scrabbled around in his mind for an explanation that she'd relate to. 'Look at Jane Austen! That character you love so much—what's his name? Captain Wentworth! Wasn't he apart from his true love for years? Didn't they go through all sorts of misunderstandings and hurt before they ended up together? They still lived happily ever after.'

'But Jane Austen's heroines don't have alopecia totalis.'

'What's that got to do with it? You're not making any sense,' he told her.

'This isn't a Jane Austen novel, it's real life,' she said. 'And the truth is, if we were meant to be together, we'd have stayed together all those years ago. I would have trusted you with my secret. You wouldn't have walked away without a fight. There wouldn't have been all those years when we didn't speak a word to each other.'

'People make mistakes,' he said. 'Nobody's perfect. No *relationship's* perfect.'

'But that's where you're wrong,' she said. 'Your parents have had a massive impact on you and how you see love, I realise that now. But my parents had a massive impact on me too. They were so happy, Ross,' she added, wiping away more tears. 'They were soulmates, and when you say no relationship is perfect you're mistaken. Theirs was. Mum would never have pushed Dad away if something like this had happened to her, and he wouldn't have let her. What we had clearly didn't come close to what they shared, and that's what I want. That or nothing.'

He had no answer for her. He couldn't wipe out all the mistakes they'd made, and he couldn't promise there'd be no more of them going forward. Life was full of errors and mishaps, arguments and misunderstandings.

Being in love, as far as he could see, didn't make you immune to imperfection. Clemmie was asking for the impossible, and he couldn't deliver that. It seemed, once again, she'd made her choice and he'd have to live with it.

'And the thing is,' she said hesitantly, 'the thing is, Captain Wentworth... In the end, he learned to trust Anne Elliot again. And I—I don't think I can trust you, Ross.'

The pain was almost too much to bear. How could she say that? He'd never hurt her the way she'd hurt him, yet here she was saying she didn't trust him? Because he'd looked at other women? Because he'd dated other women after they'd broken up? He'd explained all that to her. He'd never considered cheating on her, and he never would. She was being so unfair.

'Right,' he said heavily. 'Well, I think that's clear enough. I think I'll start shovelling the snow from the drive and getting my car ready to go. The roads should be clear soon after all.'

He got to his feet and headed for the door.

Clemmie's voice cut through him as he left the room. 'I really am sorry, Ross.'

She wasn't the only one.

## THIRTY-ONE

Ross seemed to be taking his time clearing the drive. Clemmie glanced out of the window every now and then to see what he was doing and thought he could have dug his way back to Tuppenny Bridge by now if he'd got a move on. He certainly wasn't rushing.

She supposed it was to make sure he stayed out of her way, and how could she blame him for that? She'd made a real mess of things, and wished she could put things right.

When he'd asked her for another chance she'd almost keeled over in shock. It was the last thing she'd been expecting, and for a few glorious moments she'd seen all the possibilities that a future with him might bring. She'd never, she realised at that moment, got over him. All her barbed comments and cruel thoughts had been her way of defending herself from the one unpalatable truth. She still loved Ross Lavender, and maybe she always would.

So why hadn't she grabbed the opportunity to rekindle their love affair? He'd said things to her that she'd never in her wildest dreams imagined she'd hear him say. She should be over the moon. Yet here she was, still alone, while the man of her dreams shovelled snow outside, deliberately taking his time so he could stay out of her way.

The truth was, when that initial euphoria had passed, she'd felt nothing but fear. Ross had known the old Clemmie—the girl with a full head of gorgeous fair hair, a lot more confidence than she had now, and the optimism of youth.

She might be not quite twenty-seven, but she felt as if she'd become middle-aged since they were last together. It seemed to her she'd shed her self-esteem along with her hair, and although she'd always been shy, she knew that her awkwardness and lack of confidence around other people was on a much higher scale than it had been back then.

It was difficult to admit it, but she didn't trust anyone. The fear of them finding out that she wore a wig nagged away at her constantly, and she often played out imaginary scenarios in her head of their shocked and appalled reactions if they discovered her without it. Teenagers terrified her. She had visions of them pulling her hair and dragging the wig off by mistake. In her nightmares they jeered and mocked her, drawing a large crowd of onlookers who stared at her in disbelief, or worse, pity.

Someone like Ross, who had the thick dark hair and flashing brown eyes of his Italian mother, a lean, muscular body, and easy confidence that came with knowing women found him attractive, could never understand how she felt. And before long he'd grow tired of her fears and shyness. He needed a beautiful woman by his side—one who knew her own worth and didn't feel the need to hide away from the world.

Maybe if she had the confidence to take off the wig and show her friends and neighbours who she really was; if she had the nerve to go out there with her head held high and say, 'This is me, and I'm happy with the way I look,' then she and Ross might stand a chance.

But the truth was, she *wasn't* happy with the way she looked. She missed her hair. She felt all wrong without it. How could she act so confident when inside she was curled up in a ball sobbing for the person she could never be?

Dolly had reassured her so many times that she was beautiful with or without hair, and that it really didn't matter. Now she had Ross telling her that it made no difference to him either.

But they didn't understand that it made a big difference to *her*, and it mattered to *her*. They didn't have to live with it. Telling her to be honest about it to other people as if it was as easy as that! They had no right to assume they knew what was best for her. She had no control over her hair loss, but she did have control over how she dealt with it. It was no one else's business.

Ross might think they could go back to how it used to be between them, but she knew it wouldn't work because the old Clemmie had gone. And the old Ross had gone too. She understood and accepted his reasons for dating all those other girls, and she knew she had no right to object to him sleeping with some of them. He'd been single for six years. What else could she expect? He certainly didn't owe Clemmie any loyalty.

But if she gave their relationship a second chance, how long would it be before he started urging her to be open and honest with everyone about how she really looked? She'd have to share a bed with him, and he'd see her without her wig, lying next to him every night. How could he cope with that? How long before he regretted his mistake and longed to get away from her?

She'd had to be honest and admit to him that she still didn't trust him. Didn't trust his love for her was strong enough to withstand the problems they faced. That was why she'd ended it with him all those years ago and nothing had changed.

Her happy ever after, she realised bleakly, was a thing of dreams. Time to wake up.

Dolly rang her at around half past twelve to tell her the roads had been cleared.

'You can tell Ross Lavender to sling his hook now,' she said cheerily. 'Tell you what, love, I'll be glad to get home to my own bed tonight. Shall I bring us fish and chips in from Millican's to celebrate?'

'That would be nice,' Clemmie assured her, still coming to terms with the fact that Ross could go home any time he wanted. She ought to tell him really.

It was mid-afternoon before he re-entered the house. His face was pink with cold, and he was shivering, despite all his hard work.

Clemmie warmed up the shepherd's pie for a late lunch and made them both mugs of hot chocolate. There was, she decided, no need to tell him he could go home just yet. He'd been working outside in the cold and deserved a couple of hours relaxing by the fire. She'd tell him later.

As they sat at the table, eating in silence, she wondered how they were going to get past this awkwardness, and what their relationship would look like in the future. Would they revert to never speaking and having no contact with each other? Or would they manage to forge some sort of friendship?

She couldn't bear the thought of them never talking to each other again. It had been so awful before, and now they'd shared these few days together she didn't think she could stand to go back to stony silence.

'I noticed some of the shepherd's pie was missing,' she said tentatively. 'Did you take some to Mr Francis?'

'Yeah, and some of the minestrone soup and rolls. Hope that's all right?'

'Of course. How is he?'

'He's fine. I cleared his path for him, and we had a cuppa and a chat. He's a nice old man. His daughter's coming to see him as soon as she can get through, so he'll be okay until then.'

'That's good.' Clemmie thought how kind Ross was to do all that this morning, especially when he'd been going through his own turmoil. He was a good man. She'd always known it deep down. The way she'd let Summer believe the worst of him filled her with shame. What had she been thinking? Yes, she'd been hurt, but the truth was she had no right to be. She'd broken Ross's heart, and then she'd stamped all over it for good measure. He hadn't deserved any of this.

Ross cleared his throat. 'I'm getting off home as soon as I've finished this, Clem.'

She stared at him. 'Getting off home? But the roads might not be cleared yet. You need to wait and see—'

'When I was outside the snow plough came through, just after I started digging out the car. Then a delivery van from the Lusty Tup Brewery passed me about an hour ago. I'm guessing it was taking barrels to The Farmer's Arms in the village. The point is, the brewery's on the other side of Tuppenny Bridge, so clearly the roads between here and the town are now open. If the van can get here then I can get home.'

Clemmie's heart sank. There was nothing she could say to keep him here any longer then. He was leaving, and this little whatever it was they'd had going on was over.

'What about the portrait?' she asked suddenly. 'I haven't sat for it, have I? You just did some sketches, that's all. What about the proper sitting?'

'I can manage with what I've done,' he said heavily, pushing his half-eaten shepherd's pie away. 'I can work from those, and a photo I took of you when you were standing by the window. I can already see the portrait in my mind's eye.' He hesitated. 'Clemmie, I'm guessing you want me to paint you with your hair?'

Startled, her hand flew to the wig. 'You mean, this? Of course! What else?'

'I just wondered if maybe... I don't know... Maybe if you could see how beautiful you are even without it...'

'You wanted to paint me without hair?' She gasped. 'No

way! Promise me you'll paint me with hair! I'll never forgive you if you don't! Please, Ross, please—'

'It's okay, don't worry.' He squeezed her hand reassuringly. 'It was just a question. I'm sorry.'

'I couldn't bear it,' she said, still feeling panicky. 'Don't try to bully me into doing something I don't want to do.'

'I would never bully you,' he assured her. 'It's your life. Your choice. I'll paint you as you want to be painted, don't worry.'

'Thank you.' She relaxed a little. 'When will it be finished?'

'I can't tell you at the moment,' he said. 'It has to be done in layers, and there's the drying times in between. Oils take a good while to dry. I'll let you know as soon as it's ready for you.' He scraped back his chair and nodded towards his plate. 'I'm not hungry I'm afraid. I might as well get my sketchbooks and get off home. Make a start.'

'Oh, right.' Clemmie stared up at him as he got to his feet. 'Ross, when you go home—'

He frowned. 'Yes?'

'We—I mean—we will talk, won't we? I wouldn't want us to avoid each other again, the way we've been doing all these years. It would be nice to be friends.'

'Would it?' He gave a short laugh and shook his head. 'If you say so.' His eyes softened suddenly as he looked down at her and he sighed. 'Yes, we'll talk. We're adults. You're not on Facebook any more, are you?'

She hesitated. 'Er, no. Not for years.'

No point in telling him that she'd created another account. Jay Bennett. Her middle name and her mother's maiden name. It was the only way she'd felt safe to join an online support group for alopecia sufferers. She couldn't deal with face-to-face meetings, but online there'd been a certain anonymity that had reassured her. She could be honest with these people she didn't know. People who'd never met her as she was now, let alone the Clemmie she'd once been, had learned more about her feelings than even Dolly. Talking to them had really helped her come to terms with the depression and anxiety that had plagued her for a long time after her diagnosis. She wasn't sure how she'd have coped without that support from people who knew all too well how she was feeling.

'But I mean, if we bump into each other in the street, or— something. Would that be okay?'

'Yes, that would be okay.' His voice was heavy with sadness. 'As you said, it is what it is.'

He headed into the living room to collect his sketch book and pencils and Clemmie pushed her own plate away, aware that she no longer had any appetite either.

Ten minutes later, she was standing on the doorstep, and Ross was by his car, looking as awkward and as unhappy as she felt.

'Thanks for your hospitality,' he said.

'Thanks for your cooking,' she joked, trying to ease the tension between them. 'You might just have converted me to eating salmon fishcakes.'

He gave her a faint smile and climbed into the driver's seat, slamming the door after him.

Lowering the window, he looked at her for a moment, and she wondered what he was thinking. There was so much she wanted to say to him, but she had no words.

It seemed he had none either, as he shrugged at last and said, 'Bye, Clemmie.'

He fastened his seat belt and reversed carefully out of the drive. A brief wave, then the car pulled away and he was lost to her sight as the trees shielded him from her view.

'Bye, Ross,' she said sadly, then stepped back into Wintergreen, closing the door behind her.

# THIRTY-TWO

'All I'm saying is, you've seemed distracted, as if your heart's no longer in the refurbishment.'

Ross wrinkled his nose as Boycott cocked his leg and showered the wheel of his car. Those Yorkshire terriers of his aunts had no manners whatsoever. Funny they never showered his aunt's car. It was as if she'd trained them to avoid peeing on her property.

'Ross, are you listening to me?' His aunt eyed him suspiciously. 'Meg says you haven't been the same since you got back from Wintergreen. She thinks you've quite lost interest in Monk's Folly and she's bitterly disappointed in you. Is it true that you told her to get on and refurbish the upstairs however she saw fit?'

Ross sighed. 'Aunt Eugenie, with the best will in the world I can't do everything. You asked me to get this portrait of Clemmie Grant finished so we can do a grand handover, and I'm working hard to make sure that happens. I haven't got time to faff around choosing paint and bedding right now. Surely Meg's more than up to the job? Isn't that what you're paying her for?'

His aunt's eyes narrowed. 'Hmm. You want a stranger to design your own living quarters? Surely you want the final say in that?'

Ross wondered how to admit that, right now, he couldn't care less about his living quarters. What did any of it matter anyway? At the end of the day, it was just somewhere to sleep and eat. It was hardly a home.

When he didn't reply his aunt sighed. 'Meg tells me you've been doing the portrait in the living room of the house. Why would you do that when you have a purpose-built studio to work in? I'd have thought you'd have been desperate for the chance to try it out.'

'I'll be working in the studio in future,' he said quietly. 'I just wanted to paint part of this portrait in the house. No big deal.'

'Ross, dear,' she said, her tone suddenly kind and concerned, 'is there something you're not telling me?'

He gave her a startled look. 'Such as?'

'Well, I don't know do I? If I did, I wouldn't be asking you.' She laughed, but there was clear anxiety in her eyes. 'You're not yourself, and I can't help thinking this has to do with being marooned at Wintergreen with young Clemmie Grant. Am I right?'

'I don't know what you mean,' he said, gazing over at the studio that stood where the derelict garage had once been. He shivered and pulled his coat tighter, marvelling at how an old lady of eighty-two could stand outside in the snowy car park, wearing only a jacket, skirt, and brogues, and seem immune to the bitter February air.

'Well, you and she have a history after all. It can't have been easy for you, spending time under her roof after the way she treated you. I know, I know.' She held up her hand as if to fend off protests he hadn't even made. 'It was a long time ago and you've certainly moved on since those days. Even so, it must still rankle. She treated you appallingly. I sincerely hope she didn't give you a hard time while you were stuck in that house with her.'

'Auntie, I promise you Clemmie was absolutely fine with me. We ate, we watched television, I made some sketches, we even cooked. It was all very civilised. You have nothing to worry about.'

'I'm glad to hear it.'

'But, just for the record,' he added hesitantly, 'Clemmie had her reasons for breaking up with me. Don't be too hard on her, okay?'

She raised an eyebrow. 'That's not what you said at the time.'

'No, well.' He ran a hand through his hair, wondering how to explain without giving anything away. 'Let's just say feelings were running high back then, and I've learned a lot recently. Maybe I wasn't the perfect boyfriend I thought I was. Maybe we both made mistakes. The main thing is, we're friends now, and that's got to be a good thing, hasn't it?'

'Yes,' she said, giving him a thoughtful look. 'I suppose it has. Even so, I want you to get back to helping Meg. You'll regret it if you don't at least have an input in your own rooms. She's done splendid work with the rest of the upstairs, but come on, Ross. It's not fair to put that responsibility on her.'

'You're right,' he said heavily. 'I'll speak to her, apologise. I'll get my act together, Aunt Eugenie, I promise.'

'Excellent, because I've booked a table for the two of you at The Black Swan tonight so you can make a start then. Maybe you can finally make some decisions. I want this house done, Ross. Time's running out. Be there at seven o'clock sharp and no arguments.'

He didn't have the energy to argue.

'Fine. I'll be there.'

His aunt picked up Trueman and Boycott and bundled

them into her car, seeming oblivious to their frenzied yaps of protest.

'I'm glad you've seen sense,' she said, settling herself in the driving seat. 'I expect to hear that the final decisions have been made and it's all systems go. Not long to the grand opening now!'

'People won't be getting a tour of my private quarters,' he pointed out. 'It doesn't really matter if they're not finished in time, does it?'

She fixed him with a beady stare from hooded blue eyes that may have faded, but still had the power to intimidate.

'I don't like loose ends, Ross,' she reminded him. 'If something's not quite right I like to see it sorted out. Nothing worse than unfinished business.'

As she drove away, Ross stared across the lawn to Monk's Folly, and thought of the portrait that stood on the easel by the front window. He hated unfinished business too. He just wished he could see a way to give his story a happy ending.

The Black Swan was heaving. Ross had never seen it so busy. When he arrived at just before seven, a flustered looking waitress showed him to a table in the middle of the pub, and looking round he realised that nearly every other table was occupied, and the few that weren't appeared to have reservations on them. What was going on?

'It's Valentine's Day,' Meg explained when she arrived five minutes later, and he voiced his surprise at the chaotic atmosphere tonight. 'Hadn't you realised?'

She sounded disappointed and his heart sank. Great. That was all he needed, being surrounded by loved-up couples. How on earth had he forgotten Valentine's Day? He supposed he'd just been so preoccupied with the art academy and brooding over Clemmie. And it wasn't as if he'd frequented the shops recently. He must have missed the usual advertising campaigns that swamped most of them almost the minute the Christmas decorations were taken down.

'It's hardly a great place to have a business meeting,' he complained. 'We're stuck here on this table for two with no room to spread samples and swatches out, and we're bang in the middle of the pub where everyone can see us. I don't want my private business to be the talk of the town.'

Meg laughed. 'God forbid that anyone should know what colour paint you want in your en suite.'

Ross frowned. Was she taking the mickey out of him? An uncomfortable thought popped into his head, and he tried to push it away, but it had taken root and wouldn't be banished.

Had Aunt Eugenie set them up? She must have known it was Valentine's Day. She always knew everything like that. She would have realised, surely, that there wouldn't be any real opportunity to talk business. Or, God forbid, was this Meg's idea? He thought he'd made it clear to her that their relationship was strictly business, but maybe he hadn't been direct enough. He ran a finger around his shirt collar, feeling as if it was choking him suddenly. What a nightmare.

'Relax,' Meg said. 'Shall we have a glass of wine and look at the menu?'

He supposed a glass of wine might help. Clemmie would have asked for the soft drinks menu, he thought wistfully. She hated wine. She didn't like the taste of alcohol full stop. It was one of her little quirks. God, was he ever going to stop thinking about Clemmie bloody Grant?

He ordered a large glass of house red and studied the menu.

'Do you know that couple?' Meg asked him. 'They keep looking over at us.'

He glanced up, his brow furrowed. 'Which couple?' He turned to look over his shoulder and his gaze fell on Kat and Jonah, who were tucked away in a table in the corner. Kat's eyes widened when she saw him looking at them and she murmured something to Jonah before offering Ross a guilty smile and an awkward wave. He gave her a brief nod and went back to the menu, knowing the news of his Valentine's Day date with Meg would be all round Tuppenny Bridge tomorrow.

'They're just friends,' he muttered.

'They've clearly taken an interest in you,' Meg said. 'Oh well, let's see what there is to eat. I love that they've got a special menu for the occasion, don't you? Not that I need one. I expect you know what I want, right?'

He blinked. 'Should I?'

'Oh come on! I could be hurt you know.'

He had no idea what she was talking about.

'Ooh, fancy seeing you here!'

Ross groaned inwardly as Buttercup and Clover bounded over to their table, dragging with them two awkward looking young men who clearly had no idea why they'd been forced to approach him.

'Fancy,' he said wearily.

'We're here for Valentine's Day,' Buttercup explained. 'This is my bloke, Danny, and that's Clover's bloke, Owen. Guys, this is Ross Lavender. He's a painter.'

'Really?' Owen looked suddenly interested. 'What are your rates, mate? My mam wants her through lounge decorating and I can't be arsed to do it.'

Clover nudged him. 'Not a painter and decorator, you plank! He's a proper painter. Paints pictures and that.'

'Oh, right.' Owen looked away, his interest in Ross having clearly waned.

Buttercup and Clover eyed Meg with undisguised curiosity.

'Hiya. Sorry, don't know your name,' Buttercup said.

Meg smiled. 'Meg McKenna,' she said, holding out her hand to a surprised Buttercup, who shook it warily. Evidently she wasn't used to such formal introductions.

'Oh, right. Nice to meet you.' Buttercup reddened, as if she didn't know what to do with herself now.

'Enjoy your date,' Clover said, and giggled, before the four of them thankfully moved off to their table.

Ross rolled his eyes. That was all he needed.

'So,' Meg said, as if they'd never been interrupted, 'have you remembered?'

'Remembered what?' he asked, puzzled.

She shook her head as if despairing of him. 'What I usually have to eat, of course. Come on, Ross. This is the third restaurant meal we've had together. What do I always choose?'

How the hell should he remember that? He racked his brains and recalled the dinner she'd chosen at her hotel and that first night at The Black Swan.

'Steak,' he said, concentrating hard. 'Medium rare.'

'Bingo!' She looked thrilled. 'There, that wasn't so hard, was it?'

He was getting tired of this meeting already. A crowded pub populated with too many familiar faces was no place to discuss Monk's Folly. And why was she banging on about steak anyway? Something was very wrong.

'Did you even bring samples and swatches?' he asked suspiciously.

Meg sighed. 'No, of course not.'

His heart sank. 'So this is a set-up?' he asked. 'Whose bright idea was it? Yours or my aunt's?'

'Wow.' Meg shuffled back in her chair and gave him a reproachful look. 'You don't pull any punches, do you? We came up with it together, actually. Your aunt was worried about you. She seems to think you're still hung up on some girl you used to date years ago. I told her that couldn't possibly be true.' She took a sip of wine, her brow furrowed. 'Although I'm beginning to think she might be onto something.'

'I'm sorry she dragged you into this,' he said. 'She had no right—'

'She didn't drag me into anything,' she told him with a shrug. 'She thought she was doing me a favour. So did I, come to that. I guess the truth is, you're just not interested. I'm right, aren't I?'

Ross wasn't used to someone being so forthright. He remained silent, not sure what to say. His heart sank at the thought of being with anyone other than Clemmie. He couldn't imagine dating another woman in the future.

He was right back where he'd been six years ago. In fact, it was worse now. He didn't even have the energy to persuade himself that he could start again with someone new. He couldn't deny it any longer. He wanted Clemmie back, and since she didn't want him he couldn't see himself ever settling down.

'It's okay.' She laughed. 'You made it pretty clear last time we had dinner, but I was sort of hoping you were just playing hard to get, or that I could change your mind, but obviously you meant it. Well, I'm a big girl. I can see nothing's going to happen. I think I knew that from the first date to be honest, but a girl can hope, right?'

'It's not you,' he said, feeling guilty, while at the same time thinking, *First date? We haven't been on any dates to my knowledge. They were business meetings.*

'I know. It's you,' she told him brightly. 'You're a very handsome chap, Ross, but you're not the man I thought you were. You come across at first as someone who's confident, in control, a man of the world. Truth is, there's an innocence and a naïvety about you that I wasn't expecting—especially given your reputation in this town.'

Charming. Well, at least she seemed to be taking it well, which was something. She hadn't thrown wine over him or anything like that.

'I'm sorry,' he said.

'Don't be. Now that's out in the open we can finish the job at Monk's Folly, and I'll be on my way. No hard feelings. Shall we eat?'

'That would be good,' he said gratefully.

They enjoyed a good meal of steak and chips with all the trimmings, followed by champagne and strawberry possets with shortbread, a special addition to the menu for Valentine's Day.

They talked easily over dinner, with no trace of awkwardness or resentment. Ross explained what his thoughts were about his living quarters, and Meg made some suggestions. He selected a kitchen he liked the look of from an online brochure and Meg said she'd book someone to come and measure up. They agreed they'd go to Kirkby Skimmer the next day to order whatever he wanted in the way of soft furnishings, wallpaper, and paint.

Meg had found a place in Cheshire that dealt in what she considered to be the perfect antique Regency beds. They currently had four of them in stock. Ross looked at the price of them but quickly decided he wasn't prepared to spend upwards of fifteen thousand pounds on an old bed, antique or not.

Meg dutifully—if reluctantly—came up with an alternative. A place that sold Regency-style four-posters. They perused the website on her phone, and Ross selected a style he liked: a warm oak frame with an Italian leather headboard, which he thought appropriate, given his heritage. It was still fairly expensive, but a fraction of the cost of an original. Meg promised to place the order the following day.

They ordered one last glass of wine and toasted their decisions and the successful near completion of a project. She booked a taxi to take her back to the hotel, insisting that it could make a detour and drop Ross off at Monk's Folly first. He helped her into her coat and left the waiter a large tip before they headed out of The Black Swan into the cold night air.

He felt relaxed and happy, knowing that Meg understood he wasn't interested, and that they were only ever going to be business acquaintances. Even better, she'd taken it well, and hadn't seemed upset. At least that was one nagging worry ticked off. It had been awkward at first, but there'd been no harm done in the long run.

'Goodness, I nearly bumped into you then. Sorry!'

Ross smiled as he recognised Ava Barrington and her husband, Zach, well wrapped up in thick coats and scarves.

'My fault,' he assured her. 'I wasn't looking where I was going.'

'Been for a meal?' Zach enquired, his gaze sliding past Ross to Meg, who was, he realised, leaning on him, and looking quite merry.

'That's right,' she told him. 'Are you going in the pub?'

'We are,' Ava said. 'Just for a drink, though. We've already eaten at The White Hart Inn. It's packed there. What's it like in here?'

'Heaving,' Meg told her with feeling. 'You should be able to get a drink though. If you hurry, you might be able to nab our table.'

Ava laughed and he saw the curiosity in her eyes as she looked from Meg to Ross.

'Well, darling, we'd better hurry before someone else takes it,' she told Zach. 'Goodnight, Ross. Goodnight, er, Meg, isn't it?'

'That's right,' Meg said, sounding delighted that Ava knew her name. 'Goodnight to you both. Have a lovely evening.'

Ross and Zach nodded at each other, then the Barringtons headed into The Black Swan and Ross and Meg climbed into the taxi that had just pulled up.

How, Ross wondered as he fastened his seat belt, had Ava known Meg's name?

He realised suddenly that people must be talking about her,

and if they were talking about her they were talking about him. Tonight, the two of them had been seen by the Barringtons, by Kat and Jonah, and by Buttercup and Clover, whose mother, Bluebell, was almost as big a gossip as the Lavender Ladies.

Something else nagged away at him. Something Meg had said... What was it?

He couldn't think, but something worried him. He just hoped people wouldn't say anything about this to Clemmie. Yes, he'd been out with other women before, and she'd made it quite clear they had no future.

Even so, there was a part of him that still hoped it might happen. Something that made him think that if he could just get through to her how much he loved her, and that she could trust him with her life, they could still make it work. He didn't want her getting the wrong idea and shutting down the possibility of them getting back together, however small that chance was.

It was only after he'd scrambled out of the taxi at the gates of Monk's Folly and waved goodbye to Meg that it dawned on him what was worrying him. She'd asked him to tell her what she always ate when they had dinner.

'This is the third restaurant meal we've had together,' she'd said. And she was right.

He realised suddenly that—to outsiders at least—he and Meg had been on three dates. And everyone knew he never dated anyone more than twice.

No wonder there'd been so much curiosity. People might think this was serious!

How the hell would Clemmie react to that?

## THIRTY-THREE

'Right, let's get this lot taken down then, shall we? Thank God that's over with for another year.'

Dolly, who was standing on the top rung of a stepladder, reached up to the far corner of the wall and began to unpin a string of Valentine's Day bunting that she'd felt obliged to put up in the shop, despite being possibly the most unromantic person Clemmie had ever met.

'You shouldn't be up there in those heels,' Clemmie reproved, holding tight to the stepladder, and praying Dolly wouldn't come crashing down. 'Why don't you let me do it?'

'Give over. I'm fine. Got a better head for heights than you anyway. I'll be glad to get this lot down. All that pink was giving me the heebie-jeebies.'

Clemmie couldn't help but laugh. 'How on earth do you make a living writing romantic fiction when you don't have a romantic bone in your body?'

Dolly peered down at her, a wide grin on her face. 'The clue's in the word fiction. I make it up, love. I daresay Agatha Christie never murdered anyone in real life either. Mind you, she might have wanted to.'

She chuckled and reached over to pull out another pin. 'That's it. I'll just move over to the other end. Hang on.'

She clattered down the stepladder, as one half of the bunting dropped to the floor. Clemmie moved the stepladder under where the final pins were located and Dolly quickly removed them, heaving a sigh of relief as the offending decoration collapsed in a pile, ready to be picked up and put away for another year.

She'd already taken great pleasure in popping the Valentine's Day balloons last night as soon as the shop closed. For once, Clemmie hadn't felt sad to see them go. Valentine's Day had been difficult for a long time, but this year had, if anything, been even worse.

She knew, of course, that it was a long shot that Ross would send her a Valentine's card, but it didn't stop her secretly hoping he would. When nothing arrived for her she told herself she was being stupid. Hadn't she made it clear to him that it was over? And she'd meant it, of course she had.

So why would she want or expect a card from him? Maybe it just felt like a replay of the way he'd been all those years ago. Accepting they were over so easily. Not putting up a fight for their relationship.

But that wasn't fair, and she knew it now. It was her pushing him away, not the other way around. She'd hurt him enough, so what exactly did she want from him?

Oh, that was the question! Clemmie had to admit there was a part of her that wanted him desperately, and wished with all her heart that they could be together. But the other part of her knew she could never settle for something that she'd doubt would last. There was no going back.

If she wanted a happy ending, perhaps it had to be with someone new. But since it was very unlikely she'd ever get close enough to any man to share her secret with, she had to accept that she'd never get her happy ending. Even worse was that she didn't *want* another man. Ross had been everything she ever dreamed of, and now that she knew how he'd really felt when they broke up and had a better understanding of why he'd gone out with so many women, she was even more certain that no other man could take his place.

Valentine's Day was a bitter reminder that she was destined to be alone, so for once, Clemmie didn't sigh and complain when Dolly took down the romantic trimmings.

'That's that done,' Dolly said, folding up the bunting with satisfaction. 'Mind, I can't moan. Sold quite a few romance novels yesterday, and some expensive volumes of love poetry too. It was quite busy in here, despite it being market day, when that bloody second-hand book stall usually steals all my business. It served its purpose.'

'I don't think the purpose of Valentine's Day is to sell things,' Clemmie said sourly.

'Don't kid yourself, love. What other purpose is there? You think lovers need a special day to tell each other they're in love? If they do, they're doing something wrong if you ask me.'

'You're such a cynic.'

'And you're a romantic.' Dolly patted her on the shoulder. 'And that's what we love about you. Wouldn't have you any other way.'

'Hmm.' As Clemmie carried the stepladder into the kitchen, she wished she could be more like her aunt. Dolly was so content with her life, finding fulfilment in her work and social life, and not having the slightest need for a partner. Maybe, she thought, you *can* get by without romance. If she was doomed to be alone forever, at least she had a great role model to aspire to.

There was a steady stream of customers that morning, which was encouraging. What was left of the snow had turned to slush and although it was still cold people were out and about as usual.

Clemmie and Dolly took advantage of a lull at around two o'clock to finally eat their packed lunches.

'I'm not sure about this packed lunch lark,' Dolly said gloomily. 'Ham sandwiches and a KitKat each—not exactly inspiring. Why don't you make us some of that minestrone soup tonight? We can bring a flask of that tomorrow, and some rolls. Warm us up good and proper too.'

Clemmie shrugged. 'Maybe. If I can be bothered.'

Minestrone soup. How could something so ordinary stir up so many unwanted emotions in her? Was she ever going to put bloody Ross Lavender out of her head?

Dolly eyed her worriedly. 'You're not yourself, love. Ever since you got snowed in with miladdo you've been acting proper weird. Are you sure nothing happened? Nothing I should know about, any rate.'

'Like what?' Clemmie peeled the wrapper off her KitKat, deliberately not looking at her aunt. 'I told you everything that went on. We cooked, we ate, we watched films, he sketched. End of.'

'If there is something, you can tell me you know. I won't judge.' Dolly put her hand over Clemmie's. 'Look, love, I know it must have been hard for you, being on your own with him all that time. You don't have to pretend to me. I know you still have feelings for him. I've always known. But look, it's never too late. If you want it to work out with Ross there's still time to do something about it. Why don't you give him a chance? Tell him about the alopecia. What harm can it do? At worst he'll decide it's too much, but if he does you're no worse off than you are. My betting is, though, that he won't mind at all. What you've got to understand is that there's so much more to you than that. You've forgotten how beautiful, funny, kind, and damn lovely you really are. Somewhere, the real Clemmie's got buried in all this insecurity and self-doubt. You don't see what I see, but I'll bet you any money that Ross will. He loved you to bits, he really did, and from what I've seen he's still got feelings for you. Just think about it, eh?'

She hadn't told Dolly about Ross discovering her wig. It was all too painful to go over again. 'I've told you what happened. Ross and I talked this over and agreed we'd be friends. And that's something, isn't it? Talking again after all this time? But we don't want anything more than that, so can you please just leave it?'

Dolly sighed. 'Yeah, yeah. Whatever you say. Ooh, 'ey up! Visitor incoming.'

The bell above the door jangled and in walked Clive Browning.

'Well,' Dolly said, giving him a warm smile, 'not often we see you in here. Are you looking for anything in particular?'

'I am actually,' Clive said, smiling back. 'Something very special. I don't suppose you have such a thing as a copy of *Black Beauty*? It's for Joseph.'

Clemmie and Dolly exchanged glances.

'Aw, how is he?' Dolly asked, tilting her head to one side in sympathy.

'Well, you know Joseph. Stubborn as a mule and insisting he's perfectly all right.' Clive sighed. 'I'm just glad the community palliative care nurse managed to get through to see him while the weather was bad. I've, er, moved into Whispering Willows. Did Summer tell you?' he asked, nodding at Clemmie.

'No, I haven't seen her for a couple of days,' Clemmie said. 'Why have you moved there?' Her face crumpled. 'Is he that bad?'

'Well, he's not good. The nurse has increased his long-acting painkiller. I offered for him to stay with me at Stepping Stones, but he insisted he wanted to stay in his own home, so I told him if that was the case I was going to move in there whether he liked it or not.'

'That's quite a big decision,' Dolly said. Although she didn't add to her statement, Clemmie was pretty sure she knew what Dolly was thinking. Stepping Stones was a beautiful old house, and although the downstairs was given over to the veterinary surgery, everyone knew that the upstairs was a spacious apartment that was modern, clean, and beautifully decorated.

Whispering Willows, on the other hand, was a crumbling wreck of a house that hadn't been modernised in decades. Clemmie thought Joseph would have been much better off at Clive's, although the sentimental side of her could understand why he wished to remain at his own home.

'It's the least I can do,' Clive said. 'Summer's carrying most of the burden of keeping the sanctuary going—although we're very grateful to Reuben for helping while he's here, and of course we've got our teenage volunteers at the weekend. I'm very much afraid that Ben's going to be doing extra hours at the surgery soon, and I'll have to take on a locum. I can't be over at Stepping Stones when Joseph needs me with him.'

'No. I guess not,' Dolly said soberly. 'It's awful, all this. I'm so sorry, Clive. I know you and Joseph are such good mates. I can't imagine...'

'Aye well.' Clive straightened as if suddenly determined not to get too low about things. 'So, *Black Beauty*.'

Dolly brightened, back on familiar territory, and Clemmie shared her relief that the subject had been changed. She felt terrible for Clive, and was heartbroken for Joseph, but it was so difficult to know what to say. How much sympathy was too much? Were kind words and commiserations helpful, or did they make the recipient feel worse? She wasn't sure, and it made her uncomfortable, which in turn made her feel guilty.

'I think,' she said, 'we have a couple of different editions in the children's section in the back. Although,' she added, frowning, 'surely Joseph will have read *Black Beauty* before? It's a classic, and a horse lover like him must be familiar with it.'

'Oh, he's read it all right,' Clive said. 'He was talking about it yesterday. How it was his favourite book when he was a kid. It was what inspired him to start Whispering Willows in fact. He used to have his own illustrated edition which he cherished, but when he got a bit older he gave it to Bethany, and she never gave it back apparently. I thought I'd treat him. While he's taking it easy indoors it will give him something to read.'

'That's lovely of you,' Dolly said, beaming at him. 'I'll see if we've got an illustrated edition.'

'Who's Bethany? Was she Joseph's little sister?' Clemmie queried, as Dolly hurried into the children's section to check the stock.

'Aye, that's right.' Clive wrinkled his nose. 'Well, I say little. Obviously she's a grown woman now. She'll be a couple of years younger than me, I reckon.'

'As old as that!' Clemmie said mischievously.

Clive laughed. 'Cheeky! I'm only fifty-six you know. I'm in my prime.'

'If you say so.' Clemmie's heart lifted to see the twinkle in the Scotsman's eye again. She was glad she'd been able to raise his spirits, even if only momentarily. 'So where is this Bethany now? Is she coming home to visit Joseph?'

She wished she hadn't asked the question as the light dimmed in Clive's eyes.

'Unfortunately I have no idea how to get in touch with her. She and Joseph lost contact after she left Tuppenny Bridge, and he hasn't seen or heard from her since. It's a shame. He rarely mentions her, but I know he'd love to see her before...'

His voice trailed off and they stared at each other in awkward silence. Clemmie offered up a silent prayer of thanks as Dolly returned, carrying two books in her hand.

'Right, love, these are the two we've got in stock. One paperback and one illustrated hardback.' She handed both over to him to check out. 'Obviously that's a bit more expensive,' she said, nodding at the hardback. 'Well,' she added, 'to be honest, it's a *lot* more expensive, so it's up to you.'

Clive flicked through both books. 'The illustrated hardback,' he said. 'The drawings are beautiful, and I think maybe it will remind him of his old childhood edition. Besides, the print's a lot easier to read. That paperback's font is too small. Joseph might struggle.'

'Good call if you don't mind me saying so. Would you like it gift wrapping?'

'No, there's no need for that. Just a paper bag will do fine,' Clive assured her.

Dolly obliged and handed it over. 'No, put that away,' she said, as Clive took out his wallet. 'This is on me and Clemmie.'

'Oh no, I couldn't!'

'You bloody well could,' Dolly insisted. 'It's the least we can do for Joseph. Give it to him with our love.'

'That's so kind,' Clive said, sounding emotional.

'Get away with you.' Dolly sounded pretty choked up too. 'It's just a book. We're not giving him a winning lottery ticket.'

'Thank you. Both of you.' Clive took a deep breath. 'Oh well, better get back there then.'

'Must be hard for you, seeing him like that,' Clemmie said sadly.

'Aye, it is, I'll not deny it. But life goes on, doesn't it? We've all just got to get on with it and find our joy where we can. Speaking of which...' He smiled again which gladdened Clemmie's heart. 'Have you heard the Lavender Ladies have got a new bet running?'

Clemmie and Dolly exchanged amused glances.

'Uh-oh,' Dolly said, laughing, 'which poor bugger's the talk of the town today?'

'Ross Lavender!'

Clemmie's stomach plummeted. Ross! What were the Lavender Ladies saying about him? Surely this wasn't anything to do with her, and the fact that he'd stayed at Wintergreen recently?

'Ross?' Dolly said, risking a quick peek at Clemmie. 'What's he been up to?'

Clive shook his head. 'Who knows? Now, I say the Lavender Ladies are taking bets, but really it's Rita and Birdie. They're keeping it very quiet from Eugenie, because of course, can you imagine her indignation if she found out that a member of her own family was the subject of gossip?' He laughed. 'God forbid! Anyway, apparently he's got a new girlfriend. Oh, I know, I know. What's new about that, eh?' He winked. 'But shock horror, hold the front page. He's been on a third date with her. I know! Imagine that.'

He threw back his head and guffawed, clearly finding it all very amusing.

'Oh, those two Pennyfeather sisters kill me,' he said. 'I mean, three dates and they've practically got him engaged. Mind, I suppose it is unusual for him. Never seen with someone more than twice, is he? And to take her out on Valentine's Day —well, he was asking for it.'

'Who is this miracle woman?' Dolly said, obviously not finding the subject funny at all.

'Meg,' Clemmie said dully. 'Her name's Meg.'

Clive glanced at her. 'Aye, that's right. You've heard about her then? She's his interior designer apparently. Nudge nudge, wink wink. Ah well, it's about time he settled down. He must be thirty-ish now.'

'You're a fine one to talk!' Dolly said, tapping him on the arm. 'You still haven't settled down and you're pushing sixty.'

'Aye well, I think we can all agree I'm a different kettle of fish to Ross Lavender,' he said ruefully. 'Anyway, I'd better get off. Thanks again for the book. It's a very kind gesture and I'll be sure to send Joseph your love and best wishes.'

'You do that,' Dolly said, following him to the door. 'Take care now, Clive.'

As the door closed behind him she turned back to Clemmie. 'You okay, love?'

Clemmie nodded. 'Why shouldn't I be? I told you; Ross and I are just friends. Whatever we had before, it's all in the past.'

'Well, if you're sure. I'm glad it hasn't upset you at any rate. Now, I'd best get on with tidying them shelves upstairs.'

She headed for the staircase, and Clemmie slumped against the counter, feeling sick.

This was her own fault, she reminded herself. It was what she'd wanted, wasn't it? She'd been the one who ended it with him the first time round, and it was she who'd turned him down when he'd asked for a second chance. This was all her own doing. She didn't deserve any sympathy, and if Ross was starting his own clean page with someone new then good for him. She hoped he would be happy.

It was something she knew for certain that she would never be.

## THIRTY-FOUR

Clemmie couldn't hide her shock from Summer, as much as she tried to. After leaving the house at Whispering Willows, she'd crossed the stable yard and gone to the donkeys' paddock, where her friend was filling up the hay nets in the shelter, and it took all her strength not to burst into tears as she joined her.

Summer took one look at her and put her arms around her.

'I did warn you,' she murmured.

'I know, I know. I just never imagined...'

It had been hard to act normal around Joseph when she'd seen him lying on the sofa in his living room, looking so ill, frail, and thin that it broke her heart to look at him. He'd always been lean and wiry, for as long as she'd known him, but he'd had a healthy bloom to him that came from working outdoors most of the time. Now, his face had taken on a sickly yellow hue, and his kindly blue eyes looked enormous in his shrunken face.

'Look who's come to visit,' Clive had said, his tone deliberately light and cheery as he shot Clemmie a look that warned her not to show how distressed she was feeling.

Joseph had smiled at her, his teeth looking too big for his mouth somehow.

'Clemmie Grant,' he said, his voice hoarse. 'I'm glad you came, young 'un. I wanted to say thank you.'

Clemmie could barely get the words out. 'Thank you? For what?'

'For helping Summer before we got our volunteers,' he said. 'Can't have bin easy for you. I know you've never been mad keen on horses, and that's putting it mildly.' He managed another grin, and Clemmie blinked away tears.

'That,' she said jokingly, 'is the understatement of the year. I'm flipping terrified of them! What you see in them is beyond me.'

'Ah. They're everything, lass. Everything.' Joseph's eyes glazed over as he seemed to lose himself in dreams of all things equine. Perhaps, Clemmie thought suddenly, he was reliving memories of his youth, when he'd been an accomplished horseman.

Dolly had told her that Whispering Willows had once been a grand country house, and the Wilkinsons had employed many servants. Joseph's grandparents had been super wealthy and passionate about horses. His grandfather had been a Master of Hounds with the local hunt, which Clemmie thoroughly disapproved of, but tried to make allowances for because, after all, that was the olden days before people knew any better.

Joseph had inherited his grandfather's love for horses and had dedicated most of his adult life to their care. Those days were long gone. Whispering Willows was in a state of disrepair; it was believed that Joseph had spent the entire family fortune on looking after his rescued animals, and now he himself was beyond saving. It was a sad end to what had once been a glorious story.

'Clemmie's brought you a present,' Clive said gently, and Joseph had returned to them—although he seemed to do so only with great reluctance.

Clemmie had handed him a copy of a book called *Moorland Mousie* by Golden Gorse.

'I found this on the second-hand book stall,' she told him. 'Don't tell Dolly, whatever you do. It's about an Exmoor pony. It reminded me of Barney,' she explained, referring to the little Exmoor pony she'd met while volunteering at the stables. Summer had told her that poor Barney suffered terribly from a condition called sweet itch, which meant he had to wear a protective coat and hood from early spring until October every year, and he'd won a place in her heart immediately.

'*Moorland Mousie!*' Joseph took the book from her with trembling hands. 'By heck, that takes me back. I read this when I were a lad. Did you know,' he asked, sounding suddenly stronger as he eyed her with interest, 'a trust was set up that was named after these books? It's a smashing charity, all about the welfare of Exmoor ponies, just like our Barney.'

He leaned back against the cushion, seeming drained after his sudden burst of energy. 'Thank you, lass. I'll have a read of this later. It'll take me right back...'

Clemmie glanced nervously at Clive as Joseph's eyes closed. Clive gave her a reassuring smile and they left the living room.

'Thanks for that, Clemmie. He loved reading *Black Beauty*, so I reckon he'll enjoy that.' He sighed, his eyes shimmering with tears. 'When it gets to this stage, it's all about memories I reckon. Happy, childhood memories. And for Joseph that's all about horses. Well, not quite all...'

'Bethany?'

'Aye. I need to find her. She should know that her brother hasn't got long left. Trouble is, I don't want to get his hopes up if I can't track her down, or she doesn't want to come back.'

'But surely, if she knew he was dying she'd want to be here?'

Clive shrugged. 'Who knows? Whatever went on between them it was obviously huge, because why else would they have been estranged all these years? Even so, I've got to do something. I'll do some digging around. See what I can find out.'

Clemmie glanced towards the slightly open door of the living room and blinked away her own tears. Seeing Clive visibly upset had moved her. He was usually so cool and in control of his emotions. She supposed, being a vet, you had to develop a certain detachment to sad situations. But Joseph was his best friend, and Clive was struggling, even though he was doing his best not to show it. Her heart broke for both of them.

'I didn't expect...'

She didn't know how to finish that sentence and stared at him in dumb misery.

He patted her shoulder. 'Aye, I know. I know. Hey, do me a favour. Go and ask Summer and Reuben if they want a bacon sandwich. I'm just about to fry some up.'

Now, standing with Summer in the donkey shelter, Clemmie gave way to the tears she'd tried so hard to hold back.

'I'm sorry,' she gasped, as Summer held her and comforted her. 'It should be me comforting you! I don't know how you do it every day. I didn't realise he was so ill, which is stupid because obviously I knew it really. But knowing it and seeing it for yourself are two different things.'

'I know,' Summer said soothingly. 'I've had a bit more time to adjust, Clem, remember? I was worse than you to start with. I didn't even know if I could bear to see him every day. But the good thing—or the awful thing—is that you quickly get used to it. Now it's just about focusing on the practical things: making sure he's not in pain, which is down to the doctor and his palliative care nurse; that he's being physically looked after, which is mostly down to Clive; and that his mind's at rest over the horses. That's down to me. It's all I can do really, but it's important. If he's confident our animals are being well looked after it's one less thing for him to worry about.'

Clemmie pulled away, nodding. She knew Summer was

right. Focusing on the practical things was the only option Joseph's friends had left.

She looked up as Reuben joined them, having just crossed the paddock after doing some repairs to the gate in the adjoining field. He raised an eyebrow on seeing her tearful face, and Clemmie sniffed, embarrassed.

'She's just seen Joseph for the first time in a while,' Summer said briefly.

Reuben's face creased with sympathy. 'I'm sorry. I expect it was quite a shock.'

Clemmie gave a brief laugh. 'You could say that.'

'I know,' he said quietly. 'It's a horrible situation for everyone.'

She remembered that Reuben had lost his mother to cancer, and that he'd already been through this not so long ago. It must be bringing back awful memories for him.

'Clive's making bacon sandwiches,' she said, trying to sound more positive. 'Would you like one?'

Reuben glanced at his watch. 'Not for me, thanks,' he said. 'Jonah will be here soon. There are a couple of horses that need their feet trimming, so I'm going to wash their legs and clean out their hooves before he arrives. Will you be okay, Clemmie?'

She nodded, embarrassed that she'd been so emotional when it must be far harder for the two of them. Reuben was, after all, still grieving for his mum, and Summer was devoted to Joseph. 'I'm fine now. Sorry.' She hooked her arm through Summer's. 'Come on, let's go and get that bacon sarnie.'

'He's so good,' Summer said, as they left Reuben to deal with the two horses who were about to have their hooves trimmed. 'I don't know how I'd manage without him.'

'Clive's going to try to track down Bethany,' Clemmie told her as they headed back towards the house.

'Is he?' Summer's eyes widened. 'How? I don't think even Joseph knows where she is.'

'I don't know, but he's determined to try. I'm sure she'd want to be here for him, aren't you? No one can hold a grudge against their own brother when he's dying, surely? I can't imagine anyone holding a grudge against Joseph full stop. He's such a lovely man.'

They entered the kitchen, noses twitching at the delicious smell of bacon, and Summer washed her hands, explaining to Clive why Reuben wouldn't be joining them, then they sat down at the table as he handed them plates of sandwiches.

'Joseph's fast asleep,' he said quietly. 'Looks very peaceful.'

'I've been thinking,' Summer said suddenly. 'Something Clemmie just said about not being able to imagine anyone holding a grudge against Joseph rang a bell with me.'

'Oh?' Clive managed, through a mouthful of bacon sandwich. 'In what way?'

'Miss Lavender!' Summer leaned towards him, her face eager. 'We had tea with her once, and it sort of came out that she and Joseph don't get on. She wouldn't be drawn on why, but I got the feeling it was something from ages ago. I mean, it might not be connected at all, but she's been around forever, and she must have known Bethany. If anyone would know what went on it would be her.'

'You're right,' Clive said, sounding delighted. 'I don't know why I didn't think of her before.' He pushed his plate away. 'You couldn't stay here and keep an eye on Joseph, could you? I need to pop to Lavender House.'

'What, now?' Summer asked, surprised.

'No time like the present. Is that okay?'

Summer hesitated then nodded. 'Yeah, fine. Off you go.'

Clive squeezed her shoulder, grabbed one of his sandwiches, and hurried out, leaving Clemmie and Summer staring at each other in bemusement.

'Well, he couldn't wait, could he?' Clemmie said.

'I think he needed to get out of here for a while,' Summer

said sadly. 'It's all a bit much for him, and everyone needs a break. Plus, Clive's the sort of man who needs to be doing something, to feel useful. Just sitting around feeling helpless must be a nightmare for him. Let's hope Miss Lavender can offer up some information.'

'Hmm. I'm not hopeful though, are you?' Clemmie chewed her bacon sandwich, thinking it was delicious, though she really shouldn't be eating it as she had her packed lunch back at the bookshop.

'Not really.' Summer sighed. 'So how are things with you? And don't just say they're fine because I won't believe you.' She paused until Clemmie had swallowed her food. 'I heard about the bet the Pennyfeathers are running on Ross. I wanted to ring you to see if you were okay, but it's been so full on here I didn't get round to it. I'm sorry.'

'I'm glad for him,' Clemmie said immediately. 'If this Meg woman makes him happy, then good. He deserves happiness.'

'That's quite a turnaround from you,' Summer said slowly. 'Not so long ago you hated him and blamed him for everything. What's happened to change your mind?'

'I guess when you're snowed in with someone for a few days, you finally get to talk,' Clemmie said truthfully. 'Maybe you start to see things from their point of view. Maybe you realise that not everything is as black and white as you supposed.'

'Okay, that sounds deep. Hang on.' Summer got up and walked quietly to the living room door. She peered into the room and then closed the door softly behind her. 'Still fast asleep,' she said with a fond smile. 'Right, let's unpack this, shall we?'

She sat down at the table and rested her chin in her hands, fixing Clemmie with a stern gaze. 'Go on, spill. What really happened when you were snowed in with Mr-Wonderful-formerly-known-as-Mr-Evil?'

# THIRTY-FIVE

'Don't be daft!' Clemmie gave a nervous laugh. 'He was never either of those things.'

'Really? Let me refresh your memory. You let me think for months that Ross had cheated on you and behaved really badly when you were together and made me believe he'd dropped you like a stone when something better came along. Now you're saying you don't mind that he's got a new girlfriend who he appears to be serious about, and you wish him every happiness. Something doesn't add up. You couldn't even bear the thought of him painting your portrait not long ago, so what happened? Please don't say nothing happened, because I won't believe you, and I might just have to torture you until you spill the beans.'

Clemmie swallowed. 'I suppose... Look, we just had time to talk it all out, that's all. I've already confessed that it was me who broke up with him, so really if anyone had the right to be awkward and difficult while we were snowed in together, it was him. But he wasn't. He was actually really lovely.'

Summer's eyebrows shot up. 'He was? In what way?'

'He cooked for us, he drew me, we watched films together,

we chatted and...' She broke off, a fond smile playing on her lips as she remembered, 'he was so lovely to Mr Francis.'

'Who the heck's Mr Francis?'

'He lives up the lane from us. He's quite elderly and lives alone. When we realised how deep the snow was, Ross asked if there was anyone who might need help and I remembered Mr Francis, so we packed up some food and trudged through the snow to check on him. Ross was really kind and friendly to him, and he went back to see him the next day with more supplies and cleared his path for him.'

'He did?' Summer sounded incredulous. 'I wouldn't have had Ross Lavender down as the altruistic sort.'

'That's the thing,' Clemmie said sadly. 'Maybe I'd forgotten what he was really like. How kind he actually is. I've built this narrative around him all these years, cast him as the antagonist in the story, when really he was always the hero. I think I knew that, deep down, I just couldn't bring myself to face up to what I'd lost.'

Summer looked baffled as she sat back in her chair. She blew out her cheeks as she tried to make sense of what Clemmie had just said. Eventually, she shook her head.

'I'm sorry, Clem, but I still don't get it. If Ross is the sort of person you're now saying he is, why the heck did you break up with him in the first place? Especially given that you've just said you always knew deep down what he was really like. I know you denied it, but I can't help thinking I was right first time. That it was some sort of test on him which he failed because he wasn't romantic enough. And if that's the case—well, you want your head read if you ask me.'

'He *is* romantic in his way,' Clemmie admitted sadly. 'He asked me if we could get back together. Give it another try.'

'He did what?' Summer's eyes were like saucers. 'Bloody hell, this is huge!' She frowned suddenly. 'So, hang on, why is he now with this other woman and not you? You surely didn't turn him down?' She paused then gasped, 'You *did* turn him down! Are you mad?'

'It's not that simple,' Clemmie protested. 'You really don't understand.'

'Then why don't you explain?' Summer said, clearly frustrated. 'Do you still love Ross Lavender or not?'

Clemmie bit her lip and stared at Summer miserably.

'Oh my God,' Summer breathed. 'You do!'

'Please don't,' Clemmie said. 'I don't want to talk about this any more.'

'But, Clem, you have to! Don't you see? Ross has been out on three dates with this Meg McKenna woman. He never dates a woman more than twice. This could get serious if you don't do something to stop it.'

'I'm glad he's dating her,' Clemmie said determinedly. 'He deserves every happiness. All these years he's been hoping that we'd get back together, and it prevented him from starting a new relationship with someone else. Someone who deserved him. But when I finally told him there was no going back for us—well, he's accepted it at last. He can move on. He's obviously decided Meg's the one for him, and I hope they make it work. I really do.'

Clemmie's face crumpled and she buried her face in her hands as she began to sob. Where had this come from? She'd honestly thought she had her feelings under control, and she had no right to cry about what had happened. It had been her doing. Summer would think she'd completely lost the plot.

After a few moments, she heard Summer's chair scrape back, then a piece of kitchen paper was pushed into her hand.

'Here,' Summer said kindly. 'Dry your eyes and talk to me.'

Reluctantly, Clemmie wiped her tears away and faced her friend with as much dignity as she could muster.

'There's something more to this than you're telling me,'

Summer said firmly. 'There has to be. It makes no sense otherwise.'

'We're not the same people we used to be,' Clemmie said, feeling broken as she uttered the words. 'I'm—different. And Ross has had all those women since. We can't go back. It's ruined.'

'I'm sorry?'

'You wouldn't understand,' Clemmie said wretchedly. 'I'm not being rude, Summer, but your mum and dad hardly had the perfect marriage, did they? You can't imagine what it's like to grow up with the perfect example of true love before your eyes. My parents were so wonderful together. They adored each other. That's what true love is. That's what I want.'

'So why can't you have it with Ross?'

'I've just told you! Because our relationship has been spoiled—by me. We can't go back.'

'Who asked you to go back?' Summer said, puzzled. 'Surely the whole point would be that you'd go forward? Not to your old relationship, but to a new one. A better one.'

Clemmie blinked. 'Sorry?'

'Well, you're so adamant that your old relationship with Ross is ruined and you can't go back to it, but why does that stop the two of you starting again? A clean page.'

A clean page. How wonderful that sounded. If only.

She shook her head. 'It would never work.'

'But why not?' Summer said, exasperated.

But how could Clemmie explain? She stared at her friend, wishing she could tell her everything, but too afraid to take the risk. What if Summer looked at her differently after that? What if she didn't want to be best friends with her any longer?

What if she *pitied* her?

Maybe even worse, what if she made light of it? Told her it was no big deal. Made jokes about it saving her a fortune in shampoo?

A few months after it had first happened, Clemmie had been persuaded by a specialist and a well-meaning Dolly to attend counselling sessions with a handful of other alopecia sufferers.

She'd sat and listened as they related tales of how their friends and family had reacted to their condition. There seemed to be few hair jokes and puns they hadn't heard. Some of them rolled their eyes good-humouredly, while others actually laughed out loud. Clemmie hadn't seen what was so funny. She'd felt sick with fear, and it had made her even more determined that no one should ever find out what had happened to her.

Summer's gaze was intense. 'I swear if you don't explain, you and I are going to fall out,' she said. 'This is like trying to solve a murder mystery, and my *leetle grey cells* aren't sharp enough to work out the clues. Help me out here, Clemmie.'

Clemmie closed her eyes. Could she really do this? But maybe if she didn't, she could never truly say that she and Summer were best friends, because all the time she was keeping the biggest secret of all from her there would always be a barrier between them, even if Summer wasn't aware of it. If it changed things between them—well, that would be horrible, but at least it would be honest. Maybe it was better to know.

'There's something I haven't told you,' she said, trying desperately to keep the emotion from her voice. 'Something about me, and the real reason I broke up with Ross.'

'At last!' Summer took hold of her hand. 'Don't look so scared. It can't be that bad!'

'It started just over six years ago,' Clemmie said, her voice faltering. 'Please, don't interrupt. Just let me tell you and get it over with.'

Trying to stay detached, she briefly explained to Summer what had happened all those years ago while Ross was away in the Netherlands with his mother. As she relived the despair and anxiety she'd felt at the time, though, her voice became shaky, and her hand—still in Summer's—began to tremble.

She didn't leave anything out. She confessed how she'd panicked when she saw Ross at the airport with Hendrik's daughter. How she'd assumed the worst because of her own insecurities. How she'd broken up with him before he could break up with her. How hurt he'd been. How confused and heartbroken she'd felt at the time. She explained about the talk she and Ross had had at Wintergreen recently, and how he'd begged her to believe that her alopecia made no difference to him. That he still loved her and wanted to try again. She even told Summer what he'd said about his reasons for not putting up a fight for her, and why he'd dated those other women.

When she finally finished, she felt sick with apprehension, and couldn't look her friend in the face.

There was a long silence. It seemed to stretch on forever, and eventually Clemmie couldn't stand it any longer. She raised her gaze to Summer and her heart contracted as she saw the tears streaming down her friend's face.

'Oh, Summer, don't cry!' she said, aware that she was crying herself, so it was a bit hypocritical of her. 'I never meant to upset you.'

'Upset me?' Summer half-laughed, wiping her face on her sleeve. 'Oh, Clem, I'm so sorry. I'm so, so sorry. This must have been a nightmare for you, and you've carried it with you all this time.'

She gripped Clemmie's hand tighter as fresh tears spilled onto her cheeks.

'It's okay,' Clemmie said, overwhelmed at how badly this was affecting her friend. She'd never thought, never imagined that Summer would care so much.

'I'm just so sad,' Summer admitted. 'For you and for Ross. All that love, all that potential, all thrown away. Oh, Clem, you deserve so much more than this. You both do.'

She got to her feet and put her arms around Clemmie, squeezing her tightly.

'Thank you for telling me,' she said. 'It must have taken so much courage to do that.'

Clemmie's own face was wet with tears as Summer sat down again and took her hand once more.

'It did,' she admitted. 'I wasn't sure how you'd react.'

'I get that,' Summer said. She swiped her tears away again and gave Clemmie's wig an admiring nod. 'It's ever so good. I'd never have guessed.'

'I'm not taking it off!' Clemmie said, panicked.

'Oh, Clem! I would never, ever ask you to do that,' Summer promised. 'If you don't want people to know about it then that's your choice. Nobody else's business. I'm just so honoured you felt able to share that with me.'

'I thought you'd tell me it was no big deal,' Clemmie admitted.

'But it is a big deal, isn't it?' Summer said reasonably. 'I can't imagine how distraught you must have felt.' She got up and tore two sheets of kitchen paper from the roll on the worktop. Handing a sheet to Clemmie, she sat back down and wiped her nose with the other. 'Heck, I'm a blubbering mess. I just want to hug you and hug you and never let you go.'

'But when you look at what Joseph's going through,' Clemmie said, bitterly ashamed, 'it hardly matters, does it?'

'It matters to *you*. What Joseph's going through doesn't make your feelings invalid. It's something that affects you deeply, every single day. That's important. Don't feel guilty because you're still feeling that shock and pain, Clemmie. I get it, okay? I think you're amazing.'

Clemmie could hardly see Summer for her tears. 'Thank you,' she murmured. 'I don't really know what to say.'

'You don't have to say anything,' Summer said. 'Except... Well, this thing with Ross. If he says it doesn't make any difference to him, why can't you take him at his word, like you've taken me at mine? He doesn't strike me as someone who'd stick around out of guilt. He clearly has deep feelings for you, so why not give him the benefit of a doubt?'

'But you've seen him!' Clemmie said desperately. 'He's gorgeous, Summer! And look how many women flock around him. Why would he be with someone like me?'

'Because he loves you?'

'I'm just a daydreamer,' Clemmie said sadly. 'Someone with my head in the clouds. Have you seen Meg McKenna? She was in Pennyfeather's the other day. I saw her coming out of the shop. She's so elegant and polished and perfect.'

'But Ross wanted you back,' Summer reminded her. 'I don't think Meg McKenna is his type.'

'How do you know?'

'Because *you're* his type, obviously, you numpty!' Summer spluttered with laughter and hurriedly mopped her face again with the kitchen paper. 'Oh, Clem. You need to have more confidence in yourself. I understand now why you're always so down on yourself, but honestly, you have no reason to be. You're beautiful, you really are, inside and out. Ross would be lucky to have you. So what are you going to do about it?'

Clemmie twisted her kitchen paper into a tight roll. 'Nothing. He's made his decision and I'm not going to ruin his life all over again. I can't do that to him. I'd only mess up somehow, and it would all be spoiled once more, and then what? How many new pages can you turn over? No.' She shook her head decisively. 'It's best left in the past. I just want him to be happy, and if there's a chance he's going to make it with Meg then I'm not getting in the way of that.'

Their bacon sandwiches had gone cold. She pushed back her chair and stood, feeling exhausted. 'Time I went back to work. Dolly will be fuming with me. I said I'd only be half an hour.'

'Are you sure about this, Clem?' Summer asked sadly. 'Really truly certain?'

'Absolutely positive,' Clemmie said.

They hugged, and Clemmie felt that their friendship had just moved to a new, deeper stage. She'd trusted Summer with her greatest secret, and Summer hadn't let her down. She would never forget that.

She might not have any hope of a romantic relationship in the future, but she had a true friend for life. It was time to put Ross behind her and count her blessings.

# THIRTY-SIX

Ross strode purposefully through the main gallery at Lavender House. In his hand he carried the brochures for the kitchen he was having fitted in his own quarters at Monk's Folly, as well as a list of some local artists who were interested in selling their work in the academy's shop. He knew better than to visit his Aunt Eugenie without some evidence of progress.

Nodding politely at some of the female visitors to the museum, who were eyeing him with some interest, he headed down a corridor, unlocked a door marked private, and made his way to the living quarters at the back of the house. He knocked briefly on the door of his aunt's flat. She always insisted that he had no need to knock, just because he no longer lived there, but he felt it was only courteous to do so.

'Come in!' she called from within.

He pushed open the door, walked down the hallway and entered the living room with a smile on his face.

His aunt beamed at him. 'What perfect timing! Ross, this is Reuben Walker.'

Ross nearly walked straight back out again. Only his pride made him straighten and face the loathed interloper squarely.

'Ross, pleased to meet you. I've heard a lot about you,' Reuben said, smiling widely and holding out his hand.

Ross took it tentatively. 'Who from?' he asked tersely, making sure their handshake was as brief as possible.

Reuben looked puzzled. 'From your aunt, of course. She's told me all about what you're doing at Monk's Folly. It's impressive. I'm sure I can be of help to you.'

Ross stared at him, then looked to his aunt for an explanation.

'Reuben is a website designer,' she explained. 'Just what we need. He comes highly recommended by Dolly Bennett—he's done an amazing site for her recently. You can check it out for yourself. The academy needs a good website, Ross. The one-page effort we have now simply won't cut the mustard. Time to start showcasing what we're offering, don't you think?'

He did think. In fact, he'd been mulling over the website problem for a while now, but just hadn't had the time to do anything about it. Of course he'd remembered that Reuben was in that line of work but hadn't dreamed of getting in touch with him. The last thing he wanted was contact with this man who seemed to have manoeuvred his way into Clemmie's affections.

He surveyed his nemesis with curiosity. Now that he thought about it, the man did seem vaguely familiar. Clemmie had said they'd crossed at the door of The Corner Cottage Bookshop, but Ross hadn't really taken much notice. He wasn't surprised by that. What exactly did she see in him? He was good-looking enough, he supposed, if you liked that bland sort of appearance. Fair hair, blue eyes, average height. All very nice in a tick-the-box sort of way. Personally, he couldn't see the attraction. Surely he was no real threat? No matter how he tried, he couldn't see Reuben and Clemmie as a couple.

'So you'll explain to Reuben exactly what it is we're after,' his aunt said. It wasn't a question. 'We're running out of time.

You'll be able to get us up and running quickly?' she asked Reuben.

'As soon as I know what you want I'll get started on it,' he assured her.

'And we have a deal over the rate?'

'We do indeed.'

'Excellent. I'll make tea and sandwiches while you two discuss what we need on the website,' she said, beaming at them both. 'We should have this sorted in no time.'

As she hurried from the living room, Reuben grinned at him. 'Knows what she wants, doesn't she?'

Ross couldn't deny it. 'She's, er, very clear-sighted,' he said diplomatically.

Reuben laughed and patted Boycott, who'd trotted over to investigate him more closely. 'Sorry, boy. I haven't got any treats on me.'

'It's a good job,' Ross said grudgingly. 'He's thoroughly spoilt. They both are.' He glanced over at Trueman who was snoring on the rug. 'It's a wonder they've got any teeth left.'

Reuben chuckled and ruffled Boycott's ears. 'Poor lad. Too many biscuits, eh? Well, we all struggle with that one.'

Ross had to admit Reuben had a way with him. As they discussed the website he came across as being extremely professional and also very friendly. In other circumstances he might have warmed to him. But these weren't other circumstances, and he couldn't help but see Reuben as the enemy, no matter how charming and accommodating he was.

'I don't think this will be a problem,' Reuben told him. 'Shouldn't take me long at all, and we'll have people queueing up to enrol in your classes before you know it.'

As much as it galled Ross to say it, he suspected it would be excellent. Even so, he wished his aunt hadn't dragged Reuben Walker into all this. He was the last person Ross wanted to be beholden to.

After Reuben left, full of enthusiasm and evidently unaware of Ross's less than generous thoughts towards him, Ross briefly filled his aunt in with progress at the academy.

'It's all coming on very nicely,' she said. 'And how is Meg?'

He sighed inwardly. 'She's fine. I expect she's looking forward to getting the place finished so she can head home. She's got lots more work lined up anyway.'

His aunt didn't even try to hide her disappointment. 'Oh, really? I had hoped...'

'She's good at her job, Aunt Eugenie,' he said kindly. 'But I'm afraid that's all there is to it.'

She rolled her eyes. 'Oh well, it was worth a try. I expect I'm going to have to resign myself to the fact that you're always going to play the field rather than settle down.'

He bit his lip, wondering if she was comparing him with his feckless parents. It hardly seemed fair if she was, but he didn't want to get into a discussion about that, so he said nothing further on the subject. Instead they chatted about the academy for a while, and she told him that Clive had visited, asking for information about Bethany Wilkinson, Joseph's sister.

'I couldn't be of much use to him,' she remarked, 'but hopefully there was enough for him to start with.'

After half an hour Ross kissed her goodbye and headed home. Funny how he was already thinking of Monk's Folly as home. He wondered if he'd ever stop calling it that, but it was a heck of a lot easier to say than The Arabella Lavender Art Academy.

He pulled into the car park and glanced across at the studio. Even though he knew for certain that he'd locked it when he left he couldn't resist checking. He headed over and tried the handle. Yes, locked. He patted the key that nestled in his trouser pocket, knowing he was being paranoid, but he really didn't want anyone going in there unless he was with them. He'd moved the painting of Clemmie into the studio to continue working on it, having got the background finished in the house. If anyone else should see it...

It was a painstaking process, building the portrait up layer by layer, allowing time for each layer to dry. The oils he used weren't for the impatient, that was for sure, but he knew he could do justice to Clemmie using that medium far more than he could with quicker-drying oil paints, or acrylics.

His stomach churned with nerves as he considered the way he'd chosen to paint her and its possible repercussions. This could go so badly wrong, he knew that. If it did, his name would be mud, and his humiliation complete. Worse than that, Clemmie would never speak to him again. He could drive her away for good.

Sometimes, in the dead of night, he would lie in the darkness worrying that he'd made the wrong decision, but in the light of day he would awaken with a renewed determination to see it through. He had to make Clemmie understand that he adored her, and she was the only woman for him. He'd messed up. He hadn't been romantic enough for her, he knew that. But he loved her, and whether her hair ever grew back again or not made no difference to him. The only reason her alopecia had any effect on him at all was because it hurt her, and he'd give anything to take that hurt away. Their story hadn't been perfect, but it could have a happy ending if she'd just give him another chance.

Anyway, the painting was safe. The studio was warm, well-ventilated, and spotlessly clean, and it had been left in a purpose-built drying cabinet. He was confident that it would be ready to work on again in a couple of days.

In the meantime, he had an advertising campaign to organise, interviews with prospective art teachers, menu options to discuss with Jennifer, meetings with various local craftspeople who were interested in having their creations showcased in the gallery, more art materials to purchase, all while checking over the student accommodation and making sure his own rooms were being decorated the way he wanted them.

And that wasn't even everything he had to think about. His head was whirling with the responsibility of it all, and he wondered, not for the first time, if he was up to the job.

He pushed open the door of Monk's Folly, stamped the slush from his shoes onto the doormat, and walked down the hall towards the kitchen, giving brief nods to the various workmen who were plodding up and down the stairs. The first floor was still a hive of activity as the finishing touches to the sleeping accommodation were made, and the landing and stairs were measured and prepared for new carpeting.

Meg was just coming out of the kitchen, carrying a mug of coffee.

'There you are! I'd have made you one if I'd known,' she said. 'You have a visitor waiting for you. I've made him a drink. He's in there.' She nodded over her shoulder towards the door and carried on past him.

A visitor? Perhaps Noah had dropped by. His spirits lifted at the thought, and he pushed open the kitchen door and strolled in, stopping dead in shock as he saw the man sitting at the table.

Ben Callaghan! Of all the people Ross had expected to see, Ben was the last person.

His only consolation was that Ben looked as nervous as he felt. He half got to his feet and offered Ross a shaky smile.

'Ross, good to see you.'

He might as well have added, 'After all this time', because it had been years since they'd exchanged a word. Ben looked different, he thought. Older of course. No longer the teenager he'd once hung around with. Naturally, he still had those bright blue eyes, and that floppy fringed light brown hair. But the confidence—no, not confidence, the *arrogance*—had gone from his expression. Ben had suffered and it showed in his face. Ross turned away from him, suddenly nauseated.

'Fancy seeing you here,' he said, heading straight to the kettle, his hands shaking as he flicked on the switch.

'I know.' Ben gazed around him. 'You've done an amazing job. I hardly recognised the place. Mum said it looked completely different, but I never imagined... I'm glad you've poured so much love and money into it. It deserved it and we could never have done what you have.'

Ross wasn't sure what to say to that. He quickly made a coffee and sat down at the opposite end of the table to Ben, as far away from him as he could reasonably manage.

'What brings you here?' he asked, aware that he sounded stand-offish and wishing he could be a bit warmer towards the man who'd once been closer to him than his own brother.

Ben cleared his throat. 'This is a bit awkward,' he said. 'Normally I wouldn't interfere, because, well, it's none of my business and I might be out of order here.' He gave him an awkward smile. 'Thing is, I wouldn't be here at all if not for Summer, but she's begged me to say something to you, and I suppose really you do need to be put in the picture.'

Ross frowned. 'I have no idea what you're talking about,' he said.

Ben sighed. 'I know. Look, I know you don't want me here any more than I want to be here, so let's just cut to the chase. You and Meg—'

'There is no me and Meg,' Ross said abruptly. 'What are you implying?'

'I'm not implying anything,' Ben said patiently. 'I just wondered if you were aware that the Lavender Ladies are taking bets on you and her getting together. Well, I say the Lavender Ladies. From what I gather your aunt knows nothing about it, but that doesn't stop Rita and Birdie, does it?'

'They're betting on us getting together?'

'Yes. Because you see, you've been on three dates with her,' Ben explained. 'Well, more really, if you count your little jaunt into Kirkby Skimmer the other day.'

Ross's mouth fell open. 'Who told you about that?'

Ben gave him an incredulous look. 'This is Tuppenny Bridge. It's all round the town. So as far as they're concerned you've now had four dates with Meg and, given your reputation for only dating a woman twice at the most, it's caused a fair bit of excitement and a flurry of bets.' He raised an eyebrow. 'Especially since you were careless enough to go on a dinner date on Valentine's Day, of all days.'

Ross felt the colour drain from his face. 'Does—I mean, how widespread are these rumours?'

Ben's eyes softened in sympathy. 'Like I said, you're the talk of the town.'

'So, Clemmie might know?' he asked quietly.

'Let's just say, she and Summer had a long chat, and yes, Clemmie has heard the rumours.'

Ross rubbed his face. Great. Another nail in the coffin of their relationship. Things just kept going from bad to worse.

'There's no truth in the rumours,' he said firmly. 'Meg's just a work colleague. She'll be leaving here in a few days anyway.'

'I did wonder.' Ben rubbed his chin. 'I'm glad to hear you say that, because it might just be that a certain someone was a bit upset about those rumours.'

Ross's heart leapt into his throat. 'Upset?'

'I can't believe I'm getting involved in all this,' Ben said, rolling his eyes. 'The things we do for love, eh? Summer thought you should know, that's all. Well, I've given you the news, so I'll be on my way.'

He got to his feet and Ross stared up at him, unable to help the appeal in his voice as he asked, 'But Clemmie doesn't care one way or the other. Does she?'

Ben shrugged. 'All I know is Summer thought it worth

telling you that Clemmie didn't take the news too well, even though she tried to pretend it was okay. I don't know what's going on between you two, but Summer reckons there's been a lot of misunderstandings and she thinks Clemmie's in the wrong, even though it's for the right reasons.' He shook his head, clearly bewildered by the whole thing. 'I have no idea what that means but maybe you do. Anyway, that's that done. I'll see myself out.'

He headed for the door and Ross watched him go, a whole whirlpool of emotion swirling inside him as he thought about Clemmie and about Ben. The past was such a mess, he thought. If only he could work his way through the mistakes that had haunted him for so long and put it right with both of them. They were probably the two people he cared most about in the world along with Noah and his Aunt Eugenie.

'Ben!'

Ben turned and looked at him, and Ross didn't miss the sadness in his old friend's eyes.

'Could we...' he paused, wondering what he was going to say. What was he thinking? Ben wouldn't be interested after all this time. Would he?

But there was a sudden look of hope on Ben's face, and it gave him new courage.

'Could we meet up? I think—I think we need to talk, don't you?'

Ben hesitated. 'After all this time?'

'Yes. Even after all this time.'

He held his breath as Ben considered it.

'Where?' he said at last.

'The Black Swan? Say, seven thirty tomorrow night?'

Ben nodded. 'I'll be there.' His tone was grim, and Ross merely nodded in response. It seemed Ben was as nervous and unsure about this meeting as he was. But something was telling him that now was the time to start to put things right. He'd drifted along for too long, letting the people he loved slip from his grasp.

Tomorrow night, just maybe he and Ben could—if not put things right exactly—at least start to come to terms with the past.

As for Clemmie.

He rubbed his forehead, feeling confused. What did all that mean? Was Summer mistaken in her beliefs that Clemmie had been upset about the rumours? After all, Clemmie had made it very clear that she wanted nothing more from him than friendship. He didn't understand it, and the more he tried to make sense of it the more he convinced himself that Summer had been wrong.

One step at a time. First of all he had to meet Ben.

It was time to lay some ghosts to rest.

# THIRTY-SEVEN

Clemmie would never admit it to Dolly, but she quite enjoyed market days in Tuppenny Bridge when the second-hand book stall was open, and she could have a sneaky browse through some of the books on offer.

Although The Corner Cottage Bookshop was well-stocked, there was something special about sifting through piles of pre-loved books that had once meant so much to other people.

Clemmie rarely parted with any of her own books, and it often made her wonder what had led those previous owners to give away their precious paperbacks—sometimes even expensive hardbacks.

She couldn't imagine ever being able to pass her collection on. Even if she ran out of space, she'd probably get rid of her bed and sleep on the sofa downstairs, turning over her bedroom to the bookcases. She smiled to herself, imagining Dolly's reaction if she did that.

She was, naturally, looking for romantic novels. This time, though, it was more for research. She still hadn't figured out what was wrong with Emmeline, but something was nagging away at her. The story wasn't quite right. Something jarred. She knew it but had no idea what the problem was, so had no way of fixing it.

She thought, maybe if she read a few more reputable romances they might give her some ideas. It was either that or show the manuscript to Dolly. Unbelievably, desperation was making her edge ever closer to that option, but she really wanted to fix it herself if she could.

'Gotcha!'

She jumped, her hand flying to her chest as if to save herself from a cardiac arrest.

Reuben grinned at her. 'Sorry. Didn't mean to scare you.'

'Scare me! Honestly, I nearly keeled over.'

He gave her a mischievous look. 'Why? Did you think I was Dolly?'

'Oh, you know me so well. She'd throttle me if she caught me looking on here.'

'Anything caught your eye?' he asked, picking up a hardback copy of a footballer's autobiography and surveying it with mild interest before returning it to the pile.

'Loads,' she admitted. 'But I wouldn't dare buy anything. Dolly wouldn't be impressed, would she? And I've got to go back to work in a minute. I only popped out to take some book orders to the post office.'

'If there's anything you want I can nip it under my coat for you,' he offered. 'After I've paid for it of course,' he added hastily, seeing her eyes widen in shock. 'I could take it back to Dale View for you to collect later. We'll tell Dolly I spotted it and thought you'd like it, so I bought it for you. She won't tell *me* off.'

'Don't count on it.' She laughed, but couldn't help but glance wistfully at an old copy of *Jane Eyre* that she'd spotted earlier. It was a bit battered, and there was a small tear on the front cover, but the pages looked clean, and it was an edition she hadn't read before.

'That one?' he asked, following her gaze.

'Well...'

'Consider it done.' He picked up the book and waved it at the middle-aged man who was manning the stall. 'Excuse me. Can we have this one please?'

The man beamed at them. 'You certainly can, squire. That'll be two pounds fifty please.'

'Bargain,' Clemmie told him, and he laughed.

'Thanks for tipping me off. I'll put my prices up for next week.' He stuffed the book into a paper bag and handed it over as Reuben passed him the money. 'Cheers now. Have a good day.'

'He was nice,' Clemmie said as they walked back towards the bookshop, Reuben deftly tucking the book into his inside coat pocket so it would be well away from Dolly's prying eyes.

'He was. Then again, everyone's nice round here. Haven't met anyone yet that I didn't like,' he confessed. 'Even the famous Miss Lavender that everyone seems keen to warn me about has been lovely.'

'You met Miss Lavender?' Clemmie asked. 'Well, if she's been lovely to you then you've cracked it. You're part of Tuppenny Bridge now.'

He laughed. 'I'm honoured. Mind, I was doing her a favour so that's probably why.'

'Oh? And what favour have you done for her?' Clemmie asked, intrigued.

'I'm designing a website for her, and I've agreed to do it in double quick time at no extra cost. Well, I say for her. It's for that new art academy she and her nephew are opening.'

'Great-nephew,' Clemmie murmured automatically.

'Oh right. That makes more sense, given her age. Anyway we've had a face-to-face meeting and a couple of phone conversations about the concept and what sort of information they want on there, which payment system they want to use, that sort of thing. I've been working hard on it and they're very pleased with what I've done so far. I figured if I did her a favour—well, she's got influence in this town. Recommendations from her could be quite valuable. Besides, I must admit, I liked her.' He frowned. 'He's a bit prickly, though. Doesn't give much away, but I could see he liked what he saw, even though he obviously didn't want to go overboard with the praise. Takes all sorts I suppose.'

Clemmie decided a change of subject was called for in case Reuben mentioned the gorgeous girlfriend of his 'prickly' client.

'Thanks so much for the book. Were you coming to see us at the shop, or did I steer you off course?'

'I was coming to see you,' he admitted, sounding suddenly hesitant.

'Excellent. Come in then and I'll make you a coffee to say thank you. Remember, not a word about *Jane Eyre*!'

'I promise,' he said, a twinkle in his eyes.

They pushed open the shop door and stepped inside, glad of the warmth after the chilly air outside, even though the temperature had, thankfully, risen over the last couple of days.

Dolly was serving someone, but she looked over and smiled at them as they walked towards the kitchen.

'Did you get them books posted?' she enquired, joining them as soon as the customer had left the shop.

'Of course. Got the receipt and proof of postage,' Clemmie said, rummaging in her coat pocket and drawing out two slips of paper. 'There you go.'

'Ta very much. Got to keep the accountant happy,' Dolly said with a sigh. She turned to Reuben who was leaning against the worktop. 'How's things?'

'Things,' he said warmly, 'are good. I've got plenty of work on, I'm enjoying myself at Whispering Willows, and the people in this town are lovely. I'm really glad I came here.'

'Glad to hear it,' Dolly said warmly. 'So to what do we owe

this pleasure? Or did you get dragged in here by madam? I know she can be very demanding,' she added, winking at Clemmie.

'She bribed me with coffee,' he said. 'How could I refuse?'

'Well exactly,' Dolly said. 'She's not daft.'

Clemmie rolled her eyes. 'If all it takes is a coffee, you're easily bought,' she said.

'That's always been my trouble,' he agreed. 'Actually, I was wondering if, er, you were free for dinner tomorrow night? Both of you, I mean. It would be great to have you both round again, and to be honest I'd quite like to exercise my culinary skills. I rarely bother when it's just me, and I really fancy doing a bit of cooking.'

'Tomorrow night?' Dolly tilted her head, thinking. 'Sorry, love. No can do. I've got far too much work to get on with and I daren't take another night off.'

'That's a shame,' Reuben said lightly. 'Clemmie?'

'We could do it another night,' Clemmie said, frowning at her aunt. 'It doesn't have to be tomorrow, does it?'

'Yeah but, to be honest, I'll be pretty much working flat out every night for the foreseeable,' Dolly said. 'My own fault. I do leave everything to the last minute and then it's one mad panic to meet my deadline. I never learn.' She gave Clemmie a bright smile. 'You can go on your own, though. No reason not to, is there?'

Clemmie could have throttled her. The thought of spending an evening alone with Reuben filled her with dread. Not because she didn't like him. She did. She actually liked him a lot. He was kind and made her laugh for a start. But her natural shyness meant she always needed a buffer of some sort, and Dolly was perfect for that. Without her sociable aunt's presence, she was afraid conversation would dry up and the evening would be a disaster. Surely Dolly knew that by now?

'That's great,' Reuben said. 'I'll dig out some recipes and get shopping.'

'Please,' Clemmie said quickly, 'don't go to any trouble for me. Something cheap and cheerful will do. I hate formal occasions anyway.'

'Oh, don't worry. It won't be formal,' Reuben assured her. 'Doesn't mean I can't cook something special for you though, does it? Besides, you have to come. I might have something for you.'

He winked and his fingers lightly tapped his coat where *Jane Eyre* was nestling in his inside pocket.

'Oh yes?' Dolly said suspiciously. 'And what's that then?'

'Just a little something I thought she might like,' he said airily. 'So you'll be there then? Seven-ish?'

Clemmie sighed inwardly, not wanting to appear ungracious, especially after he'd been so kind as to buy her the book.

'Seven-ish,' she agreed, trying not to sound reluctant.

'Excellent.' He beamed at her. 'It's a date! Now, how about that coffee?'

She tried not to look too appalled. What did he mean, 'It's a date'? Was it just an expression or...

Oh jeez, she thought as she filled up the kettle. How on earth did she get herself into these situations?

# THIRTY-EIGHT

Clemmie was playing one of Dolly's CDs as she drove to Tuppenny Bridge that evening. She couldn't, in all honesty, say she was a huge fan of music from the nineteen eighties, but she'd had to endure the likes of Duran Duran, Spandau Ballet, Wham, and Dire Straits so many times that she knew most of the lyrics of their songs without even having to think about it.

She therefore channelled her nervous energy about spending an evening with Reuben into singing loudly to each track.

As the car headed over Tuppenny Bridge, she caught a glimpse of someone familiar walking along Bankside and the breath caught in her throat. She quickly flicked the CD player off and stared as Ross Lavender—looking utterly delicious in dark trousers and his familiar expensive overcoat—headed into The Black Swan.

Clemmie's heart sank. So he was on another date with Meg McKenna? That would make it their what? Fourth, fifth date? Rumour had it they'd been in Kirkby Skimmer together too. They were certainly getting around.

She managed to keep her mind on the road as she turned

right onto Bankside and drove slowly past the pub and the car park, but by the time she'd safely turned left onto River Road, her thoughts were already back with Ross and Meg.

The Black Swan appeared to be their favourite place for a date. They'd had at least two meals here to her knowledge, including one on Valentine's Day, and now here they were again. Evidently it held a special place in their hearts.

Clemmie felt sick to her stomach but told herself she was fine. She was happy for Ross. It was what she'd wanted for him after all. Anyway, it was all in the past and she had a meal with Reuben to look forward to.

Once past the junction with Market Street, River Road became Lavender Lane. Clemmie drove carefully towards Dale View, trying to focus on the evening ahead and not think about Ross's date. She had enough to worry about with her own so-called date.

Summer, she suddenly realised, was probably right. Reuben must be interested in her, because look how much time he'd spent with her since arriving in Tuppenny Bridge. Okay, he'd spent time with Dolly too, but even so, she got the distinct impression that it was her he was interested in, rather than her aunt.

He had, after all, asked Summer lots of questions about Clemmie, and he'd certainly chatted easily enough to her when they'd had dinner together either at Dale View or Wintergreen. He'd seemed genuinely interested in her, wanting to know all about her. He'd been so warm and friendly she'd almost forgotten herself and confessed that she was writing a book, and even Dolly didn't know about that. Luckily, she'd reined herself in just in time.

And then there was *Jane Eyre*. He hadn't had to buy it for her. All right, it had only cost him two pounds fifty, but it had been a kind thought just the same.

The trouble was, no matter how kind and friendly Reuben

seemed, and no matter how good looking he was for that matter, it would never work between them. Even if she'd had the courage to pursue things if he was keen on her—which, given everything a close relationship would entail, she didn't—she wasn't attracted to him in that way. How could any man hold a candle to Ross? She just hoped her host wouldn't make a move on her this evening.

Reuben must have been looking out for her because he threw open the front door the minute she pulled up outside.

'Come in,' he called, before she'd even had time to shut the car door. 'Hope you like lamb.'

Clemmie frowned. 'I love lamb,' she told him. Hadn't she mentioned that once when they were having dinner at Wintergreen? She was pretty sure he'd asked her what her favourite meal was, and she'd said, without hesitation, roast lamb and all the trimmings. But surely he hadn't cooked a whole roast dinner for her tonight? She'd told him not to go to any trouble.

As he led her inside, she thought he looked edgy, nervous. Not the usual relaxed Reuben at all. She was sure he was trembling as he took her coat from her.

'Are you okay?' she asked him worriedly.

'Me? Absolutely fine. How about you?'

*Apart from feeling completely devastated because my ex has gone out to dinner with his glamorous new girlfriend, and feeling pretty terrified because I think you're going to tell me you like me tonight and I have no idea how to let you down gently, because things like this don't happen to me?*

'Yeah, fine.'

'Good, good.' He ushered her into the living room and handed her a glass of grape juice that he'd already poured for her.

'Mm, smells really good,' Clemmie told him, her nose twitching as the aroma of roast lamb drifted through from the kitchen.

'Doesn't it? Slow-roasted shoulder of lamb. It was in the oven for five hours so hopefully it will be so tender it will melt in the mouth. Sound good?'

'Sounds delicious,' Clemmie admitted, looking forward to tasting it despite her nerves.

'Make yourself comfortable. It shouldn't be long,' he told her, and left her to it.

Clemmie settled herself in the armchair and sipped her grape juice, wondering what was wrong with Reuben. His smile had been as wide as ever, and his attitude as welcoming as it always was, but she'd detected tension around his mouth, and a trace of anxiety in his eyes that she'd never seen before.

Her stomach rolled with fear. Oh heck! Was he *really* going to choose tonight to tell her he was interested in her? That must be it. She couldn't think of any other reason why he'd be nervous. Had he told Dolly what he planned to do?

She couldn't help thinking he must have. It was all very odd that Dolly had backed out of this dinner, stating work commitments. She'd thought so at the time, and had noticed Dolly had seemed evasive, as if she didn't want to be drawn on her reasons for not joining them.

Which would mean, she thought heavily, that Dolly approved of Reuben, and was hoping Clemmie would welcome his advances.

Well, the fact was, she wouldn't.

The fear that had kept her hiding in the pages of novels for so long, seeking thrills and passion only from fictional heroes—her own or other people's—experiencing romantic love only through the eyes of the heroines who populated the stories she devoured so eagerly, was as strong as ever.

Making a connection with a real-life man would bring up all sorts of problems—not least having to admit to him that she wasn't exactly as she seemed. If she couldn't cope with Ross knowing her secret, how could she bear to let a relative stranger know?

And what difference did it make anyway? Even if, miraculously, her hair grew back that very instant, she still wouldn't want to be with Reuben. She could never love him that way. Her heart belonged to another, and she had no idea how to take it back from him.

By the time Reuben called through that dinner was ready, Clemmie's nerves were in shreds, and she almost dropped her glass of grape juice as she took her seat at the table.

Maybe Reuben's own obvious anxiety should have soothed her, made her feel better, but it didn't. It was just confirmation that tonight was important, and he was about to tell her something that could change their relationship completely. She simply wasn't sure she was ready to hear it.

The meal was superb. Clemmie was no food aficionado, but she couldn't fail to appreciate how delicious it was, as Reuben explained how he'd marinated the lamb overnight in a marinade that had, with the addition of a cup of water, become the tasty gravy that Clemmie raved about. The roast potatoes were crispy on the outside and fluffy on the inside, and the broccoli, peas, and green beans were cooked to perfection.

Despite her nerves, it was simply too good not to eat, and Clemmie enjoyed every mouthful, even while keeping an eye on Reuben and hoping he wouldn't ask her any awkward questions while they were at the table.

He didn't, thankfully. Instead, the conversation was light and easy, with general chat about television programmes they'd watched recently and some discussion of the many plays and shows Reuben had seen in the West End, something which filled Clemmie—who had never been to any theatre outside North Yorkshire and only then on three occasions—with awe.

Dessert was light, which Clemmie was thankful for after such a heavy main course.

'Vanilla yoghurt panna cotta with strawberries, runny honey, and roasted rhubarb,' Reuben announced, placing a small dish in front of her. 'I'm quite chuffed with how it turned out. Got a lovely wobble on it.' He laughed. 'It's one of Jamie Oliver's recipes. I can't take credit for it.'

'But you made it!'

Clemmie had no idea how he'd managed to make what seemed to her an incredibly difficult meal, but she was glad he had. She tucked in happily, relieved to see Reuben looking more relaxed. It helped settle her own nerves.

After the meal, she insisted on loading the dishwasher while Reuben made them both a coffee, then they headed back into the living room, carrying their cups with them.

He put some music on—something middle-of-the-road that didn't invite any comments either for or against—and settled back in his chair, suddenly looking pensive.

Clemmie eyed him cautiously, her senses on alert. There was no mistaking the fact that he was anxious about something, and she had the distinct impression he was building up to saying something important.

They sat facing each other, and suddenly the atmosphere seemed strained and awkward. His throat must have been dry because he kept clearing it. She gulped down the rest of her coffee and wondered if she ought to tell him she was leaving early, because she had things to do herself and after all she had to drive all the way back to West Colby. Then she thought that might give him the opportunity to invite her to stay over, so she remained silent, her imagination fevered and her mind racing as she waited for him to get whatever it was over with.

'Oh, I've got your book,' Reuben said suddenly, and got to his feet. He opened a drawer in the dresser and passed her the Charlotte Brontë novel. 'Just tell Dolly it was a gift from me to you.'

'Thanks. It was really kind of you,' she said, her own voice suddenly cracking with tension.

'Do you want a glass of water?' he asked, as she coughed.

'Please.'

He hurried into the kitchen, and she took a deep breath and closed her eyes. Suddenly, she thought that Ross's salmon fishcakes had been even better than Reuben's slow-roasted lamb, and a fierce longing to be back in Wintergreen, snowed in with him once more, attacked her with such ferocity that she gripped the chair arm. If wishing could make things happen...

But Ross wasn't part of her life any longer. She had to face it. Oh, maybe they would be friends who'd occasionally nod or smile at each other as they passed on the street, but that's as far as it would go. He'd be too busy with his art academy to spare her a thought, and besides, he had Meg now.

She imagined the two of them right now, sitting at a candlelit table in The Black Swan. Ross would be gazing into Meg's eyes, murmuring things to her that Clemmie would never hear from him again. In her mind she saw his intense dark eyes peering into her soul. Meg's fingertips stroked the velvety smooth skin stretched over his well-defined cheekbones then moved down to gently touch his chin, brushing against the neatly clipped beard, which Clemmie had always thought gave him a certain distinction, and which she'd begged him never to shave off.

She saw, in her mind's eye, Ross helping Meg into her coat, leading her out of the pub, kissing her, asking her to go back to Monk's Folly with him. Or perhaps they'd get a taxi back to her hotel. Either way they would be spending the night together. She was sure of it.

Her eyes flew open as she heard Reuben walk back into the living room. She could see he was still nervous. His hands shook as he handed her the glass of water. She took a sip then went to place the glass on the floor. She gasped as Reuben's face brushed hers and, without thinking what she was doing, she pushed him away from her, tipping the water all over him in the process.

'What do you think you're doing? Leave me alone!'

He staggered back, wet through and clearly horrified. 'What the hell? I was just going to take the glass from you, that's all.'

'I'm sorry,' she managed. 'I thought...' Clemmie's legs felt weak, and her heart thudded while her face burned with shame.

'Well,' he said, sounding shaken, 'you thought wrong. I'm not interested in you, Clemmie. Not in that way. Far from it.'

She'd been such an idiot! How had she got this so wrong? Just because she'd seen Ross heading into the pub for his date with Meg! She'd been hurt and miserable, and so determined not to admit it to herself that she'd dreamed up an imaginary scenario in her head in which Reuben was romantically attracted to her. Why would he be?

The truth was, Reuben was just a nice man who'd cooked dinner for her, and the only reason it had been the two of them was because Dolly was too busy to join them.

She couldn't imagine how she'd ever face him again.

'I'm so sorry,' she repeated. 'I think I'd better go home.'

'You don't have to,' Reuben replied, but there was no real conviction in his voice. He seemed different. It was clear that she'd embarrassed him. More than that. She seemed to have really shaken him up. Evidently the idea that he could possibly be attracted to her had never entered his head.

'Thanks for the meal,' she said, heading into the hall to grab her coat.

She clambered into the car and fastened her seat belt, then switched on the ignition, hoping he wouldn't come out and try to persuade her to stay. She needn't have worried.

By the time she drove away from Dale View, Reuben still hadn't come to the front door, or made any attempt whatsoever to stop her from leaving.

It seemed he couldn't wait to get rid of her.

'Well done, Clemmie,' she said, gritting her teeth as she glanced at herself in the mirror. 'Now you've lost a friend on top of everything else. Dolly's going to be thrilled about this, not. Only you could mess things up quite this spectacularly.'

# THIRTY-NINE

Ben was late, which only added to Ross's nerves. Maybe, he thought, as he stood at the bar waiting to be served, he wasn't even coming. After all this time, who could blame him? And if he did come, what good would it do? It had been so long since they'd spoken properly, and even if they cleared the air tonight was their friendship too damaged to repair?

Surely, he thought, Ben must have wondered over the years? He'd never said anything to him, but Ross found it hard to believe he hadn't figured it all out. No wonder he'd avoided him. Then again, Ross had done his best to avoid Ben, too. It was all such a mess. Hard to believe they'd once been so close.

'What can I get you, love?'

He blinked as he realised the barmaid was talking to him and tried to pull himself together.

'A pint of Randy Ram please,' he said, before wondering in a sudden panic whether he should get Ben one. Did Ben drink Randy Ram? Did he drink beer at all? The last time they'd hung out together he'd been drinking all sorts, but that was different. Ben had been so drunk he hadn't really been aware what he was pouring down his throat... Oh, hell! This was such a bad idea.

'And a pint of Coke please.'

The voice behind him was unmistakable and Ross steadied himself before turning to greet Ben.

'You came.'

'Of course.' Ben sounded surprised, as if it hadn't even occurred to him not to, and Ross felt suddenly a little calmer. At least Ben didn't look as if he wanted to punch him, which was something.

'Coming right up.' The barmaid began to pull their pints, then placed the glasses on the counter.

'Shall I find us somewhere to sit?' Ben asked, and Ross nodded as he handed over a twenty-pound note.

By the time he'd waited for his change and picked up the two glasses, Ben was nowhere to be seen. Ross scoured the room and eventually spotted him sitting over at the front, at the table nearest to the door. Maybe he was making sure he could escape quickly if he needed to? Fair enough.

'I never had you down as the Randy Ram type,' Ben confessed as Ross took a seat. 'Always thought you'd be more a red wine man.'

Ross wasn't sure whether that was a dig at him or not, but decided to assume Ben was just making friendly conversation.

'I do like a good red,' he admitted. 'But there's nothing wrong with a pint of beer sometimes, and this is one of the best. You're not drinking? Are you on call?'

'Yes, what with Clive being otherwise occupied,' Ben said. 'Not that I'd drink that stuff anyway. I find anything that comes from the Lusty Tup Brewery a bit hard to swallow. Anyway,' he added, 'I'm here for now, although I can't promise I won't get called away at some point.'

Ross nodded, wondering if that was a good or bad thing. At least Ben would have a way of escaping if this all got too much. On the other hand, the last thing he wanted was to start to explain things and have the talk interrupted by Ben's phone.

He'd hoped to build up slowly to telling him what he needed to tell him, and then have some time for them to thrash things out afterwards. He had a feeling there'd be a lot to discuss. He just hoped it wouldn't end with a brawl in the street outside.

Ben was watching him carefully and Ross went to loosen his shirt collar, only to remember he was wearing a jumper. Funny that. He could have sworn his collar was too tight. How could he feel so nervous? Ben wasn't the vengeful type. But there were worse things than physical violence, he knew that. He was dreading seeing the look of disgust on his former friend's face.

'It's been a while,' Ben said at last.

'It has. Must be, er—'

'Fourteen years,' Ben said flatly.

Ross nodded. He was aware of that. Fifteen in October. He knew the date off by heart. The date Ben's older brother Leon had died in a car accident. No wonder Ben never drank beer from the Lusty Tup Brewery. It was where Leon had worked, after all, along with their father who'd died of cancer just a year later. Ben and his family had been through too much. How had he ever thought this was a good idea?

'How are you finding it at Daisyfield Cottage?' he asked, thinking that seemed a safe subject. 'Your mum seems very happy there.'

'We love it. It's been a revelation; how easy it's been to keep warm over the winter. We're not used to it. That's something I don't envy you. Monk's Folly is a nightmare to heat, I'll warn you now. You'll notice when you're actually living there.'

Ross grinned. 'It might interest you to know that I *am* living there. Well, sort of. Camping out really, although it's nearly done now. And I'm not surprised it was a nightmare to keep warm, given the state of the central heating system and the windows. It's not bad now we've got a new boiler and radiators, underfloor heating, new windows, window shutters...'

'All right, all right. Show off.' Ben said it good-naturedly though, and Ross relaxed a little. 'Mum's been telling us all about it. She can't wait to get started cooking in your swanky new kitchen.' He hesitated. 'Thanks for giving her the job, Ross. It's given her a whole new lease of life. She's so excited about it.'

'She was the best person for the job,' Ross said with a shrug. *Besides, I owed her.* 'I'm just glad she accepted. I'm, er, sorry to hear about Joseph. It must be hard for you and Summer, what with you having to cover for Clive, and Summer working flat out at Whispering Willows.'

'It's been tough,' Ben admitted. 'But I've got a locum working with me now, and Reuben's been a godsend to Summer.'

'I'm sure he has,' Ross said tightly. *Bloody Reuben Walker. Why does everything always have to come back to him?*

'Of course, he'll be leaving in a couple of weeks,' Ben continued, 'so it's going to be tricky for a little while.'

Ross raised an eyebrow. 'Is he? Are you sure?'

'Oh yes. It was only ever going to be a two-month stay as that's how long he booked Dale View for, and he arrived in early January.' Ben sighed. 'It'll be a wrench for Summer, losing him, but her stepsister Frankie's coming to stay for the Easter holidays, and she's offered to help out, and Jamie's volunteered too. He's got a girlfriend now,' he added. 'Eloise. She's said she'll pitch in, so at least Summer will have help while they're off school, and Lennox and Maya have said they'll do extra hours instead of just weekends. After that...' He sighed. 'We'll have to think again, I suppose. It depends what's happening with Joseph at that point.'

They both fell silent, and Ross contemplated the future, wondering just how long Summer could hold Whispering Willows together and what would happen to it in the long term. He suspected Ben was thinking along similar lines.

Apparently, though, Ben's mind had wandered a little

further, as he suddenly said, 'So what's this about, Ross? Why did you want us to meet up after all this time?'

Ross's pulse raced. He hadn't expected such an abrupt change of subject, nor to be thrown in at the deep end like this. He'd planned a slow build-up, but now he was faced with the thing he was dreading most. The reason he'd wanted to see Ben.

'It's—hard to explain,' he said, his hand tightening around the glass of beer.

Ben leaned forward, his elbows on the table. 'I suppose moving into Monk's Folly has thrown up a lot of memories,' he said slowly. 'I've had to do a lot of thinking myself lately, for various reasons. Coming to terms with what happened that night, trying to accept that it wasn't all my fault that Leon died.'

Ross swallowed. 'Of course it wasn't.'

'It's easy to say that now,' Ben said, watching him steadily, 'but for years I blamed myself, and it's only these last few months that I've started to forgive myself and move on.'

Ross took a long drink of Randy Ram. Was Ben about to ask him the question he'd dreaded for so long?

'I get it, you know,' Ben said quietly. 'I always got it. I've never blamed you. Not for a moment.'

Ross's eyes widened. *Ben knows?*

'I'm so sorry,' he said miserably as he placed the glass on the table. 'I've wanted to talk to you for so long. Ever since it happened. I just—I was a coward. I couldn't face it. And I was never sure if you knew already. I thought maybe you'd guessed why—'

'Why we stopped talking?' Ben leaned back in his chair and nodded. 'Oh yes, of course I guessed. And like I said, I didn't blame you. I'd have walked away from me too if I could. I was a brat. You tried to warn me not to go to Pellston, but I didn't listen. Look what happened because I ignored your advice. I know I must have hurt you, hanging out with those stupid lads and pushing you away. I'm sorry, Ross. If I could change it all I would do so in a heartbeat, for so many reasons. Leon's death obviously, but also the death of our friendship. I was a jerk, and there's no one knows that more than me.'

Ross was confused. What exactly was Ben saying? He blinked, trying to make sense of it all.

'You think I stopped talking to you because you hung out with those kids from your school?'

'Because of what it led to. If I hadn't done that, Leon would still be alive. If I'd just listened to you...' Ben shook his head sadly. 'How many conversations did we have at the time? How many times did you warn me not to bother with them because they were leading me into trouble? You begged me not to go to that party. You said it would be a disaster and you were right. More than we could ever have imagined. I'm sorry I dragged you into it. I'm just glad you got away before the police came. I never said a word, you know. Not even to Summer. No one knows you were there that night.'

He managed a wry smile. 'Your aunt wouldn't have appreciated seeing her precious great-nephew in a cell.'

'She knows all about it,' Ross said, before he could stop himself. 'I told her. I confessed everything.'

'Oh!' Ben looked surprised. 'I hadn't realised. She's never said anything, so I just assumed... Well, I hope you didn't get into too much trouble.'

Ross looked down at his lap, unable to meet Ben's gaze any longer. The shame washed over him as he remembered that fateful night all those years ago.

He'd been Ben's best friend, but because Ross attended St Edgar's school and not the local high school, Ben had started hanging out with a crowd who Ross knew were no good for him. They'd bullied Ben at first, mocking him for living in what they perceived was a grand old house, Monk's Folly. They'd assumed he was rich, which was far from the truth, and had tormented him quite mercilessly for a time.

Somehow, Ben had managed to wangle his way into the gang, becoming one of them. But it had come at a price. He started to get into all sorts of trouble, and his attitude had changed until Ross hardly recognised him any more.

Nothing Ross had said made any difference, and he'd been worried about his friend. When he saw the gang heading over the bridge to Monk's Folly that night, he'd thought nothing of it. Ben had been grounded by his parents, he knew that much, and he'd expected the boys to leave once they knew that.

Instead, they'd come running back over the bridge, laughing, and he'd been horrified to see Ben running with them.

'How did you persuade your mum to let you out?' Ross had asked, catching up with him.

'Didn't. I sneaked down the drainpipe,' Ben had replied, as if he'd done something marvellous and not something incredibly stupid.

'You'll be in even more trouble now,' Ross had said angrily. 'Where are you going anyway?'

'A party outside York. We're off to catch the train.'

Ross had grabbed his arm, tried to stop him. 'You're just causing more upset for your mum. Don't you think she's got enough to worry about, with your dad being ill?'

Ben had wrenched free of his grasp. 'Look, for your information Mum's out for the night, and if she can go out and forget all about how rubbish everything is, why shouldn't I? It's just a party, Ross. A bit of fun. Remember that?'

There was a sudden challenge in his eyes. 'You could come with us.'

'To a party? With this lot?' Ross had given him a scornful look. 'Why would I want to do that? They're all losers, and if you go with them you're a loser too.'

'Is that right?' Ben said angrily. 'Or are you just scared? Wouldn't want to annoy Auntie Eugenie, would we? Go home to your posh mausoleum—oops, I mean museum. I'm sure your aunt's got some knitting you can do or something.'

Ross had been sorely tempted to punch him in the face, but Ben had started running again to catch up with his friends, and somehow Ross had found himself running after him. It wasn't that he was stung into joining them by Ben's taunts. He was worried about him. However much Ben tried to pretend, he wasn't like those other boys. Something might happen to him if he went off to a stranger's house all those miles away for a party of all things.

He'd made up his mind at that moment to go with Ben and protect him. Whether Ben wanted him there or not, someone had to keep an eye on him.

So he'd tumbled onto the train with the rest of them, and despite being jeered at and pushed around for the entire journey, he'd stuck grimly with them. A short bus ride and they were in Pellston, and one of the boys led them to a house in a field where the party was in full swing.

He'd had a miserable time of it, he remembered. The house was heaving with people, mostly a lot older than him and Ben and the rest of the boys. There was a lot of drinking going on, and no one seemed to care that so many underage children were helping themselves to beer and spirits.

He could see Ben had got talking to a young woman who seemed to be all over him. Ben was clearly drunk and hadn't noticed they were being watched by a man of around twenty, who seemed to be taking a keen interest in the young woman. Ross could see by his face that his anger was building and hurried over to Ben to warn him.

Ben had been completely unconcerned and seemed to find it all very funny. The young woman, who was obviously older than him, had told Ross to chill out.

'Jealous, are you? I'm going to take him upstairs. You can come and watch if you like.'

'There's a man over by the door,' Ross had told her urgently, 'who looks like he's going to kill you both. Is he your boyfriend?'

She'd peered over his shoulder and giggled. 'Yeah. Well, he was. I dumped him when we got here. Telling me who I could and couldn't talk to! Who does he think he is? Well, I'll teach him a lesson all right.'

She'd kissed Ben, who by then was practically out of it, and Ross had realised that this was going to end up in disaster. Frantically, he looked around, wondering what to do.

Without stopping to think of the possible ramifications, he'd left the house and ran across the field to the lane where they'd got off the bus. He'd seen a phone box there, and he was relieved to find it in working order. He rang the police and tipped them off that a load of underage teenagers were drinking at a party and that it was getting way out of hand.

Then, angry and fed up, he'd caught the next bus back to York train station and headed home to Tuppenny Bridge.

It was only the following morning that he heard what had happened to Leon, and his world had come crashing down around his ears. He couldn't eat, couldn't sleep, couldn't stop crying. He wanted to go to Ben, to apologise, to tell him how sorry he was, but he just couldn't face it.

Eventually, he'd confessed everything to his aunt, who'd listened, held him, and comforted him, reassuring him repeatedly that he'd done the right thing, and couldn't blame himself for Leon's accident.

Would Ben feel that way, though? There was, he supposed, only one way to find out.

'Our falling out—if you can call it that—had nothing to do with what you did,' he said miserably. 'And everything to do with what I did.'

Ben looked puzzled. 'What *you* did? What do you mean?'

Ross was trembling. He drained his glass then ran a hand through his hair, hardly knowing where to start.

'It was me,' he said at last. 'It was my fault.'

'What was your fault?'

He forced himself to say the words. 'Leon's death. It was down to me.'

There was a long silence, then Ben said, 'That's impossible. What are you talking about?'

Ross took a deep breath then faced his former best friend. *Look him in the eye and explain. After all these years he deserves nothing less.*

Ben sat quite still and listened as Ross confessed it all, leaving nothing out.

'I'm so sorry,' he finished at last.

Ben seemed frozen and Ross turned to gaze out of the window at the river, seeing that same bridge how it was all those years ago, when he'd made the fateful decision to tag along to a party in Pellston.

'I always thought it was her boyfriend,' Ben said quietly, and Ross turned to look at him, hearing the shock in his voice. 'I thought he'd rung the police to get back at me. I never thought—it never occurred to me it was you.'

'I've regretted it every moment of every day since,' Ross admitted. 'I honestly thought you must have guessed. I thought maybe that was why you never attempted to talk to me. And I couldn't speak to you. I was so ashamed. I let you down so badly.'

'Let me down?' Ben shook his head, dazed. 'You didn't let me down. You were trying to protect me.'

Ross wasn't sure what to make of that. It wasn't the response he'd been expecting.

'But if I hadn't rung the police, Leon wouldn't have had to come out to fetch you and he wouldn't have had that crash.'

'If I hadn't gone to the party in the first place and behaved like a moron you wouldn't have had to ring the police,' Ben pointed out. He swilled what was left of his Coke around in the glass. 'What a bloody mess. I had no idea you were carrying all this guilt, Ross. None at all. I'm so sorry.'

Tears sprang into Ross's eyes. 'You have no reason to be sorry! It was me; don't you see that? I—'

'What I see,' Ben said, 'is that I had a good friend. A brilliant friend. Someone who looked out for me and cared what happened to me. Someone who put himself in a situation he didn't want to be in just to make sure I was okay and did the responsible thing to save me from a beating, or alcohol poisoning, or both.'

He shook his head sadly. 'It took me years to accept that Leon's death was an accident, and something I couldn't blame myself for any longer. I can't bear that you've been going through a similar thing. If I'd known how you were feeling, if I'd just realised what secret you were keeping I'd have tried to help you. It's *me* who let *you* down. You have nothing to feel bad about. Absolutely nothing.' He leaned over and patted Ross awkwardly on the arm. 'Thank you for looking out for me. I'm just sorry I was such a crap friend.'

Ross could barely see him, his eyes were so blurry. 'All these years I've wanted to tell you and I just couldn't do it. I kept away from you because I thought you'd hate me.'

'And I thought you hated me and blamed me for what happened, and that's why you were keeping away from me,' Ben said heavily. 'Like I said, it's a bloody mess. So much pain and misery, all because I went to one stupid party.'

'But you do know you're not to blame?' Ross asked anxiously. 'You have realised that now?'

'A part of me will always feel responsible,' Ben admitted. 'But I've started to see that Leon's death was an accident. He shouldn't have been on that road at that time of night, and if not for me he wouldn't have been. But the crash wasn't down to me. I don't know what happened on the road and I don't think we ever will know. But I wasn't to blame for it, and neither were you.'

They were both quiet suddenly. Ross felt mentally exhausted and thought Ben probably felt the same. It was a lot to process. They'd lost so many years of friendship and it saddened him. Was there any going back for them, or was it all too late?

'So what happens now?' Ben asked.

Ross's eyebrows lifted. 'I have no idea,' he admitted. 'I suppose we both try to get on with our lives and accept that, while we each played a part in this tragedy, neither of us was ultimately responsible for Leon's death.'

'And what about us?' Ben said, tilting his head to one side and watching Ross thoughtfully. 'Does this mean we can stop avoiding each other at events?'

'Or ducking into a shop when we spot each other in the market place?' Ross managed a wry smile. 'Been there, done that.'

'Me too. Many times.' Ben grinned, and just for a moment Ross saw a trace of his old friend—the boy he'd loved like a brother before it all went so horribly wrong.

'Maybe...' His voice trailed off, too nervous and unsure to finish the sentence.

'What?' Ben asked, but Ross couldn't find the words.

'Maybe,' Ben finished for him, sounding hopeful, 'we could start again? We can't pick up where we left off, because where we left off was a bloody awful place. But a new start perhaps? We've got a lot of catching up to do after all.'

Ross's heart lifted. 'We do! And I'd like that. I really would.'

'Great.' Ben got to his feet. 'So why don't I get us another round and then we can start to fill in what we've missed.' As Ross handed him the empty glass he added with a knowing smile, 'And you can start by telling me what's going on with you and Clemmie.'

# FORTY

The atmosphere at The Corner Cottage Bookshop the following morning was strained, to say the least. Clemmie realised, a bit too late, that she should never have told Dolly what had happened at Dale View the previous evening.

Reuben had tried ringing her several times, but Clemmie had ignored her phone, which Dolly vehemently objected to.

'If you'd just talk to him!'

Clemmie wasn't budging.

'I don't want to talk to him. I don't want to see him or speak to him, or even think about him, ever again. So can you please stop going on about him? Oh!' She glared at her phone in exasperation as it began to ring again. 'When is he going to take the hint?'

Dolly marched over to the counter, snatched up Clemmie's phone before she could stop her, and answered the call.

'Hiya, Reuben. No, it's me, Dolly. Yes, she's here right now. Just a sec.'

Defiantly, she handed Clemmie the phone. Clemmie gave her a sweet smile, then pressed the end call icon. As Dolly shook her head, she switched her phone off and put it under the counter.

'There, now he can't call me, can he? Can we just leave it at that please?'

'Anyone would think he'd done something wrong,' Dolly said, returning to her dusting. 'You ought to remember, it was you that ballsed everything up, not him.'

'Thanks so much for reminding me,' Clemmie said, her face pink with embarrassment. 'I can't believe you're having a go at me. As if things weren't bad enough.'

'Aw, love.' Dolly gave her a contrite look. 'I'm sorry. I wasn't having a go at you. Just, it's so frustrating seeing you two fall out like this. Look, you made a little mistake. It happens. You thought he was interested in you in a romantic way, and he wasn't. We've all been there, trust me.'

'I don't want to talk about it,' Clemmie said stubbornly.

'But the point is, up until then he was a good friend to you. You were getting on really well. Don't let embarrassment ruin that for you. We all need friends, and you'd be daft to turn your back on him because of one teeny error of judgment.'

'*Teeny error of judgment?*' Clemmie couldn't let that pass without comment. 'It was a catastrophic error of judgment more like! How did I get it so wrong? Oh! I still blush when I think about it. You should have seen his face, Dolly.'

Now that she thought about it, it was almost funny. Poor Reuben. Dolly was right and she knew it. It was she who'd ballsed everything up between them. She should apologise. Pride had a lot to answer for.

'You just took him by surprise, that's all. Why don't you listen to what he's got to say? Go to Dale View and let him explain. Maybe you two could come to an understanding.'

'I think we already have. I'm a prat and he completely understands that.' Clemmie grinned at her aunt. 'Oh, all right.

I'll talk to him. I suppose I owe him that much since I practically accused him of trying to assault me.'

If nothing else, she thought, she and Reuben knew where they stood now. She wasn't interested in him, and he wasn't interested in her. Maybe, once she'd apologised to him, they could be even better friends in future, now all that doubt was out of the way. She glanced over at her aunt, surprised to find her watching her with a worried look on her face.

'What?'

'Nothing, nothing.' Dolly glanced out of the shop window. 'Look at them clouds. It's going to chuck it down later, you mark my words.'

'Good. Might wash away the last of the slush. I'm absolutely sick of it, aren't you?'

She switched on a smile when a customer entered the bookshop, the first of what turned out to be many that morning. She didn't mind being busy, but since Dolly had taken it upon herself to give the shop a good spring clean, which meant Clemmie was left to handle the sales, she didn't have the opportunity to work on her novel.

She was quite glad about that though. She was growing heartily sick of Emmeline, who was refusing to tell her what was wrong with her. It was odd how easily she could write her hero, but then again, maybe that was because she'd already fallen in love with him. He did, after all, bear more than a passing resemblance to Ross.

Just as the shop quietened at around twelve, the door opened and Reuben walked in.

Dolly was upstairs helping a customer choose a couple of non-fiction books, so Clemmie had no choice but to face him.

He headed over to the counter and they stared at each other for a moment.

'I'm sorry.'

They'd both said it at exactly the same moment, and as they realised that they grinned at each other.

'I didn't mean to scare you,' Reuben said, shaking his head. 'Honestly, I felt so bad when I realised what you'd thought I was about to do.'

'I was a numpty,' Clemmie admitted. 'You know what I'm like. Too much imagination. I should have known you'd never launch yourself at me like that.'

'The thing is, Clemmie,' he said, the twinkle in his eyes suddenly dimming, 'I—I'm not interested in you in that way. It's not that you're not attractive,' he added hastily. 'But the truth is...' He hesitated then said in a rush, 'I've actually got a partner back in Hampstead.'

Her eyes widened. It hadn't even occurred to her that he was already seeing someone. But if that was the case, why had Reuben come all the way here for two months after his mum died? Surely his girlfriend wanted to be with him, to help him grieve?

'It's okay,' she admitted 'I'm not interested in you that way either. That's what freaked me out. I mean, you're very nice and everything, but... Anyway, tell me about your girlfriend. What's her name?'

He smiled. 'His name actually. It's Matt, and he's lovely.'

Clemmie beamed at him. 'How long have you been together?'

'Three years,' he said. 'We met at college, but we lost touch. Then we bumped into each other at a friend's party, and it was instant fireworks. You know what I mean?'

'Yes,' Clemmie said, thinking of how it had been when she and Ross had first got together. 'I know exactly what you mean. I'm so glad for you, Reuben, I really am. I was worried about you going back to Hampstead all alone. You should have told us.'

'Yeah,' he said sheepishly, 'I should have. I suppose I was waiting until I was sure.'

'Sure of what?'

'Sure you'd be okay with it.' He sighed. 'Believe me, not everyone is, even in this day and age. But the fact is, I love him, and I'm very happy with him. Can you forgive me for keeping it from you?'

'Of course!' Besides, she was still keeping something from him, and she couldn't imagine a time when she'd ever be brave enough to share it with him. She knew all too well what it was like to worry about other people's reactions. She was just glad Reuben had someone by his side and wouldn't be all alone in the world when he went home.

'So are we good?' he asked.

She leaned over the counter and gave him a quick hug. 'We're good,' she told him.

They both swung round as Dolly called out to them from where she was leaning over the staircase railings, grinning at them. 'Thank God for that, cos I've just sent you a text message, Reuben. You're invited to afternoon tea at our place, three o'clock on Sunday, and no arguments.'

At around twelve thirty, the rain started. Dolly had been right. It did 'chuck it down'. The raindrops bounced off the pavement outside, and the market place emptied quickly as people hurried inside shops or the pubs to take shelter, or rushed back to their cars and headed home.

Market Place was soon full of puddles, as overhead the first rumbles of thunder sounded.

'Bugger, and I only washed them windows a couple of days ago,' Dolly grumbled. 'If that isn't typical!'

'What the heck's Summer doing out in this?' Clemmie pondered, peering out over the square where Summer was dodging puddles as she ran, holding her coat hood up over her head because it was too big and always fell down, something which never ceased to annoy her.

As she watched, Summer glanced up and saw her standing there. She gave her a cheery wave then seemed to pause before rushing towards the bookshop.

'She's coming in,' Clemmie told Dolly, who sighed.

'Great. She can drip all over my clean floor.'

Summer burst through the door and threw off her hood. 'Bloody hell, have you seen it out there?'

'No,' Dolly said, deadpan. 'Haven't noticed a thing.'

At that moment, thunder rumbled again, and Summer pulled a face. 'I've got to go back out in this, can you imagine?'

'What are you doing here anyway?' Clemmie asked.

'Just popping to the chemist to collect Joseph's meds.' Summer leaned against the door. 'I didn't think it would be raining this fast but it's really coming down now.'

'How is Joseph?' Dolly asked.

'You know.' Summer shrugged and Dolly and Clemmie exchanged glances. She clearly didn't want to talk about it.

'I've got to refill the stationery shelves upstairs,' Dolly said. 'Are you sticking around for a bit, love, until the rain eases off?'

'I may as well.' Summer glanced at her watch. 'Joseph's meds aren't urgent, and Reuben's just arrived at the stables.'

As Dolly headed upstairs Summer hurried forward and said eagerly, 'So, did you get your invitation?'

Clemmie frowned. 'Invitation?'

Summer leaned on the counter, a look of surprise on her face. 'You mean you didn't? Oh well, maybe it'll be waiting for you when you get home. Ours only arrived today. There's going to be an open day at Monk's Folly next month. Sorry, I mean The Arabella Lavender Art Academy.' She wrinkled her nose. 'No one round here will ever call it that, you know. It's always going to be Monk's Folly to us.'

'An open day?' Clemmie thought wistfully that she'd love to attend that. She was dying to see what Ross had done to the house. Then again, the thought of him wafting around Monk's Folly with the drop-dead gorgeous Meg on his arm would be too much to stomach.

'I'd probably be working anyway,' she said lightly.

'No you wouldn't. It's on a Sunday. The third of March.' She eyed Clemmie thoughtfully. 'So, will you go?'

'I don't know. I'll see if I get an invite first.' Clemmie shrugged nonchalantly. 'You're not going are you? I mean, Ben wouldn't want to, surely?'

'We're both going,' Summer said, sounding a little uncomfortable.

'Really? I wouldn't have thought Ben would accept an invitation from Ross. Although,' she conceded, 'I suppose the chance to see what they've done to his old home is too tempting to resist.'

'It's not just that though, Clem,' Summer admitted. 'Ross and Ben have made up.'

'Made up?' Clemmie's eyes widened. 'After all this time? How did that come about?'

Summer looked awkward. 'Oh, er, they bumped into each other one day, and Ross asked Ben to go for a drink with him, which he did. They had a good talk and apparently it all got sorted.'

'As easy as that?' Clemmie couldn't believe it. After she'd tried to talk to Ross at Wintergreen about his relationship with Ben he'd closed her down completely. He'd seemed certain there was no going back for them. It was incredible that whatever problems had driven them apart had been resolved so easily.

Well, however it had happened, she was glad for him. Ross needed a friend, and so did Ben. It was brilliant that they'd found their way back to each other. 'So, did you find out what they fell out about?'

Summer hesitated and cast a look towards the staircase. There was no sign of Dolly so she leaned forward and murmured, 'I did, but it's between you and me, okay? Ross told Ben it was okay to share with me, but he didn't say I could share it with someone else.'

Clemmie nodded. 'Of course.'

'It turns out that it was all to do with Leon's death. You know that night when Ben went to the party?'

Briefly, she filled Clemmie in with all the details, and Clemmie listened, her heart breaking for Ross and for Ben, and everyone whose lives had been shattered by the events of that night.

'All that time we were together,' she said sadly, 'and he never mentioned a word of how he was feeling. I could have helped him.'

'He was too ashamed,' Summer said. 'Awful, isn't it? Seems they've both been drowning in guilt all these years for something that, when it comes right down to it, wasn't their fault at all. I'm glad they made it up. At least they each understand what the other has been going through all this time, and I'm sure that talking to each other and hanging out again will ease the burden.'

'So they're hanging out again?' Clemmie asked.

'Do you know what, Clem? Ben says it's like all those years have just rolled away. He thought it would be a bit awkward at first, but he says they ended up chatting as if they'd only spoken a few days before. He got called away to a sick cow, so they had to leave it there, but they met up again yesterday and honestly, Ben seems so much lighter and happier. It's brilliant.' She gave a contented smile. 'Ross has invited us round for something to eat on Saturday. Can you imagine? Must admit I'm dying to see what the house looks like. Last time I was there it was like Wuthering Heights.'

She frowned suddenly. 'Sorry, is that insensitive? You don't mind me going do you? Because if you do—'

'Of course not! Why should I mind?' Clemmie gave her a bright smile. 'I'm glad Ross and Ben are friends again, and it's only natural that you should get to know him too.'

Dolly clattered down the stairs, a big grin on her face.

'Result! Found a packet of Jammie Dodgers in the stock cupboard. I'm buggered if I know what they were doing in there, but it's okay. I checked the sell-by date and we're good to go.'

Summer pushed away from the counter as Dolly opened the packet.

'Ooh, I do love a Jammie Dodger!'

She flashed Clemmie a wide smile, and Clemmie smiled back. Inside, though, her heart was sinking.

She was glad that Ross had rekindled his friendship with Ben. Of course she was. And it was good that they had each other to talk to if things got too much for them. But Ben and Summer were a couple, and that meant Ross would be hanging out with them both. And maybe, in time, Meg would be hanging out with them too.

If they started to spend time as a foursome, where would that leave her?

She'd already lost Ross. Was she about to lose Summer too?

## FORTY-ONE

There was no invitation waiting for Dolly and Clemmie when they arrived back at Wintergreen that night, and it didn't arrive the following day, or the day after that either. After the third day Clemmie gave up waiting. It was obvious that Ross had no intention of inviting them to the open day.

So much for them being friends.

Then again, maybe it was for the best. She tried to tell herself it didn't matter, and that she hadn't wanted to see Monk's Folly anyway. The truth was, she was dying to see it restored to its Regency glory, but if the price of that was seeing Ross and Meg swanning around together, she didn't think it was worth paying.

Summer had gone there with Ben for a meal and called Clemmie on the Sunday morning to tell her it looked amazing, but Summer's passions didn't lie with historical houses, and she hadn't taken in any of the details that Clemmie wanted to know. It was frustrating but there was nothing she could do about it.

Her bigger problem was the feelings of jealousy that had attacked her as Summer related how she, Ben, and Ross had eaten a meal that Ross had cooked especially for them—

Summer couldn't remember what it was but said it was something Italian, which made sense—and how they'd had an astonishingly good evening together.

'Did he say anything about me?' Clemmie had asked hesitantly.

There was a pause. 'Sorry, Clem, but he didn't, and I thought it best not to bring the subject up after everything that's gone on. Did I do the right thing?'

'Of course!' Clemmie rushed to reassure her, even as she battled her disappointment. 'I don't want him to even think about me, so you did *exactly* the right thing.'

Summer sounded thoughtful. 'To be honest, it's the first time I could understand what you saw in Ross Lavender,' she said. 'He's actually really nice, and quite funny too. Who'd have thought it?'

Quite funny? So Ross was clearly in a good place then. Making jokes, having fun, cooking for his new friends... Clemmie tried not to let it get to her, but she was sick with jealousy and grief. He wasn't pining for her at all, was he?

*For God's sake, Clemmie! You know he's not! He's with Meg now. It was your choice, remember? Let it go.*

Every word that Summer had told her was dissected and analysed, until she thought she was going mad.

*This won't work. We've been through all this. Our relationship has been damaged beyond all repair, and he's moved on. Time for you to move on, too.*

At least she had afternoon tea with Reuben and Dolly to look forward to, and she was eager to find out more about Reuben's boyfriend, Matt, and maybe learn why he'd remained in London while Reuben came all the way to Tuppenny Bridge alone.

Dolly, never usually the most domesticated of people, had pulled out all the stops, preparing an afternoon tea that made Clemmie hungry just looking at it.

'You do know it's Reuben coming over?' she asked, giving her aunt a cheeky grin. 'It's not the Prince and Princess of Wales.'

'I want it to be nice for him,' Dolly said obstinately. 'You realise he's leaving in a week's time? I want him to have happy memories of this place when he goes.'

'Happy memories?' Clemmie wrinkled her nose. 'Of tuna and cucumber sandwiches and mini chocolate eclairs?'

'You know what I mean,' Dolly said, giving her one of her looks. 'Aw, I'll miss him when he's gone, won't you?'

'I suppose I will,' Clemmie admitted, realising it was true. Now the pressure was off with Reuben she thought she'd miss him very much. He'd become a friend. 'I'm glad he's got a boyfriend to go home to, though. I'm dying to know more about him.'

'Hmm, well don't push him on the subject,' Dolly warned. 'I mean it. Let him get a word in edgeways, love, okay?'

'Jeez, you'd think this was an important meeting the way you're going on,' Clemmie said indignantly. 'Do you want to write a script for me? Make sure I don't big up my part?'

Dolly pursed her lips but said nothing else on the subject. After a moment's silence she turned and popped a macaron into Clemmie's mouth, so Clemmie knew they were still friends.

Reuben arrived at three o'clock as arranged, looking smart in dark jeans and a red shirt. Now she knew he wasn't dressing to impress her, Clemmie told him how nice he looked, and made him very welcome, ushering him into a chair while Dolly brought in the food.

'Blimey, this is posh,' Reuben joked, as he gazed at the plates of sandwiches, cakes, and scones that sat on the coffee table in front of him. 'I wasn't expecting all this.'

'You're honoured,' Clemmie assured him. 'Dolly doesn't do catering as a rule. I was raised on bread and jam,' she added, giving him a wink as her aunt straightened and fixed her with an indignant stare.

'Don't stand on ceremony,' Dolly urged them. 'Tuck in. It's there to be eaten.' She hurried into the kitchen, returning with a tray of teacups and a pot of tea, which she placed next to the food, before sitting on the sofa beside Reuben.

Clemmie was halfway through her fourth sandwich when she noticed Dolly giving Reuben odd looks. He was, she realised, looking incredibly tense suddenly, and had barely eaten a thing, which was strange because, considering Dolly had done the catering, this afternoon tea was scrummy.

'Is everything all right?' she asked.

Reuben started, as if just hearing her voice was enough to scare him to death. 'Of course. Absolutely fine.'

Clemmie finished her sandwich slowly, surveying them out of the corner of her eye. She saw Dolly nod towards her, her eyes fixed on Reuben, as if urging him to say or do something.

Reuben looked like a deer caught in the headlights of a fast-moving car. What on earth was going on?

Dolly heaved a big sigh. 'Right, one of us has got to make a start,' she announced, 'so it might as well be me.'

Clemmie finished her sandwich and eyed her aunt with trepidation. This was weird behaviour even by Dolly's standards, and she couldn't begin to understand what was going on.

'Okay,' Dolly said heavily. 'Confession time. I'd never met Reuben until he turned up in our shop that day, and I never knew his dad either.'

Clemmie's mouth dropped open. 'What?'

She fixed her gaze on Reuben, who was looking at Dolly with some horror.

Dolly shrugged. 'Time it all came out, and you weren't going to start the ball rolling.'

'I was building up to it,' he protested. 'You didn't have to land that on her so quickly.'

'Well, it's done now, so you can take it from here,' Dolly said.

'Hang on a minute.' Clemmie wondered if she was having some sort of wild dream. 'That morning he walked into our shop, you said he was the son of an old friend of yours. Your old accountant. You gave him air kisses!'

She'd known that was suspicious, even at the time, she recalled. Dolly never gave air kisses.

'Why would you greet someone you didn't know like that? And why lie about knowing his dad?'

Dolly glanced at Reuben, but he seemed frozen to the spot. She rolled her eyes and picked up a sandwich.

'Okay,' she said, waving it in the air as she spoke, 'here's what happened. I got a letter from Reuben here and it knocked me for six, I won't lie. You remember you kept asking me if I was keeping something from you, and I made up all that guff about being nervous about the awards do in London?'

'I *knew* you were being weird!' Clemmie cried. 'I couldn't believe you were so worried when normally you're as confident as anything about stuff like that. So what was in the letter?'

'Hmm, that's a bit complicated. Suffice it to say Reuben wanted to get to know us. Well,' she gave Clemmie an apologetic look, 'you really.'

'Me? But I don't get it.' Clemmie turned to Reuben. 'You didn't even know me. We'd never met. Or had we?' She frowned, trying to remember.

'It's not that simple,' he managed at last.

'So explain.'

Dolly took a bite out of her sandwich and chewed as she waited. When Reuben didn't reply she gave him a sharp nudge.

'Go on. It's over to you now, I think. Finish what you tried to start the other night before madam here got the wrong end of the stick and ruined everything.'

Reuben took a deep breath, clearly steadying himself.

'There's no easy way to tell you this, Clemmie, so I may as well just take a leaf out of Dolly's book and say it straight out.'

His eyes softened with sympathy suddenly, and Clemmie had an awful feeling of foreboding.

'I'm your brother, Clemmie.'

She heard his words, and she knew he was speaking English, yet somehow she couldn't absorb his meaning. She could have sworn he'd said he was her brother, but that was impossible. Of course it was impossible. She'd have known about him, and it didn't even add up. She felt a sudden gnawing fear in the pit of her stomach and fought to stay calm.

'You can't be,' she said faintly.

'I'm sorry, but it's true. Well, half-brother anyway.'

'You've made a mistake.' Clemmie gave her aunt an appealing look. 'He can't be, can he? It's impossible.'

When Dolly didn't reply, she turned furious eyes on Reuben.

'You're lying! My mum and dad were together from high school. They were only thirteen when they started going out together. They loved each other from that moment on. You've got this all wrong.'

'I haven't got it wrong, Clemmie,' Reuben said quietly. 'I'm sorry, but it's true. Your dad was my dad. He and my mum—'

'Stop it!' Clemmie jumped to her feet. 'Tell him, Dolly!'

Dolly's eyes glistened with tears, and that, more than anything, told Clemmie Reuben wasn't lying. Her aunt wasn't given to tears. Moreover, she was no one's fool. She'd have checked this out. There was no way she'd have taken Reuben's word for it. Clemmie dropped back into the armchair feeling utterly stunned and sick to her stomach. This couldn't be happening.

'But Mum and Dad,' she whispered. 'They loved each other.'

'They did, love,' Dolly reassured her. 'Of course they did.

But what you've got to understand is that they got together at a very young age. Some might say too young. Your dad loved your mum, but there came a time when—well—when he thought the grass might be greener on the other side of the fence, shall we say.'

'He met my mum at a retreat in Derbyshire,' Reuben explained. 'It was for creative people of all kinds. He'd signed up for a course on poetry, and she was teaching a pottery class. She lived in Derbyshire at the time. Your dad's course only lasted a fortnight, but—I guess they fell for each other pretty quickly.'

Clemmie couldn't speak. She sat dumbly, trying to take in what these two people were telling her about the father she'd adored all her life.

'When his course ended, he left and went back to your mum,' Reuben said gently. 'A few weeks later, Mum found out she was expecting me.'

Dolly was watching her closely. Clemmie couldn't take all this in and had no way of responding to the information they were giving her. It was like she wasn't really there at all. As if she was asleep, and someone was reading a bedtime story that was drifting into her dreams somehow. She could hear it, but it didn't make sense.

'Mum wrote to him to tell him she was pregnant,' Reuben continued. 'She wasn't sure if she should, but in the end she felt he had a right to know.'

Clemmie's eyes flickered as something penetrated the fog at last. 'Dad knew about you?'

Reuben glanced at Dolly, who nodded.

'So did your mum, love. Your dad confessed it all to her.'

'*Mum knew?*'

'It was an awful time,' Dolly admitted. 'Your mum was devastated, heartbroken. She threw your dad out and we both thought he'd gone to be with Reuben's mum. I moved in to take care of her because she was in no fit state to be on her own.' Her mouth tightened. 'It was a bad time all right. I never thought they'd get through it. I had them in the divorce courts with the judge stamping the papers. Just shows you.'

'Your dad did come to see Mum,' Reuben told her. 'From what Mum told me they knew from the start that it would never work between them. What they'd had at the retreat had just been a holiday fling. Nothing more. Besides, your dad loved your mum and wanted her back, and my mum knew that and had no desire to break up a marriage. She told him to go and get her, and promised he could see me whenever he wanted.'

'And—and did he?' He *couldn't* have done. He would never have been able to keep that a secret from her, surely? And what about Mum? It would have broken her heart if he'd kept in touch with that woman.

'Your dad went back home and threw himself on your mum's mercy,' Dolly said. 'Told her he loved her, that he was sorry. He'd been feeling trapped. As if he'd missed out on something, getting tied down so young. He knew he'd made a huge mistake and he swore it would never happen again.'

'And Mum forgave him?' Clemmie asked incredulously. 'Just like that?'

'Not just like that at all,' Dolly said, shaking her head. 'Far from it. It was bloody hard work. Especially once Reuben arrived and your dad wanted to see him. It was difficult for your mum to forgive him. Somehow, she had to find it in herself to trust him when he visited Reuben and his mum, and your dad did all he could to reassure her and make sure she knew he loved her more than anyone. They both put in a lot of hard graft to get past it, love, but they did it because they loved each other, and neither one of them wanted to be without the other.'

'My mum told me that, when I was around six months old, your dad brought your mum with him to meet me. After that, she came with him for almost every visit. She was nice to me,'

Reuben said, a wistful smile on his lips. 'She never made me feel unwanted or unwelcome. I liked her.'

'You knew my mum?' Clemmie's mind whirled. 'But—but how come I never knew about you?'

'Reuben had turned three when you were born,' Dolly explained. 'Your mum and dad used to leave you with me when they went off to see him, but they did have him to stay once at your house. You'd only have been about a year old at the time.'

'I remember you though,' Reuben told her, smiling. 'You were a chubby little thing with fair hair and these big blue eyes. Just like now. I was told you were my baby sister, and I've never forgotten that day.'

'But your mum and dad were worried about how to explain things,' Dolly said. 'As you got older, they knew you'd start asking questions that they didn't feel you were ready to hear the answers to, so they decided to keep the two of you apart. They planned to tell you when you were older, and they felt you could understand. Sadly, they never got the chance.'

'Then why didn't *you* tell me?' Clemmie demanded tearfully. It was as if she'd woken up from the dream, and real life was intruding all too clearly. 'Why keep this from me for all these years?'

'I wanted to,' Dolly admitted. 'I just didn't know how. You've got such an idealised view of love, and of your parents' marriage. I didn't want to be the one to shatter that illusion.'

'Are you okay, Clemmie?' Reuben asked anxiously.

She stared at him. 'Why now?'

'I'm sorry?'

'All these years you've known about my parents, about me. You've never said a word. Why now, all of a sudden?'

Reuben rubbed his face, looking weary. 'I suppose,' he said, 'it's because I lost Mum. When she was dying, she begged me to find you. Reminded me I had a half-sister in the world, and she didn't want me to be alone. I didn't see the point. I thought too long had passed and I told myself I didn't need any family but Matt. But then, after she died, I started to feel differently.'

He glanced at Dolly. 'I found you pretty easily. I knew you were a writer, because I remembered Clemmie's mum telling me proudly all about her sister's books. I soon found your website online.' He gave her a crooked grin. 'Sorry, but it made me cringe. What a mess! Anyway, we fixed that for you, didn't we?'

When she nodded and smiled at him, he turned to face Clemmie as he continued.

'I sent a letter to her publisher, explaining I had important personal business with her, and asking if they'd put me in touch with her. I enclosed a photo of me as a baby with your mum and our dad. I knew she'd get what that meant.'

'And I did. That was the letter I got in January,' Dolly explained. 'The one that sent me into a spin. I knew who he was straight away. Reuben had put his phone number in the letter, so I gave him a call. He told me about his mum dying, and how he wanted to meet you, so we arranged for him to visit Tuppenny Bridge. We cooked up the story of his dad being my old accountant as a way of explaining how I knew him. The plan was, he was going to stay in a B&B, and I'd offer him a room at Wintergreen so he could get to know you, but when he arrived he'd booked Dale View until March which threw me a bit.'

'I thought it would be better to have some distance to start with,' Reuben admitted. 'I didn't want to rush it or pressure you.'

Dolly sighed. 'I'm so sorry, love.'

'Wow, I really have been stupid, haven't I?' Clemmie said, shaking her head. 'Oh no! And I thought you were trying it on with me!'

'Yeah, that was a bit of a shock,' Reuben admitted. 'It was my fault. You were bound to think I had designs on you, the way I was showing such an obvious interest in your life and inviting you to dinner like that.'

'Did you actually have a dad?' Clemmie asked. 'I mean, apart from mine.'

'Oh yes, that was all true. Everything I said about mum and dad was real, except he wasn't Dolly's accountant. He accepted me and he accepted that I had a relationship with my real father. He was wonderful.'

'You've had a lot of loss, love,' Dolly told him gently. 'Your parents splitting up when you were fourteen, losing your biological dad when you were sixteen, then your real dad at twenty-one. Now your mum's gone, too. I'm sorry.'

'We've all lost people we loved,' Reuben told her. 'You lost your sister, and Clemmie lost both her parents. That's why it's even more important that we hang on to the family we still have, don't you think?'

He gave Clemmie a pleading look. 'You're my half-sister, and you're all the family I've got left in the world. I don't expect you to accept that straight away, but I hope, in time, you'll start to see me as a positive addition to your life, and not an unwelcome intruder who almost shattered your family.'

'You did no such thing,' Dolly said firmly. 'A baby's always a blessing in my opinion. In the end both dads and both mums got on well, and they always had yours and Clemmie's welfare at heart. Nothing to feel bad about there.'

Easy for her to say! Dolly and Reuben had known about this for years. It was all new to Clemmie, and she still couldn't believe that her mum and dad had kept something so massive from her. She had no words.

Dolly and Reuben exchanged glances.

'Love?' Dolly asked hesitantly.

Clemmie stood. 'I think I'm going to go upstairs for a lie down,' she said. 'I really don't know what to think, and I've got nothing to say right now. To either of you.'

As Reuben opened his mouth, Dolly put her hand on his arm in a warning gesture. 'Fair enough, love. You do that. Tomorrow's another day.'

Reuben clearly took the hint.

'I'd better go home,' he said, getting to his feet. 'Thank you for listening. Oh!' He fumbled in his coat pocket and brought out a paper bag. 'You left this.'

Slowly, Clemmie took the battered copy of *Jane Eyre* from his hand.

Reuben met her gaze, and she saw how troubled he looked and wished for a moment that she could tell him everything was okay.

'I hope—'

But Clemmie was already leaving the room. She had an awful lot of thinking to do.

# FORTY-TWO

Clemmie heard the tentative knock on her bedroom door and gave an inward groan. She just wanted to be left alone. Why couldn't Dolly understand that?

The door was pushed open, and her aunt peered round, waving a white tea towel.

'Am I safe to come in?'

Clemmie glared at her. 'You think this is funny?'

'No, love. I don't. Far from it.'

Dolly sighed and walked into the room, closing the door behind her. Despite Clemmie giving out obvious signals that she didn't want her here, she chose, for reasons known only to herself, to sit on the bed beside her niece and gaze sadly down at her, the tea towel on her lap.

'This is a pretty pickle, isn't it?' she said at last.

Clemmie rolled her eyes. 'Wow, you do have a way with words. No wonder you're a writer with a talent like that.'

'All right, snarky!' Dolly tutted. 'Look, I know you've had a bit of a shock—'

'A *bit* of a shock? Dolly have you heard yourself?' Clemmie sat up on the bed and stared at her aunt in amazement. 'Have you any idea how I feel, knowing you've been lying to me all these years?'

'I didn't lie,' Dolly protested. 'I just didn't tell you.'

'Same difference! And then to lie to me again in cahoots with Reuben! Finding out that I've got a half-brother I never knew existed. And as if all that wasn't bad enough, as if things could get any worse, I learn that my dad—my darling, perfect, wonderful dad—cheated on my mum.'

She threw herself back on the bed again, yelping as she banged her head on the headboard.

'You shouldn't have done that,' Dolly observed. 'Give yourself concussion carrying on like that.'

'Go away, Dolly,' Clemmie said wearily. 'I've got nothing to say to you.'

'No, well, I've got plenty to say to you,' Dolly said firmly. 'So you can take that petulant look off your face and listen to me, right?'

'Well, that's nice!' Clemmie gave her an indignant look. 'Haven't I been through enough?'

'We've all been through plenty,' Dolly said. 'You think Reuben's had an easy time of it? At least you had your dad with you right up until the end. He was lucky to see him once a month. And he's lost both his dads, and now his mum. He's still grieving for her, have you thought of that? Remember what that feels like?'

Clemmie bit her lip. 'As if I'd ever forget.'

'Well, there you go then. Have a bit of compassion for the lad.'

'It's not Reuben who's the problem,' Clemmie said. 'It's you, lying to me. And even more than that, it's Mum and Dad. They're not who I thought they were after all. I've been so stupid.'

'They were exactly who you thought they were,' Dolly replied. 'Good, decent people, who loved you to bits and wanted nothing more than your happiness.'

'But their life together was a lie.'

No matter which way she looked at it, Clemmie couldn't see a way around that. The perfect couple. Childhood sweethearts who'd fallen in love at school, married at twenty-one, and had idolised each other throughout their entire marriage. That's how she'd seen them. They'd been her role models. It was their relationship she viewed as the perfect example. Now it was all ruined. It had been a lie from start to finish.

'Nothing about their life together was a lie,' Dolly said. 'Okay, your dad messed up spectacularly, but he also confessed to your mum. He didn't keep Reuben a secret. He had the courage to face her and tell her the truth. And she had the courage to give him another chance. They worked hard to make their marriage work, because they loved each other, and neither of them wanted to say goodbye.

'You think that was easy? Of course it wasn't. It was bloody agonising at times, for both of them. But they stuck at it, and gradually they fell in love all over again, deeper this time because they understood all too well what they'd almost lost. You were a celebration of their love, of forgiveness, of courage. If you can't appreciate and understand that I don't know what else to say to you.'

'You should have told me,' Clemmie said tearfully. 'I don't know why you kept it from me all these years.'

Dolly sighed. 'I wanted to tell you so badly, and I nearly did, so many times. But you're such a little romantic, Clem.' She stroked Clemmie's cheek affectionately. 'You had this vision of your mum and dad in your head, and I just couldn't bring myself to shatter it. You see,' she said sadly, 'I lacked your mum's courage. I was never as brave as her. I'm so sorry.'

When Clemmie didn't reply she reached for the book on the bedside table and leafed through it, frowning.

'Is this new? Well, not new obviously but... I haven't seen it before. It's a bit tatty.' She eyed Clemmie suspiciously. 'Where did you get it from?'

'Reuben bought it for me,' Clemmie said truthfully. 'Although,' she added in the interests of honesty, 'only because I told him I really wanted it, and you didn't approve of me buying books from the second-hand book stall on the market.'

'Got it from the market, did you? Charming.' Dolly grinned and continued browsing. '*Jane Eyre*, eh? Now, her and Rochester had a bit of an uppy-downy time of it, didn't they? He told a proper big fib. A secret wife in the attic if you please! Jane must have been very forgiving to get past that one.'

Clemmie eyed her suspiciously.

'Of course, Jane and Rochester were meant for each other. That "cord of communion" Rochester talked about, remember? Like a piece of invisible string attaching his heart to hers. When you're connected like that it doesn't matter how many bumps there are along the road, or even if you're separated for a long time. Somehow, you'll find your way back to each other. That, if you ask me, is true love. Anyone can stay with someone when the going is easy and it's all hearts and flowers. It's the obstacles along the way and how you deal with them that's the real test. Shows that all the pain of staying together is better than the pain of being without them.' She put the book back on the table. 'That's what I reckon, anyway. But, hey, what do I know? I only wrote the romantic saga of the year.'

Clemmie tutted. *Okay, no need to hammer home the point.*

'Funny thing about this book,' Dolly continued. 'All the romantic stuff going on between Jane and Rochester is fine and dandy, but do you know which passage is my favourite?'

'Surprise me.'

Dolly ignored the sarcasm. 'What always gave me goosebumps and brought tears to my eyes was Jane's passionate outburst after she discovered Rochester had a secret wife and he'd tried to persuade her to stay and be his mistress. Now, naturally, Jane's tempted. She loves the fella after all. And then she wonders who'd really care if she sacrificed her ideals. And there it comes. Four little words! "*I care for myself.*" By heck, it gives me the shivers.'

She shook her head. 'Poor, plain, friendless Jane Eyre had the courage to stick to her principles, and enough self-esteem to do what she believed was right, no matter what. You know why? Because she knew her own worth, and loved herself no matter how badly other people treated her. And your mum was the same. Oh, she was devastated by your dad's affair, just like Jane was when she found out about poor Bertha. But she also knew she wanted to be with him, and that gave her the courage to give him one more chance, but only on the understanding that one chance was all he'd ever get.'

'But how?' Clemmie asked, drawn in despite herself. 'How could she possibly trust him after all that?'

'Because, like Jane, she knew her own worth. She knew that if he messed up again that was his problem not hers. If he couldn't see what he had in her then it would be his loss, and she'd cope. Oh, she'd be upset. Heartbroken. But she knew she'd survive. The way she saw it, she had nothing to lose. She did what made her happy knowing that whatever the outcome she'd be okay, and she'd given it her best shot. Any failure after that would be down to him. But it didn't fail. He never let her down again. See, he saw it too. What she was worth. And he wasn't daft enough to let her go again, was he?'

She winked and gathered up the tea towel. 'I'm cooking a chilli. Let me know when you're hungry.'

As she closed the bedroom door behind her, Clemmie sat up and reached for *Jane Eyre*. She hadn't really looked at it properly because Reuben had turned up just after she'd spotted it at the stall. Now, as she flicked through the pages she realised someone must have been studying the book for a course or something, because there were pencil notes in most of the margins.

Bits of narrative and dialogue were underlined, some of them with exclamation marks and circles around them. Whoever had owned the book previously had written footnotes in the bottom of each chapter, sometimes scribbling out part of what they'd written.

It was a mess really. What with the tear on the cover and the dog-eared pages...

Clemmie hugged the book to her, realising that none of those things would stop her from becoming absorbed in the story that lay within. That she would instantly be transported to Lowood School and Thornfield Hall, and that she wouldn't even notice the state of the book.

The love story of Jane and Rochester would be all that mattered.

Jane could have chosen a clean page and married St John Rivers after all. But instead she'd returned to the ruins of Thornfield and the damaged Edward Rochester.

Her mum could have turned her back on her dad and ended their marriage. She'd had cause to, and no one could have blamed her. But she'd chosen to work on their relationship, finding the beautiful love story hidden under the crossings out and mistakes.

Because she'd trusted herself.

Because she'd known her own worth.

Clemmie grabbed her notebook from the drawer and turned to the back, rifling through the notes she'd made as she'd gone over and over *The Marquess Wants a Wife*, trying to figure out what was wrong with it.

Emmeline! It was so obvious now what was wrong with her.

In parts she came across as petulant, naïve, and childlike. She pushed Rollo away and refused to listen no matter how many times he assured her that his heart was true. Clemmie hadn't been certain why she reacted that way, and had come up with all sorts of half-baked attempts to explain why she treated him so badly.

But when it came right down to it, it was quite simple. Emmeline had no faith in herself, and therefore no faith in Rollo's love for her. Somehow, she had to believe that she was good enough for him, and that when he said he loved her he meant it. Right now there was no way she could ever trust in Rollo, and she'd make them both miserable. That was why her ending had felt all wrong, and why she wasn't convinced they'd really found their happy ever after.

Emmeline had to learn to love herself.

She had to be more like Jane Eyre!

Clemmie put the notebook back in her drawer and lay back on the bed, her eyes closed.

And Emmeline wasn't the only one. She'd pushed Ross away. She'd told herself it was because she didn't trust him. She'd convinced herself that at some point he'd force her to reveal the truth about herself to others, even when she didn't want him to. And she'd been so sure that he'd grow tired of her, that even though he promised he loved her, that love wouldn't last when he had to lie with her every night, seeing who she really was.

But it wasn't Ross she didn't trust, was it? It was herself. Deep down, she didn't trust that she was good enough. And her lack of self-esteem had ensured that she could no longer believe in him, or in their love for each other.

Ross had told her he loved her, and her alopecia didn't matter to him. He'd sworn to her that he wasn't interested in other women. And she'd refused to listen, because she didn't believe someone like him could possibly love someone like her.

It wasn't Ross who'd let her down. It was she who'd let herself down.

Why hadn't she seen the truth sooner? Now he was with Meg, and from what Summer had said he seemed happy.

She'd learned her lesson. Sadly for her, she'd learned it too late.

## FORTY-THREE

It was a very nervous Clemmie who knocked on the door of Dale View a couple of days later. She knew Reuben wasn't at Whispering Willows that morning, and Dolly had given her the morning off to visit him and, hopefully, have a civilised conversation with him. She just hoped he wasn't too busy working on a website to see her.

She swallowed as she heard the latch on the door being lifted. The door opened and Reuben stood there. Her half-brother. She could barely believe it, even though she'd spent all yesterday trying to come to terms with it.

To her relief, his face lit up when he saw her.

'Clemmie! Do you want to come in?' he asked, opening the door wider to allow her to pass through.

'I think it would be a good idea,' she said. 'I suppose we have a lot to talk about.'

He nodded and ushered her through to the large kitchen/diner. Without even asking he poured her a glass of apple juice and helped himself to a glass of wine. She supposed he felt the need for some Dutch courage, which made her feel a bit guilty.

'How are you doing?' he asked, sitting at the table beside her. 'I was going to come and see you, but I thought maybe you needed some time to process everything. I know it was a lot to take in.' He sighed. 'I'm sorry, Clemmie. I'm sorry for the way it was sprung on you like that.'

'I don't suppose it would have mattered how the news was broken to me,' she admitted. 'It was always going to be a shock.'

'I know. How are you feeling about things now?'

'Honestly? Still shaken. I had such an idealised image of my mum and dad's relationship. I honestly thought they'd never put a foot wrong in all the years they knew each other. Finding out Dad strayed was hard. Really hard.'

'I can imagine.' Reuben sipped his wine. 'He was a good man. I mean, I didn't see nearly as much of him as you did, but I loved him. He was a good dad to me—as good as he could be, anyway. And your mum was really kind.'

'She was obviously a very strong person,' Clemmie said. 'She didn't crumble, even though it must have broken her heart, what they did to her.' No offence,' she added hastily.

'None taken. You're right. It must have. She obviously loved him very much to take him back after what he did, and to accept me. I'm glad they made it work, even after everything that happened with my mum.'

'So am I,' Clemmie said fervently. 'I wouldn't be here otherwise, would I?'

It was a sobering thought. If her mum had been just a little less forgiving, if she'd chosen to walk away, if she hadn't decided that her love for her husband was stronger than her hurt and sense of betrayal, Clemmie wouldn't exist. What if she and Ross were destined to have children one day? What if her stubborn refusal to give their relationship another chance meant they never got to be born?

She mentally shook her head. It was impossible to think like that. She'd never know, would she? Even so...

'I'm glad your mum found someone of her own,' Clemmie said. She realised how that sounded and added quickly, 'I'm sorry, I didn't mean *of her own* as a criticism. I just meant, I'm glad she found someone she could love who could be with her. And that he loved you, too.'

'I'm very glad about that as well,' he said. 'You know, Mum always felt guilty about what happened, Clemmie. She was at a low ebb when she met your dad, and she knew they'd behaved badly. I really wouldn't want you to think she was a bad person because she wasn't. It was just...'

'Circumstances,' Clemmie said with a shrug. 'I don't blame her. Well, I did at first,' she admitted, 'but thinking about it, how can I? It was at least as much Dad's fault as hers, and he was the married one. She wasn't cheating on anyone.'

'Has it made you feel differently about him?' he asked gently.

She tilted her head, considering. 'Not really. He was still my dad, and he was a good dad. I was lucky to have him. As for their marriage—well, I suppose it just proves how strong it really was. Look what they overcame.'

'I'm glad you see it that way,' he said. 'I was worried you wouldn't be able to once I saw your reaction. That's a very mature way of looking at things, Clemmie.'

'Maybe I've had to do a bit of growing up lately,' she said, taking a sip from her apple juice.

'And what about me?' he asked quietly. 'How do you feel about me, now you know I'm your half-brother?

She smiled. 'It's weird,' she admitted. 'I've always been an only child, and unlike you, I had no idea I had a sibling out there in the world. It's going to take some getting used to.'

'Do you think you'll ever manage that?' he asked hopefully.

She hesitated, then put her hand on his. 'I think I can live with it,' she said. 'It's quite nice to think I have a big brother. Don't worry, I won't ask you for pocket money,'

He laughed. 'I'm so glad, Clemmie. Not about the pocket money! About you being able to live with it. You know, I really wasn't sure what to expect when I came here, but you've surpassed all my expectations. Even if you weren't my sister I'd like you. You're a good person. I hope we can get to know each other properly over time.'

'I'd like that,' she admitted. 'And I'd like to meet Matt, too. How come he didn't come with you to Tuppenny Bridge? He must be missing you.'

'We're missing each other,' Reuben said. 'But we talk every day. He knew this was something I had to deal with myself. He's a very understanding man. I'm so lucky to have him.'

Clemmie blinked away tears. 'I'm glad for you. I really am. I'd love to meet him one day.'

'I'm sure that can be arranged.' He looked suddenly sheepish. 'You might find a wedding invitation arrives in the post in a couple of months. We're getting married.'

'No way!' Clemmie squealed and gave him a hug. 'So I'll have a new brother-in-law, too?'

'You will. Will you come to the wedding? You can bring Dolly, of course.'

'Wild horses wouldn't keep us away,' she promised. 'Gosh, a trip to London. I can't wait.'

And the funny thing was, she meant every word.

'It's such a shame he's going back to Hampstead,' she said to Dolly, as she recounted their meeting when she got back to the bookshop.

'I suppose it is, love,' Dolly agreed. 'Mind you, he doesn't have to go just yet. I know Dale View will most likely be booked up after he leaves as it'll be March and we all know how quickly these holiday lets go, but we've got a spare room. If he wants to stay here a bit longer he's more than welcome.'

'Really? Do you think he'd want to? What about Matt? I know he's missing him.'

'Matt could come and stay with us, too.'

Clemmie's eyes widened in delight at the thought of it. 'Do you think he would?'

'Only one way to find out.'

Clemmie asked Reuben how he felt about moving in with them for a little while, just so they could get to know each other properly, and if Matt would like to stay with them, too. Matt had been able to get the second week in March off work and was delighted to accept their offer, saying he was looking forward to meeting them and to finally seeing this beautiful little town that Reuben kept telling him about.

Reuben would be moving into Wintergreen when his rental period was up on the first of March, although he'd made up his mind to return home with his partner on the fifteenth of the month because he had his mum's house to put on the market, and he and Matt had wedding plans to finalise.

Although she still felt weird whenever she realised that her beloved dad was also Reuben's dad, she was glad to have her newly found big brother around. There was, after all, no one else alive who was related to Dad apart from the two of them. She had Dolly as a reminder of her mum, so it felt right to have them both under the same roof as her—even if it was only temporary.

She hadn't told anyone that he was her half-brother, not even Summer. She was still coming to terms with it all and was worried that people would think differently of her dad. The last thing she wanted was for people to remember him as a philanderer. And there was another reason.

'I know it will come out at some point,' she told Dolly, 'but right now I just want to get to know Reuben without anybody gawping at us or gossiping. You know what this place is like. We won't get a minute's peace once they know. It's probably best if we introduce him as my half-brother just before Reuben goes home. That way we'll get to spend time together in relative calm.'

Reuben was happy with that, so while he was still at Dale View they continued meeting up when neither of them was working, or he wasn't volunteering at the sanctuary. Now that she knew he had no romantic interest in her, it was surprising how much more relaxed she felt around him. The protective shield had dropped, and she found herself listening to him without a warning voice in her head, and as a consequence discovered she really liked him.

'Are you going to tell him?' Dolly asked her one grey, drizzly Saturday. 'About you know what.'

'You can say the word,' Clemmie told her. 'About the alopecia? No. I'm not ready for that, and he doesn't need to know, does he?'

'He is your brother, though,' Dolly pointed out. 'Family.'

'It's too soon for all that.' Clemmie couldn't imagine that it would ever be the right time. Reuben might be her closest living relative, but she didn't see any reason to confide in him about something so personal. Three people knew already. That was quite enough.

She glanced out of the window and pulled a face. 'I hope the weather cheers up before Matt gets here. I'd hate his first sight of Tuppenny Bridge to be so grim.'

The snow had been annoying, but the endless rain and grey skies which replaced it were no better. The dismal weather seemed to match the mood of everyone Clemmie spoke to, as no one seemed to be in high spirits.

'It's Joseph, more than anything,' Kat confided. 'Everyone's so depressed about him. I don't think it will be long now, you know.'

She'd popped into The Corner Cottage Bookshop to order a book. Her knitting classes were starting up in The Crafty Cook

Café and this particular book gave handy hints about teaching beginners one step at a time. A nervous Kat had decided she needed all the help she could get, whatever Jonah and her aunts told her.

'I know,' Clemmie said sadly. 'Summer says he's in bed most of the time now. It's awful, isn't it?'

'Terrible. Has Clive had any luck tracing Bethany?'

It was pointless asking Kat how she knew about that. There were few secrets in Tuppenny Bridge, and besides, look who Kat's aunties were.

'Summer hasn't said anything since he went to see Miss Lavender.'

'Hmm.' Kat sighed. 'I thought she'd have been more help to be honest. I guess if she doesn't know where she is there's no hope.'

Miss Lavender, according to Summer, who'd got it from Ben, who'd got it from Clive, had remembered that, a few years after Joseph's sister had left home, she'd read in the papers that Bethany had married someone called Ted Marshall who lived in Somerset.

Ted, apparently, was loaded, so Bethany had done all right for herself. However, Miss Lavender had tracked down an obituary in a London newspaper which had stated that Ted had died over a year ago, and which gave his wife's name as Helena, which could only mean Bethany and Ted had divorced—or worse, Bethany had already died.

There was no mention of where Bethany was now if she was still alive. Clive was currently searching for Helena Marshall to see if she knew where Bethany might be, but it seemed the address given in the obituary was no help, as the house was shut up and for sale, and the estate agent was unable to pass on her personal details.

'Let's just hope he finds her in time,' Kat said, crossing her fingers. She picked up her umbrella and gave Clemmie a wry look. 'Oh well, time to brave the rain again. Wish me luck!'

Market Place was surprisingly busy. Plenty of people had braved the market, despite the gloomy weather, and Dolly was quite chuffed that the shop had a steady flow of customers, even though she swore market days were usually dire.

Clemmie had always thought her aunt imagined that. Dolly's insistence that prospective customers spent their money at the second-hand book stall instead had never rung true to her. They were looking for different things, after all. The brand-new pristine books on the shelves of The Corner Cottage Bookshop were very different from the battered old books on the stall. Some of those were decades old, and you could discover a real gem if you looked hard enough and were lucky.

Like *Jane Eyre*.

Clemmie sighed then glanced up as Dolly came clattering down the stairs with a padded envelope in her arms.

'I'm taking this book order to the post office before it shuts,' she announced. 'Do you want anything while I'm out?'

'No thanks. Are you driving?'

Dolly laughed. 'Of course not! It'll only take me fifteen minutes there and back.' She put the box on the counter and hurried into the kitchen, returning a moment later wearing her coat.

Clemmie eyed the sky doubtfully. 'I don't know. Looks to me like it's going to pour down in a minute,' she warned her aunt.

'Give over. It's been threatening all morning, but it's only managed a drizzle. I'll be fine. See you soon.'

Dolly grabbed the parcel and headed out into the market place. Clemmie thought she was taking a risk, but she couldn't say she hadn't been warned. She switched on a smile as a young woman entered the shop and enquired about children's books, directing her to the back room.

A few moments later, the heavens opened, and the rain poured down. Poor Dolly was going to get caught in it, no doubt about it. She'd probably nip into The White Hart Inn, knowing her aunt, and take shelter there. Clemmie grinned to herself. She shouldn't expect to see her back within the next half hour, not if Sally offered her a glass of wine while she waited.

Never mind, it would give her a chance to get on with the rewrites she'd started. *The Marquess Wants a Wife* was already flowing much better, and Clemmie realised she liked Emmeline now a whole lot better than she had previously. At last it made sense why Rollo loved her!

Ten minutes later the door flew open again and a trio of middle-aged women hurried in, laughing, and making jokes about it being great weather for ducks.

'Just browsing, love,' one of them said, and Clemmie nodded, aware that they'd probably only popped in to get out of the rain and had no intention of buying anything. The young woman came back carrying a copy of a lift-the-flap picture book, suitable for a toddler, and Clemmie put her notebook and pen back under the counter.

She put the picture book in a paper bag and took the woman's debit card, glancing up as the doorbell jangled again.

Her heart jumped into her throat as she realised Ross had entered the shop. His dark hair was plastered to his head, and his coat was soaking wet, yet he still managed to look gorgeous.

'Excuse me, I think that's gone through.'

Clemmie blinked, realising the young woman was waiting for her. She glanced down at the card reader and shook her head.

'I'm so sorry. Would you like a receipt?'

She handed the young woman the book and thanked her for her custom. The three older women were, she noticed, currently browsing adult fiction. Maybe one of them would buy something after all.

'Hi, Clemmie.'

He was standing right by the counter, so close to her she could easily touch him if she wanted to. Or had the nerve. It was the first time she'd seen him since they'd said that awkward goodbye outside Wintergreen.

'Hi, Ross.' She forced a smile. 'What brings you here? Looking for a romantic novel?'

Why had she said that? She was such an idiot!

He shook his head and drops of rain spattered on the floor, a couple of them flicking Clemmie. Jeez, he was drenched, poor man!

'I came to give you these.' He put his hand inside his coat and pulled something from his inside pocket.

Clemmie stared at the invitations on the counter.

'I'm so sorry they're late,' he said. 'I honestly thought my aunt had sent them. There was a bit of a mix-up. You see—you see the painting's finished, and she wanted to have a big unveiling at the opening, before handing it to you. But I said no.' He gave her a nervous smile. 'Tell me if I'm wrong, but I thought you'd hate all that fuss.'

Clemmie managed to stop herself from shuddering at the thought. 'I would,' she admitted. 'I can't think of anything worse.'

'That's what I thought you'd say. Initially, Aunt Eugenie was going to invite you to this grand handover herself, but when I vetoed her plan she assumed I was going to send you an invitation, but I assumed she'd already sent it. Then Summer mentioned that you hadn't been invited and I was mortified. You must have been really annoyed with me.'

Clemmie wasn't sure how to respond to that. *Annoyed? I was devastated* didn't seem appropriate.

'It's okay,' she said with a shrug. 'These things happen.'

'But you will come?' he asked her, sounding hopeful. 'And afterwards I can give you your portrait. I'll have to take a photo of you with it to please Aunt Eugenie, and to prove you received your prize, but it will be away from prying eyes. Is that okay?'

Was she mistaken or did he sound and look anxious?

She stared at him, not sure what to say. *Have you any idea how beautiful you are? Look at those eyes. I could drown in them. I don't even care that you're dripping water on the counter.*

'Dolly, too, of course,' he said quickly, as if her silence was because she thought her aunt hadn't been invited. Dolly hadn't, she admitted to herself, somewhat ashamed, even entered her head.

'I'm sure we'll both be there,' she managed.

His gaze was intense. He seemed to be analysing every part of her face, and she wondered if he was comparing the real-life Clemmie to the one he'd painted and assessing how good a job he'd done. Or was he, God forbid, checking out her wig? Was he taking the time to marvel at how realistic it looked? Or was he picturing her without it? Uh-oh. She was doing it again, wasn't she?

*No, he's not doing that, Clemmie. Get a grip. He's not even looking at your hair. He's looking into your eyes. He's practically hypnotising you. Lord, I can't even move. How is he doing that? You must look like a rabbit caught in the headlights. Say something. Anything.*

'I'm glad you sorted things out with Ben.'

The words were out before she could stop them, and she stared at him in horror. What if he guessed Summer had told her everything? He'd be furious. There'd be a huge showdown. Ben would have to take Summer's side and then he and Ross would fall out all over again, and it would all be her fault.

'I—I mean...'

'It's okay,' he said kindly. 'I knew Summer would fill you in as soon as I gave Ben permission to tell her what had happened. So now you know. I think, in a way, I was hoping she'd tell you, so I'd never have to.'

Clemmie felt a rush of sympathy for him. 'I don't see why you didn't tell me all those years ago,' she said. 'I could have helped you come to terms with it. It wasn't your fault. I think you did the right thing. You were a good friend to Ben.'

'I was worried you'd hate me,' he admitted. 'I'd hated myself long enough as it was.'

'I could never hate you,' Clemmie said.

Their gaze held and for a moment Clemmie thought about reaching out to him, but then she remembered The Big Problem.

'I—I wanted to tell you,' she said, looking down at the counter and trying not to sound too miserable. 'I'm really pleased to hear about you and Meg. I hope you'll be very happy together.'

'Me and Meg?' The tone of his voice made her look up sharply. 'There is no me and Meg.'

'But I thought...' She swallowed. 'Rumour has it that—'

'Oh, rumours! I can imagine. Meg was my interior designer, and we met up purely to discuss the plans for the house. Nothing else. Meg's not my type. She's practical, brisk, focused.'

He gave her a wistful smile. 'When you've loved a dreamer, how can you love someone who's forgotten how to dream?'

Clemmie's heart raced and she stared at him, unable to take her eyes off him, even though the doorbell jangled again.

From a million miles away she heard Dolly say, 'By hell, it's like a monsoon out there. Oh! Fancy seeing you here, Ross. To what do we owe this pleasure?'

Ross turned to greet her. 'Just dropping off your invitations to the open day next Sunday. My apologies for their lateness. Clemmie will explain, I'm sure.'

He nodded at Clemmie. 'I'd better be going. I hope to see you there.'

With that, he left the shop, leaving Clemmie dazed and confused.

'You look like you've been hit by a truck,' Dolly remarked. 'What's happened?'

What *had* happened? Clemmie really wasn't sure. Had Ross just been nice to her? Or was he telling her something much more important—that *she* was the dreamer, and he could never love anyone but her?

But even after the way she'd behaved? Even though she'd rejected him a second time?

Surely she could never be that lucky.

# FORTY-FOUR

Although it was overcast, the rain had, luckily, held off, which was a good job as there was a long queue of people waiting to enter The Arabella Lavender Art Academy that Sunday afternoon.

The event was invitation only, but it was clear that most of the town had been invited, and a great many of those had taken Ross up on his invitation.

As Clemmie and Dolly queued, they spotted many familiar faces. Ben, Jamie, and Eloise were just ahead of them in the line, and Ben told them that Jennifer and her new assistant had been working in the kitchen, and had prepared a buffet for everyone to enjoy after the tour.

Further up in the queue they saw Zach and Ava with their two children, and Kat and Jonah without theirs. Maybe the aunties were babysitting Tommy and Hattie, although Clemmie would be surprised if they were. Surely the Pennyfeathers, of all people, wouldn't want to miss out on this event?

'Summer's minding the kids,' Ben explained when she voiced her thoughts. 'They were going to bring them with them, but then they decided the little ones wouldn't have the patience, so Kat was going to stay home, but Summer volunteered. Well, we've already seen the house, so she wasn't fussed. I'm only here to support Ross and Mum.'

Bluebell, Clover, and Buttercup were way behind Clemmie and Dolly, and looked pretty fed up about how far down the line they were.

Sally and Rafferty had wangled a couple of hours away from the pub and were right at the top of the queue near the doors. Rafferty was passionate about art and would probably take lessons here himself. Everyone looked very eager, and there was a buzz of excited conversation. The new academy was the talk of the town, and everyone wanted to see how Monk's Folly had been transformed.

Reuben hadn't been invited, but when Clemmie had suggested that she ask Ross if he could attend, he'd told her there was no point because he'd be needed at Whispering Willows.

Clive was also absent for obvious reasons, although Clemmie wasn't sure he'd have attended anyway. She didn't know much about Clive's interests but couldn't imagine the art academy would be one of them.

At two o'clock sharp, the doors opened, and everyone flooded in. There were lots of gasps and exclamations of delight as people wandered through the rooms, admiring the Regency splendour of what had once been—and to most would always be—Monk's Folly.

The hallway—now a light and airy space painted in powder blue—had a small table at the end that held a rack full of leaflets for local tourist attractions, restaurants, and pubs. Miss Lavender was quick to point out that this should bring extra visitors to the town and the surrounding area.

Miss Lavender steered people through the house, explaining the purpose of each room in turn. The front living room would be used for guests to relax in peace and quiet at the end of the day, while a smaller room housed computers and printers so the students could print off their digital photos, which would be taken to enable them to finish the landscape paintings they'd start on location.

There was a spacious dining room, big enough to seat up to fourteen people comfortably, and the large kitchen with its state-of-the-art units and cooking facilities, where a shy-looking Jennifer and her cheerful assistant paused in their work to exchange pleasantries with the visitors.

The front room on the opposite side of the hallway from the living room had several low-level bookcases with a wide variety of art books to peruse. Several of Ross's paintings were on display, though it was Arabella's artwork that took prominence. There was also another room which would, according to Miss Lavender, be used as a gallery for local artists' work in the future.

Clemmie was enraptured. She loved the beautifully painted walls—a different colour in each room—and the warm white ceilings, cornices, and ceiling roses. The fireplaces were stunning. The sash windows with their shutters were enchanting.

The furniture, although authentic looking, was comfortable and clearly new. Rather than being a disappointment, this only added to Clemmie's pleasure. After all, the Regency furniture in Jane Austen's time would have been new, too. It looked welcoming and romantic and everything she'd hoped it would be.

Upstairs on the first floor were four en suite bedrooms. Two were large doubles, one was a twin, and one was a single. There were two further double bedrooms with small, en suite shower rooms, in what had once been a dusty old attic, but certainly didn't fit that description any longer. All had flat-screen smart televisions, as well as tea and coffee making facilities.

Miss Lavender explained that each residential course would have a maximum of six participants to ensure they received individual attention, but that students' partners who didn't wish to take part in the courses were welcome to stay with them at a reduced cost.

Clemmie noticed the first-floor front rooms were marked private and no one was shown around them, and she guessed they were Ross's own rooms, which gave her a thrill of anticipation as she wondered if she'd ever get to see what lay behind those doors.

The studio itself was of less interest to her initially, although when she discovered that it was Ross showing them around it her interest surprisingly soared. She could tell from the enthusiastic way he talked about it that it meant as much to him—if not more—than the house.

'As you can see, we have everything that our students could possibly need,' he said, his eyes shining as he opened various cupboard doors. 'Easels, oil paints, acrylics, watercolours, pastels, charcoal, pencil.' His hand rested on one of the work benches as he indicated the sinks where students would be able to clean their equipment—and themselves,

Clemmie couldn't take her eyes off him as he handed someone a bundle of leaflets and asked him to pass them around.

'We're offering day tuition, and I'll be hiring an expert tutor to work alongside me with our day students. Our residential courses will run for either three or six days, and there are several courses to choose from as you can see in the leaflets. There'll be opportunities for students to work in this studio or outside, either in the grounds of the academy, or further afield. Our minibus will take students to a variety of locations in the area. Given the stunning landscape this town sits in, there'll be no shortage of locations for them to paint.

'I'm also liaising with local craftsmen and artists to give demonstrations to students in their own premises, or here at the academy if appropriate. There will also be the opportunity to visit our local museum and gallery, Lavender House, to study the work of the renowned Georgian artist, Josiah Lavender.'

Dolly nudged Clemmie. 'Eugenie's idea, no doubt. Doesn't miss a trick, does she?' she said, grinning.

'Would you expect anything less?' came a voice over their shoulders, and they spun round, embarrassed, to see a smiling Noah who clearly hadn't taken offence, much to their relief.

'What do you think of it all?' he whispered to Clemmie. 'Done an amazing job, haven't they?'

'It's incredible,' Clemmie said. 'From what Summer told me about the state of Monk's Folly, I know this must have taken an awful lot of work.'

'Ross poured his heart and soul into this place,' Noah said, watching his little brother fondly. 'Oh, don't get me wrong. Aunt Eugenie put the funds in place, and Meg helped with the design and sourcing the materials to decorate and furnish the house, but it's Ross's baby. He's come up with all the courses, and everything concerning the actual art and business side of things is down to him. I'm so proud of him.'

'No Isobel?' Dolly asked, peering over his shoulder. 'Thought she'd be here on such a big day for your family.'

Noah's smile faded. 'Sadly, she wasn't feeling well,' he said. 'Excuse me, I said I'd check in on the catering. See you later.'

As he hurried off, Dolly pursed her lips. 'Hmm.'

'Hmm, what?'

'Them two. Noah and Isobel. Bet you a tenner they're divorced before the year's out.'

'Don't say that!' Clemmie said, shocked. She glanced quickly around. 'If the Pennyfeathers heard you there'd be a book running on it by the time we got home today.'

'Not if Eugenie had anything to do with it there wouldn't,' Dolly said. 'Even so. You wait and see.'

The guests were led outside to show them the spectacular views of Tuppenny Bridge and the stunning countryside beyond, which the students would have the pleasure of sketching and painting. Then Ross pointed out the brand-new eight-seater minibus which was parked behind the house, and which was to be used to ferry the students on day trips to various locations where they could further practise their landscape skills—weather permitting, naturally. Clemmie tried to catch his eye, but he seemed oblivious to her presence, which was disappointing. She supposed he had other things on his mind right now.

After that it was time to return to the dining room, where the buffet had been laid and genuine champagne was flowing, along with orange juice for the teetotallers and under-eighteens.

'I'll say one thing for Eugenie,' Rita said, piling up her plate with a variety of sandwiches and baked goods, 'she doesn't skimp on the grub.'

'Or the bubbly, thank God,' Bluebell added, before murmuring, 'Sorry,' as Zach joined her at the table where the champagne flutes were standing.

'Oh, don't worry,' he assured her. 'I think we can all be grateful to God for this smashing feast—and for the company of such wonderful friends and neighbours, naturally.'

'Yeah,' Bluebell said, giving a knowing Ava a sheepish look. 'That's what I meant.'

There was to be another open day, this time for prospective students, the following week, but although this was an informal gathering to show the residents of Tuppenny Bridge around the academy, Ross seemed to be busy, nevertheless. Every time Clemmie looked over at him he was surrounded by people asking him questions or making conversation, and she thought she'd probably never get close to him at this rate.

She was desperate to know what he'd meant by his comments in the bookshop, and needed to talk to him to find out if what she was hoping could possibly be true. She'd imagined he'd seek her out at some point today, but he'd made no attempt to find her, and although she looked over at him frequently he never seemed to be looking back at her. Had he even noticed she was there?

'Why don't you go over to him and speak to him?' Dolly asked her at last, evidently growing fed up with talking to Clemmie and getting no response as her attention was elsewhere.

'Sorry? Who do you mean?'

'Pur-lease.' Dolly rolled her eyes. 'You've been in a state of fevered impatience ever since that fella walked into the shop last Saturday. It's obvious you've changed your mind about him. You *have* changed your mind about him, haven't you?'

There was no point in Clemmie denying it. She knew it had been written all over her face after Ross had told her there was nothing between him and Meg.

'Do you think he'd give me another chance?' she whispered to Dolly. 'I know he's single, but even so. I did mess him about a lot. And then there's...' She pulled a face, thinking of the elephant in the room—her alopecia. 'Well, you know.'

'Which he knows about and accepted without any qualms,' Dolly reminded her. 'He told you so, didn't he? Said it made no difference to him. Take him at his word and go and throw yourself at him before some other woman does. Seriously, love, what have you got to lose?'

Clemmie knew she was right, though it didn't make the thought of going up to Ross any easier. Still, he had said he'd be giving her the portrait when the madness had died down, and she could remind him of that. Maybe ask him where she should go to receive the portrait. It was as good an excuse as any.

It seemed ages before the crowd around thinned out enough for her to stand in front of him.

'Can I have a word with you?'

There was something different about him today. The way

he'd looked at her last week bore no resemblance to the dispassionate way he was looking at her now.

'Of course. What about?' He took a sip of champagne and waited, leaving Clemmie feeling flustered.

'Well, about the portrait,' she said uncertainly. 'You told me you'd be handing it over after the buffet was done and I was just wondering—'

He looked down at his feet as if avoiding her gaze. 'Oh yes. Sorry about that. Fact is, I haven't brought it with me. It's safely stored at Lavender House, so I'll have to give it to you another time. Don't worry, I'll make sure it arrives safely.'

Clemmie didn't know what to say to that. There was no mistaking the coldness in his tone, nor the way he was avoiding eye contact. It was as if he had no interest in her at all and wanted to look at anyone but her.

'Oh,' she said disconsolately, unable to think of anything else to say. 'Right.'

His gaze suddenly rested on her, and there was a slight thawing in his attitude.

'Do you—do you like it?' he asked, waving a hand around as if to encompass the entire house.

'It's beautiful,' she said, meaning it. 'You've done an amazing job. Captain Wentworth would look right at home here.'

'Huh.' He nodded slowly, staring at the glass in his hand as if it contained something fascinating. 'I'm sure he would.' He hurriedly downed his champagne and gave her a bright smile that didn't reach his eyes. 'I'm glad you like it. If you'll excuse me, I've got business to see to.'

With that, he hurried out of the room, leaving Clemmie staring after him in disbelief.

'Well?' Dolly asked, hurrying to her side. 'How did it go?'

Clemmie's eyes filled with tears. 'I was right all along,

Dolly. It's too late. I should have known that and left our relationship in the past where it belongs. Can we go home now?'

'But, love—'

'Please.' Clemmie put her glass of orange juice on the table and turned away from her aunt. 'I can't stay here any longer.'

'All right, love, all right.' Dolly's voice, so gentle and concerned, only made the tears harder to hold back, but somehow she forced herself not to cry. There was no way she could risk Ross knowing how much he'd hurt her, because then he'd realise that she'd been stupid enough to dream.

'How can you love someone who's forgotten how to dream?' he'd asked her.

Well, maybe it was time she tried to forget.

After all, what good had dreaming ever done her?

# FORTY-FIVE

Ross threw back the cover on the painting and stared bleakly at the canvas. He'd thought it was finished, ready to hand over to Clemmie. Now, as he looked at it with fresh eyes, he realised he had a lot of work to do on it to turn it into something she'd be happy with.

What had he been thinking? As if she'd want this! He'd been so caught up in his dreams of their future, sure that if he could just make her see how much she meant to him, she would give him another chance. Give *them* another chance.

Now he knew he'd been living in a fool's paradise. Rumour had reached him just that morning that Reuben Walker had left Dale View and, rather than going home to London, had moved into Wintergreen with Clemmie.

So they were officially a couple then.

His eyes filled with tears as he stared at her beautiful face on the canvas before him.

'Why?' he asked her. 'Why did you push me away? Why can't you see how much I love you? How right we are together?'

The face on the canvas was turned away from him. The real Clemmie was, he realised now, as unreachable as her portrait.

His last bit of hope had died that morning, yet she'd stood right in front of him earlier, smiling shyly up at him as if nothing had happened. As if she hadn't just blown his world apart. She hadn't even had the courtesy to tell him Reuben had moved in with her. All she'd been bothered about was this damn thing. Well, time to put right his mistake.

He knew what he had to do, but even as he turned to the cabinet where he kept his brushes and paints, he knew he wasn't up to the job. Not yet. Not today.

He turned back to the portrait and drank it in, not wanting to change a single part of it, even though he knew deep down that there was no way he could hand this over to her. Maybe he could keep it and paint another one for her? A similar painting but with one major change.

And what, he wondered, would he do with this one? Hang it in his bedroom so he could be tormented every night by thoughts of what could never be? Better to burn it.

His mind in turmoil he recovered the canvas and stormed out of the studio, locking the door behind him.

He'd decide what to do with Clemmie's portrait tomorrow. He'd had more than enough for one day.

# FORTY-SIX

The Crafty Cook Café was surprisingly busy when Ross climbed the stairs and looked around for a spare table. Evidently, Kat and Daisy's new venture was taking off. There'd been plenty of customers browsing downstairs in the shop, too. He was pleased for them. It was good to see a new business thriving in Tuppenny Bridge.

He managed to find an empty table over by the window and took a seat, giving the menu a cursory glance, even though he had no intention of ordering anything other than a coffee.

The café, he thought, was larger than he'd expected it to be, although since it had once been Kat's two-bedroomed flat he supposed he should have realised it would be a decent size. Most of the rooms had been knocked into one large seating area, but the old bathroom was now the customer toilets, and there was an area over in one corner that had comfy chairs, a table, and a cabinet stocked with craft materials.

That, according to the posters on the walls, was where the craft lessons would take place. Kat was running various knitting classes and Birdie and Rita were teaching crochet—his lips twitched at the thought of it—while a woman from Lingham-on-

Skimmer had booked the place to hold various other classes such as needle felting, and paper crafts.

He wondered if he should order a coffee or if he should wait for Jonah, who was meeting him to discuss business. Kat had wanted to sit in on the meeting so it seemed easier to meet at her workplace, where they could at least be comfortable and have a drink as they talked.

At that moment he heard boots on the stairs, and sure enough Jonah stepped into the room, followed by Kat, who immediately went to the counter to order drinks from Daisy.

When Jonah spotted him he called, 'Have you got a drink?'

Ross shook his head. 'A flat white please.'

Kat placed the order as Jonah joined Ross at the table.

'Sorry I'm a bit late,' he said. 'I've come from Kirkby Skimmer way. Traffic was a bit slow.'

'It's okay, I haven't been here long myself,' Ross assured him. 'So, what I wanted to talk to you about was firstly, displaying some of your work in our gallery, and secondly, the demonstrations you're going to be giving to some of my students.'

Jonah nodded. 'It's going to have to be booked well in advance. I'll need to plan my farrier work around the blacksmithing, and right now the horses are my priority.'

'Although,' Kat said, smiling as she took a seat beside him, 'that could all change very soon.'

'Not *very* soon,' Jonah corrected her, 'but eventually.'

'Oh?' Ross raised an eyebrow. 'What's this?'

'Jonah's taken on an apprentice,' Kat said excitedly.

'For the farrier work?'

Jonah nodded. 'That's right. The plan is to train up someone who can eventually work for me full-time. Then I can cut some of my hours and spend them doing more in the forge. Mind, it'll be a long process. It'll take four years for the lad to qualify so this isn't going to be an overnight thing.'

'And this is what you want to do?' Ross asked.

Jonah rubbed his chin. 'I love being a farrier, and I wouldn't want to give it up completely. But I can't deny I enjoy firing up the forge and getting stuck into the artwork. More and more I enjoy working in there rather than driving for miles every day in that van. This way I'd get the best of both worlds.'

Daisy arrived with a tray of drinks. She placed them on the table with a cheery smile and said, 'Enjoy,' before heading back behind the counter.

'Good coffee,' Ross said, after taking a tentative sip.

'You should try the cake,' Kat told him enthusiastically. 'It's to die for.'

'Best not,' Ross said, smiling. 'I might not be able to stop at one slice.'

'Probably a wise decision,' she agreed. 'It's far too handy for me to pop upstairs and nab a slice. I've put pounds on lately. Jonah will be going off me.'

Jonah winked at her. 'That'll never happen, my love.'

She beamed at him, and Ross tried to quell the sadness he felt at their obvious love for each other. He was pleased the two of them had got together, but it was yet another reminder of how lonely he felt. It was a loneliness that was gnawing away at him day and night, and seemed to be getting worse, not better. Maybe if he got rid of that damn painting instead of staring at it every day, punishing himself...

'Ross?'

He blinked back into awareness and gave Jonah an apologetic smile. 'Sorry, I was thinking of cake. What were you saying?'

'I was asking how many students there'd be and how often I'd be expected to give demonstrations.'

'Oh. Oh right. Well, there'd be no more than five or six. We're limiting the numbers on our residential courses to make sure they get enough individual attention. Of course, not all the courses will include trips to the forge. It depends on the course and the students' interests. I'm arranging various ones for them to choose from, which will run over three or six days. Then, of course, there are the day students, but they'll only be doing drawing or painting with our new art teacher.'

'You have a new art teacher?'

'I've drawn up a shortlist. I've just got to interview the final candidates and make a decision. He or she will be dealing with most of the day students, while I take the residential courses, although I'll help with day classes if we have a lot of applications and it's between courses.'

'It sounds amazing,' Kat said. 'I have to say, we were so impressed with what we saw at Monk's Folly, weren't we, Jonah? It doesn't look like the same place. You've done a great job with it, Ross.'

He smiled. 'Thanks. I'm glad you approve. Coming from you two that means a lot, given your history with the place.'

'Well, you were part of that history,' Jonah reminded him. 'I can still see you and Ben hanging round the house, annoying us when we were trying to be all grown up and sophisticated. Feels like another lifetime.'

'It does.'

They were quiet for a moment, contemplating how much time had passed since those days that had ended so abruptly over fourteen years ago.

'I'm glad to see you're back in touch with Ben,' Jonah told him. 'It's good to see the two of you hanging out together again.'

Ross laughed. 'Hanging out together? Well, I suppose we are. It's like we were never apart really.'

'Aye.' Jonah sighed. 'Well, when it's meant to be it'll always feel natural if you ask me, and true pals always find their way back to each other.'

'Mm.' Ross supposed he should be grateful that at least one of the people he cared about most was back in his life. Perhaps that was all he could ask. Perhaps Ben had been sent back to him as compensation for Clemmie. He couldn't have everything. Maybe he just expected too much.

He sipped his coffee. 'Have either of you heard how Joseph's doing?'

Jonah looked sombre. 'I was at Whispering Willows a couple of days ago. You know how it is. Just a matter of waiting, isn't it?'

'There is some good news, though,' Kat told him.

'Oh?' Ross leaned forward, interested. 'What's that?'

'Clive's managed to track down Helena Marshall. You know, the widow of Bethany's ex-husband?'

'That's great,' Ross said. 'So did she know where Bethany is?'

'She does,' Jonah told him. 'Unfortunately she refused to give Clive her whereabouts. Reckons Bethany's abroad at the moment.'

'But,' Kat added, 'she did promise to pass on the message and give her Clive's contact details when she got back to England.'

Jonah sighed. 'I just hope it's not a long trip. I wouldn't like to put money on how much time Joseph's got left.'

They all sat in gloomy silence, contemplating the future, and wondering if Joseph would get his last wish to see his sister.

'Anyway,' Kat said, her voice brisk as if she'd decided a change of subject was called for, 'Jonah's made another decision. He's going to start selling some of his stuff online, aren't you?'

As Jonah nodded, Ross took a sip of his coffee and eyed them approvingly. 'I think that's a great idea,' he said. 'But this time, make sure your prices reflect your talent and the time it takes to make the artwork. I remember when you took the stall at the sheep fair last September, you were seriously undercharging.'

'Don't worry,' Kat said firmly, 'I'll make sure he doesn't make that mistake again.'

'And we're even getting a proper website done,' Jonah said proudly. 'Got that Reuben fella to work on it for us. Had a meeting with him the other day and it's going to look bloody brilliant when it's finished.'

Ross's stomach turned over with dread and jealousy. He drained his coffee and pushed the cup away. 'Well,' he managed, 'I can vouch for his work. He's done an amazing job with our website for the academy.' He wondered how he was managing to be so generous. He should be warning Jonah off and telling him not to touch Reuben's work with a bargepole. Trouble was, that wouldn't be true. The website for the academy was fantastic and Ross couldn't deny it. 'Good to have someone local doing it for you, too.' *Bloody hell, I deserve an Oscar for this little performance.*

'Well, hardly,' Kat said. 'He went back to Hampstead yesterday.'

Ross's eyes widened. 'He did what?'

'Went back to Hampstead,' she said. 'Didn't you know?'

'No,' he murmured, bewildered. 'I didn't. But I thought he was living with Clemmie now? Aren't they—' He broke off as a thought occurred to him. 'Clemmie.' He had to ask even though he dreaded the reply. 'Has she gone with him?'

Kat frowned. 'Why would she?' She exchanged glances with Jonah then said, 'You haven't heard, have you?'

'Heard? Heard what?'

'About Reuben! Oh my word, Ross, you're behind the times. It all came out the day before yesterday. It's all round the town. How have you missed it?'

His jaw tightened. What had he missed? Had Reuben Walker hurt Clemmie in some way?

'It's been one of the Lavender Ladies' biggest failures,' Jonah said laughing. 'Not surprised your auntie hasn't mentioned it. She must be mortified. Right under her nose an' all!'

'What was?' Ross asked, exasperated.

'Reuben. He's Clemmie's half-brother.'

Ross stared at Kat, hardly able to take in what she'd just said. From what seemed far away he heard her voice explaining how Reuben had come to Tuppenny Bridge to meet Clemmie and find out more about her before revealing his true identity to her.

'But I thought they were...'

'So did I to be honest,' Kat admitted. 'But evidently there was never anything romantic between them. In fact, Reuben's gay. His partner, Matt, has been staying at Wintergreen with him for the past few days. We didn't get to meet him but by all accounts he's a nice lad. They're getting married in the summer.'

Ross shook his head. 'Reuben's gay? And he's Clemmie's half-brother?' He could hardly believe it.

'Clemmie's had an awful shock, according to Dolly,' Kat continued, clearly having no idea the effect her words were having on him. 'She didn't have a clue, and she always thought her parents had the perfect marriage, didn't she? But she's dealing with it now apparently. She and Reuben seem to get along well, which is good. It's nice for Clemmie to have another family member, other than Dolly.'

'You're sure about this?' Ross asked.

'Absolutely positive.' Kat frowned as Ross got to his feet. 'Where are you going? Aren't we going to discuss—'

'Can we take a rain check?' he pleaded. 'I'm sorry. There's something I really have to do, and it can't wait another minute.'

# FORTY-SEVEN

'There you go, sir. That's all gone through for you.' Clemmie tore off the receipt and handed it to the middle-aged man who was standing at the counter, looking slightly embarrassed.

'Thank you.' He put his credit card back in his wallet and picked up the book he'd just purchased. 'And you say the other one I wanted will be out later this month?'

'That's right,' she said. 'Publication date is March the twenty-eighth. I'll put you a copy aside.'

'That's good. It's just, I wouldn't want to disappoint my wife. They're both for her birthday, you see.'

Clemmie smothered a smile. This was the third time the man had told her it was for his wife. God forbid that she should think he'd ordered a romance novel for himself!

As he headed towards the door, she shook her head slightly and glanced at her watch. Half past four. Still another half an hour to go before she could shut up shop and go back to Wintergreen. Dolly had taken the day off to do some work at home, and Clemmie hoped she'd have her tea cooked for her when she got back. She was tired and didn't feel like cooking for herself.

The doorbell jingled moments after the man had exited the

shop, and Clemmie looked up, surprised to see Ben staggering into the shop, carrying a large parcel, with Summer following behind, Joseph's Bichon frise, Viva, on a lead beside her.

'Brought your wallet, Ben?' she joked as he carried it carefully over to the counter and laid it down before her.

Ben pulled a face. 'I wish. No, this is for you. It's from Ross.'

Clemmie felt her face drain of colour. 'Ross?'

No prizes for guessing what it was then. So he hadn't even bothered to give her the portrait himself? He really had lost all interest in her, hadn't he?

'Well,' Summer said, picking Viva up and giving her a cuddle, 'aren't you going to open it?'

Clemmie stared at the package, wrapped in brown paper and tied with string, just like Julie Andrews sang about in *The Sound of Music*. She had an awful feeling, though, that this wasn't going to be one of her favourite things.

'How come you've brought it?' she asked.

'You might well ask,' Ben said with feeling. 'Apparently I'm an errand boy now. I was just coming back from a call-out and I found myself driving behind Ross. He flashed me to pull over and asked me if I'd do him a favour. Next thing I knew I had this bloody big parcel in my back seat with instructions to hand it over to you. For your eyes only.'

'And I was taking Viva for a walk before teatime and spotted Ben pulling into Market Place. Lucky the market stalls close by four in the winter, or he'd never have been able to get parked and he'd have had to carry that thing from Stepping Stones.' She nodded towards the package. 'Come on, Clem. I'm dying to see this, aren't you?'

Hardly. It occurred to Clemmie that, if Ross had lost interest in her, he might have decided to do the unthinkable. What if she opened this package and revealed what she was most afraid of to Ben and Summer?

Ross wouldn't paint her without her wig, would he? He'd

promised. But that was then, when they'd seemed closer, and she'd hoped they could remain friends if nothing else. Now there was this distance between them again, and he might feel he owed her nothing. Maybe, considering the way she'd rejected him, he might even see it as an opportunity for revenge?

She swallowed. He wouldn't. He couldn't have. That wasn't Ross.

Yet the fear persisted. She couldn't bear it if Ben and Summer saw her like that.

'Can I—would you mind if I opened it in the kitchen?' she asked nervously.

Ben and Summer exchanged glances. Ben shrugged. 'If you like. We'll mind the shop for you. Here, I'll take it through for you.'

Clemmie nodded gratefully as he carried the parcel into the kitchen and returned a moment later, smiling. 'There you go. I hope it's everything you want it to be.'

Oh, so did she! She took a steadying breath and headed towards the kitchen door then paused as a thought occurred to her. Turning to them she said, 'You can come, too, if you like, Summer.'

If the worst had happened she would need her best friend's support. She'd also need her help to come up with a way of destroying the painting so no one else ever got to see it. She didn't relish the thought of Summer seeing a portrait of her without her hair, but at least she knew about the alopecia so it wouldn't be as much of a shock to her as it would be to Ben.

Summer handed Viva to Ben and followed her into the kitchen.

'What's wrong, Clem?' she asked quietly as she shut the door after her.

Briefly, Clemmie voiced her worries to Summer.

'He wouldn't do that,' Summer said confidently. 'He's not vindictive. I've seen a whole new side to Ross Lavender lately, and honestly I don't believe he'd do something so horrible. Besides, he thinks far too much of you to hurt you like that.'

Clemmie nibbled her thumbnail. 'You think?'

'Trust him, Clemmie,' Summer told her. 'This is Ross we're talking about.'

She was right. She knew Ross. She knew the type of man he was. He would never do anything to hurt her, she realised that now.

Her fingers trembled so much she could barely untie the string and Summer had to help her. Between them they removed the brown paper and turned the canvas round to face them.

There was a collective gasp and Clemmie leaned against her friend, staring at the portrait in disbelief.

'Oh my word,' Summer breathed. 'Clemmie, it's *stunning!*'

Clemmie couldn't speak. She could only stare at the portrait in amazement.

'But—but what does it mean?'

Summer burst out laughing. 'Well what do you think it means, you numpty? Could he be any more obvious? Oh, Clemmie! This is so exciting.'

There was a tap on the door and Summer inched it open.

'Sorry,' Ben said, sounding thoroughly sheepish. 'I totally forgot that Ross gave me this for Clemmie, too.'

'Thanks.' Summer gave Clemmie an enquiring look.

'It's okay, Ben,' Clemmie said. 'You can come in now.'

He pushed open the door and entered the room, Viva in his arms, then stopped dead, whistling in approval at the portrait.

'Bloody hell! That's—that's fantastic! He's one talented man, isn't he?' His eyes narrowed. 'Is it what you were expecting?'

Clemmie puffed out her cheeks as Summer handed her something. 'I'm not sure what I was expecting, but it definitely wasn't this.' She looked down at the envelope in her hand. 'What's this?'

'Open it and find out,' Summer said.

Clemmie leaned on the counter wondering how many more shocks she could take today and tore the envelope open. It was a letter from Ross.

But Ross never wrote letters.

She began to read, tears blurring her eyes, her heart racing as she absorbed the words he'd poured onto the page.

*My darling Clementine,*

*I'm writing to you—correction, I'm attempting to write to you—to tell you how sorry I am about the way I behaved at the open day. I was rude and unkind, and I can't tell you how bad I feel about that.*
*It was my fault entirely. I got the wrong end of the stick. You see, I thought Reuben had moved in with you at Wintergreen because you and he were together. I couldn't stand it, Clemmie. It broke my heart. I could barely bring myself to be civil to you. Earlier today I learned the truth about your relationship, and I couldn't believe it. I was such an idiot. Can you ever forgive me for the way I behaved?*
*I know you said we're over and I should put our relationship behind me and move on, but I can't. I must ask you one more time if there's any chance at all that we can be together?*
*You know me, Clem. I'm rubbish at romance and putting my feelings into words, so I've taken some inspiration from your favourite sea captain. As Captain Wentworth says:*
*"You pierce my soul. I am half agony, half hope. Tell me not that I am too late, that such precious feelings are gone for ever. I offer myself to you again with a heart even more your own than when you almost broke it, eight years and a half ago." (Except it was six*

*years ago, obviously.) "For you alone, I think and plan. Have you not seen this? Can you fail to have understood my wishes?" Well, I think that's quite enough from him, but he's only said what I feel, Clem. I wish I could be more romantic for you. I wish I had a way with words so I could tell you how much you mean to me.*

*All I have is my art, so with this portrait I've tried to show you that I love you completely, and this is how I see you, even though I can't express myself verbally. And maybe, just maybe, if you look at it enough you'll see that we do have a future together, if you'll only let me back into your heart.*

*If there's really no hope you're free to do whatever you wish with the painting. I'll honour my commitment and paint you in a more conventional manner. Whatever you like.*

*But please, please, Clemmie, don't make any hasty decisions. Think about what we had. Think about what we could have again.*

*I love you, like Mark Darcy loves Bridget Jones. "Just as you are."*

*Always yours*
*Ross xxx*

'Clemmie?' Summer's voice came to her as if from a distance, and she stared blankly at her friend, barely able to focus on her for the tears that were welling in her eyes and spilling down her cheeks.

'Oh, Clemmie! What's he said?' Summer cried, putting her arms around her, and hugging her tightly. She turned to Ben. 'What was in that letter?' she demanded fiercely.

'I don't know,' Ben assured her, sounding deeply worried. 'Honestly, he didn't say. He just told me to give it to Clemmie, and that he'd be waiting in the churchyard if there was any return message—'

'In the churchyard?' Clemmie wiped her tears away and turned desperate eyes on Ben. 'Are you sure?'

'Absolutely positive. Though why he's waiting there I can't imagine. You could have just sent him a text message if you had anything to say and—'

She didn't wait to hear any more.

'Drop the latch when you leave,' she yelled at them as she ran into the shop and wrenched open the door. 'I'll be back to close up properly.'

If they replied she didn't hear them. She sped across the market place, not even stopping to think about what she was going to say. Ross was waiting at All Hallows, and deep down she knew he was hoping that she'd be the one to come to him, not Ben.

For once in her life, she wasn't going to disappoint him.

# FORTY-EIGHT

Somehow, Clemmie knew exactly where Ross would be, and she wasn't wrong. He was standing by Leon's stone in the Garden of Ashes and seemed a million miles away.

She slowed as she approached him, but her footsteps on the gravel path gave her away, and he looked up, a wary expression in his eyes when he saw her.

'I hoped you'd come,' he told her as he went to sit on the bench. 'I was just making my peace with him.' He nodded at the stone, where a vase of daffodils now stood. 'I'm hoping he's forgiven me.'

Clemmie sat down beside him. 'There was nothing for him to forgive you for. It wasn't your fault.'

He was silent for a moment, then he turned to her. 'And what about you, Clemmie. Have you forgiven me?'

'Forgiven you? For what?' She shook her head, almost blinded with tears. After everything she'd done to him he was asking for *her* forgiveness?

'For the way I spoke to you at the open day. For not being the romantic man you wanted. For not being there when you needed me all those years ago. For not making it obvious that I loved you and you could trust me. For so many failures I don't know where to start.'

'Ross,' she said tearfully. She took his hand in hers. 'You were hurt at the open day. You thought me and Reuben—' She shook her head. 'He's my half-brother. I have a half-brother, Ross.'

'I know.' He gave her a gentle smile. 'So do I. I can highly recommend them. I wouldn't be without mine.'

She smiled back. 'It was such a shock. I thought Mum and Dad—well, you know what I thought. It made me realise that I was wrong in so many ways. Dad was a real romantic, always quoting poetry and telling Mum how much he adored her, yet look what he did to her! I couldn't get my head around that. It really hurt. Their marriage wasn't what I thought it was at all.'

'But they loved each other, Clem,' he told her. 'Everything you've ever told me about them proves that. Please don't doubt it. Please don't lose your faith in love because he made one mistake.'

'But that's just it,' she explained. 'I haven't. If anything, it's made my faith in love stronger.'

As he lifted his eyebrows in surprise she said, 'I thought it had to be perfect, you see. I thought that if one partner made a mistake, deep down things could never be the same again. I'd made so many mistakes with you and I didn't see how you could possibly feel the same way about me again, no matter how much you told me you could. But Mum proved me wrong. She forgave Dad completely, and their marriage grew stronger and stronger. They even had me! I was so stupid.'

'Not stupid,' he said firmly. 'Never stupid.'

'Naïve anyway,' she amended. 'Gullible perhaps.' She gave him a rueful smile. 'A dreamer.'

He squeezed her hand. 'The world needs more dreamers, Clemmie. It's full of hard-bitten, cynical people. Someone has to remind us that this can be a beautiful place. That good, kind people still exist, that love in all its forms is real and worth fighting for, that dreams really can come true.'

'The portrait,' she said falteringly. She hardly knew how to put into words how she felt about it.

He waited, and she saw the anxious look in his eyes and gave him a reassuring smile.

'It was perfect. Beautiful. I never expected...' She shook her head. 'I don't deserve...'

'Just tell me it's what you want,' he said urgently. 'Just tell me I didn't make a mistake.'

'You didn't make a mistake, Ross,' she said. 'Any mistakes have been mine. It wasn't you I didn't trust. It was me. I pushed you away because I didn't believe someone like you could ever want someone like me, and I didn't listen to what you were trying to tell me. I'm so sorry.' She swallowed down a sob. 'I love you so much.'

'Clementine.'

His arms were around her and he held her tightly, soothing her, telling her everything was all right, as long as they had each other.

'Your letter was beautiful,' she whispered. 'It must have taken you hours.'

He gave a short laugh that was also a half sob. 'It poured out onto the page. Honestly, once I'd looked up old Captain Wentworth's letter for inspiration everything else seemed easy. It was like I had all this stuff in my heart, and I just had to get it out there, so you'd know what I felt. How much you meant to me. How much I love you.'

He pulled back and cupped her face in his hands. 'I do love you, Clementine. So very much. You know that, don't you?'

She nodded. 'I know.'

When he kissed her, Clemmie thought briefly of Anne Elliot, and how she must have felt when Captain Wentworth finally declared his love for her after all those years of waiting.

Then her passion for Ross took over, and she forgot all about Jane Austen's hero. After all, she had her own hero now. For keeps.

Ben and Summer had kindly dropped the latch of The Corner Cottage Bookshop, but Clemmie fished in her pocket for the key and she and Ross stepped inside, the bell jingling as they did so.

Clemmie locked the door behind them and took Ross's hand, leading him into the kitchen where the portrait stood on the counter, leaning against the wall.

They stood, arms wrapped around each other's waists, and gazed at it.

'I still can't believe it,' Clemmie admitted. 'When I saw it I just... I can't explain. It was everything, Ross. Everything I could ever have hoped for or dreamed of.'

'It was *my* dream,' he said. 'I knew it was a risk, but it was one I had to take. I had to know if there was any chance at all, and this was the only way I could think of to make you see that we could be together, that we *belonged* together.'

It had, Clemmie thought, shown her that all right.

She eyed the portrait hungrily, devouring every loving brushstroke. Because they must have been loving, she thought. Love poured from this painting.

The living room of Monk's Folly, which she'd seen and admired so much at the open day, served as the background for the portrait. Ross had painted her standing by the window, her head turned to the side as she gazed through it.

Her hair was à la Hollandaise—a style which Regency buff Clemmie was familiar with. A row of wispy curls fell around her hairline, while her long hair was gathered into a high bun. She wore an empire line dress in a simple, white cotton muslin.

Behind her stood Ross, his hands curled around the top of

her arms, looking every inch the Regency gent in a white shirt with a starched chin-high collar, ivory cravat, and ivory jacquard waistcoat.

He, too, was gazing out of the window, and there was a faraway expression in their eyes.

Some might suppose they were looking out across the river towards Tuppenny Bridge, but somehow Clemmie felt they were looking beyond that. It was as if they were gazing into their own future, and the contentment on their faces showed it was a pleasing sight.

'Anne Elliot and Captain Wentworth,' Ross said, sounding half-embarrassed.

She turned to him and put her arms around his neck.

'No,' she said firmly. 'Clementine Grant and Ross Lavender.'

He smiled and kissed her again.

'I'm so happy,' he murmured. 'I never expected to feel this way again.'

She stepped away from him suddenly. 'But there's one thing, Ross. One thing you have to be sure about before we can know for certain that this is forever.'

He frowned. 'What is it?'

She closed her eyes, wishing she could control her nerves. Taking a calming deep breath she opened her eyes again and, as carefully as she could manage in her anxious state, removed her wig.

Placing it on the counter, she waited. It was the most terrifying moment of her life, but she had to know for sure. And so did he. Could he really deal with this?

'This is the real me,' she told him, raising her chin, and meeting his gaze with some defiance, despite her fear. 'This is who I am, and it's probably who I'm always going to be. My hair will never come back, Ross. I know that deep down, and if you can't—'

He stepped forward and put his arms around her, pulling her close, then gently kissed the top of her head.

As he held her, she whispered through her tears, 'What are you thinking? Really?'

He looked down at her and smiled, and she saw the love shining in his eyes.

'I'm thinking, what the hell did someone like me do to deserve someone as completely and utterly wonderful as you?'

She might never, she realised as they held each other, standing in front of the portrait that had brought them back together, have the courage to reveal the truth about herself to anyone else. Dolly, Summer, and Ross knew but she couldn't imagine ever telling another person, even Reuben.

Many women in a similar situation to herself had the courage to go out there and tell the world, 'This is me, and I'm not going to hide it'.

And they were right to, she knew that. There was nothing to be ashamed of, after all. She'd seen them. Admired them. Realised how beautiful they looked, and that having no hair had taken nothing away from them at all.

But Clemmie had always been a shy person, shunning attention, hiding from any kind of spotlight. It wasn't in her nature to do anything that might attract people's notice.

But maybe, she realised, that was okay too. Everyone was different, after all, and what was right for one person wasn't necessarily right for another. The main thing was, it was her choice, and she was free to make it.

She had no pressure on her from the three people who knew her secret. The three people, she realised, that she loved most in the world. How lucky was she to have them in her life? Dolly, who'd cared for her since she was a heartbroken child. Summer, who'd befriended her almost from the moment they'd met, even though, on the surface, they had very little in common. And now Ross.

He was back in her life, accepting her, loving her, adoring her just as she was. She couldn't ask for anything more.

'Would you like to come back to Monk's Folly?' he asked her, his eyes shining with sudden excitement. 'I'd love to show you what I've done with my flat, and my car's only parked in Market Place.'

'Is that a proposition?' she asked in mock outrage.

'No,' he said, a twinkle in his eye. 'A gentleman would never be so discourteous. I just want you to see what it looks like, Clemmie, because I think you'll approve. You wouldn't be surprised to find one of your Jane Austen heroes in there, honestly.'

'In that case, I'd be delighted,' she said. 'Why don't you take the portrait to the car while I give Dolly a call? I need to warn her I'll be late home.'

He nodded and picked up the canvas, then kissed her again before carrying it out of the shop.

Clemmie quickly rang Dolly and gave her a brief explanation of what had happened, promising she'd fill her in on all the details later.

'You'd better do! I'm so pleased for you, love. This is everything I hoped for. You're going to make each other very happy; I know it. Now, don't you worry about me. No rush to come home if you get my drift. I'll see you when I see you.'

Amused, Clemmie rolled her eyes, then paused when a sudden thought occurred to her.

As new confidence flowed through her, she said, 'When I get home I'll have something to show you.'

'Oh? And what that might be?' Dolly enquired.

'You'll see. Catch you later, Dolly.'

She ended the call, wondering how her aunt would like *The Marquess Wants a Wife*. She was sure she'd adore Rollo. Best of all, she was pretty sure now that she'd love Emmeline, too, just as she did.

Carefully, she replaced her wig and checked herself in the mirror.

There she was, the Clemmie everyone knew. But the real Clemmie was loved too, by the people who really mattered. She had no doubt of that now, and maybe if they loved her so much, it proved she really was worth loving after all.

Squaring her shoulders, she smiled to herself, flicked off the lights and made sure the shop was secure.

Then she headed across Market Place to where Ross Lavender, the hero she'd dreamed of all her life, was waiting for her.

# A LETTER FROM THE AUTHOR

Dear reader,

A big thank you for reading *Snowflakes and Surprises in Tuppenny Bridge*. I hope you enjoyed following Ross and Clemmie on their journey towards true love! If you want to join other readers in hearing all about my new releases and bonus content, you can sign up here:

www.stormpublishing.co/sharon-booth

If you enjoyed this book and could spare a few moments to leave a review that would be hugely appreciated. Even a short review can make all the difference in encouraging a reader to discover my books for the first time. Thank you so much!

I've loved being back in Tuppenny Bridge again. The characters feel like old friends to me now, and I've been longing to dive into Ross and Clemmie's story.

Right from the start I knew their relationship wasn't going to be what it seemed. Clemmie did a very good job of leading Summer to the wrong conclusion about Ross, and his behaviour didn't help his case. I knew, though, that Ross wasn't at all how the townspeople assumed him to be. I found that quite fun to write. A town lothario who turned out to be a loving, kind, supportive man, whose heart belonged only to Clemmie. Aw!

I'd been thinking about writing a character with alopecia for some years. I had a friend whose hair was extremely thin, and she was very self-conscious about her scalp being visible through it. When she started to wear a wig she became so much more confident about her appearance, and I thought, what must it be like for a woman who's lost all her hair? How must that affect her? And how much worse would it be if the man she loved was incredibly handsome, popular with the women of the town, and oozed charisma?

From the beginning of the Tuppenny Bridge series, I knew this was Clemmie's secret. I also knew Ross was the love of her life, and that she'd left him before he could leave her. I felt quite mean at times letting people think he was a bit of a cad. I hope I redeemed him in your eyes, because frankly, I adore him!

I read up a lot on alopecia on the NHS website, and on websites such as Alopecia UK (www.alopecia.org.uk) which has loads of useful information. A recent survey conducted by the organisation showed that nearly 70% of participants had suffered with depression because of their alopecia, while nearly 65% had suffered anxiety. Younger age and more severe alopecia were higher risk factors, which made me think that Clemmie must have gone through an awful lot, coming to terms with her hair loss.

I also read Gail Porter's autobiography, *Laid Bare*. It's a good read, and there's so much more to her story—and to Gail herself—than hair loss. But it did give me an insight into how she'd felt when her hair fell out and she was forced to accept that it would probably never grow back. Gail has taken an open approach to her alopecia. She's not hidden it, and made the decision early on not to wear a wig as it wouldn't make her feel comfortable.

I knew, however, that Clemmie wouldn't react like that. Clemmie is a shy young woman and doesn't like attention. She blushes when someone compliments her and has no self-confidence. Doing anything that would draw attention to herself wouldn't be right for her, so I had to allow Clemmie to deal with her condition in a way that was true to her.

That doesn't mean I think Clemmie's way is right for everyone. As I've tried to make clear, it's a very personal decision, and it's entirely up to each individual to decide how they handle their alopecia. There's no right or wrong way, only what feels best for that person.

Similarly, while Clemmie chose not to undertake treatment, I'm aware that many people do, and that for some it's at least partly successful. Clemmie's circumstances were such that, when I read some NHS papers on the treatment for alopecia totalis, I decided it wasn't right for her. This in no way is meant to dissuade anyone else from doing what they feel is best for them.

Clemmie also felt uncomfortable in her face-to-face support group. I must stress that, again, this was purely driven by the character. Knowing her as I do, knowing how difficult she finds any social occasions, I thought it would be something she would shy away from. That doesn't mean I think they don't work for others. As I said previously, people must do what they feel is right for them. She did find some comfort in her online social media support group, and that felt more realistic for her character.

I send lots of love to anyone who has found themselves in a similar situation to Clemmie.

If you'd like to know more about alopecia please visit the website mentioned above.

I've loved spending time with Clemmie and Ross, and I hope you have, too.

Thanks again for visiting Tuppenny Bridge. I love to hear from my readers so please do feel free to get in touch.

Love Sharon xx

www.sharonboothwriter.com

facebook.com/sharonbooth.writer
x.com/Sharon_Booth1
instagram.com/sharonboothwriter

## ACKNOWLEDGMENTS

It takes more than one person to produce a book, even though there may only be one person's name on the cover. I'm lucky to have a whole team of talented people at Storm Publishing who have been with me every step of the way from the moment I handed in the manuscript.

Huge thanks go to Kathryn Taussig and Emma Beswetherick for the brilliant job they did on the editing. Their insightful comments and guidance made me look at Clemmie in a whole new light, which enabled me to shape this into a much better book as a result.

Thank you to Shirley Khan for the copyedits, and to Liz Hurst for the proofreading. I'd also like to thank Debbie Clement for the beautiful cover, which I absolutely love, as I've loved all the covers she's created for this series. And thanks, too, to Elizabeth Bower, who is narrating the audio version of this story, as she's narrated the first two Tuppenny Bridge books. I feel very lucky that she agreed to it as she's done an amazing job.

There are so many other people who are part of this fantastic team who deserve my thanks. Thank you to Oliver, Alex, Anna, Elke—I'm feeling a bit like an Oscar winner who's desperately trying not to forget anyone in her speech! I hope I haven't forgotten anyone, but if I have that's a reflection on my terrible memory and not on your amazing work. Thank you!

On a more personal note, I must thank The Husband, long-suffering as he is. He takes such good care of me I could never do all this without him. Over forty years together and he still makes me laugh every single day, just as he did when we were teenagers. I think that says a lot. He's just redecorated my office—again. We only did it last year and I decided I didn't like it and preferred the old look, so he's had to put it all back the way it was. I don't know how he puts up with me, but I'm very glad he does.

I'm lucky to be part of The Write Romantics, whose other members this book is dedicated to. Over ten years as a group and we're still supporting each other and cheering each other on. I'm so proud of how far we've all come in that time. It just shows you. Never give up on your dreams.

Thank you to the fabulous ladies of our local writers' group, who make me laugh so much at our monthly meetings and keep me going in the darkest times. Jeevani Charika, Jenni Fletcher, Linda Acaster, Sylvia Broady, Val Wood, Alex Weston, Julie Heslington, and Lynnda Worsnopp, you're all amazing! As is Eliza J Scott who has become a "real life" friend over the last couple of years and is such a lovely person. Online, the writing community is so supportive, and I've made so many friends over the years that I can't possibly name everyone. I hope they all know how much I appreciate them.

Special thanks, as ever, to Julie, AKA Jessica Redland, who's my absolute rock in what can sometimes be turbulent waters. She's always there to listen, support, encourage, advise, console and cheer. Anyone who forgoes pudding because their bestie is on a diet has to be worth hanging on to! Hugs, Julie.

And finally, a massive thank you to you, the reader. None of this would be possible without you. I'm so very grateful for all your support. I hope you'll keep in touch and that you'll continue to enjoy my books. You're a star!

Happy reading and lots of love, Sharon xx

Printed in Great Britain
by Amazon